Studia Fennica
Folkloristica 23

Storied and Supernatural Places

Studies in Spatial and Social Dimensions
of Folklore and Sagas

Edited by Ülo Valk and Daniel Sävborg

Finnish Literature Society • SKS • Helsinki • 2018

STUDIA FENNICA FOLKLORISTICA 23

The publication has undergone a peer review.

This volume was supported by institutional research funding from the Estonian Ministry of Education and Research (project IUT2-43 Tradition, Creativity and Society: Minorities and Alternative Discourses).

A digital edition of a printed book first published in 2018 by the Finnish Literature Society.
Cover Design: Timo Numminen
EPUB: Tero Salmén

ISBN 978-952-222-917-5 (Print)
ISBN 978-952-222-994-6 (PDF)
ISBN 978-952-222-993-9 (EPUB)

ISSN 0085-6835 (Studia Fennica)
ISSN 1235-1946 (Studia Fennica Folkloristica)

DOI: http://dx.doi.org/10.21435/sff.23

BoD – Books on Demand, Norderstedt, Germany 2018

Contents

Ülo Valk, Daniel Sävborg

Place-Lore, Liminal Storyworld and Ontology of the Supernatural.
An Introduction

Places are far more than geographical locations; they are sites of memories and venues of extraordinary encounters in storytelling. Some of them have an intimate relationship with us as places of dwelling that determine our belonging; others are distant or remain in the world of imagination. Places can be monumental, grand, small, cosy, homely, holy, scary or repulsive, natural or man-made, familiar or strange – either belonging to our daily surroundings or being beyond our direct experience – and they can also be meaningful to us in a variety of ways. This collection of articles offers a variety of approaches to the construction of places in narrative genres, the relationship between tradition communities and their environments, the supernatural dimensions of cultural landscapes and wilderness as they are manifested in folklore and in early literary sources, such as Old Norse sagas. The storyworld that is evoked by these multiple modes of verbal expression can be conceptualised as a liminal realm between factuality and fiction, where everyday reality is transformed by imagination and where the subtle magical power of words evokes the supernatural. Sceptical folks, however, question the reality of this narrative enchantment, reinforcing the cognitive boundaries between the 'real' and 'imagined', between fact and fantasy. However, even analytical minds are often carried away by the ideological currents that shape societies. The folklore of place can thus become a part of national agendas and be used for political goals.

The book consists of three parts that investigate these topics, expounding the dimensions and levels of narrative construction of places, and the broader framework of research. The first part "Explorations in Place-Lore" offers a set of case studies and analysis of local legends from North European traditions past and present. The second part "Regional Variation, Environment and Spatial Dimensions" broadens the comparative and historical aspects of place-lore, and shows the role of beliefs, legends and ritual practices in shaping the environment of tradition communities both in their daily surroundings and in the fictional landscapes of sagas. Thirdly, the last part of the book "Traditions and Histories Reconsidered" examines former scholarship, its historical formation and sources from reflective and critical perspectives. It carries the discussion from local traditions and single case-studies to the level of statehood, national ideologies and geopolitical spaces. The introduction addresses the conceptual framework of the book, focussing on the basic notions of place-lore, the supernatural and genres of expression. It also links folkloristic approaches with current debates in some related disciplines, such as religious studies, anthropology and ethnology.

Place-Lore and Narrative Gravitation

Environment is not a mere background or surrounding for stories, songs and other expressive forms, it is a sensed and intimately known reality. Places acquire meanings – both personal and shared – through lives, experiences and narratives (Knuuttila 2006). We can talk about the stratification of places as they store their histories, and about their simultaneity, as multiple interconnected places often co-exist and overlap with each other (Knott 2005: 127). Some significant places emerge due to perceptual strategies by means of which certain landscape features are prioritised and perceived as special, charging local topography with the quality of sacrality (Anttonen 2014a: 120). Such an overall dynamism of places – either sacred or profane, emergent or with waning significance – indicates that they cannot be identified through some essentialist features, but are situational, undergo constant remaking and are lodged in changing circumstances (Heynickx et al. 2012). As seen from a folkloristic perspective, telling and listening to stories is the quintessential practice of building places. Frank J. Korom who has studied oral narratives about the advent of the local deity in a West Bengali village has shown that although stories often rely on widely spread traditional motifs, each narrative is born as a creative and independent work of verbal art. The relationship that people develop with locality, the belief systems and narrative theologies they share – and their very place in the world is thus unique, and differs from that of neighbouring communities. (Korom 2016.)

Some places grow in time and accumulate meanings, layer by layer, although the same places can also obtain personal significance as awareness of them grows together with life experience and memory. Keith Basso (1996: 107) has noted that relationship with place is both reciprocal and dynamic: "When places are actively sensed, the physical landscape becomes wedded to the landscape of the mind, to the roving imagination, and where the latter may lead is anybody's guess". Because it is animated by thoughts, emotions and memories, place becomes a powerful agent that attracts, inspires and bounds people. Edward S. Casey (1996: 25) has talked about the capacity of places to hold and gather, to generate particular configurations and senses of ordered arrangements of things. Places also hold their inhabitants within their boundaries and offer them protection, bringing people together. In some religions, the power of deities to reward and protect their devotees is limited to the vicinity of the abodes of these deities, thus people are firmly bound to place (Tuan 2001 [1977]: 152–153). In belief narratives, places can also act in a straightforward manner, without involving any supernatural agents: forests lead people astray or hide cattle, sacred places punish transgressors who violate taboos, displeased lakes travel long distances to new locations. Human misdeeds trigger the dramatic reactions of places and those extraordinary events are remembered in local legends. Other places display the activities of giants, ancestors, saints or heroes who have left visible traces in the environment. Yi-Fu Tuan notes that among native peoples, mythic history is recorded in the landscape, in rocks and waterholes that these peoples can see and touch. A native finds there "the ancient story of the lives and deeds of the immortal beings from whom he himself is descended, and whom he reveres" (Tuan 2001 [1977]: 158). Places thus store collective memories of the mythic past, as is also shown by Cristina Bacchilega, in her monograph *Legendary Hawai'i and the Politics of Place* (2007). She has explored such "storied places" in Hawaiian traditions, focussing on *wahi pana* – significant and celebrated places that appear in *mo'olelo* – a narrative genre of the indigenous folklore. Bacchilega discusses how local stories have been translated and re-interpreted within the framework of Western notions of folklore genres and applied to produce legendary Hawai'i, primarily for non-Hawaiian audiences.

Places thus appear differently to local people and to outsiders, and the related narrative traditions are transformed when they circulate in various media and across boundaries. Not only is folklore local, but there are also multiple folkloristic research traditions, bound to different languages and sociocultural contexts. In the 1990s a new concept emerged in Estonian folkloristics – *kohapärimus*, 'place-lore', which soon became a distinct field of studies, the importance of which has only increased in the years since. Growing public interest in place-lore has brought about several publications, both in hard copy and in digital form, and has led to a place-lore revival. In its "second life" (Honko 2013a [1991]), obsolete folklore is resurrected from archives and other dormant forms and brought back into circulation. Conserved place-lore resumes its life in the environment – often in its original dwelling places, with landscape becoming narratively re-loaded.

According to Mari-Ann Remmel (2014: 67), place-lore is "mostly narrative lore, which is strongly bound to some toponym, site or landscape object, and which includes (place) legends, place-bound beliefs, descriptions of practices, historical lore, memories etc". Mall Hiiemäe has characterised place-lore as a set of traditions that focus on natural and cultural surroundings, such as hills, valleys, forests, wetlands, lakes, rivers, fields, rocks, old trees, graveyards, chapels, churches, roads, and terrain. She notes that the very existence of these objects in the neighbourhood supports the continuity of the related place-lore, which in turn attributes value to sites and objects, safeguarding them from destruction. Hence, place-lore is a concept that refers to a symbiotic relationship between tradition communities and their environment, between tangible reality and the storyworld. (Hiiemäe 2007 [2004]: 364, 370.) When the Estonian term *kohapärimus* appeared, it seemed problematic to find a suitable equivalent in English. It was explicated as "place-related oral tradition", and it took many years before "place-lore" gained traction as a more fitting translation (Valk 2009). Its definitions above reveal that place-lore is not an analytical label that pinpoints a certain genre but a synthetic concept that highlights a variety of expressive forms that manifest close bonds between humans, places and the environment.

Characteristically, place-lore contains elements from different time periods, but place-lore is also in constant formation as new memory places are being created (Remmel & Valk 2014: 387). The concept has close affinities with the notion of environment mythology (Finnish *ympäristömytologia*), defined by Veikko Anttonen (2014b: 76) as a web of meanings that come into being through the interaction between mobile humans and both rural and urban landscapes that are never natural in themselves but become naturalised through various practices and discourses. Ergo-Hart Västrik has noted that folkloristic interest in place-lore correlates with recent shifts in the humanities that have changed the research focus to include human relationships with the environment. This 'human' aspect has appealed to local communities and municipalities in Estonia, which have recognised the value of place-lore in regional identity building as well as in nature and heritage tourism. (Västrik 2012: 26–27.)

Thus, place-lore has the power to unite people, to protect them (Casey 1996), and to move them to action in their endeavours of protecting remarkable places in their locality. In addition, certain distant destinations enthral people into making long journeys. Places with historical importance, such as sites of crucial battles, the birth places, homes and graves of great heroes and celebrities, and monuments of the past are visited by thousands of travellers. Innumerable pilgrims have been drawn to holy places by miracle stories of saints and of miraculous cures to receive blessings and return home with fresh stories to tell. However, as Jacob Kinnard notes, "there is nothing inherently sacred about any place or space or physical object; human agents give them power and maintain that power" (2014: 2). Places are empowered through narratives that are recycled in countless variants and which mark them out as extraordinary locations. Hence, we can talk about the social gravitation that certain sites exert through storytelling. This narrative gravitation field can fluctuate in time, increasing or waning, depending on the changing status of the place. The landscape, as it becomes storied, turns from a passive surrounding into an active participant in creating the supernatural environment. Lisa Gabbert has written about "performative landscapes" that participate in creation and shaping of the liminal reality where this world and the other world meet. People who enter this environment beyond the boundaries of everyday reality transform themselves ritually into story characters and become participants in the legendary realm. (Gabbert 2015: 162–164.) Thus, the storyworld, landscape and people all participate in the creation of this realm, in the supernaturalisation of places.

Regina Bendix (2002) argues that tourism relies to a great extent on narration and narrative potential to attract travellers – those who crave for something new, genuine and authentic – to the "aura of the touristic experience". Here Bendix refers to Walter Benjamin's understanding of aura as the irresistible attraction of certain works of art which bring into material proximity something which is felt to be inaccessibly remote. (Bendix 2002: 473.) Aura in Benjamin's understanding is also a form of perception that endows a phenomenon with the "ability to look back at us", to open its eyes or "lift its gaze" (Hansen 2008: 339). Notorious places appear as animated; they generate a sense of personal relationship and emotional awareness.

Places are of different kinds. They can be familiar, homely or unknown, or mysterious, or even dangerous. Places can become lived experiences and as such they can evoke different feelings. Visiting a cemetery can generate a sense of peace and tranquillity or bring back sweet memories, yet the same surrounding can evoke feelings of loss or regret, even mystery and fear, when the graveyard appears in the darkness of the night. American folklorists have studied the tradition of legend questing and legend tripping – visits to haunted places and scenes of horrific tragedies (Ellis 1996; Kinsella 2011; Gabbert 2015; Tucker 2015). Analyses of the psychological side of these visits reveals a strongly emotional aspect – on the one hand the need to induce fear, and on the other hand developing methods to cope with it, such as relying on comforting companionship (Thomas 2007: 58–59).

Place-related legends and traditions about the supernatural are the focus of the largest single group of chapters in the present volume. In his piece, Terry Gunnell examines Icelandic legends directly connected with specific places in the landscape, *álagablettir* ('enchanted spots'). They were seen as cursed and dangerous to visit. Legends have served to preserve knowledge of these places as well as the belief in their status as enchanted, even up to the present day. Three chapters in the volume are concerned with a certain type of place, the church. Kaarina Koski investigates the role of church buildings in Finnish folk belief. She describes how the "supernatural otherness of the church" is expressed in many folk traditions and legends. They depict dangerous encounters with otherworldly beings in the church at night as well as the different kinds of spirits found there. The special status of church buildings is closely connected with their sacrality and the special rituals conducted there. Church buildings in folk tradition are also in focus in Sandis Laime's chapter. He develops what he calls "place valence approach", an understanding of why a certain place has the capacity to attract certain narrative motifs. In his piece he specifically analyses the motif of churches sinking underground in Latvian folklore. John Lindow devotes his chapter to the churchyard and the Scandinavian folk legends that relate to it. He emphasises the liminal status of the churchyard, situated inside the church wall, but outside the church building. In many folk legends, the churchyard is a place where the dead communicate with the living. In Ülo Valk's chapter another type of place is in focus. He examines stories of hauntings in a particular hospital in Tartu. Here the *place* of the supernatural encounter is further emphasized by the fact that the hauntings are connected with specific areas within the hospital. Kristel Kivari investigates several phenomena that are generally seen as pseudo-science, including place-related ideas such as "energy lines" in the earth, which are supposed to influence dowsing rods and pendulums. In an important way this chapter also problematizes the concept of 'supernatural', since firstly, the idea of energy lines has a connection with accepted sciences such as geology, and secondly, the direct purpose of some of the investigations of the phenomenon in her discussion was to give the supernatural *natural* explanations.

Regional Variation, Environment and Spatial Dimensions

The physical environment is closely connected to narrative traditions. Folklore is always born in certain social and physical settings and is shaped by these surroundings. Carl Wilhelm von Sydow, who was interested in the dissemination of traditions, noticed that in the course of transmission folklore becomes adapted to a certain milieu – i.e. it appears in ecotypes. He remarked: "The narrower the cultural area is, the more uniform will be the development and the more distinct the oicotypification" (von Sydow 1948: 16). Later research has revealed that folklore cannot be considered an isolated phenomenon of culture and that the notion of 'uniform tradition' is incompatible with its endless live variation, and is, in fact, an oxymoron rather than a useful theoretical construct. However, there is no reason to doubt that folklore of the pre-Internet age bears a regional character. It is not only recorded in local dialects from people who reside in certain places, but it is often flexibly harmonized with nearby sites and adjusted to surrounding landscapes. Lauri Honko (2013b [1981]: 174) called these processes the 'milieu-morphological' adaptation of folklore, which he sees as consisting of operations and devices, such as familiarisation and localisation, "linking a certain tradition to a spot or place in the experienced physical milieu". The fusion of boundaries between the narrative plot and its physical and social environment is one of the distinctive features of legend as a genre. According to Timothy Tangherlini, local traditions reflecting culturally-based values and beliefs exert influence upon legends. Therefore, the legend can be considered as a highly ecotypified genre (1990: 385).

Ecotypes and regional variation in legends and traditions are discussed in three of the chapters in the present volume. Frog examines ATU 1148b, "The Theft of the Thunder-Instrument", a tale that is spread over the Scandinavian and Baltic area; his main focus is regional variation. He particularly analyses how the ATU 1148b tradition has been attached to local landscapes in Sámi traditions to a specific sacred site and in some Norwegian versions to a road through scree. Madis Arukask presents several aspects of the role of the herdsman, both certain rituals and different kinds of supernatural connections in the Vepsian culture area. He points out some features that differ remarkably from the traditions of herdsman magic in southern cultures, and explains them as differences between burn-beat agriculturists and cattle breeders on the one hand and large-scale corn cultivators on the other. Bengt af Klintberg conducts a survey of the legends and beliefs about bracken and its magical flower that blooms at Midsummer Night. The chapter shows close connection between spatial and temporal dimensions in legends and the role that belief narratives play in the supernaturalisation of the everyday world. Bracken legends can transform the well-known environment into the realm of the supernatural, manifesting the "chronotope of enchantment", to take up the term that Camilla Asplund Ingemark has used to characterise the generative principle of some narrative genres (Asplund Ingemark 2006). Bracken legends often merge with legends about buried treasures and express one more aspect of place-lore – namely the awareness that some singular places close to human neighbourhoods remain hidden, even inaccessible, and they only occasionally reveal their secrets. The temporal aspect of legends – the magical time of special nights – plays an active role in making the supernatural places.

These three chapters address the impact of folklore upon the perception of local natural surroundings which sometimes then acquires an otherworldly character. Lotte Tarkka (2015: 17) has drawn a distinction between "the environmental or social spaces that are the 'other', such as the forest or neighbourhood village" on one hand, and the empirically inaccessible otherworlds (such as the land of the dead) (cf. also Tarkka 2013: 327–428). For Max Lüthi the contrast between the nearby and a remote otherworld was found in the distinction between the down-to-earth legend and the marvellous folktale (German *Sage* vs. *Märchen*). He states that "folktale characters do not feel that an encounter with an otherworld being is an encounter with an alien dimension" (Lüthi 1986 [1982]: 10), while the opposite is the case in the legend. When it comes to physical or geographical distance, Lüthi (1986 [1982]: 7–8) describes a sort of paradox: although the legend emphasises that otherworld beings belong to another world, they are physically close to human beings, living with or close to them; in the folktale the opposite is true: hero has to wander far and wide before he meets otherworld beings, whose dwelling places remain distant. Lüthi concludes (1986 [1982]: 8–9): "In legends otherworld beings are physically near human beings but spiritually far. In folktales they are far away geographically but near in spirit and in the realm of experience."

The next chapters in the volume explore the relationship between the remote and nearby otherworlds and spatial dimensions in sagas. Daniel Sävborg discusses the generic features of Icelandic sagas, focussing on the relationship between supernatural elements and spatial distance. He applies Max Lüthi's contrastive model of legends (*Sagen*) as two-dimensional narratives and folktales (*Märchen*) as one-dimensional stories to Old Norse literature. It appears that two-dimensionality is a characteristic of stories about events in the vicinity of tellers, whereas one-dimensionality increases with geographical distance. Mart Kuldkepp addresses other aspects of distance in Old Norse literature, analysing travelogues about the spiritual quest of two heroes who convert to Christianity and start preaching in their home countries. Imaginary holy lands outside everyday experience function as gateways from the natural to the supernatural realm and display liminal qualities. The geographical distance between places is converted into spiritual distance between heathendom and the holiness of Christianity. Kuldkepp's approach successfully reveals a common pattern in two sagas usually treated as belonging to entirely different genres.

Nation, People and Folk: Traditions Reconsidered

Folklore studies from the 19th century often express a craving for the glory and wisdom of the distant past. Several monumental source publications were conceptualised as memorials to past generations. Folklore was seen as revealing their spiritual heritage and was envisioned as a treasury, as a resource-rich asset to be deposited in the national archives and to be used for the development of literary culture. Awareness of the historical value of folklore thus did not mean that the glance of scholars was turned backwards only. The approaching 20th century engendered high expectations of general progress, enlightenment, modernisation, and liberation of peoples from poverty, ignorance, and social and political suppression. Patriotic idealism, folklore collecting, the publication of epics, interest in and research into pre-Christian mythologies and histories all created a sense of ethnic unity, in several cases leading to the foundation of nation states. Folklore represented their national heritage and was labelled with ethnonyms as a marker of ownership. When folklore was designated as Estonian, Finnish, German, Latvian, Russian, Swedish or some other ethnic heritage, these compartmentalisations also charted the geopolitical map of European nation states. The temporal dimension of folklore thus came together with the notion of countries as territorial units. Early folklorists were often provincial scholars with in-depth knowledge of local dialects and lore that was specific to places and which marked off these places as unique. It was not only differences in landscape and material culture that distinguished sites from each other, but also differences in local psyche and tradition, including beliefs in magic and the supernatural. These traits marked folklore as fundamentally different from the intellectual traditions of the educated urban people. However, the opposition between the 'superstitious' folk and the rationally minded 'elite' might be nothing more than a cognitive construct of modernist thinkers who were drawing sharp boundaries between their own enlightened mindset and the backward mentality of the past. In his chapter, Jonathan Roper problematises this distinction. While folklorists have for a long time been concerned with folk belief as opposed to educated scepticism, Roper argues that we also have to take the concepts of folk disbelief and educated belief into account. He shows that sceptical narratives that contradict the pattern of depicting the folk as credulous have often been recorded by open-minded non-folklorists. It appears that their works sometimes offer a more nuanced picture of the intellectual life in the countryside than those of the folklorists with their bias towards focussing on tale types and supernatural beliefs. The chapter by David Hopkin also addresses narrative traditions among local communities. Whereas Roper looks for alternative sources to study the mentality of the people, Hopkin examines folklore collections to study peasant history. He shows that historical legends of the peasantry express social divisions and group ideology and can be re-examined as important sources for studying the history of peasant emancipation. Because of their 'truth value', legends can help scholars to understand why people behaved as they did, they are also expressions of 'peasant historiography'. However, Hopkin argues that "legends, despite their historical character, are not really about the past, they are about the present and future." Hence they have a great role to play in the formation of social identities and political realities. Hopkin's article also discusses the construction of the Celt in France. In the 18th century, the division of the French population into three estates – the clergy, the nobility, and the commons – was frequently connected with the allegedly different origins of the classes: the nobles were descendants of the

Franks who had conquered and oppressed the Roman-Celtic population, whose descendants were the commons. Diarmuid Ó Giolláin sheds light on a common assumption about folklore – the idea of its national quality, which has led to the perception of folkloristics as being a 'national science'. Ó Giolláin discusses the construction of the concepts *Baltic*, *Nordic* and *Celtic* and the interest in collecting the folklore of these supposed cultures. These attempts, as well as the founding of folklore societies and university chairs, are analysed in connection with national movements and nation building in the 19th and 20th centuries.

The three articles in the third section of the book lead us from the rural communities – i.e. from the grassroots level of folklore – towards folklore's political uses in constructing and reinforcing national identities. From places and localities we reach the concept of homeland and geopolitical spaces. Romantic national ideologies, in turn, became important factors of collecting folklore, which leads us back to a small community, tied to a place, which is "an extremely meaningful component of individual identity", as Alan Dundes (1989: 13) argues in his essay "Defining Identity through Folklore", where he demonstrates the complexity of the dynamics of belonging and self-identification. The last chapters thus also illustrate the multi-layered nature of folklore in relation to social, political and territorial identity formation.

Ontology of the Supernatural

Our analytical and reflexive era of knowledge production presupposes a critical examination of the categories that we use. We have discovered that many concepts have roots in European epistemological traditions and their potential to illuminate and encompass other cultural realities can either be limited or even distorting. Thus, 'religion' has turned out to be a problematic term, as it is too often understood 'prototypically', which means viewing its diverse phenomena through the lens of some particular religion, usually that of Christianity (Alles 2005: 7704). Several authors argue that religion as a category is pre-theoretical, culturally constructed and ineffective, especially if we look beyond the boundaries of the Abrahamic religions: Judaism, Christianity and Islam. Along the same lines, the fundamental dichotomy between nature and society, human and non-human in Western epistemology appeared as a late construct, which spread with the ideas of modernity, only becoming firmly established quite recently (Latour 1993). Anthropologists representing the ontological turn have rejected the notion of inanimate nature, which lacks agency and personhood, and have shown the human relationship with the environment in a new light. In Western epistemology, personhood as a category can only be applied to self-conscious individual humans, but this is not the case for many peoples who are not affected by the theory of the great divide between nature and culture. In addition, animals, birds, fish, spirits, deities, rocks and trees can be recognised as (other-than-human) persons – as far as they relate to humans (and to each other) in a particular way (cf. Harvey 2012).

These interactions reverberate in the indigenous theories that Eduardo Viveiros de Castro (1998) has called perspectivism – consistent ideas in Amazonian cosmologies concerning the way in which humans, animals and spirits see themselves and one another. According to this outlook "animals (predators) and spirits see humans as animals (as prey) to the same extent that animals (as prey) see humans as spirits or as animals (predators)" (Viveiros de Castro 1998: 470). Philippe Descola (2013) has developed the theory of basic configurations, how humans are related to nature, and described animism as one of those cognitive modes. He points out that in animist ontologies, plants, animals and other elements of the physical environment are endowed with a subjectivity of their own; and that different kinds of person-to-person relationship are maintained with these entities. In animist thought, both humans and non-humans possess the same psychological dispositions (interiority) with the latter also being bestowed with social characteristics (Descola 2011: 19). The counterpart of animism is the prevailing Western ontology of naturalism, which "can be defined by the continuity of the physicality of the entities of the world and the discontinuity of their respective interiorities" (Descola 2013: 173). Thus, in the Western world, humans are singled out by their intellectual and ethical capacities and are seen as surpassing the rest of living nature, although they share essentially the same substance of their physical bodies.

Graham Harvey (2005: 185) notes that animistic thought does not require concepts such as 'nature' nor 'supernature' because various persons, such as animal-, tree- or human-persons, and according to some animists, places as relational persons, co-exist and interact within the same domain. In light of these deliberations, the category of the supernatural might seem problematic. The compound *super-naturalis* reflects some basic Western dichotomies of matter and spirit, body and mind, nature and something which is superior to physis. It implies a hierarchical world where the divine consciousness transcends the earthbound biological reality that is governed by the laws of nature. Morton Klass (1995: 27) finds the term 'supernatural' uncomfortable, especially in cross-cultural study, because many societies make no distinction between the two realms of Western ontology, and the concept is "irremediably ethnocentric and thus leads inevitably to confusion and misinterpretation". (However, Klass [1995: 28] finds it a perfectly acceptable term in certain contexts, such as "tales of the supernatural".) In 2003 a special issue of *Anthropological Forum* was published, dedicated to the notion of 'supernatural' as a contested concept in anthropology with its controversial cultural baggage and the implied dichotomy it bears with the 'natural' world, something which in non-Western cultures may be associated with colonial domination (Lohmann 2003). Some authors reject it, especially as an etic category, although others find it cognitively useful. Thus, according to the provisional definition of Thomas Raverty (2003: 188), the supernatural is "a general categorical perspective, whether insider or outsider (emic or etic), wherein human metaphorical and analogical capabilities, especially in imaginatively enlarging upon sense data and empirical reality, are given free rein". This notion of the supernatural, which refers to imaginative cognition, seems broad enough to encompass non-Western ontologies beyond Christian theology. In the same issue of *Anthropological Forum*, Susan Sered (2003: 217–218) found the concept useful, bearing in mind the differences between cultures in the extent to which they recognise spheres that are distinct from the 'natural'. Finding unified theories and neat dichotomies problematic, she recommends thinking about the supernatural as 'enhanced natural' or ultra-natural, rather than as 'not natural'.

We, editors of the current volume find these more nuanced approaches to the concept more appealing than strict avoidance of the term simply because of some theological and philosophical connotations. The supernatural has become an emic notion, at least in the Western world, with vernacular equivalents in many languages; it rarely causes misunderstandings in fieldwork or when analyzing textual sources. Folklorists have a long history of discussing the supernatural and using it as an etic category. In some early works, it seemed to indicate irrational superstitions in contradiction to a scientific worldview and to reality as the scholars themselves perceived it (cf. Klass 1995: 30). However, the term today does not usually have pejorative connotations, and has been used by some researchers as a cognitive category, testifying to the unknown, mysterious and transcendental aspects of reality. Thus, Barbara Walker (1995: 2) notes:

> The existence of the term [supernatural] itself is a linguistic and cultural acknowledgement that inexplicable things happen which we identify as being somehow beyond the natural or the ordinary, and that many of us behold beliefs which connect us to spheres that exist beyond what we might typically see, hear, taste, touch, or smell.

Other scholars demonstrate the continuity of the supernatural as a persistent topic in folk narratives that has never faded away, either in religious or in secular contexts (Gay 1999; Dégh 2001). As a consistent but boundless realm, the supernatural thus appears in oral and literary traditions throughout all ages and in all societies, and it can be studied as a more or less distinct field. As the unknown domain beyond the limits of our understanding, the "'supernatural' world lies beyond the defining parameters of natural law, allowing the human imagination free rein in the shadowy margins of knowledge and ignorance" (Reeve & Van Wagenen 2011: 1).

Imaginary Realms of Genres

Folklore, which is to a great extent a verbal practice, has its more or less recognisable discursive modes, called genres[1]. Different genres evoke different kinds of outlook, feelings and dispositions to believe or disbelieve. They make people perceive the world from a variety of perspectives and to reflect upon it in multiple ways. The supernatural in folklore can be considered a generic phenomenon – not only a form of artistic expression or representation, but of realising the generic potential of generating imaginary realms that coalesce with socio-physical reality. Proceeding from Frog's discussion about enactment as an aspect of genre, the supernaturalisation of the environment can be considered as something that "genres may do", if they "actualize something as reality at a mythic level" (Frog 2016: 62–63). Expressive imagination evokes the supernatural as a kind of aura, a numinous halo that can enshroud the 'ordinary world' with a mysterious veil of anomalous otherness. From a folkloristic perspective, the supernatural appears "as a social phenomenon, located in the context of a verbal performance and metanarrative reaction rather than an existential one," as Bill Ellis has noted (2015: 196). In belief narratives, other-than-human persons gain agency and interact with people. Trees, lakes, cliffs and other elements of nature wake to life, animals and birds communicate important messages, such as omens of death or accidents; spirits appear, often intentionally, and intervene in the lives of humans, who are the closest kin of the 'others'; the dead come back from the otherworld to visit the living. Belief narratives animate the world by fostering relationships between humans and the non-humans, which are bestowed with personhood and individuality. The supernatural is evoked through imagination and storytelling as a kind of liminal reality, which is never fully comprehensible or complete, but compelling in its powerful presence. And this storied world of the supernatural manifests basic elements of the daily reality while remaining open-ended and uncertain, and implying the vast space of the unknown beyond the realm of human existence.

Lotte Tarkka (2015: 27–30) has noted the overlap of wakefulness, dream-world and utopias, and the expressive power of their relationships. In her account, folklore genres appear as "differentiated yet interconnected spheres of vernacular imagination: they offer the expressive means and set the expressive constraints for imaginative processes and their communication" (2015: 30). Genres actualise during the process of oral or literary production and sometimes take easily recognisable forms, such as myths, legends or sagas, while at other times remaining indefinite. Genre categories often seem irrelevant if they are used merely as labels for sorting, but if we consider genres as tradition-bound creative practices they offer insightful perspectives with which to comprehend textual production. Through their expressive and cognitive power, genres explicate this world while at the same time envisioning otherworldly realities. Myths are among the mightiest genres that can evoke the supernatural and relate it to the basic conditions of human existence. Anna-Leena Siikala has characterised myths as narrative and poetic expression of mythic consciousness. Although they are persistent, and rely on a long history of fundamental symbolism, myths are far from static; rather they are kaleidoscopic. Mythic images are in constant motion and derive "their force from the implicit significance of these symbols" (Siikala 2012: 19). Frog (2015: 33) has explicated the mechanisms of mythic discourse which generate stability and produce variation through the concept of a symbolic matrix – "a term which refers to the constitutive elements of a mythology or mythologies in a cultural environment and conventions for their combination". He has noted that mythical symbols are invested with emotion, "because they are socially recognized as being meaningful to people in powerful ways [...]" (Frog 2015: 38). Genres of the supernatural have a personal aspect as they are emotionally charged, evoke memories and offer frames for life experiences, while as communicative practices they actualise in social settings and become a shared resource.

Whereas mythic imagination is often expressed in poetry and envisions otherworldly realms, legendary discourse is much more bound to ordinary social realities. Legends are not detached from the environment, they are embedded into familiar settings, they take place. According to Kaarina Koski, the narrative time-space in legends is flexible, as the "narrators can adjust the distance between the narrated world and the real world" (2008: 337). She has shown that "The closer to the reality the narrator locates the narrated events, the more realistic the story is bound to be" (ibid.). The scope of the supernatural element in legends can vary but predominantly, legend as a narrative genre depicts unexpected encounters between a human character and supernatural powers (Lüthi 1976 [1971]). This confrontation becomes more dramatic if the numinous power takes a personified form – of a spirit, ghost, devil, revenant, nightmare, witch or some other human or non-human entity. Legends are oriented to everyday life, and the events described therein usually happen to real people in real surroundings, known well by the storytellers and their audiences. These stories draw from the inscrutable realm of the unknown, of the otherworld, and enchant the social and physical world by shifting elements that derive from legendary discourse and move into the daily environment. Through this synthesis of social and narrative realities, legends transform the ordinary world into an unsafe realm of frightening encounters with the supernatural. Legends are not only dramatic and entertaining stories, they are also guidelines for behaviour in critical situations and instructions on how to avoid unwanted contacts with the otherworld. As legendary plots get localised into familiar settings, these stories mould the local landscapes and charge certain places, such as groves, lakes, graveyards, churches and other buildings with supernatural aura (cf. the chapters by John Lindow, Kaarina Koski and Ülo Valk in this volume). The numinous radiation of the genre empowers these places and transfers them into the realm of unknown. Caution and ritual behaviour, which is prescribed by legends but acted out in real life situations, shows how compelling this genre is for those individuals and communities who live in its liminal world, where the supernatural, natural and social co-exist. The numinous radiation of the genre empowers these places and transfers them into the realm of the unknown. Caution and ritual behaviour, which is prescribed by legends but acted out in real life situations, shows how compelling this genre is for those individuals and communities who live in its liminal world, where the supernatural, natural and social co-exist. Remarkably, in contemporary legends, the otherworld can appear not only in the form of spiritual entities but also as "extraterrestrial aliens, ethnic, religious and other minorities, criminals, mental patients, new technology, as well as the faceless power of the state and big commercial companies" (Koski 2016: 131). Thus both places and social spaces can reveal a supernatural dimension.

The current book analyses the hybrid realm where the supernatural and social realities merge in the fabric of legendry. It has its roots in the discussions that were held at the Nordic-Celtic-Baltic folklore symposium at the University of Tartu in June 2012. This international forum, with nearly one hundred participants, was organised by the Department of Estonian and Comparative Folklore, the Department of Scandinavian Studies, and the Tartu NEFA group of the University of Tartu in cooperation with the Centre of Excellence in Cultural Theory. It was the sixth symposium in the series of international meetings, which began with one organized in 1988 by the Department of Irish Folklore, University College, Dublin. Other symposia followed: in Galway (1991), Copenhagen (1993), Dublin (1996) and Reykjavík (2005) (for a brief history of the meetings see Gunnell 2008: 17–22). The first forum in Dublin had addressed the supernatural in Irish and Scottish migratory legends. The following symposia extended the geographical and thematic range of studies, focusing on the supernatural (Galway), minor genres (Copenhagen), maritime folklore (Dublin) and folk legends (Reykjavík). The sixth Nordic-Celtic-Baltic folklore symposium, in Tartu, was entitled "Supernatural Places", and it addressed place legends as a versatile genre in international folklore, exploring local tradition dominants such as holy groves, churches, haunted houses, cemeteries, grave mounds, hills, forests, lakes, and locations of hidden treasures. Narration of the supernatural aspects of environment was considered as a practice with social impact, shaping everyday life and the behaviour patterns of tradition bearers. Several papers discussed the localisation of legend plots in the environment and analysed how legends are entangled with social realities, in both rural and urban settings. Others scrutinised the otherworldly realms of the imagination, such as paradise, the land of the blessed, purgatory, the netherworld, and hell. In addition to empirically-oriented papers, the symposium offered critical reflections on the history of folklore research, and conceptual and theoretical discussions of genres, the pragmatics of folklore and its social functions. The current volume cannot represent the Supernatural Places forum in its full richness.[2] It offers a selection of papers that have been reworked, sometimes to a considerable extent, together with some chapters which have been written especially for this volume.

Acknowledgement

The editors express their gratitude to the two anonymous reviewers whose valuable comments helped to improve the manuscript to great extent. We are also indebted to the language editors Daniel E. Allen and Jonathan Roper, and also to Helen Kästik and Ergo-Hart Västrik for their editorial assistance. This book was supported by institutional research funding from the Estonian Ministry of Education and Research (project IUT2-43 Tradition, Creativity and Society: Minorities and Alternative Discourses).

NOTES

1 For a comprehensive discussion of 'genre' as a concept, its history and usage from the perspective of folklore studies, see Frog, Koski and Savolainen 2016. For 'genre' as a text-type category and a flexible theoretical model for analysing and interpreting both emergent and 'classic' folklore, see Frog 2016.
2 For the programme and abstracts of the sixth Nordic-Celtic-Baltic Folklore Symposium "Supernatural Places", held in June 2012 at the University of Tartu, see Siim 2012.

Sources

Alles, Gregory D. 2005. Religion (Further Considerations). In *Encyclopedia of Religion.* 2nd edn. Lindsay Jones (ed.). Detroit: Macmillan. Pp. 7701–7706.

Anttonen, Veikko 2014a. Religious Studies as Landscape Studies: Perceptual Strategies and Environmental Preferences in Religion and Mythology. In *New Trends and Recurring Issues in the Study of Religion.* Ábrahám Kovács & James L. Cox (eds.). Budapest: L'Harmattan. Pp. 113–132.

Anttonen, Veikko 2014b. Kotona maisemassa. Mytologian spatiaalinen rakentuminen. In *Ympäristömytologia.* Seppo Knuuttila & Ulla Piela (eds.). Kalevalaseuran Vuosikirja 93. Helsinki: Suomalaisen Kirjallisuuden Seura. Pp. 74–88.

Asplund Ingemark, Camilla 2006. The Chronotope of Enchantment. *Journal of Folklore Research* 43(1): 1–30.

Bacchilega, Cristina 2007. *Legendary Hawai'i and the Politics of Place. Tradition, Translation, and Tourism.* Philadelphia: University of Pennsylvania Press.

Basso, Keith H. 1996. *Wisdom Sits in Places. Landscape and Language among the Western Apache.* Albuquerque: University of New Mexico Press.

Bendix, Regina 2002. Capitalizing on Memories Past, Present, and Future. Observations on the Intertwining of Tourism and Narration. *Anthropological Theory* 2(4): 469–487.

Casey, Edward S. 1996. How to Get from Space to Place in a Fairly Short Stretch of Time. Phenomenological Prolegomena. In *Senses of Place.* Steven Feld & Keith H. Basso (eds.). Santa Fe, New Mexico: School of American Research Press. Pp. 13–52.

Dégh, Linda 2001. *Legend and Belief. Dialectics of a Folklore Genre.* Bloomington, Indianapolis: Indiana University Press.

Descola, Philippe 2011. Human Natures. *Quaderns* 27: 11–25.

Descola, Philippe 2013. *Beyond Nature and Culture.* Chicago, London: University of Chicago Press.

Dundes, Alan 1989. *Folklore Matters.* Knoxville: University of Tennessee Press.

Ellis, Bill 1996. Legend Trip. In *American Folklore. An Encyclopedia.* Jan Harold Brunvand (ed.). New York, London: Garland. Pp. 439–440.

Ellis, Bill 2015. The Haunted Asian Landscapes of Lafcadio Hearn: Old Japan. In *Putting the Supernatural in Its Place. Folklore, the Hypermodern, and the Ethereal.* Jeannie Banks Thomas (ed.). Salt Lake City: The University of Utah Press. Pp. 192–220.

Frog 2015. Mythology in Cultural Practice: A Methodological Framework for Historical Analysis. In *Between Text and Practice. Mythology, Religion and Research.* Frog & Karina Lukin (eds.). A special issue of *RMN Newsletter* 10. Helsinki: University of Helsinki. Pp. 33–57.

Frog 2016. "Genres, Genres Everywhere, but Who Knows What to Think?" Toward a Semiotic Model. In *Genre – Text – Interpretation. Multidisciplinary Perspectives on Folklore and Beyond.* Kaarina Koski, Frog, & Ulla Savolainen (eds.). Studia Fennica Folkloristica 22. Helsinki: Finnish Literature Society. Pp. 47–88.

Frog, Kaarina Koski & Ulla Savolainen 2016. At the Intersection of Text and Interpretation. An Introduction to Genre. In *Genre – Text – Interpretation. Multidisciplinary Perspectives on Folklore and Beyond*. Kaarina Koski, Frog, & Ulla Savolainen (eds.). Studia Fennica Folkloristica 22. Helsinki: Finnish Literature Society. Pp. 17–43.

Gabbert, Lisa 2015. Legend Quests and the Qurious Case of St. Ann's Retreat. The Performative Landscape. In *Putting the Supernatural in Its Place. Folklore, the Hypermodern, and the Ethereal*. Jeannie Banks Thomas (ed.). Salt Lake City: The University of Utah Press. Pp. 146–169.

Gay, David E. 1999. The Supernatural World of Christian Folk Religion in Twentieth-Century America. In *Studies in Folklore and Popular Religion. Papers Delivered at the Symposium* Christian Folk Religion 2. Ülo Valk (ed.). Tartu: University of Tartu. Pp. 51–63.

Gunnell, Terry 2008. Introduction. In *Legends and Landscape. Articles Based on Plenary Papers Presented at the 5th Celtic-Nordic-Baltic Folklore Symposium, Reykjavik 2005*. Terry Gunnell (ed.). Reykjavik: University of Reykjavik Press. Pp. 13–24.

Hansen, Miriam Bratu 2008. Benjamin's Aura. *Critical Inquiry* 34(2): 336–375.

Harvey, Graham 2005. *Animism. Respecting the Living World*. London: Hurst.

Harvey, Graham 2012. Things Act: Casual Indigenous Statements about the Performance of Object-persons. In *Vernacular Religion in Everyday Life. Expressions of Belief*. Marion Bowman & Ülo Valk (eds.). Sheffield, Bristol, CT: Equinox. Pp. 194–210.

Heynickx, Rajesh; Thomas Coomans, Harman De Dijn, Jan De Maeyer & Bart Verschaffel 2012. Introduction. In *Loci Sacri. Understanding Sacred Places*. T. Coomans, H. De Dijn, J. De Maeyer, R. Heynickx & B. Verschaffel (eds.)Leuven: Leuven University Press. Pp. 7–11.

Hiiemäe, Mall 2007 [2004]. Poollooduslike kooslustega seonduvast. In *Sõnajalg jaaniööl*. By Mall Hiiemäe. Eesti Mõttelugu 73. Tartu: Ilmamaa. Pp. 363–370.

Honko, Lauri 2013a [1991]. The Folklore Process. In *Theoretical Milestones. Selected Writings of Lauri Honko*. Pekka Hakamies & Anneli Honko (eds.). Folklore Fellows' Communications 304. Helsinki: Academia Scientiarum Fennica. Pp. 29–54.

Honko, Lauri 2013b [1981]. Four Forms of Adaptation of Tradition. In *Theoretical Milestones. Selected Writings of Lauri Honko*. Pekka Hakamies & Anneli Honko (eds.). Folklore Fellows' Communications 304. Helsinki: Academia Scientiarum Fennica. Pp. 173–188.

Kinnard, Jacob N. 2014. *Places in Motion. The Fluid Identities of Temples, Images, and Pilgrims*. Oxford, New York: Oxford University Press.

Kinsella, Michael 2011. *Legend-Tripping Online. Supernatural Folklore and the Search for Ong's Hat*. Jackson: University Press of Mississippi.

Klass, Morton 1995. *Ordered Universes. Approaches to the Anthropology of Religion*. Boulder, Oxford: Westview.

Knott, Kim 2005. *The Location of Religion. A Spatial Analysis*. London, Oakville: Equinox.

Knuuttila, Seppo 2006. Paikan moneus. In *Paikka. Eletty, kuviteltu, kerrottu*. Seppo Knuuttila, Pekka Laaksonen & Ulla Piela (eds.). Kalevalaseuran vuosikirja 85. Helsinki: Suomalaisen Kirjallisuuden Seura. Pp. 7–11.

Korom, Frank J. 2016. A Telling Place: Narrative and the Construction of Locality in a Bengali Village. *Narrative Culture* 3(1): 32–66.

Koski, Kaarina 2008. Narrative Time-Spaces in Belief Legends. In *Space and Time in Europe: East and West, Past and Present*. Mirjam Mencej (ed.). Ljubljana: University of Ljubljana. Pp. 337–353.

Koski, Kaarina 2016. The Legend Genre and Narrative Registers. In *Genre – Text – Interpretation. Multidisciplinary Perspectives on Folklore and Beyond*. Kaarina Koski, Frog, & Ulla Savolainen (eds.). Studia Fennica Folkloristica 22. Helsinki: Finnish Literature Society. Pp. 113–136.

Latour, Bruno 1993. *We Have Never Been Modern*. Cambridge: Harvard University Press.

Lohmann, Roger Ivar 2003. Naming the Ineffable. *Anthropological Forum* 13(2): 117–124.

Lüthi, Max 1976 [1971]. Aspects of the *Märchen* and the Legend. In *Folklore Genres*. Dan Ben-Amos (ed.). Austin: University of Texas Press. Pp. 17–33.

Lüthi, Max 1986 [1982]. *The European Folktale. Form and Nature*. Bloomington, Indianapolis: Indiana University Press.

Raverty, Thomas D. 2003. Starting with the Supernatural: Implications for Method, Comparison, and Communication in Religious Anthropology and Inter-religious Dialogue. *Anthropological Forum* 13(2): 187–194.

Reeve, Paul W. & Michael Scott Van Wagenen 2011. Between Pulpit and Pew. Where History and Lore Intersect. In *Between Pulpit and Pew. The Supernatural World in Mormon History and Folklore*. Logan: Utah State University Press. Pp. 1–16.

Remmel, Mari-Ann 2014. The Concept, Research History and Nature of Place Lore. Summary. In *Muistis, koht ja pärimus II. Pärimus ja paigad./ Monuments, Site and Oral Lore II. Lore and Places*. Heiki Valk (ed.). Muinasaja teadus 26(2). Tartu: University of Tartu. Pp. 64–70.

Remmel, Mari-Ann & Heiki Valk 2014. Monuments, Lore Places, and Place Lore: Temporal and Spatial Aspects. Summary. In *Muistis, koht ja pärimus II. Pärimus ja paigad./ Monuments, Site and Oral Lore II. Lore and Places*. Heiki Valk (ed.). Muinasaja teadus 26(2). Tartu: University of Tartu. Pp. 387–398.

Sered, Susan 2003. Afterword: Lexicons of the Supernatural. *Anthropological Forum* 13(2): 213–218.

Siikala, Anna-Leena 2012. Myths as Multivalent Poetry. Three Complementary Approaches. In *Mythic Discourses. Studies in Uralic Traditions*. Frog, Anna-Leena Siikala & Eila Stepanova (eds.). Studia Fennica Folkloristica 20. Helsinki: Finnish Literature Society. Pp. 17–39.

Siim, Pihla Maria 2012. *6th Nordic-Celtic-Baltic Folklore Symposium Supernatural Places. June 4–7, 2012 Tartu, Estonia. Abstracts*. Tartu: University of Tartu. Available at https://www.flku.ut.ee/sites/default/files/www_ut/sp_abstracts.pdf [Accessed April 15, 2018]

von Sydow, Carl Wilhelm 1948. On the Spread of Tradition. In *Selected Papers on Folklore Published on the Occasion of his 70th Birthday*. Copenhagen: Rosenkilde and Bagger. Pp. 11–43.

Tangherlini, Timothy R. 1990. "It Happened Not Too Far From Here…": A Survey of Legend Theory and Characterization." *Western Folklore* 49: 371–390.

Tarkka, Lotte 2013. *Songs of the Border People. Genre, Reflexivity, and Performance in Karelian Oral Poetry*. Folklore Fellows' Communications 305. Helsinki: Academia Scientiarum Fennica.

Tarkka, Lotte 2015. Picturing the Otherworld: Imagination in the Study of Oral Poetry. In *Between Text and Practice. Mythology, Religion and Research*. Frog & Karina Lukin (eds.). A special issue of *RMN Newsletter* 10. Helsinki: University of Helsinki. Pp. 17–33.

Thomas, Jeannie Banks 2007. The Usefulness of Ghost Stories. In *Haunting Experiences. Ghosts in Contemporary Folklore*. Diane E. Goldstein, Sylvia Ann Grider & Jeannie Banks Thomas (eds.). Logan: Utah State University Press. Pp. 25–59.

Tuan, Yi-Fu 2001 [1977]. *Space and Place. The Perspective of Experience*. Minneapolis, London: University of Minnesota Press.

Tucker, Elisabeth 2015. Messages from the Dead. Lily Dale; New York. In *Putting the Supernatural in Its Place. Folklore, the Hypermodern, and the Ethereal*. Jeannie Banks Thomas (ed.). Salt Lake City: The University of Utah Press. Pp. 170–191.

Valk, Ülo 2009. Narratives of Belonging: Comparative Notes on Assamese Place-Lore. In *Folklore. The Intangible Cultural Heritage of SAARC Region*. Ajeet Cour &

K. Satchidanandan (eds.). New Delhi: Foundation of SAARC Writers and Literature. Pp. 38–50.

Viveiros de Castro, Eduardo 1998. Cosmological Deixis and Amerindian Perspectivism. *The Journal of the Royal Anthropological Institute* 4(3): 469–488.

Västrik, Ergo-Hart 2012. Place-Lore as a Field of Study within Estonian Folkloristics: Sacred and Supernatural Places. In *Supernatural Places. Abstracts. 6th Nordic-Celtic-Baltic Folklore Symposium, June 4–7, 2012, Tartu, Estonia.* Pihla Maria Siim (ed.). Tartu: University of Tartu. Pp. 26–27. Available at https://www.flku.ut.ee/sites/default/files/www_ut/sp_abstracts.pdf [Accessed April 15, 2018]

Walker, Barbara 1995. Introduction. In *Out of the Ordinary. Folklore and the Supernatural.* Barbara Walker (ed.). Logan, Utah: Utah State University Press. Pp. 1–7.

Explorations in Place-Lore I

Terry Gunnell

The Power in the Place:
Icelandic *Álagablettir* Legends
in a Comparative Context

The stories people tell change things. They have effects not only on the way people see the storyteller, but also on the way in which they understand and experience both the surroundings of the performance and the world around them in general. Legends directly connected to these surroundings function alongside place names to give landscape depth, history, personality and mysticism (see de Certeau 1984; Gunnell 2005; 2009a). However, for listeners, they also provide a kind of map of how one should behave in this landscape: what is right, what is wrong, *when* are they right or wrong, and *how* punishment is likely to descend on you if you transgress the largely unwritten moral rules imposed by society.

The legends that will be discussed in the following article are among the most common legends still told in the countryside in Iceland, but are less rarely recorded on paper because they are so short, so similar and only really relevant to those living and working on the farms in question. The legends relate to so-called *álagablettir* (lit. 'enchanted/ cursed spots'), the first part of the word suggesting that some sort of ban has been placed on them by some other party, while second part of the word, *blettur* (lit. 'spot') underlines that they are seen as being separate from their surroundings in some way. These are places with potential: when you step into this space, you step into legend.

The national belief survey we carried out in Iceland in 2006/2007 (Ásdís A. Arnalds et al. 2008; see also Gunnell 2007; 2014a) underlined that while only 2% or 3% of the c. 1,000 people asked had personal experience of something bad happening to them at these sites, around 55% believed that it was quite possible, if not *probable*, that something could happen. Around 10% were certain that bad things could occur. The reason for these high figures is essentially based on the numerous living legendary accounts telling of experiences that have occurred at such sites. These accounts have served to perpetuate the beliefs, if only because so many of them take the form of memorates and go out of their way to underline exactly when the incidents in question occurred and to whom (cf. Oring 2008). In a sense, as one archaeologist has suggested (Omland 2007; 2010), legends of this kind have served as a very effective form of preservation order for the sites in question, perhaps more effective than any official government order. There is no question that this has helped these beliefs survive for several centuries, perhaps even from the time of the settlement of Iceland (in around 870 AD) (see below).

An *álagablettur* is essentially an area of grass that is not allowed to be harvested or disturbed in any way, but can also take the form of a few bushes or a rock. If we concentrate here on the more common grassy spots, these tend to stand apart from their surroundings in some natural way, in the form of a small hillock, mound, tussock, knoll, a depression in the local landscape, or an islet in a river, lake or pool. They might also be part of a marsh, or be easily recognised by being close to a particular rock or a cliff that stands out in the landscape (see images in Bjarni Harðarson 2001). These spots, usually situated close to farms, are found all around Iceland. While the Sagnagrunnur database of over 10,000 printed Icelandic legends (see Sagnagrunnur) only provides around 50 examples of legends relating to these phenomena,[1] Árni Óla's *Álög og bannhelgi* (1968) contained over 170 examples from all over the country. Bjarni Harðarson's more recent (2001) detailed collection of all the living legends in just one particular southern county, Árnessýsla, however, lists around 60 examples, 55 more than those noted in the same area by Árni Óla. The mere fact that over 800 examples of such legends[2] (sometimes in 'potential legend' form: see below) can be found in the sound recordings of the Arnamagnean Institute in Iceland (most made in the 1950s and 1960s: see Árnastofnun) implies that one might expect most counties to have a similar number of sites to those recorded by Bjarni in Árnessýsla, the majority perhaps being in the south, west and north of the country, and especially those areas in valleys and flatlands where farming was the main means of subsistence. These figures suggest that the *álagablettir* legends are probably the most common form of legend known in the Icelandic countryside, and probably have been so for some time – even if they are not told on a daily basis.

These sites have obvious similarities and sometimes close relationships to the Icelandic 'elf rocks' previously examined by Valdimar Tr. Hafstein in connection with road building (Valdimar Tr. Hafstein 2000; see also Sigvardsen 2009 for parallels in the Faroes). Here I deliberately want to keep to those legends connected to the grassy spots, areas which were more tempting for people in need, and thus more regularly dangerous.

As noted above, Icelandic *álagablettir* legends can be very short, so short that it is questionable whether they are legends at all. Some are little longer than what the Swedish folklorist von Carl Wilhelm Sydow called "dites" or belief statements indicating that this or that place was not harvested or tampered with in any other way because it could have "dire consequences", as occurs in the following two short examples from southern Iceland:

> In the homefield at Prestbakki in Síða there is a hillock which must never be harvested. If it is harvested, there will be a storm which will blow all the hay away. (Árni Óla 1968: 178; unless otherwise stated, all translations in this article are by the author.)

> At Mannskaðahóll [lit. 'human danger hillock'], there is a spot on the farm mound which must never be harvested; that will cause bad luck to animals or people. Old people still living say that, without exception, animals have died when a scythe has been used on that spot. (Árni Óla 1968: 143.)

This second account could stop after the first sentence. The second sentence nonetheless underlines that this is a belief statement with potential; what I would call a 'potential legend'. It refers to oral traditions, and could clearly be taken further into a legend format, as happens in most cases if the informant is encouraged to explain, as often occurs in the extant written and spoken records. The following example from the islands of Breiðafjörður in the west of Iceland is fairly typical of how the account might continue:

> There is an old story about Rúfey island which says this patch on the island called Kirkja [church] should not be harvested. There was a farmer called Þórður, who lived on Rúfey. One summer, he set out and harvested the spot, and decided to ignore everything that was said about that place. But he was a little disturbed by the fact that that autumn, he lost his cow. Þórður didn't let this change his mind and harvested the spot again the following year, and things got worse, because now he lost his boat, which was either smashed on the rocks or sunk so that it couldn't be used. But Þórður still refused to abandon his stubbornness, and harvested the spot for a third summer. Nothing happened until the autumn, and people had started thinking that nothing new was going to happen until one day in late autumn, Þórður went out alone to an island and never came back. And when people began wondering where he had got to, they started searching and he was found lying in a depression in the ground, his clothes all torn and tattered, and he himself covered in bruises, black and bloody. Þórður was the best of men, but he was exhausted and had to be supported back to his bed. He lay in his bed all winter, and at last got better again. Þórður never wanted to say what he had encountered on that island, but he swore he would never harvest Kirkja again, and people believed that his life had been spared on that condition. When Þórður died, his daughter María lost her mind, and the same thing was blamed for that as had caused Þórður's injuries. She was sent to Hallgrímur Bachmann in Bjarnarhöfn to be cured, and with his help recovered her health; indeed, it was said that he knew a thing or two. (Árni Óla 1968: 75–76; based on a manuscript by Friðrik Eggerz from 1852.)

This account not only adds details about the unfortunate events that can occur if local belief is ignored, providing an archetypal list of increasingly worrying accidents; it also contains a strong element of horror and supernatural mystery in the account of Þórður's disappearance, while the final sentence about a famous doctor brings the supernatural into a clear relationship with a reality that listeners knew.

The role of the supernatural in the *álagablettir* legends seems to grow proportionally as the accounts lengthen in the hands of more confident storytellers, commonly extending themselves with what might be referred to as 'the Icelandic dream motif', well recognised from the medieval sagas. Such longer accounts tell of how during, prior to, or after the harvesting of the site (or the removal of the bushes or stone) takes place, either the main protagonist or (more commonly) his wife dreams of a woman who firmly requests that the activities be halted. The following early legend, recorded by Ólafur Sveinsson from Purkey on Breiðafjörður is fairly typical:

> In Látrar in the Flatey parish, lived a man called Ingimundur. He was a prosperous man, and his grandchildren are still alive (around 1840). This Ingimundur, he was a very active, tough character. On his land was a small islet, which, I am told, was called Múli. People weren't allowed to harvest that, and it was never harvested, although there was a lot of grass on it. It irritated Ingimundur to see that islet having so much grass on it which couldn't be used. He couldn't put up with that any longer and asked his men to harvest the islet. His wife asked him not to let them do that. But he took no notice and had the islet harvested against his wife's wishes. So, the islet was harvested, and the grass was well used; a lot of hay came from that islet, and people thought that Ingimundur had made a good decision in having it harvested.
>
> Later that autumn, the couple dreamt of an anguished woman who said she had had to have her cow put down because Ingimundur had harvested the islet. And he would pay for it, while his wife would be rewarded for having asked him not to harvest the islet. She then took Ingimundur's hand and said, "You'll never feel a firmer grasp." Then she went away, and he woke up with a pain in his hand. It then withered, and he could never work with it again. "And it's all true!" Ólafur writes at the end. (Árni Óla 1968: 72–73.)

In most cases, the implication is that the dream woman in the account is an *álf-* or *huldukona*, the Icelandic equivalent of a nature spirit, an idea often supported by the name of the site in question (or others around it) which suggests it is an *álfhóll* (lit. "'elf" hillock'), or by additional statements concerning local beliefs about the site. This motif takes the account (and the spot in question) directly into the field of the supernatural. When it is lacking, listeners are free to imagine that the accidents that have taken place *might perhaps* be coincidental, although the implications of most accounts are that few saw things that way: listeners *know* that the protagonist was playing with fire, and view him (he is usually male) as foolhardy. What is interesting about the dream motif, however, is that as listeners, we still have to trust the experiences of those involved. The storyteller never states directly that people *saw* the nature spirits. They only dreamt of them; they say they *felt* (Icelandic: '*þóttust*') they saw them in their dreams. Secondly, it is noteworthy how often the 'other world' in these dream accounts tends to be represented by a female figure, a motif which has very old roots in Icelandic culture, going back to ideas of *valkyrjur* and females (such as Hel and Freyja) ruling the world of the dead. Whatever its age, the conflict of interests in the accounts is personified as a clash between a male harvester and a female nature spirit who represents the other world, with the male doomed to lose for not following local tradition (which seems to favour the female).

Also worth noting is the way in which these legends seem to be effectively updating themselves all the time, as can be seen in the following two examples recently recorded by Bjarni Harðarson in Árnessýsla, in which the cows, horses, and sheep commonly lost as a result of *álagablettir* transgressions are replaced by equally valuable mechanical objects.

The first runs as follows:

At Blesastaðir, there is an enchantment on Grænhóll that says it mustn't be mown, and that the area closest to the knoll must be left alone. Nothing must be touched on the knoll, and its inhabitants must not be disturbed, the belief being that hidden people live in the Grænhóll. Ingibjörg Jóhannsdóttir, the farmer at Blesastaðir told the author that this belief has always been respected, even though her husband, Hermann Guðmundsson, had not paid much attention to superstitions like this. Ingibjörg and her daughter Hildur said that they had respected the knoll as it was a kind of sacred space. All the same, one time there was talk of flattening the knoll, and a bulldozer was got in to carry this out. It was standing by the stable-door when those living on the farm went to sleep, the idea being that work would begin next day. That night, the bulldozer caught fire, and all ideas of flattening the hillock were abandoned. (Bjarni Harðarson 2001: 275.)

Another account deals with a hillock called Krosshóll:

Krosshóll is a hillock about the height of a man, just north-east of the farm at Kílhraun á Skeiðum. It is believed that there was an *álfa*-settlement in the hillock, and it was said that the hillock shouldn't be harvested or messed with in any way. Guðmundur Þórðarson (born 1939) once suffered from the result of burning crop residue near that hillock: the fire reached the hillock itself and burnt everything. Within a month of that happening, both of the cars owned by the farmer were damaged. He had an accident in one, but with the other one a tyre burst on the way over to Laugarás, which led to the car overturning. That was in 1980. Farm animals have since grazed on the outside of the hillock, but he drives them off. [...] That hillock is now protected with a fishing net. (Bjarni Harðarson 2001: 276–277.)

As noted earlier, there are obvious connections between these accounts and those modern Icelandic legends related to 'elf rocks' which stand in the way of new roads, legends which also involve potential damage to equipment and contact with nature spirits through the medium of dreams (Valdimar Tr. Hafstein 2000). Such rocks, though, tend to be simply rocks, and are less economically valuable to farmers (until they are in danger of being destroyed). They thus tend to be less part of the daily life of the farm.

Obvious parallels exist between these legends and the widespread Nordic migratory legends (Christiansen 1958: ML 8010, and af Klintberg 2010: V51–69) about people who try to break into grave mounds to steal treasure, and then break a taboo of silence by commenting on the vision of a farm or church seeming to be on fire in the distance, or an even more miraculous sight, such as that of seven headless roosters wandering by a carriage. Such legends are also found all over Iceland in connection with grave mounds, but they are essentially different to the legends under discussion here. Both legends have the function of protecting the space and clothing it with a veneer of taboo, but the *álagablettir* legends, while they are occasionally connected to grave mounds, and sometimes suggest that the sites in question light up at night (as often occurs with Icelandic treasure sites), are less connected with greed. They involve no illusions and less fantasy or humour. Furthermore, while those treasure-hunting only lose access to the treasure, those disturbing *álagablettir* lose their entire livelihood, in the form of cows, horses or sheep, if not their own wits or health. These are not legends told as mere entertainment for others either. They tend to be recounted as part of a walk around the landscape or as an element of job preparation, when a new worker begins, a child grows up, or a farm is sold. In short, they occur on a need-to-know basis; or if the farmer is asked about such sites, at which point they start pouring out in a long list, as can so often be heard in the sound recordings in Árnamagnean Institute.

As the evidence presented above demonstrates, *álagablettir* legends are still very much alive in Iceland; and they still actively protect the sites in question as they adapt to new lifestyles and new threats. And they are clearly not new phenomena: as noted above, the early folk legend collections demonstrate that they were also known all around the country in the 19th century, marking off the landscape into sacred and non-sacred areas just as they still do today.

What can have brought these slightly impractical legends and beliefs about? Why should people choose to mark off sites on their farms in this fashion? Admittedly, many of these sites are not easy to harvest, but as noted above, the legends regularly underline how attractive they were in hard times, not least because the grass they contained was good, and there was a lot of it. So why are these legends so widespread?

In recent years in Iceland, various explanations have been given for these beliefs, one being that the *álagablettir* might have been mass burial sites for animals that had died from outbreaks of disease (an anthrax outbreak being referred to as a consequence in one legend: see Árni Óla 1968: 120–122). Others suggest they might be old Catholic sites, where crosses or churches used to stand (Ólafur H. Torfason 2000). While the first explanation might be supported by several other legends telling of how livestock suddenly sicken after the harvesting takes place, and while the second might receive some support from one or two place names, like Krosshóll (lit. 'Cross Hillock') or Krosshólar ('Cross Hillocks'), they fail to explain many other sites (not least those taking the form of islets in rivers, lakes or streams).

Bearing the above in mind, it is noteworthy that no one has yet commented on the fact that similar practices, beliefs and legends, albeit sometimes in a slightly different form, are actually also found in all of Iceland's neighbouring countries, and most particularly in Ireland, where, as in Iceland, the beliefs are still very much alive. In Ireland, however, the sites in question tend to be connected to archaeological sites going back to the early Iron Age: referred to as "fairy forths", *ráithes*, or *sidheán*, they are sometimes seen as being places where the old gods (or Tuatha de Danaan) vanished into the earth only to re-emerge as the modern-day 'fairies'. Most commonly found on hilltops, these sites can also be found on hillsides where they stand out of the peat fields, areas of rich peat which no sensible farmer dares touch or visit after dark (personal experience in County Mayo). The sites in question are sometimes connected to migratory Irish legends of the Rip van Winkle kind, in which a man agrees to enter a fairy hill for a quick drink, and then joins a dance or learns how to play the fiddle before leaving, only to find that it is now fifty years later, and that his wife has remarried or died.

The most common *daily* Irish legends about such 'power spots' nonetheless tend to deal with more mundane occurrences, serving to warn people to be careful when visiting these sites, just as they are supposed to show respect for the so-called 'fairy hawthorne trees' found growing alone in the landscape.

As Séamas Ó Catháin and Patrick O'Flanagan (1975: 268) write:

Many of the bastions of the otherworld, especially the *sidheáin*, are believed to act as entry and exit points to and from the otherworld. Some people are believed to have vanished into the *sidheáin*, having been abducted by the fairies [...]. Interference with *sidheáin*, or indeed *carragáin, ballógaí* "old ruins", *claidhtheachaí* "ditches" or suspect stones of any kind which might harbour the fairies, was to be avoided at all costs. Such interference would lead to bad luck, even death, and was frowned upon and warned against by the community at large.

Numerous accounts of such beliefs can be found in earlier works, like those by Patrick Kennedy (1870: 141–142); Lady Wilde (1887: 46–47, 142, 234–235); Elizabeth Andrews (1913: 3–5); Lady Gregory (1920: see Gregory 1976: 255–273); and most recently in a work by Eddie Lenihan and Carolyn Green (2003: 124–131). The following account from Fermanagh on the border with Northern Ireland, collected by Henry Glassie (1995: 66–67), reflects well how such beliefs come up in conversation:

Many of Fermanagh's little hills are topped by rings of trees, rooted in Iron Age earthworks. Only some people believe these "forths" are the homes of fairies, but few will cut the trees or disturb the branches that fall within their dark, twisted circle. Tommy Lunny told me of a forth with a double ditch at the Battery down the Skea Road from Sessiagh Bog. Within the district, there is a forth on Crozier's Hill, another at Quigley's in Rossawalla, and one on Tommy's own land. "When you are raised hearin about the forths from the old people," Mr. Lunny said, "you hear that it is bad luck to cut a stick or lift a stick in it. I don't know is there anything to it, but I never did cut a stick there. The cows go in it, and it is wet. But it is good land, the best. I wish all my fields were land so good."

In *The Penguin Book of Irish Folktales*, Glassie includes a legend told by another of his Fermanagh informants, Ellen Cutler, which demonstrates the consequences that can take place should such a spot be disturbed:

Well, a forth: it's round as a ring. And there's trees growing all around the edge of it. And the grass grows inside./ And you're not allowed to take anything out of a forth. Because it belongs to the Good People./ And I remember my husband one time./ He had killed pigs/ for the market./ And he went out to this forth to get a piece of skiver to put in the pig./ And he got the piece of stick, or rod, and he went out the next morning, the best pig he had, his two hams were broken. Because he cut that out of there./ I said for him not to go out there, so he went on. Went out the next morning to get the two pigs for the market, their hams were broken./ They were broken that they were past using, you see./ He brought the pig to the market, and he didn't get half price for it./ There was another time, a man went out into a forth with an axe. He was after buying the new axe./ And they had no firing./ And he says to the mother, "I'll go up to the forth and get a fire out of the windfalls," out of the whitethorns that was down./ So he went up with the new axe,/ and he hit the whitethorn,/ and the hatchet went into pieces,/ and blood flew out of the tree./ So he was very glad to leave it there./ And so would I. (Glassie 1985: 158–159.)

Moving on to the Gælic Highlands of Scotland, it is clear that a very similar phenomenon used to exist there until it was deliberately banned by the Church Elders of Scotland in the late 16th century. Briefly mentioned by Sir Walter Scott (1830; see Scott 2001: 58–59), Edward Tylor (1903 [1871]: II, 370), and William Carew Hazlitt (1905: 283); and described in most detail by Joseph McKenzie McPherson (1929: 134–141) and Emily Lyle (2013), the so-called 'Goodman's Croft' was essentially:

> a piece of land dedicated to the devil and left untilled. It got various names, the Halyman's Rig, the Goodman's Fauld, the Gi'en Rig, the Deevil's Craft, Clootie's Craft, the Black Faulie. These names almost indicate a change in the point of view. Originally land dedicated to the Great Spirit worshipped there, it came through the influence of Christianity to be regarded as land consecrated to the Evil Spirit. Be he good or bad, none dare touch it with spade or plough. This belief was not restricted to the Northern corner of Scotland. (McPherson 1929: 134.)

McPherson also mentions parallels in Devon, but concentrates on the Highlands, quoting a verse which once again underlines the quality of the grass often found on these sites:

> The moss is soft on clootie's craft,/ And bonny's the sod o' the Goodman's taft/ And if ye bide there till the sun is set,/ The Goodman will catch you in his net. (McPherson 1929: 135.)

Marion McNeill (1989: 58) effectively summarises McPherson's findings as follows:

> There were two kinds of "croft". First we have the traditional open sites, visible from a distance, and long venerated as places of sepulchre and worship. Then there were the space "private" crofts, one of which was found on practically every estate, usually on the Mains, or home farm.

It is clear that in spite of the aforementioned church law which forced people to cultivate these sites, similar activities were still going on into the 19th century amongst new farmers setting up farms (see further Davidson 1955: 22). Beliefs associated with the Scottish equivalent of the Irish fairy tree, the so-called 'Cloutie Tree', a name which connects it to the aforementioned 'Cloutie's Craft' tradition, are still alive in Scotland, often in association with Cloutie Wells (see Cloutie Wells). The alleged associations with the Devil were almost certainly something that originated with the church, the expression 'Goodman' being more probably related to other expressions for fairies, like the 'good people' and 'good neighbour' (Bruford 1991: 131), here probably referring to some kind of protecting *individual* spirit. Particularly worth of note here is the way in which some of these sites, which do not seem to have been as closely associated with archaeological remains as those in Ireland, were actively established by new farmers wanting good luck with their crops (see above). McPherson's evidence also suggests that like the *álagablettir*, the sites contained good grass and were protected by legends and memorates.

Another interesting feature of the 'Goodman's crofts' is the suggestion that offerings (of stones or milk) were sometimes given to them, both when they were set up and afterwards (see Davidson 1955: 20, 22; McNeill 1989). While such practices are not mentioned in the modern accounts known from Iceland and Ireland, they offer close parallels to beliefs, legends and traditions known in the Nordic countries (especially in western Norway), which are once again associated with sites on farms that should be left untouched (see Sande 1992 [1887]: 69–71; Shetelig 1911; Birkeli 1938; Olrik & Ellekilde 1926–1951: I, 242; Omland 2007; 2010; for similar beliefs in Estonia, see Jonuks 2009: 30–35; 2011: 85).

In most of these cases, the beliefs in question are once again associated with archaeological remains, and first and foremost with grave mounds situated close to farms that appear to have been seen as the homes of powerful individual spirits which protected the farm. The beings in question went by various names, such as the *rudningskarl* (lit. 'clearing man'), *haugtusse* (lit. 'mound spirit'), *gardvord* (lit. 'farm protector'), and, more recently, *nisse*, a word nowadays used for the Christmas spirit in Norway and Denmark. This temperamental figure is well known in mainland Nordic legends (see examples in Kvideland & Sehmsdorf 1988: 238–247), and the same applies to the protective traditions associated with grave mounds which existed all over Denmark and Norway, and were particularly widespread in western Norway right up into the early 20th century.

The following early account from Denmark is fairly typical for this kind of legend and has obvious similarities to those legends already noted from Iceland and Ireland. Here, however, one notes that the earlier original single inhabitant has become a group of beings (a development which is not uncommon):

West of Vadum Church in Vendsyssel there is a small mound called Plomgårds Mound which is inhabited by the Hill Folk. They always lived on good terms with the farmers around there; however, it did occasionally happen that they revenged themselves if any sort of harm was done to their mound. It is said, for instance that long ago there were several trees on the mound, and that one of them served as a boundary marker between two men's fields. One day one of these men was at this spot, busy driving a cow home. As the cow was running about wildly, he broke a branch off this tree, because he had nothing else at hand to control her with; but this breach of the rules was punished immediately, for as soon as he struck the cow with the branch she fell to the ground lifeless and never revived.

On another occasion, the parish priest wanted to have the mound levelled because he was shocked by all the stories the people told about it, but no sooner had his servants stuck a spade into the ground than a sickness came over him and he did not recover until he gave up his plan. (Thiele 1843 [1818] II: 240; transl. Simpson 1988: 183.)

In Norway, however, it was not enough to leave the mound untouched. In many cases, one also had to leave newly-made food and drink on the mound on holy days (sometimes each week), a tradition which has evolved over time into the cream porridge (*römmegraut*) still left out for the *nisse* in Norwegian homes at Christmas. As with any disturbance of the mound, which included the harvesting of grass or the removal of branches and stones, failure to keep up such offerings could have drastic consequences. Farms would burn; all livestock would die; children would be forced into service (see especially Sande 1992 [1887]: 69–71; Birkeli 1938; Olrik & Ellekilde 1926–1951 I: 242, and Gunnell 2014b).

It is clear that this tradition, once again aided and abetted by local legends, was also brought to Orkney and Shetland (see Hibbert 1822: 205–207; Saxby 1888: 202–203; Black & Thomas 1903: 20–22, 207; Bruford 1991: 120; Muir 1998: xi–xii, 125; Marwick 2000: 38–42), where both respect and offerings were paid to Neolithic mounds like that in Maeshowe, Orkney, as well as other particular stones, the receiver now having morphed into the figure of the Scottish Brownie who served a similar protective function on the farm to the Norwegian *gardvord*.

These Nordic traditions of giving offerings to mounds seem to be very old (Gunnell 2014b);[3] and like Emil Birkeli, I believe there is reason to connect them to local ancestor cults that survived into folk tradition. There is no good Christian reason for why bread, butter and beer should have been 'wasted' on early grave mounds, or for why these traditions should have been so widespread. It seems logical to connect them with early medieval Nordic laws, which vainly attempted to ban such veneration (*Den Eldre Gulatingslova* 1994: 52; *Guta saga* 1999: 4–5).

Iceland, however, was only settled in around 870, and unlike Shetland, Orkney, Norway, Scotland and Ireland, had no ancient mounds or earthworks from before this time. The land was (initially) empty of forefathers and sacred sites. Many of the first settlers from Ireland, Scotland and Norway were already Christian. It might seem questionable to suggest that some of the modern Icelandic *álagablettir* traditions described at the start of this article might go back to the time of the settlement, especially when most evidence of such activities comes from the last three centuries. Nonetheless, as with the earlier-noted Nordic grave mound legends I have discussed in more detail elsewhere (Gunnell 2014b), it is difficult to understand why the Icelandic (and Faroese) *álagablettir* traditions should have come into being and spread as widely as they have done. It is also a little foolhardy to ignore the comparative evidence from the Gælic and the Nordic areas, which suggests that the original Icelandic (and Faroese) settlers would probably have all grown up with similar traditions around them, albeit in connection with ancient remains like graves and iron-age forts.

Furthermore, there is evidence in early medieval Icelandic accounts suggesting that from the time of the settlement, people were marking out 'sacred sites' in the landscape, sites which were not only protected in story and tradition, but also demanded both respect and offerings (as later occurred in Norway and Scotland). From the start, many of these sites (like those in Norway, Shetland, Orkney and Ireland) were connected to spirits of the dead, nature spirits or both. An obvious example is Helgafell (lit. 'Holy Mountain'), which, according to *Eyrbyggja saga* (1935: 9) and *Landnámabók* (1968: 98), was believed to be the dwelling place of those who died in the settlement below it. Similar hills of the dead mentioned in the sagas are found at Krosshólar (*Landnámabók* 1968: 140); and Kaldbak (*Brennu-Njáls saga* 1954: 192–194, ch. 14). All of these sites stand out from the surrounding territory like some of the *álagablettir* noted at the start. It is also noteworthy that some of them resemble large grave mounds in shape.[4]

Meanwhile, *Kristni saga* and Þorvalds þáttr viðförla (*Biskupa sögur* 2003: 7–8, 60–68) contain accounts of the Celtic settler Koðrán's dedication of a rock at Stóra Giljá to a supernatural *ármaður* (lit. 'good year man') who demanded and received respect in return for help with the fields; and *Kormáks saga* (1939: 288) describes a blood sacrifice which is given to the *álfar* (nature spirits) living in a local *hóll* ('hillock') in the hope that they would help cure a wound.

The most interesting of all is a homily in the Icelandic *Hauksbók* manuscript from the early 14th century which tells how:

> Some women are so stupid and blind with regard to their needs that they take their food out to cairns, [placing it] on or under slabs of rock, and dedicate it to nature spirits and then eat it, so that the land spirits will be loyal to them and so that their farming will go better than before. And there are some who take their children and go to a crossroads and drag them through the earth for their health. And so that they will be in better form and do well. (*Hauksbók* 1892–1896: 167.)

The passage in question is not found in the French original of this section of the text by Cæsarius of Arles. It is clearly meant to refer to local Icelandic practices known at the time. The parallels with the modern *álagablettir* legends from Iceland and Ireland, the legends about Norwegian and Orcadian grave mounds, and even those concerning the Goodman's croft are obvious.

Is it then possible that in spite of the lack of ancient remains, the new settlers in Iceland with their apparent creation of new 'sacred' sites like those noted above were deliberately attempting to recreate the 'sacred' areas they had known and respected in their old home landscapes, in a somewhat similar way to Scottish farmers with their 'Goodman's croft' spaces, believing that all farms needed sites that remained as they were before man arrived, sites which 'belonged' to the 'others' be they the dead, the spirits of the land, or both?

The word 'survival' has become a dirty word in folkloristics, but if the protracted Icelandic tradition of *álagablettir* is not a form of polygenesis and does have roots in the Gælic traditions from Ireland and Scotland, then it must go back to before 1400 when direct connections with that part of the world broke down. The same would apply to any roots in Norwegian culture with which (as noted above) direct regular contact also apparently broke down around the time of the Black Death.

The actual age and origin of the *álagablettir* beliefs will, of course, never be determined (unless new archaeological evidence comes to light) and, when it comes down to it, are perhaps beside the main point. Most interesting for the author at this present point in time is the way in which very basic legends or simple statements of belief can protect a small area of grass from outside intrusion for centuries. Accidents are, of course, prevalent in societies like those of Iceland, Ireland, Scotland and the Nordic countries which lived on the edge, and the *álagablettir, ráithes*, Goodman's crofts and grave mounds naturally provided useful explanations for bad luck that was bound to occur at one time or another. Over and above this, however, these living legends might also be said to reflect our apparent need to see something sacred, mysterious and dangerous about the landscapes that we inhabit.

NOTES

1   Helgi Guðmundsson & Arngrímur Bjarnason 1933–1949 III: 437–441; Guðni Jónsson 1940–1957 VIII: 20–21, 27–29, 33–34; Arngrímur F. Bjarnason 1954–1959 II.1: 39–40, 64–67; 171; and III.1: 15–20, 81–82, 140; Jón Árnason 1954–1961 I: 24, 36–37, 39, 232–234, 278, 480–483; III: 70; Oddur Björnsson & Jónas Jónasson 1977: 205–206, 240–243; Ólafur Davíðsson 1978: 157; Jón Þorkelsson 1956: 28–29; Torfhildur Hólm 1962: 167; and Þ. Ragnar Jónsson 1996: 118–120.
2   It might be borne in mind that the collection contains around 12,000 recorded legends in total.
3   It might be noted that regular, direct connections between Orkney, Shetland and Norway broke down around the time of the Black Death in the mid-14th century.
4   I am grateful to Luke Murphy for drawing this to my attention.

Sources

Árnastofnun. Available at http://www.ismus.is/ [Accessed January 1, 2018]

Andrews, Elizabeth 1913. *Ulster Folklore*. London: Elliott Stock.

Arngrímur F. Bjarnason 1954–1959. *Vestfirzkar þjóðsögur*. 3 vols. Reykjavík: Ísafoldarprentsmiðja.

Árni Óla 1968. *Álög og bannhelgi*. Reykjavík: Setberg.

Ásdís A. Arnalds, Ragna Benedikta Garðarsdóttir & Unnur Dilja Teitsdóttir 2008. *Könnun á íslenskri þjóðtrú og trúarviðhorfum*. Reykjavík: Félagsvísindastofnun Háskóla Íslands.

Birkeli, Emil 1938. *Fedrekult i Norge: Et forsøk på en systematisk-deskriptiv fremstilling*. Skrifter utgitt av Det Norske-Videnskaps-Akademie i Oslo II: Hist-filos. Klasse 5. Oslo: Jakob Dybwad.

Biskupa sögur I 2003. Sigurgeir Steingrímsson, Ólafur Halldórsson & Peter Foote (eds). Íslenzk fornrit, XV2. Reykjavík: Hið íslenzka fornritafélag.

Bjarni Harðarson 2001. *Landið, fólkið og þjóðtrúin: Árnessýsla*. Selfoss: Sunnlenska bókaútgáfan.

Black, G. F. & Northcote W. Thomas (eds.) 1903. *County Folk Lore III: Orkney and Shetland*. London: David Nutt.

Brennu-Njáls saga 1954. Einar Ólafur Sveinsson (ed.). Íslenzk fornrit XII. Reykjavík: Hið íslenzka fornritafélag.

Bruford, Alan 1991. Trolls, Hillfolk, Finns and Picts: The Identity of the Good Neighbors in Orkney and Shetland. In *The Good People. New Fairylore Essays*. Peter Narváez (ed.). Lexington: The University Press of Kentucky. Pp. 116–141.

Certeau, Michel de 1984. *The Practice of Everyday Life* I. Steven Rendall (transl.). Berkeley: University of California Press.

Christiansen, Reidar 1958. *The Migratory Legends: A Proposed List of Types with a Systematic Catalogue of the Norwegian Variants.* Folklore Fellows' Communciations 175. Helsinki: Academia Scientiarum Fennica.

Cloutie Wells. Available at http://ichscotland.org/wiki/clootie-cloutie-wells [Accessed January 1, 2018]

Davidson, T. D. 1955. The Untilled Field. *The Agricultural History Review* 3(1): 20–25.

Den Eldre Gulatingslova 1994. Bjørn Eithun, Magnus Rindal & Tor Ulset (eds.). Norrønne tekster 6. Oslo: Riksarkivet.

Eyrbyggja saga 1935. Einar Ólafur Sveinsson & Matthías Þorðarson (eds.). Íslenzk fornrit, IV. Reykjavík: Hið íslenzka fornritafélag. Pp. 1–184.

Glassie, Henry 1995. *Passing the Time in Ballymenone.* Bloomington: Indiana University Press.

Glassie, Henry (ed.) 1985. *The Penguin Book of Irish Folktales.* Harmondsworth: Penguin.

Gregory, Lady 1976. *Visions and Beliefs in the West of Ireland.* Gerrards Cross: Colin Smythe Ltd.

Guðni Jónsson 1940–1957. *Íslenzkir sagnaþættir og þjóðsögur.* 12 vols. Reykjavík: Ísafoldarprentsmiðja.

Gunnell, Terry 2005. An Invasion of Foreign Bodies: Legends of Washed Up Corpses in Iceland. In *Eyðvinur: Heiðursrit til Eyðun Andreassen.* Malan Marnersdóttir, Jens Cramer & Arnfinnur Johansen (eds.). Tórshavn: Føroya Fróðskaparfelag. Pp. 70–79.

Gunnell, Terry 2007. 'Það er til fleira á himni og jörðu, Hóras'. Kannanir á íslenskri þjóðtrú og trúarviðhorfum 2006–2007. In *Rannsóknum í félagsvísindum* VIII (Félagsvísindadeild). *Erindi flutt á ráðstefnu í desember 2007.* Gunnar Þór Jóhannesson (ed.). Reykjavík: Félagsvísindastofnun Háskóla Íslands. Pp. 801–812.

Gunnell, Terry 2009a. Legends and Landscape in the Nordic Countries. *Cultural and Social History* 6(3): 305–322.

Gunnell, Terry 2014a. Modern Legends in Iceland. In *Narratives Across Space and Time: Transmissions and Adaptations. Proceedings of the 15th Congress of the International Society For Folk Narrative Research (June 21-June 27, 2009 Athens), I.* 3 vols. Aikaterini Polymerou-Kamilaki, Evangelos Karamanes, Ioannis Plemmenos (eds.). Athens: Academy of Athens, 2014. Pp. 337–351.

Gunnell, Terry 2014b. Nordic Folk Legends, Folk Traditions and Grave Mounds: The Potential Value of Folkloristics for the Study of Old Nordic Religions. In *New Focus on Retrospective Methods.* Eldar Heide, Karen Bek-Pedersen (eds.). Folklore Fellows' Communications 307. Helsinki: Academia Scientiarum Fennica. Pp. 17–41.

Guta saga: The Story of the Gotlanders 1999. Christine Peel (ed.). London: Viking Society for Northern Research, University College.

Hauksbók 1892–1896. Finnur Jónsson (ed.). Copenhagen: Kongelige nordiske oldskrift-selskab.

Hazlitt, William Carew 1905. *Dictionary of Faiths and Folklore: Beliefs, Superstitions and Popular Customs.* London: Reeves and Turner.

Helgi Guðmundsson & Arngrímur Bjarnason 1933–1949. *Vestfirzkar sagnir.* 3 vols. Reykjavík: Bókaverzlun Guðmundar Gamalíelssonar.

Hibbert, Samuel 1822. *A Description of the Shetland Islands Comprising an Account of Their Scenery, Antiquities and Superstitions.* Edinburgh: A. Constable and Co.

Jón Árnason 1954–1961. *Íslenzkar þjóðsögur og ævintýri.* 6 vols. Reykjavík: Þjóðsaga.

Jón Þorkelsson (ed.) 1956. *Þjóðsögur og munnmæli.* 2nd edn. Reykjavík: Bókafellsútgáfan.

Jonuks, Tõnno 2009. *Hiis* Sites in the Research History of Estonian Sacred Places. *Folklore: Electronic Journal of Folklore* 42: 23–44. Available at https://doi.org/10.7592/FEJF2009.42.jonuks [Accessed April 14, 2018]

Jonuks, Tõnno 2011. An Archeology of Holy Places. Can We Find 'Forgotten' Sacred Sites. In *Kultūras Krustpuntkti: 5. Laidiens*. Juris Urtāns (ed.). Rīga: Norvik. Pp. 78–88.

Kennedy, Patrick 1870. *The Fireside Stories of Ireland*. Dublin: M'Glashan and Gill; P. Kennedy.

af Klintberg, Bengt 2010. *The Types of the Swedish Folk Legend*. Folklore Fellows' Communciations 300. Helsinki: Academia Scientiarum Fennica.

Kormáks saga 1939. In *Íslenzk fornrit* VIII. Einar Ólafur Sveinsson (ed.). Reykjavík: Hið íslenzka fornritafélag. Pp. 201–302.

Kvideland, Reimund & Henning K. Sehmsdorf (eds.) 1988. *Scandinavian Folk Belief and Legend*. Minneapolis: University of Minnesota Press.

Landnámabók 1968. In *Íslenzk fornrit* I: 1–2. Jakob Benediktsson (ed.). Reykjavík: Hið íslenzka fornritafélag. Pp. 29–397.

Lenihan, Eddie & Carolyn Eve Green 2003. *Meeting the Other Crowd*. Dublin: Gill and Macmillan.

Lyle, Emily 2013. The Good Man's Croft. *Scottish Studies* 36 (2011–2013): 103–124.

Marwick, Ernest 2000. *The Folklore of Orkney and Shetland*. Edinburgh: Birlinn.

McNeill, Marion 1989. *The Silver Bough* I. Reprinted. Edinburgh: Canongate.

McPherson, Joseph McKenzie 1929. *Primitive Beliefs in the North-East of Scotland*. London: Longmans, Green and Co.

Muir, Tom 1998. *The Mermaid Bride and Other Orkney Tales*. Kirkwall: The Orcadian Limited.

Ó Catháin, Séamas & Patrick O'Flanagan 1975. *The Living Landscape, Kilgalligan Erris County Mayo*. Baile Atha Cliath: Comhairle Bhealoideas Eireann.

Oddur Björnsson & Jónas Jónasson 1977. *Þjóðtrú og þjóðsagnir*. Steindór Steindórsson (ed.). 2nd edn. Akureyri: Bókaforlag Odds Björnssonar.

Ólafur Davíðsson 1978. *Íslenskar þjóðsögur*. 4 vols. Þorsteinn M. Jónsson (ed.). 3rd edn. Reykjavík: Þjóðsaga.

Ólafur H. Torfason 2000. *Nokkrir Íslandskrossar*. Reykjavík: Ólafur H. Torfason.

Olrik, Axel & Hans Ellekilde 1926–1951. *Nordens gudeverden*. 2 vols. København: G. E. C. Gads Forlag.

Omland, Atle 2007. *Stewards and Stakeholders of the Archaeological Record. Folklore, Local People and Burial Mounds in Agder, South Norway*. Acta Humaniora 305. Oslo: Faculty of Humanities, University of Oslo.

Omland, Atle 2010. *Stewards and Stakeholders of the Archaeological Record. Folklore, Local People and Burial Mounds in Agder, South Norway*. BAR International Series 2153. Oxford: Archaeopress.

Oring, Elliott 2008. Legendry and the Rhetoric of Truth. *Journal of American Folklore* 121: 127–166.

Sagnagrunnur. Available at http://sagnagrunnur.com/en [Accessed January 1, 2018]

Sande, Olav 1992 [1887]. *Segner fra Sogn*. Bergen: Norsk bokreidingslag l/l.

Saxby, J. 1888. *The Home of the Naturalist*. London: J. Nisbet.

Scott, Sir Walter 1830. *Letters on Demonology and Witchcraft, Addressed to J. G. Lockhart, esq*. London: John Murray.

Scott, Sir Walter 2001. *Letters on Demonology and Witchcraft*. Ware: Wordsworth Editions.

Shetelig, Haakon 1911. Folketro om gravhauger. *Maal og minne*: 206–212.

Sigvardsen, Peter Jacob 2009. *Hin heimurin 2*. Tórshavn: Forlagið Búgvin.

Simpson, Jacqueline (ed. and transl.) 1988. *Scandinavian Folktales*. London: Penguin.

Thiele, J. M. 1843 [1818]. *Danmarks folkesagn*. 2 vols. Kiøbenhavn: C. A. Reitzel.

Torfhildur Þorsteinssdóttir Hólm 1962. *Þjóðsögur og sagnir*. Reykjavík: Almenna bókmenntafélagið.

Tylor, Edward Burnett 1903 [1871]. *Primitive Culture. Researches into the Development of Mythology, Philosophy, Religion, Art, and Custom.* 4th edn. London: J. Murray.
Valdimar Tr. Hafstein 2000. The Elves' Point of View. *Fabula* 41: 87–104.
Wilde, Lady Francesca Speranza 1887. *Ancient Legends, Mystic Charms, and Superstitions of Ireland.* London: Ward and Downey.
Þ. Ragnar Jónsson 1996. *Sigfirskar þjóðsögur og sagnir.* Reykjavík: Vaka-Helgafell.

John Lindow

Nordic Legends of the Churchyard

The churchyard represented a particularly interesting space in traditional Nordic society. It was inside the church wall or other boundary, but outside the walls of the church building. The walls of the church building marked off the sacral realm proper (thus the baptismal font was just inside the church door, and baptism and churching ceremonies began at the door). However, the secular only began beyond the church wall. The horizontal distribution of space and the holy continued as one entered the church building. Even in small churches there might be a vestibule, and even in the smallest churches there was a division between the nave (the space where the congregation sat) and the altar area; in Lutheran churches this might even be marked off by a low fence separating the parson from those who were taking communion from him. Thus the binary of the sacred–profane distinction was complicated within the church building, with ever more sacred space as one approached the altar.

The binary was similarly complicated in the churchyard, not least through the notion of the status of the location of graves. The very fact that there were often graves inside the church building as well as in the churchyard disturbed the binary, as did notions of status in the location of graves outside. To be close to the church was higher status than to be farther away, and the southern and eastern portions were the areas more often used, in accordance with the privileging of these directions in Christian doctrine in Europe. Indeed, the north side of the churchyard might be shunned, and the place to put those whose salvation was in doctrinal question, such as unbaptised infants and suicides, might well be on the north edge of the churchyard. The liminality of the churchyard was thus obvious.

Furthermore, the graves, and especially the gravestones with their specific naming of the dead, created a link between the dead and the living, and this constituted a vertical rather than horizontal connection: the dead in the earth and the living on top of it. Church and bell towers, along with the soaring roofs that larger churches achieved, must have accentuated this vertical connection, and with the dead below and the towers and God above, the living were again placed in a liminal location.

There was also a kind of temporal liminality. Many Nordic churches were old, and legends told how they had been built long ago, by master builders like St. Olof or giants; sometimes large stones in or near the churchyard had been thrown there long ago by giants, and these giants had departed because they could not bear to hear the sound of the bells set high in towers. Alongside those events in the distant past, the living could also confront events in the future, namely the Last Judgment, which was of such great doctrinal importance. As we shall see, the churchyard was a place where the mystery of Judgment Day was to some degree confirmed.

Besides this long-term temporal dimension stood a short-term dimension, although it manifested itself more inside the church itself than in the churchyard. For the living, the church was usually sacred and thus safe, if in a numinous kind of way. But come to church at the wrong time, and you might be in trouble, as the widely known legend of the midnight mass of the dead shows so clearly (see also Koski in this volume, 68–71).

The other link between the dead and the living existed and was perpetuated in legend tradition. In this paper I intend to survey legends that are set in the churchyard and exemplify that link. I will begin with the legend I just cited, ML 4015, "The Midnight Mass of the Dead". Here is an example collected before 1840 by Carl Fredrik Cavallius, a rural deacon in Småland and the father of Gunnar Olof Hyltén-Cavallius, the famous ethnographer and editor of Sweden's first edition of folktales.

> An old woman who had no clock came too early to the church for the early Christmas service. She saw the church all lit up and hurried in. But surprise on top of surprise. The dead minister was preaching and those listening were all dead persons.
>
> Near the door sat her dead godmother, who gestured to her and said: "Undo the hook on your cloak and run!"
>
> This she did. But in the doorway a hundred hands clutched at the cloak. It fell off, but she got away.
>
> In the light of day there lay a piece of her black cloak on every grave in the churchyard. (Printed in Sahlgren & Liljeblad 1939: 276.)

Here the times are switched and the church is dangerous, but the church door still constitutes a boundary. The dead person saves the living woman sits near it, and 100 ghostly hands grasp at her right in it. When time has become clear again, the tokens of her close call are found neither inside the church nor beyond the churchyard, but rather in the liminal space of the churchyard itself, and indeed, according to the story, on each of the graves in the churchyard. This legend certainly thus presents the churchyard as the locus of continuing potential contact between the living and the dead.

Although Kerstin Johansson (1990: 162) reported that sometimes the fragments of the garment are found "scattered through the church or over the graves" – that is, on both sides of the boundary between church and churchyard, Reidar Th. Christiansen (1958: 61) described the location of the torn scraps as "on the doorsteps of the church", that is, on the churchyard side and at the boundary between church and churchyard. In either case, the legend builds on the contrast between the church itself and the churchyard outside it.

For the sake of completeness, let me point out that Bengt af Klintberg (2010) separates out this widely-known type, in which the congregation as a whole threatens the protagonist (his C31A "Woman Comes too Early to Christmas Service"), from a more rare version he calls C31B "Lady of Castle Threatened by Two Dead Husbands". Although the type as he describes it takes place in a castle chapel, which might allow escape into the castle rather than the churchyard, the version he included in his *Svenska folksägner* (af Klintberg 1972: no. 196) takes place in a normal church. Following the advice of the usual dead donor, the woman rushes out the door right through the middle, "because on each side stands one of your dead husbands". She escapes, and when the parishioners arrive at the proper time for the early Christmas service, they see bits and pieces of her jacket scattered over every grave.

ML 4015 is to some extent anomalous, in that the dead in the church are not unquiet for some obvious reason related to their lives on earth or the deaths that terminated those lives. The usual explanation is that the legend calls upon the idea of the dead being up and about after dark, and those variants that are set on Christmas Eve probably conceive of Christmas as a topsy-turvy time, when lots of spirits would be about. I would add that during the normal hours one would expect the parson to be in the church. He was the one member of human society most able to cope with the potentialities associated with the numinous in the church, and his presence or absence coincides, then, with the temporal valence of the church: safe or dangerous. Most churchyard legends, however, do not rely on this temporal mechanism to open the worlds between the dead and the living, and, as we have already seen, the church and the churchyard occupy rather different spaces.

So: the church door is one important boundary to the churchyard, an 'inner boundary' if you will. The outer marker of the boundary of the churchyard, often a wall, is perhaps even more important, and it drives other legend types.

The closest analogue to "The Midnight Mass of the Dead" and similar might be the Lenore legends (ATU 365), as they are usually called, after Bürger's ballad. An example collected in 1861 at Hvammur in Skagafjörður in Iceland and sent to Jón Árnason for inclusion in his folktale edition is interesting on a number of levels, and it shows both of the boundaries I have been discussing. When the girl Guðrún has rejected a marriage proposal, her spurned suitor says ominously that they will ride together to church next Christmas, come what may. During the year he dies, but he still comes to ride to church with her. We must infer that he has not joined the blessed, since he calls her Gárún, apparently because he can no longer pronounce the first syllable of her name, *Guð-*, which is homonymous with the word for god (one may wonder if she notices that and attaches the first syllable of what he does call her with the verb *gára*, which can mean 'tear apart'). I take up the story when they arrive at the churchyard wall. Speaking in spooky supernatural-style verse, he tells her that he must stable the horse, "eastward of the churchyard, churchyard."

> Then he disappeared with the horse, and she flung herself over the wall and ran up to the door of the church. Just as she was about to enter, someone grabbed her from behind, but her overcoat was lying unfastened over her shoulders, so whoever grabbed her got only the coat, and Gudrun escaped into the church. (Collected by Páll Jónsson in 1861 from Guðrún Guðmundsdóttir at Hvammur. Printed in Jón Árnason 1954–1961 III: 353. Translation in Kvideland & Sehmsdorf 1988: 93.)

Here, because the time is right, the living are in the church, and the church is safe rather than dangerous. The primary binary is at the church door, but in this version the churchyard, which first separates Guðrún from the dead assailant, is still not safe. This version is of course a mix of two types, "The Midnight Mass of the Dead" and "Lenore". Thus, in most versions of the Lenore legend the boundary of the churchyard is the crucial point. Here is such a version.

> Finally they came to the church where he had been buried. He leaves her alone on the horse on the road and makes his way into the churchyard. But then she thinks that she has been betrayed and goes off down the road to escape from him. (Collected by the tailor's apprentice Johan Magnus Pettersen before 1840. Printed in Sahlgren & Liljeblad 1939: 48.)

After this parting at the churchyard wall, she escapes by running into someone's house and saves herself by writing the name of Jesus over the door.

Before moving on to the churchyard as the abode of the dead, let me just mention that the churchyard also plays into legends involving nature beings. Here the status of the churchyard is not in question: being Christian, it is unambiguously safe. A familiar example is the widely known type that Christiansen designated ML 6045 "Drinking Cup Stolen from the Fairies". In typical recordings of this type, someone asks the supernatural nature beings for a drink. They give him a cup, and he pours out the contents, frequently singeing the hair of his horse with it. He then sets off with the trolls in pursuit. The mechanism of his escape, as is so frequent in Nordic legend tradition, calls on the safety of Christianity: he rides across the furrows of a ploughed field, thus creating crosses, or the church bells disperse the trolls. Relevant to my topic are those versions – and they are many – in which he escapes into the churchyard, where the trolls cannot pursue him. The sanctuary of the churchyard accords particularly well with the motif, when it is present, of the gift of the drinking cup to the church, where it remains as a token of the legend. This token, frequently kept on the altar, adds a deep temporal dimension to the legend. It may suggest that the contrast between churchyard and church, made possible by the notion of the dead being afoot at certain times, is neutralised when it is the supernatural nature beings that are involved. Nevertheless, we should probably ask ourselves why sanctuary in this type, and in most other legends in which humans flee supernatural beings, should be in the churchyard, or the person's home, or in daybreak – a kind of temporal sanctuary – and not in the church itself, as it properly was, for example, during the Middle Ages. I hope that the answer to this question will become clearer as we proceed.

Nature beings cannot enter within the churchyard walls, but the dead live there. As in Lenore, many legends set up the churchyard boundary as the site of the living–dead binary. One such group of these involves transporting the dead to the churchyard for burial. When the dead person was not bound for salvation, or occasionally when the Devil intervened, the coffin would become so heavy as to be immovable. Here the boundary of the churchyard, often made manifest by a wall, marks off the sacred ground within it from the non-sacred outside it. In these legends, passage across that boundary is disrupted. Roughly speaking, there are two outcomes. In the happier cases, intervention, often by a clergyman, makes it possible to complete the journey. In others, the horses simply cannot go on and the dead person is buried outside the churchyard. Here is an example from Norrland, Sweden, collected by Ulla Odstedt in 1925.

There is a place on the other side of Lake Näckten, beyond the village Tunvågen, which is called Göle. In that place there lived long ago a powerful gentleman whose name certainly also was Göle. He made a bet once with a farmer in Bulägden, who also was probably rich, about who should have the most splendid horse on Christmas morning. And I think it was Göle who won. He had silver shoes on the horse, and the nails were studded with silver leaf.

That Göle was a wicked and difficult person, who did violence to women and children and did every other kind of evil. When he was dead, he was so heavy that the horses could not manage to pull him; rather they had to dig a grave for him where he was.

When she was a child, one of my mother's friends went by where he was supposed to be buried, and she spat and said "Fie on you, Göle, who did so much evil". But that night she became terribly sick. (Collected in 1925 in Fäste, Hackås sn. Jämtland by Ulla Odstedt from Brita Månsson, born 1851. Printed in Odstedt 2004: 21, no. 5.)

This recording is interesting for several reasons. On a textual level, the betting on the horses and the violence to women and children of the living Göle find themselves echoed by the inability of the dray horses to pull the dead Göle and in the sickness that assails the person who insulted him and spat on his grave, presumably a female child. I assume that Göle inflicted the illness, but there is ample room for ambiguity, since spitting on graves is hardly something that children should do. But from the point of view of my topic, of greater importance is the inscription of the name Göle on the landscape. The legend locates that place in relation to the churchyard that the corpse never reached, and that location, in turn, being out of the churchyard, permits the kind of disrespect of the dead engaged in by the friend of the informant's mother, even it if it turns out to be dangerous. That location must indeed be on the road to the churchyard, which further suggests a model of the church as centre and the social world as peripheral. The other interesting feature of this recording is that it happened long ago. Most etiological placename legends would need to be set long ago, for obvious reasons, but it is noteworthy that in Sweden the type as a whole is frequently associated with Vrål, Sweden's last giant, as Arvid August Afzelius called him, but almost certainly a historical man of normal proportions who lived in Bohuslän in the Middle Ages, as Bengt af Klintberg (1978) has shown. Whoever or whatever the historical Vrål was, calling him a giant puts him in the distant past. This extreme time depth of the legend accords with the time depth of the church, perhaps also built by or threatened by giants. If the grave of Vrål or Göle can be seen along the road to the churchyard, the centre-periphery model has been around for a very long time.

Thus legend tradition bears out the analytic finding of the special position of the churchyard, located horizontally between the sacred and the profane. As I mentioned above, there is also a vertical boundary, separating the living from the dead, and interaction across this boundary forms the subject of most of the legends of the churchyard. To generalise, these legends fall into three broad categories: legends focusing on the unquiet dead; and – a smaller category – legends in which a human interacts with the remains of the dead; and, most interesting, legends in which the living hear pronouncements from the dead. All of these involve communication between the living and the dead. I begin with legends concerning the unquiet dead.

There are many sorts of revenant legends in older Nordic tradition, few of which, however, involve the churchyard directly. The reason is, of course, that revenants must haunt because of something they did in life, and people did very little in the churchyard. Thus boundary ghosts lurk out by the boundary stones they moved, misers count their money in the storehouse, those who issued false accusations come to the homes or even bedrooms of those they accused to beg forgiveness, or those who were improperly prepared for burial seek the appropriate item of clothing or the shroud they need – or occasionally a body part – at their former homes. Nevertheless, when Reidar Christiansen gathered all these disparate legends into a single ML type, 4020, "The Unforgiven Dead", he indicated the importance of the churchyard as a site for communication between the unquiet dead and the living. In the opening portion of his summary of the structure of the type, he offers three allomotifs for the site of the haunting; two of these are in the churchyard.

> Some person (A1), having no peace in his grave, was constantly wandering as a ghost (A2), or his body was found unmoldered in the coffin (A3) or his skeleton was constantly worrying the grave digger (A4). (Christiansen 1958: 64.)

The allomotifs for solving the problem of the haunting include this possibility: "the corpse of the ghost [...] was placed outside the church wall" (Christiansen 1958: 64). Christiansen does not cite many variants for this type, but a few of them do indeed contain that motif, which clearly indicates the importance of the church wall as a boundary between the living and the dead. Once outside the church wall, the corpse tells what the problem is, and the issue is resolved. In order to recount the problem, the corpse has to be returned to the social world, where whatever caused the haunting took place.

One connection between the living and the dead likely to be found in the churchyard was the bones of the dead and buried. Af Klintberg distinguishes a few types here (af Klintberg 2010: C51–53, 126), but they can be reduced to a common plot: a bone is removed from the churchyard, and it must be returned. What varies is the way the bone is removed and the way the message is conveyed to the living people saying that it must be returned. Ways the bone can be removed are accidental or purposeful. Accidental removal of a bone can include its sticking to someone's shoe or other paraphernalia, or being removed along with grass that has been cut in the churchyard. Purposeful removal is for magical purposes. No matter how the bone is removed, it needs to go back. To retrieve the bone, usually the dead person comes haunting to ask for it; in one perhaps more jocular legend type reported by af Klintberg, the shoe or walking stick in which the bone became lodged in the churchyard bounces up and down (2010: C53).

Parallel to these legends are ones about purposeful removal of coffin wood, to be re-used (for the case of wood from the church building, see Koski in this volume, 67–68). This is not a good idea. Ragnar Nilsson and Carl-Martin Bergstrand (1955) print a legend from Värmlandsnäs in which the churchyard caretaker finds a coffin that has not rotted. I take up the story in the middle.

> He knocked the coffin apart and tossed the old man down into the grave, just as he was. He took the planks home with him. But that very night it was as if he was squeezed apart, and he died in the morning. (Värmlandsnäs, collected from Johan Nilsson, born 1871. Printed in Nilsson & Bergstrand 1955: 70.)

While it is obvious that mistreatment of the corpse of the old man contributed to the caretaker's undoing, it is worth thinking about those coffin planks. To some degree they clearly parallel the bones that make trouble when they are removed from the grave, thus suggesting the coffin and its contents as a single artefact. This makes sense, since they are treated as a single object at the moment of burial. But it is also worth considering the parallel between the built environment above the earth and outside the churchyard with the metaphorical built environment in the grave, suggested by the fact that the coffin can be knocked apart and the planks repurposed, just as could be done with any serviceable wood in the community of the living. The gravestone marks off the dwelling of a single person, and the coffin is that dwelling, a house under the earth. It is in this light that we should regard the type that af Klintberg styled "Discontentment with Coffin" (2010: C94).

> A dead person haunts his/her former home by night, because there is water in the coffin (the coffin was made from stolen boards, position in coffin has changed). The haunting stops when the nuisance has been removed. (Af Klintberg 2010: 66.)

In order to haunt, the dead person goes from his/her home in the ground to his/her former home above ground: up the vertical axis to the world of the living (in the churchyard) and then out to the social world beyond the churchyard. The complaints the dead person lodges can involve the inverted equivalent of a leaky roof (there is water in the coffin), and the stolen boards used in the coffin of others who haunt suggest that traffic between the worlds in illicit lumber is two-way.

48

Here the dead–living binary is more important than the sacred–profane binary generally involved with the churchyard, for there are also legends in which people attempt to repurpose stones taken from ancient pagan graves, with no luck. Indeed, taking anything from a pagan grave is a bad idea. In this, recent legends echo the medieval Icelandic tale, usually called *Kumlbúa þáttr* (Þorhallur Vilmundarson & Bjarni Vilhjálmsson 1991: 451–455) and probably written down in the Benedictine monastery in Helgafell, about a man who removes a sword from an old pagan grave, meaning to return it in the morning. The owner comes to him in a dream that night and threatens him.

There is more important traffic between the worlds than body parts and lumber. Of primary importance is messaging. As I have already indicated, grave stones do that, silently and, if they are worn, mysteriously. But there is also verbal messaging. The dead know things that the living do not, as they sometimes indicate. Perhaps the most important thing they know is when Judgment Day will come. Af Klintberg assigns two types here and places both in the churchyard. In the first (2010: C42 "How Long Is It to Judgment Day?") some youths are dancing…

>…close to a churchyard. They hear the dead saying in old-fashioned language: "Here you dance, and here we rest. Heavy is the earth and cold. How long is it to Judgment Day, can you say?" (Af Klintberg 2010: 59.)

In the second (C43), it is the dead who are singing or dancing in the churchyard. They say: "You do not know when Judgment Day will come, but we do." Marjatta Jauhiainen offers the parallel from Finnish tradition to af Klintberg's youths dancing close to a churchyard: "Card Players, Ball Players in the Cemetery." The reference to the difficulty of waiting for Judgment Day now is issued, according to Jauhiainen, explicitly as a warning. (Jauhiainen 1998: C 1191.)

Jauhiainen also reports 23 recordings of a legend from Finland in which the dead predict the day of death of one of the living: "Annika, housekeeper, will be here this coming Thursday", and the prediction comes true (1998: C 1241). The living read the past on the gravestones; the dead read the future and let the living hear it.

Not all legends of communication from the dead to the living are located in the churchyard. The speaker, not infrequently, is a murdered child buried or hidden in nature, far from the churchyard, telling of Judgment Day. For such a being, Judgment Day takes on a special importance, for then the child's mother (almost always the murderer in legend tradition) will face her maker and be doomed to eternal torment. Occasionally, too, the speakers are supernatural nature beings, and in this case the legend plays on the ambiguous status of these beings within the Christian belief system: in the most famous case, will the *näck* achieve salvation? Legends in which the supernatural nature beings know when Judgment Day will occur suggest that at least some of them will achieve salvation, just as only some humans will.

The issue of the percentage of the blessed is taken up in one churchyard legend. Here is an example from northern Sweden, classified by af Klintberg (2010) as C44 and by Jauhiainen (1998) as C 1221.

> There was someone here in Skinnarbyn, the wife of a gravedigger, and the church
> gate had opened up, so her cows had got into the churchyard, and she went in and
> drove them out. But while she was crossing the churchyard she chanted: "Blessed
> are those who sleep, have peace at night". But then there was such a heavy sigh
> below her and she heard: "We don't all sleep so well". (Odstedt 2004: 110, no. 421.
> Collected from Albertina Jonsson, Bydgeå sn, Västerbotten.)

Another mechanism for indicating this division of blessed and damned is
for someone in the churchyard to welcome all the Christians. This occasions
wailing, and the person adds "and non-Christians too" (af Klintberg 2010:
C46). Or one of the dead might respond: "What about us unbaptized?"
(Jauhiainen 1998: C 1211).

Another form of text messaging, and perhaps the dominant one, is
through signs. Just as the percentage of those who will be blessed remains
unknown to the living, so too does the fate of each individual after death:
blessed or doomed. Guilt or innocence in the case of a crime poses a parallel
problem in each world, and sometimes there is messaging within the
churchyard to resolve the question. Evald Tang Kristensen collected a legend
in Jutland that touches on this and some other concerns that I have raised
in this essay.

> There was a serving girl in Åbjerg who was accused of bearing and murdering
> an illegitimate child. She was convicted and executed. But on the day she was to
> be beheaded, she stepped up and proclaimed her innocence and she asked that
> they put a big stone over her grave and knock a hole in it, and as little as she was
> guilty, so little could the hole be kept dry. The stone was put there, and there was
> always water in it. They tried to take away the water and to dry the hole with
> their handkerchiefs, and a few minutes later there would be water in the stone
> again… (Collected from Jens Kr. Brink, Lem Bjærg Mark. Printed in Kristensen
> 1932: 87, no. 348.)

That is the legend itself. This narrator went on to say that the stone was
removed and used to water cattle. The cattle died immediately after drinking,
and the stone was restored to the churchyard. Af Klintberg's (2010) type C47
is similar. In it a girl has died without receiving the last rites. Her status as
saved is confirmed when a hymn is heard coming from her grave.

Churchyard signs can bring bad news too. In a legend parallel to the
one I just mentioned about the girl wrongly executed for allegedly killing
an illegitimate child, Kristensen collected a legend about a man who freed
himself in court with an oath: if he was telling the truth, let a rose grow on
his grave, but if he was lying, a hawthorn. After he was dead and buried,
a hawthorn grew over his grave (Kristensen 1932: 88, no. 351). An unusual
story along these lines also comes from Kristensen's collections.

> In Lime Church a monk is supposed to have hanged himself on the bell rope, and
> when he was buried just east of the church, the nail on his big toe grew so much
> that it finally came up to the surface and spread out into a big thorn bush, which
> today still stands in Lime churchyard. (Collected from M. Møller, Sir. Printed in
> Kristensen 1895: 125, no. 643.)

Legends set completely within the churchyard include those in which the manifestation of unrest occurs there and the parson binds the revenant to the grave. Af Klintberg assigns type numbers to several legends that in general involve binding the corpse; of these, only two take place wholly within the churchyard.

These legends form the background to Christiansen's ML 3005 "The Would-Be Ghost"; af Klintberg calls it "The Parson and the Would-Be Ghost" (2010: L121), and this is a more accurate title (it is also Jauhiainen 1998: C 1326). In legends of this type, a parson exorcises into the churchyard ground a serving-boy who has dressed up in a sheet to frighten the parson or some other person. Key to the legend is the silence of the would-be ghost when asked by the minister whether he is human. Kathleen Stokker (1991) has associated this motif with issues of confession and salvation, but we might also note that because the churchyard is a place for communication, keeping silent is wrong. A parallel legend has the would-be ghost simply kicked out of the churchyard by the dead or the church grim, or even killed by them (af Klintberg 2010: C71). A version from Värmlandsnäs has the would-be ghost stand in the church door, thus right between the churchyard and the church; something unseen squeezes him, and he is lame ever after (Nilsson & Bergstrand 1955: 71). Another, from Skåne, has the girl he is trying to frighten lock him into the church. The following morning, his body is found there in the vestibule, torn apart by the church grim (Wigström 1881: 340–341). Here we see again the enormous danger of the interior of the church when the time is wrong.

Just as there are few legends about interaction among supernatural nature beings, not between them and humans, so there are few about what goes on below the earth in the churchyard. One exception is af Klintberg's (2010) C97 "Rich and Poor Buried Side by Side".

> The relatives of a dead person dislike his/her grave being situated beside the grave of a poor person. They have the grave moved, but the dead person haunts them, asking to be taken back to the first place. (Af Klintberg 2010: 67.)

The worlds below and above the churchyard soil are indeed different. Below rest the dead, no longer concerned with social distinctions, and knowing deep things that we cannot know. Above, we the living may walk occasionally, but we cannot graze our cattle or grow our vegetables there. Eva Wigström has a story in which a coachman rests his horses in the churchyard at Halmstad in Skåne: carriage, horses, and hay are all thrown summarily far out onto the adjacent road by an unseen hand (Wigström 1881: 340). When we are in the churchyard, we can hear or see messages from the world of the dead, but we have very few ways of communicating with that world, and indeed we probably have little of value to communicate. But that place where communication can occur is a place of sanctuary, sanctuary from the threatening dead or the church grim within the church itself and sanctuary from the threatening nature beings who live beyond the social world.

I end with a legend that helps show the relationship between living and dead in the churchyard. Christiansen labelled it ML 4065 and reported ten recordings in Norway, mostly from northern coastal areas. In the version I will quote, collected in Nordland in 1870, a boy has gone down to the boathouse to fetch spirits on Christmas Eve. There he encounters a headless *draug* – an unburied sailor lost at sea. The boy swings at the *draug* with the lid of his pot and runs up the path by the sea.

> [...] but all at once he heard a strange commotion behind him, and when he looked around, he caught sight of a tremendous number of *draugs* coming up from the shore. The graveyard lay right in his way, and the flock of *draugs* would catch up with him again if he ran around it. So he hopped over the graveyard fence, sprang across the graves, and cried:
>
> "Up, up, every Christian soul, and save me!"
>
> At the same moment the clock struck twelve midnight, and the earth shook under the boy's feet. When he was well over the fence on the other side, he looked back. He saw the flock of *draugs* coming after him in hot pursuit like a flock of sheep, in over the graveyard. But there they were met by a great host of dead souls who wanted to help the boy and stop the unholy *draugs* from coming onto consecrated soil. It was a bitter struggle [...] (Collected by O. T. Olsen in Nordland c. 1870. Printed in Olsen 1912: 15. Translation in Christiansen 1964: 53–54.)

It was a bitter struggle, but the churchyard dead won.

As this legend shows clearly, along the vertical axis in the churchyard run the communication and communion that highlight the distinction between living and dead; the horizontal axis, the mundane or worldly axis, on the other hand, focuses on the distinction between sacred and profane and situates the living within it. Communion between humans and the dead is thus hardly universal. It is the dead who are in the churchyard, lying under consecrated soil as the narrator has it here, the dead who have properly undergone the final Christian ritual, with whom the living form a community, not with the dead outside it. In rising from the graves the Christian dead become for the time of the battle unquiet dead, like the poor sailors who were lost at sea and had no Christian burial. Since unquiet dead are unhappy dead, this motif shows the extent to which the churchyard dead will go to indicate the community that they share with those who can commune with them from above the churchyard earth. And this legend shows the ability of the human community to imagine that the churchyard dead, in order to help one of the living, will re-enact – or rather, perhaps, pre-enact – the moment when they will rise on Judgment Day. That is no small thing.

Sources

ATU = Uther, Hans-Jörg 2004. *The Types of International Folktales. A Classification and Bibliography. Part I: Animal Tales, Tales of Magic, Religious Tales, and Realistic Tales, with an Introduction.* Folklore Fellows' Communications 284. Helsinki: Academia Scientiarum Fennica.

Christiansen, Reidar Th. 1958. *The Migratory Legends. A Proposed List of Types with a Systematic Catalogue of the Norwegian Variants.* Folklore Fellows' Communications 175. Helsinki: Academia Scientiarum Fennica.

Christiansen, Reidar Th. 1964. *Folktales of Norway.* Pat Shaw Iversen (transl.). Chicago, London: University of Chicago Press.

Jauhiainen, Marjatta 1998. *The Type and Motif Index of Finnish Belief Legends and Memorates. Revised and Enlarged Edition of Lauri Simonsuuri's Typen- und Motivverzeichnis der finnischen mythischen Sagen.* Folklore Fellows' Communications 267. Helsinki: Academia Scientiarum Fennica.

Johansson, Kerstin Louise 1990. The Midnight Mass of the Dead. *Arv. Nordic Yearbook of Folklore* 46: 157–167.

Jón Árnason 1954–1961 [1862]. *Íslenskar þjóðsögur og ævintýri. Nýtt safn.* Árni Böðvarsson & Bjarni Vilhjálmsson (eds.). 6 vols. Reykjavík: Bókaútgáfan þjóðsaga.

af Klintberg, Bengt 1972. *Svenska folksägner.* Stockholm: Norstedts.

af Klintberg, Bengt 1978. Sveriges sista jätte. In *Harens klagan. Studier i gammal och ny folklore.* Stockholm: Norstedts. Pp. 145–150.

af Klintberg, Bengt 2010. *The Types of the Swedish Folk Legend.* Folklore Fellows' Communications 300. Helsinki: Academia Scientiarum Fennica.

Kristensen, Evald Tang 1895. *Danske sagn. Som de har lydt i folkemunde,* vol. 3. *Kjæmper. Kirke. Andre stedlige sagn. Skatte.* Silkeborg: Ny Bogtrykkeri (K. Johansen).

Kristensen, Evald Tang 1932. *Danske sagn. Som de har lydt i folkemunde.* Ny række, vol. 4. *Personsagn.* København: Reitzel.

Kvideland, Reimund & Henning K. Sehmsdorf 1988. *Scandinavian Folk Belief and Legend.* Minneapolis: University of Minnesota Press.

Nilsson, Ragnar & Carl-Martin Bergstrand 1955. *Folktro och folksed på Värmlandsnäs.* Folkminnen från Näs härad 2. Göteborg: Gumperts.

Odstedt, Ulla 2004. *Norrländsk folktradition. Uppteckningar i urval med kommentar.* Bengt af Klintberg (ed.). Acta Academiae Regiae Gustavi Adolphi 84. Uppsala: Kungl. Gustav Adolfs Akademi för svensk folkkultur.

Olsen, Ole Tobias 1912. *Norske folkeeventyr og sagn. Samlet i Nordland.* Kristiania: J. W. Cappelen.

Sahlgren, Jöran & Sven Liljeblad 1939. *Sagor från Småland. Upptecknade av prosten Carl Fredrik Cavallius och andra.* Svenska sagor och sägner 3. Stockholm: Thule.

Stokker, Kathleen 1991. ML 3005 – "The Would-Be Ghost": Why Be He a Ghost? Lutheran Views of Confession and Salvation in Legends of The Black Book Minister. *Arv. Nordic Yearbook of Folklore* 47: 143–152.

Wigström, Eva 1881. *Folkdiktning, visor, folktro, sägner och en svartkonstbok. Samlad och upptecknad i Skåne.* Göteborg: Torsten Hedlund.

Þórhallur Vilmundarson & Bjarni Vilhjálmsson (eds.) 1991. *Harðar saga. Bárðar saga. Þorskfirðinga saga. Flóamanna saga. Þórarins þáttr Nefjólfssonar. Þorsteins þáttr uxafóts. Egils þáttr Síðu-Hallssonar. Orms þáttr Stórólfssonar. Þorsteins þáttr forvitna. Bergbúa þáttr. Kumlbúa þáttr. Stjörnu-Odda draumr.* Íslenzk fornrit 13. Reykjavík: Hið íslenzka fornritafélag.

Kaarina Koski

The Sacred and the Supernatural: Lutheran Church Buildings in Christian Practice and Finnish Folk Belief Tradition

In Finnish belief narratives, the church building has been a popular theme and a setting of terrifying events. Folk legends about the church use dramatic vernacular imagery: people who enter the church at night are attacked by devils or the deceased, or simply found slaughtered in the morning. These strong images are accompanied by first-hand experiences of the distinction of the church and rituals which both express reverence and ward off the possibly harmful influence of the church. While legends and magical rites show the church as possessing supernatural otherness, reminiscences about ecclesiastical life and Christian customs in the 19th century portray the church as the positive centre of public and religious life. In this article, I use different theories of the sacred to conceptualise these different approaches to the church building's sacrality. The concept of sacred is here understood widely as a socially marked category that is set apart from everyday life. This setting apart can refer either to authority and hierarchy, which form the centre of society and is thus sacred and inviolable, or to the otherworldly and supernatural, which are kept outside the social order (Paden 1996). Typically, these sources of sacredness merge and overlap. In the 19th century, the Lutheran church was sacred, firstly, as a symbol of the social order and shared values, and secondly, because of its supernatural character. Both characteristics of the church have been manifested in the reverent behaviour of churchgoers and in belief narratives.

I contextualise ambiguous folklore materials with the Christian tradition concerning the status of the church building and the principles and practices of ecclesiastical life in Lutheran Finland in previous centuries. The nearest church historical context of this folk belief tradition includes Lutheran orthodoxy, which reached its peak in the 17th century and left a profound imprint on popular Christianity up to the beginning of the 20th century. The central points of Lutheran orthodoxy were the extension of the Lutheran doctrine to all fields of public life and strict church discipline, which included the regularly controlled obligation to learn sufficient reading skills and the basic chapters of the catechism. Reading controls were still, at the beginning of the 20th century, feared by less fluent readers. (Laine 2002: 20–30.) The church authorities controlled the churchgoers' behaviour and very strictly defined the right ways to practice and interpret the Lutheran faith. Sanctions and punishments were on offer for those who failed to live up to the norms. Narratives and rites reflect conceptions of the church building's sacredness and also handle the fears and other negative feelings about the church. They reflect and comment on prevailing norms, ontological questions, moral dilemmas and also on the ecclesiastical life of the 18th and 19th centuries.

Folk legends and practices relating to the church as a building are never only about the building itself. In vernacular tradition, the building as well as religious objects are often a symbol of much more, such as church discipline or Lutheran teaching. The church is an umbrella term that can mean the institution or the order established in ecclesiastical law. It can also mean the Lutheran doctrine and the way it was interpreted and practiced by local ministers. It can mean the Christian congregation, i.e. the society that both controlled its individual members and gave them a collective identity as humans. In the colloquial speech of rural Finns, the word 'church' denotes the whole church village, the centre of public life. People needed to travel "to the church" for various errands. Until the 20th century, people carried out many kinds of business around the church before and after attending the church service, and even during it. (Kuuliala 1939: 6.)

My research materials mainly consist of Finnish belief legends and rite descriptions that were collected in the Folklore Archive of the Finnish Literature Society (SKS. KRA) in the late 19th and early 20th centuries. Collections of The Lexical Archive of Finnish Dialects in the Institute for the Languages of Finland (SMSA) have also been used. The archived materials also include written reminiscences of church life and Christian traditions handed down at home. Part of the reminiscence material belongs to Viljo-Kustaa Kuuliala's collections (VKK), gathered in 1953 and housed at the University of Turku in the Archives of History, Culture and Arts Studies. While belief narratives and ritual descriptions show only one side of the whole picture, oral history and church historical studies accomplish the religious context of the narratives. These various sources present different spheres of reality, as well as different attitudes, voices and discourses.

The Sacrality of the Church Building in Christian Tradition

No place or building is sacred for its own sake. It is people who give a place its sacred meaning and sustain it by their reverent and ritual behaviour. Sacredness is constructed in a constant process that includes negotiation, confirmation and restoration of the sacred status. (Bossuyt 2005: 192; Hamilton & Spicer 2005: 3–4, 16.) In Christian tradition, sources of sacredness generally have a connection to the divine in common. Theological grounds for a consecrated place of worship have been diverse, reflecting the changes in social and political conditions of religious life. Harold Turner has compared two influential views on the sacredness of the church building: the *domus ecclesiae*, which refers to the church building as the meeting house of the congregation, and *domus dei*, which looks at the church as the house of God. While the study of the Bible finds the former as the main principle, the latter seems to have been more influential in Christian practice. (Turner 1967: 157.)

According to biblical studies, early Christians underlined the omnipresence of God and consequently the irrelevance of a special building for worship. Their congregation had no established position, and they regarded the state between places or on a journey a propitious context for divine encounters and conversions. (Sheldrake 2001: 33–34.) A persistent conception from the time of the Apostles up to Protestant theology was that baptised Christians themselves were the place of God. From Antiquity into the Middle Ages, holiness and supernatural powers were increasingly associated with exceptional individuals, who functioned as mediators between this and the other world. This notion formed the core of the Catholic cult of saints, which, in turn, had a close relationship to holy sites. (Sheldrake 2001: 37–38.) The tombs of holy men and women attracted burials of ordinary people as well. Combining the memorial sites of the family ancestors and the saints made these places significant sites of sacred power. Gradually, church buildings were integrated with these sacred sites and it became customary to include tombs or relics in the altar. This moved the locus of the sacred away from the congregation and towards the building itself. (Hamilton & Spicer 2005: 5–6; Sheldrake 2001: 48–51; Turner 1967: 164–169.)

In addition to the material link to the divine, human activities in and relating to the church sustained its sacred status. Shrines were made sacred by consecration ceremonies and the regular performance of liturgical rites. In medieval Europe, the existing sacredness of the church was regularly confirmed with cleansing and restoration rites. These could include ritual washing or sprinkling of holy water, as well as burning incense and candles. The scent and light only fill a restricted area and so mark out the sacred space from its surroundings. Incense also covers up worldly foul smells and repels evil spirits. (Bossuyt 2005: 189–192; Hamilton & Spicer 2005: 1, 6–8.)

In the Middle Ages, the distinction of the church as a sacred site was shown by architectural and artistic means and by organising the space around the church. The system of sacred zones, maintained by religious and mundane authorities together, formed a gradual escalation of holiness from a distance towards the shrine and its holiest parts. (Hamilton & Spicer 2005: 1, 5–9.) The atrium in Central European churches, as well as the weapon room in Finnish churches, was a liminal space between secular and sacred. In this entrance room people were to prepare themselves for a transition to a sacred place; disarming oneself was one part of this. Inside the church, boundaries of the holiest parts were designated by architectural means, such as railings or mosaic floor decorations and, as in Finnish medieval churches, high wooden fences between the nave and the choir. (Hamilton & Spicer 2005: 10–11, 18; Hiekkanen 2007: 20, 41; Turner 1967: 185–186; see also Lindow in this volume, 40.)

Medieval church buildings were loaded with meaning and symbol. In Gothic cathedrals, architecture helped to create an expression of God's presence and of a transition from the material to the spiritual. The church was a metaphoric gate to paradise, bringing heavenly Jerusalem to the Earth. Church buildings were strong symbols of medieval Christian cosmic order, which defended the faithful against evil forces, regulated human relations with the sacred and provided a link to the sustaining divine power. The church building embodied a miniature of the world order, a microcosm in the macrocosm, including all relevant information about the world in itself. (Bossuyt 2005: 194; Scribner 1993: 477–479; Sheldrake 2001: 51–60.)

During the Reformation the sacredness of church buildings was questioned and reconfigured. The Reformers invoked the early Christian view of the irrelevance of special buildings for worship. In Martin Luther's view, the magnificence of Catholic church buildings indicated holiness attached to objects, and the consecration of churches was regarded as a papist imposture. Instead of a tangible location of the sacred and its worship, Luther underlined the specifically demarcated time of worship. The sacrality of the occasion stemmed from God's word and the true belief of the participants, not from a sacred building. (Isaiasz 2012: 21–22; Sheldrake 2001: 61–62.) The point was to emphasise the church's role as a meeting place, not as a *domus dei* (Turner 1967: 205). Recent studies underline the continuity from medieval Christianity to Protestant practices. After a reconfiguration of the source of sacredness, the Lutheran policy on church buildings added up to a constant construction of the sacred in opposition to the profane. In the Middle Ages, church buildings had had multiple roles in public life and in a network of political and economic actions. After the Reformation, a clear line between sacred and profane buildings was drawn and the use of sacred space for other purposes was forbidden. (Isaiasz 2012: 20, 35–36.) In the later stages of the Reformation dedication ceremonies were developed for protestant churches to separate churches and their furniture from the secular world. Despite similarities, the dissociation of these rituals from their Catholic counterparts was sharply emphasised. (Hamilton & Spicer 2005: 21; Isaiasz 2012: 28; Spicer 2005: 210–211.)

The dispute about what made the church sacred also included the furnishings. Reformers criticised the visual and material aspects of medieval Christianity. The disapproval of materiality was part of the argument that instead of conforming to the ritual requirements of the church, a Christian should, in Luther's view, have faith and trust Christ himself. Luther regarded material objects, such as relics and altars, as unnecessary and warned about worshipping saints and their statues instead of Christ. While Luther did not oppose visuality *per se*, more radical groups insisted in removing from churches all images because they were to be regarded idolatrous. The theological endeavour to replace material symbols with God's word developed into iconoclasms which were realised by agitated crowds in some cities in the Baltic countries and Germany in the 16th century, giving rise to violent removal and destruction of statues, crucifixes, altars, triptychs and relics from churches, monasteries and convents. (Ruutu 2004: 42–46.)

In 16th century Europe, the evangelical movement had political and social motivations. It was typical that influential interest groups supported these to improve their political status. (Ruutu 2004: 68–71.) In the Nordic countries – in Denmark, which included Norway, and in Sweden with its eastern province Finland – it was the king who introduced the Reformation. The Swedish king Gustav Vasa found in this new religious movement a suitable motive to reduce the wealth and political power of the church. At the same time, he shifted power from the local level to the crown. These reformations were not widely accepted among the people, and the new religious and political situation caused uprisings. In both Sweden and Denmark, the introduction of the Reformation was supported with military force. Consequently, the actual changes in theology and liturgical practices began slowly and cautiously in order to avoid unrest among the people. (Amundsen 2010: 118; Kouri 1995: 44–56; Nyman 2009: 77–83.)

Negotiation of religious practice and sacred space reflected political interests and local circumstances. In the Nordic countries, the sanctity of church buildings and the divine service was reassessed peacefully. To avoid provoking the common people and 'for the sake of the weak', new church regulations in the first half of the 16th century preserved most of the old traditions while giving them new interpretations. (Amundsen 2010: 118; Rimpiläinen 1971: 98–100.) In the church interior, side altars and relics, which were thought to encourage 'abuse' and improper interpretation of the Bible, were removed or changed during the first decades. Triptychs and statues of the saints were generally not destroyed but moved to more appropriate places in the church. (Amundsen 2010: 121–122; Hiekkanen 2007: 49–50.) New, Lutheran elements were introduced to the church interior by the end of the 16th century. At the core of this development was the replacement of the Catholic pictorial universe with a Lutheran textual one and the elevation of God's word to the fore. Crucifixes and altarpieces were in many cases substituted with texts. Following German models, so-called catechism altarpieces, which instead of images included written sentences, were introduced to Denmark and Norway; tablets and boards with sentences from the catechism were hung on church walls to support preaching showing how reading and reflecting on God's word were important in Lutheran piety. They also gave God's word a visual and tangible form and thus made it more real to the congregation. (Amundsen 2010: 118, 126–129.) Before the Reformation, relics had been worshipped objects that created a link to the divine and made Catholic shrines special and holy. Now God's word fulfilled the same function. The word was what created the connection between God and man, and the preaching of God's word was what made the church sacred.[1]

The new Lutheran church interior was to teach the believers a new spatial symbolism which signified the duties of parishioners and their relationship to God. The Danish bishop Peder Palladius outlined in his visitation book the symbolic meanings of the Lutheran church interior in the divine service. Preaching and listening to God's word as the new function of the divine service were highlighted in the furniture: the pews and galleries kept the congregation organised and their gazes towards the minister and the altar. The minister in the pulpit was to point with his hands to the font and the altar. The altar reminded the congregation members about their life-long commitment to the divine through the sacrament of Eucharist, while the other sacrament, baptism, was represented by the font situated behind them by the door. The textual universe was also crucial in Palladius' symbolism. He presented the sacraments as seals on the 'letter of indulgence', which had been handed down from God and which included the Ten Commandments, the creed and the Lord's Prayer. These were also among the texts written on the boards in the church. (Amundsen 2010: 126–132.)

While trends of radical Reformation – such as catechism altarpieces – were realised in churches in Denmark and Norway, Sweden and Finland followed a slower path. The Catholic traditions and interpretations lived strong especially in the countryside until the end of 16th century. In Finland, even the clergy was inclined to them. (Nyman 2009: 83; Pleijel 1970: 16–17; Rimpiläinen 1971: 130–131, 148.) Among the Finnish folk, old interpretations such as the necessity of sacrifice as implementation of a reciprocal relationship with God still permeated religious life in the 18th century. For example, the believers found it important to bring offerings, such as wool and squirrel skins, to the communion table. Lutheran authorities regarded this popular behaviour as superstitious, but common people were distressed by the reduction of ritual, which they found essential. (Juva 1956: 33–35; Kuha 2016: 91–102; Laasonen 1991: 186–187.)

The Reformation had sought to separate sacred and mundane issues, but the era of Swedish great power in the 17th century tied the church to political cooperation with the crown. Uniformity of the Lutheran confession and people's loyalty to the church and the crown were required for the sake of the integrity of the state. This period was distinguished by strict Lutheran orthodoxy and church discipline. Ecclesiastical law and consequently the social life were based on the doctrine of the three estates. Hierarchy and obedience were emphasised in both sacred and secular matters. The authorities made very clear the importance of respect for the Church, the word of God and holy days. These values were displayed by harsh chastisement of religious transgressions such as disorder in church or blasphemy. (Juva 1956: 35; Pleijel 1970: 20–22.) For example, a brawl during divine service in Liperi church in Eastern Finland resulted in a death sentence in 1729. Punishments for both physical violence and swearing were more severe when the offence took place in church or on a holy day. (Kircko-laki ja ordningi 1686: 64–71; Manninen 1917: 72–73.) Churchgoers were given clear instructions on how reverence towards the church and God's word had to be expressed. A church law from 1686 ordered the congregation to stand up when certain texts were read during the church service and kneel during others (Kircko-laki ja ordningi 1686: 7). Local practices also included kneeling and praying when entering the church, as well as bowing or curtsying every time the name of Jesus was mentioned in the service. These practices were well internalised and survived in church life up to the 20th century. (For example, VKK Tampere III/Kuorevesi/Alma Autio 4:2; VKK Kuopio/Keitele/Kusti Heimonen 4:2; Hurmerinta 1982: 11–12, 16–18.) Thus, through the obligatory practices of church life the sacredness of the church was constantly performed and strengthened. One of Luther's main points was to shift the emphasis from deeds and obedience to personal faith. Political authorities, however, required an outward manifestation of a uniform confession.

Sacred Order and Supernatural Power

In the so-called old Lutheran ecclesiastical life, which reflected the 18th century legal ideals and continued in various parts of the country up to the 19th or even to the beginning of the 20th century, hierarchy and social order were an important value which occasionally seemed to surpass the importance of the divine. William Paden has outlined a conception of the sacred that is based chiefly on the inviolability of social order itself. According to this model of sacred order, the sacred is what is defended and institutionalised: the ideal order that society holds on to. Even though this type of religious system deals with a divine authority, its emphasis is in protecting the community's territory, tradition, honour and authority from violations, either concrete or moral. Instead of the relationship to the other world, the main concern is in society's own integrity. Obedience to authority and strictly defined status hierarchies are critical features of maintaining order. (Paden 1996: 3–5.) Paden introduced the sacred order model to complement the anthropological discussion of the sacred which had, in his opinion, been dominated by the view he labelled the mana model. This model views the sacred as a manifestation of otherness and a numinous or superhuman power. While the mana model deals with the supernatural and expresses alterity, the sacred order model is more secular and correlates with social organisation and integrity. Paden exposes alterity and integrity as two mutually conditioning aspects of sacrality. Rather than being contradictory tendencies, supernatural power and the sacred order work together in the construction of a religious worldview. (Paden 1996: 3–5, 10, 15.)

When applied to the religious field of 19th century Finland, the sacred order model can be enhanced with the idea of central values, proposed by Edward Shils. Shils writes that sacred status in society is given to authorities, institutions and elites which form the central zone of the community. Its centrality is strengthened by the close connection with values that society holds to be sacred and with the ruling authority. These elites both represent and shape society's central values. (Shils 1975: 4–5.) The integrity of the central values decreases towards the peripheries. Shils declares that the lower in hierarchy, or territorially further from the centre, we go, the less appreciation of authority we are likely to meet. The social and geographical margins may maintain their own, alternative value systems alongside the central ones. (Shils 1975: 10.) In Finnish rural areas, a great many parishioners lived at the social periphery, both geographically and mentally at a distance from the church village. From the scattered farmhouse perspective, the official centre could seem like a remote otherness. Even though people at the margins recognised and partially conformed to the Lutheran central values, they could also follow their indigenous social codes, beliefs and practices. Different value systems were applied according to the context. Thus, in different situations, the same people could identify themselves as decent members of the congregation or as farmers living their lives far from the church and concentrating on survival rather than on spiritual matters.

Centrality and otherness are combined in Murray Milner's study on the sacred. Milner has defined sacredness as otherness which expresses a high status, either religious or profane. Sacred status is maintained by the worshippers' reverent behaviour, which expresses conformity and association. Conformity means obeying the norms set by the sacred authority. Association means deference for the superior and at the same time the improvement of one's own status by association with it. (Milner 1994.) In Lutheran Finland, the ecclesiastical and mundane authorities, which maintained the sacred order, represented social otherness to the common folk. God and the church building represented supernatural otherness. (Koski 2014.) People at the periphery could improve their status in public life by conformity and association, i.e. by obeying Christian norms and participating in ecclesiastical life. As the folklore materials show, association was not only an outwardly social phenomenon expressed by frequent churchgoing and diligent learning. Spiritually, it involved commitment and Christian identity. It was a question of taking sides and appealing to Christian symbols and helpers instead of pagan ones. The more devoted to God an individual was, the better he or she was protected from evil threats. (Koski 2011b: 19.) While deeds of association improved the worshipper's social status, inward commitment improved his or her spiritual status. These were supposed to go hand in hand: the educational aim of the church discipline was that the collective custom would gradually generate spiritual engagement (Laasonen 1991: 162).

Popular Christianity, which was handed down in homes, was in many respects in accordance with the ideals of the sacred order, and the improvement of social status was an important motivation to invest in Christianity. However, especially in vernacular ritual and narrative traditions, sacredness was much more interpreted as supernatural otherness. Christianity was to provide blessing and protection, but Christian objects also posed a threat. According to belief narratives, an inappropriate contact with the church could cause illnesses, and especially during the night the church was inhabited by frightening creatures. This can partly be seen as a result of the demonisation of the dead in the church. However, another reason is that the folk applied to the church building their own, non-Christian conceptions of the sacred.

The old Finnish system of social categorisation was based largely on the division between 'own' and 'other', or internal and external. Phenomena and processes that were outside the ordinary or beyond society's control, yet were vital to society, were handled ritually. Veikko Anttonen (1996a: 52–55) has suggested that transformations and anomalies, as well as transgressions of spatial, temporal and bodily boundaries with social value, fell into the category of Finnish prehistoric sacred. As a bipolar category the vernacular sacred comprises both an area of positive values and an area of pollution and destruction. In narrative and ritual traditions, the concept of *väki* expresses the ambiguous dynamic potential of the sacred. In Finnish folk belief tradition, *väki* refers to an intentional or contagious force, or even a crowd of beings, which resided in all significant and powerful entities. *Väki* could be seen as a threat, but specialists who were capable of confronting it could also use it to productive ends. (Anttonen 1993: 36–37; Koski 2008: 48–49; 2014.) Some folklorists have highlighted that *väki* belonged especially to objects which were connected with the supernatural world (for example, Apo 1998: 76–77; Siikala 2002: 203–204). On the other hand, supernatural or mythical attributes were given to entities that had a special status in the community. In folklore, supernatural and social otherness are frequently paralleled: the asocial is identified with the non-human, and spaces that are not occupied by humans, or 'us', have supernatural inhabitants. While *väki* was a property of various natural, supernatural and social entities, the potential danger depended on the entities' relations to each other. The categories have been flexible: a phenomenon could be part of one's own life in one situation, but in another, a source of a threatening contagion. (Koski 2003; Stark-Arola 2002a: 67–70; about *väki* see also Apo 1998; Stark-Arola 1997; Tarkka 1998.) *Väki* was set in motion when inappropriate contacts between separate categories occurred. To ward off the possibility of failure, ritualisation was needed in liminal, transformative processes, and often also in relations between the sexes, between humans and the natural environment, as well as between the living and the dead. Ritual management could also be useful when handling for example fire or iron, or when going to church. In Lutheran Finnish folk tradition, the *väki* of the dead and the church are deeply intermingled. For example when the magical use of bones or parts of dead bodies is described in belief narratives, it is the church *väki* that brings the desired or undesired consequence. The church and the dead form almost a unified category in this tradition.

The Church and the Dead

The Church building and the deceased have, since early Christianity, had a special relationship. As indicated above, shrines were established in the proximity or even on top of tombs. Later, bishops and pious individuals were buried in churches or remains of saints were transferred there as relics. Over the centuries the sanctity of Catholic shrines has increased significantly through the use of saints' relics, either local or brought from abroad. The supernatural powers of the relic could make the church a place of pilgrimage and miraculous healing. In Catholic regions, the worship of relics still strengthened the Catholic identity and the status of the local church in the post-Reformation era. (Koudounaris 2013: 103–104, 117–122.) The coexistence of the living and dead in church buildings continued up to modern times. Not only the remains of the holy but also of the ordinary dead established a connection from this world to the divine hereafter and thus increased the sanctity of the church. The sanctifying effect of the deceased was guaranteed by a segregation of the dead: criminals, the executed and suicides were not allowed among the blessed. The practice of burying the inappropriate dead outside the churchyard continued from the 11th to the 19th century even though there were no theological grounds for it. The deceased and the shrine had a mutually sanctifying effect on one another. The holiness of the church was, in turn, an advantage to the deceased who rested inside it. (Ariès 1987: 32, 42–45; Hamilton & Spicer 2005: 11, 19.)

Despite the continuity in burial practices, the Reformation brought changes in the attitude towards the dead. In medieval Catholic thinking the living and the dead formed a dual congregation. The deceased and the living members of this congregation supported each other in their spiritual efforts. Paid requiems and intercessions were a concrete form of taking care, and it was the church that mediated the love of the survivors to the departed. The Reformation sought to break the cult of saints and the close relationship with the deceased. They were seen as a corruption of the Christian faith and a continuation of the pagan ancestor cult. (Koski 2011a: 98–100; Lehtonen 1931: 374, 383–384.) Among the rural population in Finland, the ancestor cult had preserved its significance in the rituals and customs of the annual cycle and of people's livelihoods. The disapproval of this and the endeavour to stop it materialised clearly after the Reformation. The folk needed to be estranged from the deceased. Lutheran teaching in the 17th century was characterised by a tendency to demonise spiritual phenomena which were not in accordance with the Lutheran interpretation of the Bible (Olli 2004: 118–119). Since Luther had declared there was no purgatory, it was not possible for the dead to return to this world. The official stance of Protestant churches was that visions of the departed were not real but apparitions of evil spirits. As a consequence, the deceased as a collective were portrayed as dangerous and frightening. In popular folk legends, they were evil spirits which tried to take the living to damnation. (Koski 2011a: 100; Sarmela 1994: 59; Thomas 1971: 587–591.)

After the Reformation, the deceased were nevertheless still buried in the church. The church and the churchyard as consecrated ground were the only appropriate way to the hereafter. In the 17th and 18th centuries, inhabitants of the remote areas in Finland had the tendency to bury their dead in illegal burial sites instead of bringing them to the church. This was done for practical reasons or to avoid burial payments, while the Lutheran authorities emphasised the importance of a proper funeral service and burial in consecrated ground. (Laasonen 1967: 70–71, 281–282; 1991: 78.) The church building continued to be the spiritually ideal place for one's earthly remains. The statuses of burial places reflected the hierarchy of sacredness inside and outside the church building: the best, the most expensive and thus the most prestigious places were in the church near the altar and the pulpit. Outside, it was ideal to rest by the church wall where the rain drops were sanctified by the sacred building's roof. Probably more persistent than these beliefs, which the Lutheran church regarded as superstitious, was the aspiration to use the tomb as a manifestation of social status. (Hamilton & Spicer 2005: 19–21; Koski 2011a: 101–103; Laasonen 1991: 77; Lempiäinen 1990: 8; Wirkkala 1945: 17–18.) The clergy started to speak against the old custom of burial under the church floor in the 18th century. Because of the smell of corpses and of the work involved in tearing up the floor for every burial, the custom would have in many areas been easily rejected by the common folk. However, the established classes were more reluctant to give up this privilege. Especially in areas where social distinctions were significant, the attempt to ban burial in church was strongly opposed and thus it continued until the 1820s. (Laasonen 1967: 283–286; 1991: 326;

Wirkkala 1945: 28–29.) In addition, belief in the beneficial impact of the presence of the deceased was not totally extinct either. This can be seen in the narratives connected to the famous sacrifice churches. Pyhämaa church, on the western Finnish coast, was known especially by seamen as a church which fulfilled wishes or helped when it was given or promised an offering. The miraculous power of the church was attributed to the deceased:

> When somebody was in distress and promised money to Pyhämaa old church, then at once he got help. Sure in the old church's yard there are those who are in the kingdom of heaven. (SKS. KRA. Pyhämaa. Lauri Laiho 3481. 1936.)

There are also reminiscences about the authorities' order to stop burial under the church floor and to remove all earthly remains form the church to the churchyard. This, as one narrator declared, decreased the power of the sacrifice church (SKS. KRA. Uusikaupunki. V. Heltonen KT 3:93. 1938), which had been stronger while the bodies were inside. These statements clearly represent a deviant view and are connected to exceptional churches. However, the dead represent the church in other contexts as well. They guard the church property. Among other things, they prevent enemies from stealing the church bells (for example, SKS. KRA. Saarijärvi. Otto Harju KRK 69:110. 1935.) Such stories are, however, consistent with the image of the dead as aggressive and dangerous.

In Lutheran Finnish parishes, the tombs inside the church were important chiefly not because of the spiritual effect but because it was a means to manifest hierarchy and social values. The nobility and upper classes also purchased epitaphs, coats-of-arms and flags to the church (Laasonen 1991: 77). These celebrated both the late supporters of the central hierarchical values and the living members of the mighty families. The church building was thus not only a place for divine services but also an arena presenting the whole social order. This suggests that by the 19th century, the dead who rested in the church displayed and strengthened the religious and mundane hierarchies. Even so, the presence of the dead bodies and the ghosts of the departed was not entirely forgotten. Even though the majority of the late parishioners rested in the churchyard, it was the church as an institution that managed the bodies, took care of the souls of the dead and also protected the living from the potential threat of evil spirits. This was a major positive function for the church in folklore. In folk belief tradition, the church door and the churchyard fence were boundaries that kept frightening ghosts and bodies in order and prevented them from wandering. The church and the surrounding churchyard being dedicated not only to God but also to the dead increased the otherworldly characteristics that the church building had in folk belief tradition.

That the church has been portrayed as a nest of ghosts in folk legends probably stems from more than the fact that there were tombs in the church. In the Middle Ages, it was the church that functioned as a channel to the dead through requiems and intercessions. And, even later, it was the church that was thought to control and console the souls of the departed. The graveyard was just an outer part of the complex, the heart of which was the building itself.

Blessing and Contagion: The Supernatural Otherness of the Church

In folk belief tradition, the sacrality of the church building has various aspects that are manifested in different contexts. The central values taught by the ministers and controlled by the authorities are present in folk rituals and legends. However, folk belief tradition also applies its own social categorization to the church that portrays the church as otherness with a potentially threatening *väki*. The ritual means of utilising its beneficial influence and warding off risks include procedures which were considered blasphemous and illegal by the authorities. The supernatural character of the church building is threefold. First, the church and the divine service have power, which can be either dangerous and contagious or ritually channelled for a beneficial purpose. Second, the church is described as an agent that realises intentional actions with moral judgment. Third, the church is portrayed as an otherworldly realm inhabited by supernatural beings. This realm is dangerous to laymen but it can be visited by religious specialists (*tietäjäs*) who master the correct rituals.

People who went to the church or passed the building were disposed to its impact, which could, in accordance with the vernacular worldview, bring either blessing or harm. If the contact with the church was appropriate and expressed reverence, the outcome was likely to be positive. Therefore, a devoted participation in the church service was considered a blessing that the churchgoers could even bring home with them. Swedish church ethnologist Hilding Pleijel has analysed a custom that was still known in the 19th century and was called 'to give the mass' (*ge mässe*). Church-goers used to bring the blessing home by shaking hands with those who had stayed home and greeting them with the Swedish words *mässe, in Guds namn*, 'mass, in the name of God'. According to archived reminiscences, old people who had become too weak to travel to church, found this mediated blessing very important. There was also information on reciting these words over a cradle and covering the baby with a garment which had been worn in the church. (Pleijel 1970: 173–178.) In Finland, the custom of church greetings survived up to the 20th century but had a more ambiguous tone. As a positive custom, the words "greetings from the church" were uttered, to which the people in the house could respond with thanks or the words "good Jesus". (VKK Hollola/Asikkala/Einar Toppola 2:10; VKK Hollola/Padasjoki/M. Myyrä 2:10.) The ambiguity emerges when we parallel the church with the bathhouse, a parallel that was frequently drawn in Finnish tradition. Parents taught their children that the sauna cleans the body and the church cleans the soul (for example, VKK Hämeenlinna/Renko/Sylvi Kaloinen 1:4). It has been explicitly stated that the sauna was like the church and that both places required reverence and decent behaviour. They both functioned as places in which the boundaries of life (birth and death) were ritualised, and had a supernatural dimension as places in which encounters with otherworldly beings were more likely than elsewhere. Therefore, it is not totally surprising that greetings were also made when returning from the sauna. Greetings from the bathhouse, spoken aloud when one comes back to the house, are known to date. However, it is questionable whether it has been desirable to bring the influence of the church or sauna home. In the light of the vernacular distinctions between one's 'own' and the 'other', when a boundary between the home and the otherworldly is transgressed it is more likely that one would hope that any ambiguous influence would *not* follow. Indeed, there are archival texts about expressing these greetings in a charm-like formula which derives from the words "Jesus help from the bathhouse/church". These words concern both the church and the sauna, and both leaving and returning. (Koski 2014; SKVR VII: 728; SKVR VIII: 690–695.) Pleijel (1970: 176) also mentions a case in which parents used to say "mass in the name of God" to their children when leaving for the church. While the influence of the external sphere could be ambiguous, the rituals aimed to receive positive effects and ward off unwanted ones.

Ritualisation was also needed during the journey to the church. There are documents about the need for a prayer (Uotila 1982: 48) as well as the necessity of a protective charm when the church first became visible in the distance. One reason given for the protective rituals for churchgoers was that they helped to prevent evil beings coming from the church. (Koski 2014; SKS. KRA. Väinö Laajala 73. 1939; SKS. KRA. Sirkka Korhonen 574. 1950.) The contact with the church, which represented otherness, needed to be established in an appropriate way to ensure a safe departure as well. It is important to note that in both discourses – the Christian and the folk belief tradition – ritualisation was needed even though each chose legitimate verbal formulae from their own religious vocabulary.

In popular thinking, the positive influence of the church could be ritually directed to improve one's luck. Hunting luck could be developed for example by keeping snares under the church threshold during divine service (Varonen 1891: 109). Magical manipulation of one's luck was, on the one hand, a good addition to other means of practicing one's livelihood. On the other hand, it was regarded sinful because the magic could only change the division of limited resources and was thus a theft from others. From the Lutheran point of view, attaching magical power to ecclesiastical objects presented the wrong interpretation of Christianity and was therefore regarded as blasphemy by the authorities. Especially exceptionable were practices which included usurping or violating sacred objects. This was also judged as blasphemous in many belief narratives that favoured Christian morals. Among the blasphemous tricks was the charming of a gun to strike its target by shooting a communion wafer from it. In morally laden narratives, the person who performed this went insane after seeing how the violated wafer transformed into Christ's body. (Issakainen 2012: 83–86; Koski 2014.)

The danger lying within objects with a supernatural aspect, as well as the *väki* previously mentioned, derived both from their otherworldliness and their inapproachability. That the church building itself could be contagious can be interpreted as coming either from its supernatural nature, or according to the sacred order model, which would view the infection as a punishment for violation. The next excerpt, recorded in 1938 in eastern Finland, reports a farm mistress's description how her husband became infected by touching the church:

> The narrator's husband had, long ago in his youthful stupidity, tried to see if the church doors would open by themselves in the night, as he had heard the old people tell. When they didn't, he peeped in through the window. But he wasn't careful and his cheek slightly touched the windowsill. He got a terrible rash on his cheek, and no doctors' medicines could help. They then went to show it to the sorcerer Paavo Takkinen, who immediately knew what had caused it. "You boy have messed with the church!" He made an ointment, which cured the rash quite quickly. (SKS. KRA. Haukivuori. T. Nurmi 604. 1938.)

It is evident that the endeavour to enter the church at night was a breach of the norm. The man tried to imitate great sorcerers who could enter the church and perform rituals there. Folk belief tradition emphasises that dangerous rituals should not be performed without a proper reason and definitely not without the proper skills (Koski 2011a: 229). Thus, the reason for the contamination was not only that the man violated a norm, contrary to sacred order, but also that he was not capable of handling the power of the church. Touching or taking church materials caused infection, especially if the contact was not appropriate or if the person was frightened by the situation.

> The servant of Tervola's parsonage had once at dusk gone to peep into the old church window. At the same moment there was some kind of crash in the church. The servant got a terrible fright, became ill, withered and wasted away, lay in bed like a pair of fence poles and finally died. People believed that church *väki* had infected the servant. (SKS. KRA. Tervola. Elina Pallari KT 222:8. 138.)

> In Mietoinen there is a 'Chapel hill'. There used to be a church before. There was old timber left. An old woman went and took some timber, intending to burn it. But she had to take it back as she got abscesses all over. (SKS. KRA. Mietoinen. V. Saariluoma 1116. 1915.)

In popular tradition, supernatural power persisted in the materials of the church even when the building had been repurposed from its ritual use. Sometimes old wooden churches, which were either too small for local use or worn out, were torn down and the materials were sold. Selling the church and using the material for other purposes was something of which the folk did not approve (for example, SKS. KRA. Pirkkala. Frans Kärki 2532. 1945; SKS. KRA. Valtimo. Siiri Oulasmaa 266. 1936). It has been said that in 1823, the parishioners of Eno protested against the auctioning of their old church by burning it. (SKS. KRA. KKY Eno 3/III, 13–14; SKS. KRA. KKY Eno 12/III, 2.) This fear and disapproval is also expressed in narratives which involve haunting and death after using church materials for secular purposes (for example, Koski 2011a: 234; SKS. KRA. KKY Juva 1/III:2, 7–8). In Enontekiö parish in Finnish Lapland, for example, an old church was sold and transferred as lumber to a farmer, who used it to build a house. According to local reminiscences, the pulpit and all the church furniture was brought to the house and the wood from the altar and galleries was used for the granary's grain bins. The inhabitants started to suffer and many of them died before the family decided to move away in fear. They also lost a lot of cows, horses and sheep because their cowshed burned. After the perdition of the family the house was deserted for 25 years. Later it was torn down and built again, but still the locals feared it. One narrator refers to the agency of the building itself: that the church had a strong power and that negative consequences came because it was moved against its will. In another narrator's words, the *väki* of the church accompanied the materials and started haunting the house. It was also said that this was the result of church spirits which came with the church. (SKS. KRA. Enontekiö. S. Paulaharju b) 14259. 1930, SKS. KRA. Muonio. S. Paulaharju b) 14349. 1930, SKS. KRA. Enontekiö, Hetta. Samuli Paulaharju b) 14263. 1930.) These comments crystallise the typical range of consequences of inappropriate management of the sacred in vernacular tradition. They are often conceptualised as the work of *väki*, which can simply cause death and illness or manifests itself as audible or visible haunting or spirits. The impact of *väki* on people seldom derives from a merely mechanical contagion through touch. Traditional explanations involve the victim having some form of vulnerability, for example he or she is frightened,[2] or there is a reason for the *väki* to be angered, for example the breach of a norm. (Koski 2011a: 220–227.)

A Place of Terrible Encounters

The image of the church building as an otherworldly place has been strengthened by widely known belief legends. In Finnish tradition, the most popular legend types about the church are about church services for the dead on a festival night, about sorcerers who conduct rituals in a church crowded with ghosts and evil spirits, and about fake hauntings and those who accept dares and enter the church defiantly – and who quite often pay the ultimate price for their norm breach.

The legend about the church service for the dead is an internationally known type (C 1341 and C 1821 in Jauhiainen 1998; C31 in af Klintberg 2010; 4015 in Christiansen 1958; ATU 779F* in Uther 2004), which has been a popular horror story in the Nordic countries and is most often connected to the Christmas mass in Finland and Sweden (for example, Johansson 1991: 150–166; Koski 2011a: 280–282; Köhler 1987; see also Lindow in this volume, 43–47). An example is as follows:

> The church service of church folk [the dead]. It is between midnight and three o'clock when they have their church service. A woman went to church then, took a seat on a pew and saw her neighbour, who had recently died. She sat there among the other deceased. There a minister preached and mould was dripping from his face, and likewise everybody's faces were mouldy. When the neighbour saw the woman, she told her to leave immediately. Otherwise they will kill you, she said, and also advised the woman to put her coat only loosely on her shoulders and jump over the threshold with both feet together! The woman hurried out. When she jumped out of the door, the coat was snatched from her shoulders and the door slammed shut and was locked. When the woman returned there in the morning, her coat had been torn into thousands of pieces. Church spirits and the dead have their church service like that. The ministers who are dead and buried

preach there. Humans have that kind of form there when they are dead. It is that sort of spiritual world. (SKS. KRA. Turtola Samuli Paulaharju b) 14323. 1930.)

In most versions the woman arrives at the church too early to attend Christmas mass; she is mistaken, for example because she is too poor to have a clock. This is relevant: in Finnish versions, the woman escapes without exception because she had meant no harm but tried her best to participate in the divine service.[3] The legend portrays the church in the night as an otherworldly space that, at least during this special time, belongs to the dead. The intention of the deceased to kill the living who enter their realm is explicit in many versions and it is also compatible with other Nordic belief legends about the dead (Johansson 1991: 32–33). The church building itself is more than just a setting for the events. It seems autonomously to perform certain functions that are normally handled by people. In many versions it is said that the building is lit during the church service for the dead, and when the ceremony ends, it immediately becomes dark. The advice to jump across the threshold with both feet is a particular Finnish motif and also belongs to legends about the sorcerer in the church (Johansson 1991: 83–84, 104). The church door works as a gate between the worlds, opening and closing at strategic moments and special knowledge is required to pass through (see also Lindow in this volume, 43–44).

Legends about those who accept dares and jokers who imitate ghosts (C 1311–1331 in Jauhiainen 1998) are based on the norm that the church is feared and an inapproachable place in the night. The legends about dares describe the fate of a defiant man who makes a bet that he dares visit the church at midnight. Similar stories are common in relation to graveyards and storehouses with dead bodies. To prove his visit, the dare-taker is supposed to leave a mark – for example to hammer a nail into the altar. The motif that the nail catches his clothing and he thinks that a dead person pulls him back when leaving is also known as ATU type 1676B "Frightened to Death". In the versions that most strikingly emphasise the norm, the man is found dead in the morning:

> A man made a bet that he would take shears and cut off the beard of the dead minister whose body lay buried beneath the church floor. He goes about his business at night. In the morning the man is found fallen across the coffin, the shears deep in his breast. (SKS. KRA. Jalmari Saario 36. 1904.)

The outlook on sacred values has been variable, and the defiance and testing of one's own and other's courage has been a popular sport among young men. The legends about those accepting dares are not only a comment on the taboo itself, but also on fear and bravery and the drive to test them. The story does not always include a supernatural intervention. If the protagonist dies, the explanation can, instead of a supernatural intervention, be that he died of fright or a heart attack. In addition, some stories include an extra twist: another man is sent to play a prank on the dare-taker and to frighten him. Thus, the ghost encountered in the story is claimed to be fake. Nevertheless, the person accepting the dare can also win the bet. In the humorous versions, he is fearless and responds arrogantly to both real and fake ghosts. But he may also accidentally kill his fake-ghost friend while he thinks he is preventing the dead from carrying out a haunting. The consequences of defying the norm can be fatal even though the story does not involve any explicit supernatural agent. It is possible to interpret the outcome as a punishment, although one could also use the story to state it was superstition and fear that killed the dare-taker. These legends – both in narrated and in ostensive, acted form – have been part of a constant negotiation of local values. On the one hand, they point out that the conception of the church and the dead as inviolable has been questioned, especially by young men. On the other hand, they prove that these particular norms were strong enough to pose a real challenge.

The motif of frightening also appears in legends about the parsonage's farmhand (C 1321 in Jauhiainen 1998; cf. also ATU 1676, Lindow, 51 and Roper, 230–231 in this volume). He poses as a ghost to scare the parson's serving maid who is sent to the church to fetch communion wine at night. Here, however, there is no negotiation, but instead a harsh punishment:

> The minister needed communion wine in the night and told his maid to go and fetch it from the church cellar. But the farmhand hurried before her a white bed sheet on his back to frighten her. And the devil had torn the farmhand so that in the morning, there was nothing left but pieces of bone and shreds of the bed sheet. (SKS. KRA. Nummi. Raakel Saario KRK 55:97.)

This story always follows the same line; only the gruesome details about the farmhand's death and the interpretation of the agent that caused it vary. That the farmhand is found in the morning skinned in the church corridor and his skin on the pew (for example SKS. KRA. Loimaa. KT 19. Urho Järveläinen 51. 1938) may hint it was the work of the devil. Sometimes it is stated that, "the church spirits killed him and put one limb to each pew" (SKS. KRA. Teuva. S. Korpela 27. 1889). One version says that the maid utters a blessing every time she passes through a door in the church and does not look back even though she hears a snap after her. She experiences no harm and returns safely, but the farmhand cannot be found anywhere. At last they find him in the church:

> When they went to the church porch they found the farmhand's legs and a piece of bed sheet, and in the church there was the farmhand's torso and a piece of bed sheet, and in the sacristy there was the farmhand's head and again a piece of bed sheet. God had thus punished the farmhand for bullying. (SKS. KRA. Pori. F.V. Hannus 42. 1890.)

Here, the church doors executed the farmhand by slicing him into pieces, although the actual intention and agency are attributed to God. Interestingly enough, the parts of the dead man are found in parts of the church that correspond in their importance. He lost his legs when profaning the entrance, his body when profaning the nave, and his head when continuing his blasphemy in the sacristy.

There are also narratives in which a person ends up in the church at night by accident, although not a special night. Therefore, there is no special occasion such as the divine service for the dead and no particular norm breach such as defiance to be punished. In those legends (types C 1301 and E 1231 in Jauhiainen 1998), a person who has for example fallen asleep in catechism school and cannot get out of the locked church before morning is tormented by devils or church beings. The person can be safe only in the altar, where the devils and church spirits cannot reach them. The beings lose their power and disappear by dawn and the person is rescued.

A Place of Secret Rituals

The legends presented above portray the church at night as a dangerous and threatening place to ordinary Christian people. Other legends show that once evil and threatening beings are kept in check, the church provides a supernatural resource. The holiest parts may have a particularly beneficial influence, for example in healing. The main character in the narratives about the ritual utilisation of the church in the night (D 311–331 in Jauhiainen 1998) is usually the specialist practitioner of vernacular belief tradition, the *tietäjä*. The real danger is also present in these narratives, as well: if something goes wrong, the beings attack even the specialist (Koski 2011a: 293). Entering the church has been considered a feat for a *tietäjä*. Stories about visits to the night church emphasise his or her skill and power:

> To a sorcerer, even the church doors open. Once Santala had gone to the church with his apprentice, the church doors opened to him. The sorcerer stepped briskly in, but the apprentice had to jump with both feet together. They met in the church a devil, with whom the sorcerer shook hands with a bare hand, but the apprentice was given a stick with which he could shake hands with the devil. (SKS. KRA. Jalasjärvi. Uuno Yrjänäinen KRK 206: 22.)

The rituals that make the church doors open have been richly described in legends. They include walking around the church, blowing in the keyhole and uttering magic words. Sometimes it is said that the church doors open themselves and the lights are switched on when the *tietäjä* comes. (Koski 2011a: 292.) These narratives are often told from the point of view of a witness, or a client or patient of the *tietäjä*.

> A horse was stolen from a farmhouse. The farmer went to consult a sorcerer. They went to Renko church in the middle of the night and walked around the church nine times. After each round the witch blew in the keyhole and after the ninth time the door opened. The sorcerer gave the farmer a whetstone and said that when ghosts started coming out he must not give his hand to them. But the farmer got scared and escaped, and thus they did not get any information. (The farmer has told this himself.) (SKS. KRA. Renko. Arvo Heino 1426. 1936.)

The church and the graveyard were places in which the *tietäjä* either gathered magical objects or performed rituals. The legacy of shamanism has given rise to the motif of visiting the other world or the abode of the dead to receive knowledge or to negotiate with the spirits about the cure for a patient (Siikala 2002: 84, 216–219). Finnish belief tradition has transformed visits to the otherworld into visits to the night church, which functions as the other world. The *tietäjä* rules both the church building and the beings that he meets inside it: the dead, church spirits, or the devil.

In folk legends, church spirits are mentioned both in singular and in plural. In plural, they denote the *väki* of the church – a crowd that represent the intention or interests attached to the church building. A church spirit, in singular, is a guardian spirit of the church. Usually it is said that the first person buried in the churchyard becomes the guardian spirit of the church (for example, SKS. KRA. Lappajärvi. Jaakko Loukola KRK 184: 211). However, in medieval churches, the spirit's name tends to be the same as the church's patron saint (Kuujo 1954: 1–3) and is probably a reminiscence of the saint. When the guardian spirit is mentioned with a human name, it is he or she that opens the door to the *tietäjä* and allows him to use the church for his purposes. Church spirits can be in the same story both in plural and singular: the beings have a leader, from which the *tietäjä* collects his information or who "drives his people up" to give their help (SMSA. Karvia. L. J. Kaukamaa. SatO. 1930).

The healing capacity of the church and its altar can be thought to derive from Catholic Christianity, which, in turn, had a firm link with the saints. Up to the 19th century European Catholic tradition involved beliefs about certain churches or chapels in which diseases and injuries can be healed or stillborn children can be brought into life for a moment to enable baptism. These miracles were attributed to the saints whose relics were located in those particular churches or chapels. (Devlin 1987: 51–52, 64–65; Koudounaris 2013: 120–122.) In Finland, these beliefs have parallels in stories in which the patient has to stay overnight alone in the church – often specifically in the altar – and in the morning he or she is cured (for example, SKS. KRA. Korpilahti. Vieno Vanhala KT 59:14. 1938). As mentioned earlier, the altar is also a sanctuary: it is the only place where a lay person is safe in the church at night, because the dead and the devils cannot enter it:

> Church beings cannot go to the altar. They try to lure a nightly visitor away from the altar in order to be able to tear him. (SKS. KRA. Selma Soihanen KT 56:22. 1938.)

The altar is special in various ways that can seem controversial in its relation to the otherworldly beings in the church. The altar is often also a curing place when the *tietäjä* performs the healing rituals (SKS. KRA. Suonenjoki. Eero Kansanen 64. 1938). The choir and the altar form the core of the church, where the church spirit can be spoken to (for example, SKS. KRA. Rautalampi. Pietari Munukka KRK 130:26). Thus the altar is both a place into which threatening beings cannot go and a place in which their leader is contacted. What these traditional conceptions have in common is that the altar is powerful and its role is positive from the human visitor's point of view. The pulpit, which had an important role in Lutheran worship, has been mentioned in the legends mainly when a headless or mouldy minister has preached at the midnight mass of the deceased. While it was sacred as furniture of the church, it seems to have no special status in magic. In addition to the altar and choir, the sacristy is mentioned as the place where communion wine and many sacred utensils were stored.

One informant explains that the leader of the church spirits, the *päämänningäine*, was in the choir and had before him a book so terribly big that when he turned the page its corners nearly touched the ceiling. Everything in the world was written in the book and therefore answers to any questions the *tietäjä* asked could be found there. (SKS. KRA. Perho. Väinö Laajala 61. 1936.) The huge book of the church spirit is an interesting detail. Books and learning were part of the elite and religious culture with prestige and authority. Ministers had large books to keep records of each and every parishioner's particulars, their attendance at communion and their reading skills (Laine 2002). On the other hand, as an inversion of the acknowledged authority of the learned, there were also stories about black books and learned men who had their knowledge from the devil. The example with the book corroborates the inference that the vernacular conceptualisation of the sacredness of the nightly church was not only an occupation of the church by non-Christian powers. The books, the authority, the impact of devils, the dead in and around the church, and the prohibition to manipulate Christian objects for one's personal purposes, were parts of Christian culture. The *tietäjä*'s actions in the church were, naturally, deemed blasphemous by the authorities. The folk, however, also told stories about ministers who made people stay overnight in the church. While the *tietäjäs* helped with mundane problems such as diseases and stolen goods, the minister's undertaking was to save people from the devil's power (E531, E551 in Jauhiainen 1998; L61 in af Klintberg 2010).

Legends about terrible encounters and rites in the church at night have gained popularity especially because of their dramatic plots and terrifying details, but they have also resonated with the attitudes and fears of their audiences (Koski 2007: 14–15). They discuss commonly held values and norms in relation to the church, the dead and the authority of local sorcerers. The church service for the dead, in which the living person only narrowly escapes the furious departed, is perhaps the most dramatic of them. Its imagery looks quite fabulous compared to the majority of Finnish belief tradition. Indeed, descriptions of the dead as rotting corpses who attack the living in the church decidedly differ from most traditional belief narratives in which otherworldly beings are usually sensed only partially. In more mundane settings, spirits or ghosts are transparent or visible only for a short moment. Contextual information, however, indicates that stories about the terrible Christmas mass have earlier been taken seriously. For example, people who came to the Christmas service in the morning used to wipe the pews before sitting down because of the possible dirt left by the deceased. (Johansson 1991: 138–140; Koski 2011a: 287–288.) The motifs present in the *tietäjä*'s rites in the church are even more closely attached to everyday concerns and local people and frequently narrated in the first person (Koski 2011a: 297). A central point of these legends was that the church really was special – particularly at night, and especially if somebody committed such a norm breach as to enter the sacred building outside its proper ritual context.

In all these stories, the events happen in the night, which emphasises the alterity of the church. According to the temporal division of 'own' and 'other' in the popular worldview, the daytime is fitting for work and social activities while the night is void of human activity and belongs to the dead and other spirits (for example, Koski & Enges 2010: 28; Geiger 1937: 1067; see also Pócs 1989: 17–20). Midnight or festival nights are also considered as breaks in the temporal cycle and thus liminal moments when the supernatural phenomena can penetrate the reality of the living (for example, Kropej 2008: 193–194). A church in the night is thus, for two reasons, a setting where the boundary between this world and the supernatural is permeable. Norm breaches make a third reason because they crack the socially upheld reality and provoke supernatural agents.

Christian tradition holds that the source of sanctity is the contact with divinity. Models for the vernacular sacred connect sacrality with liminality and boundaries. Consequently, it has been suggested that the sacredness of the church is based on its position as a place between this and the other world: it is a setting of category transformations and represents a boundary between the dead and the living and between the human and the divine (Eilola 2004: 150; see also Anttonen 1996b: 77). In folk legends, however, the building itself also presents the other world. This idea was present in medieval church building symbolism: the church was not only the gate to the heavenly Jerusalem but, especially during the divine service, became heaven itself on earth (see Sheldrake 2001). Similarly in Finnish belief tradition, a special time or occasion evoked its otherworldly nature to show itself. That the church itself is supernatural in the night is manifested, first, by the supernatural beings that inhabit and rule the place so that it is alien and hostile to a human. Second, entering and staying in the church generates miraculous and terrifying incidents, such as harsh punishments, the source of which is unseen. The explanations deducible from the narratives are that the source is either the supernatural agent – be it a church spirit, devil, or God – who governs the church or it is the church itself as an intentional actor. Third, the church door functions as a gate to the other world, and passing through it requires ritual knowledge.

Conclusions

The basis for the church building's special status is in Christian tradition. Vernacular beliefs concerning the church carry traits of Catholic tradition and also present popular reactions and comments to Lutheran practices. Rituals concerning contacts with the church building, as well as frightening stories about its supernatural nature, express the otherness of the church in relation to the common people's everyday life world. This life world has also been surrounded by otherness of the forests, lakes and rocks, which have similarly involved *väki* either as an effective force or in the form of beings. The *väki* of the church was decisively strengthened by its integral relationship with the dead as well as by the strong normative pressure exercised by the Lutheran church authorities.

I have applied William Paden's sacred order model to describe the Lutheran legislation's method of constructing the sacred. The Swedish crown had recruited the church to protect the religious integrity of the kingdom, which had led to the strong emphasis on the church discipline. In local folk traditions, the otherness of the church derived from its religious status and from the social gap between the social centre and the periphery. The vernacular model of the sacred involved a dynamic relationship between the internal and external spheres of social life. The contacts with areas and categories that were external or other had to be ritualised in order to ensure safety or to improve one's own wellbeing. In addition to the ritual behaviour that was appropriate in popular ecclesiastical life, folk legends described rituals that belonged to exceptional and partly hypothetical situations. These legends portray *tietäjäs* as specialists in folk belief tradition who rivalled the official church authorities in their ability to manage rituals in the church.

The legends about the night church clearly express fear towards both the deceased and the church itself. There was good reason to be scared, especially for those who were rough-mannered and not well versed in Christianity. In addition to divine services, the church building was the site of teaching and of the control of Catechism knowledge. While the church building was a symbol of salvation and blessing, it was also a symbol of control, punishment and shame. The legends of the nightly church described healing rituals that apparently were really performed and reflected continuities of belief tradition. They also provided a symbolic means to express some hidden feelings towards the sacred centre of socially shared values.

Notes

1   The idea that God's word made a place sacred is well represented in Finnish tradition. In remote areas, certain stones have been regarded as sacred because sermons, communions or other Lutheran practices were performed there when there had been no opportunity to go to a proper church. (For example, SKS. KRA. Tervo. Juho Oksman 834. 1936, SKS. KRA. Suomussalmi. A. Alopaeus KRK 235: 1194.)

2   Frightening was a common explanation for illness. Laura Stark (2002b: 99–100) has proposed that individuals were protected against infections and harmful interaction with their environment by their own internal power. When a person got a fright, fell or thought about the possibility of infection, this shock briefly reduced the protection and gave access to the infection.

3   In Europe, it has been more common that people who participated in the mass of the dead soon die themselves (for example, Köhler 1987: 933–934; Koski 2011a: 281). This is also the case in Swedish-language tradition in Finland, especially if the person happened to drink the 'communion wine', which was actually blood with bits of flesh. (FSF 1931: 12–16.)

Sources

Unprinted

KKY: General inquiry into ecclesiastical folk tradition. Folklore Archives, Finnish Literature Society.
SKS. KRA: Folklore Archives. Finnish Literature Society.
SMSA: The Lexical Archive of Finnish Dialects. Institute for the Languages of Finland.
VKK: Viljo-Kustaa Kuuliala collections. Archives of History, Culture and Arts Studies, University of Turku.

Literature

Anttonen, Veikko 1993. Pysy Suomessa Pyhänä. Onko Suomi uskonto? In *Mitä on suomalaisuus*. Teppo Korhonen (ed.). Helsinki: Suomen Antropologinen Seura. Pp. 33–67.
Anttonen, Veikko 1996a. Rethinking the Sacred: The Notions of 'Human Body' and 'Territory' in Conceptualizing Religion. In *The Sacred & its Scholars. Comparative Methodologies for the Study of Primary Religious Data*. Thomas A. Idinopulos & Edward A. Yonan (eds.). Leiden: E. J. Brill. Pp. 36–64.
Anttonen, Veikko 1996b. *Ihmisen ja maan rajat. 'Pyhä' kulttuurisena kategoriana*. Suomalaisen Kirjallisuuden Seuran toimituksia 646. Helsinki: Suomalaisen Kirjallisuuden Seura.
Amundsen, Arne Bugge 2010. Churches and the Culture of Memory. A Study of Lutheran Church Interiors in Østfold, 1537–1700. *Arv. Nordic Yearbook of Folklore* 66: 117–142.
Apo, Satu 1998. "*Ex cunno* Come the Folk and Force". Concepts of Women's Dynamistic Power in Finnish-Karelian Tradition. In *Gender and Folklore. Perspectives on Finnish and Karelian Culture*. Satu Apo, Aili Nenola & Laura Stark-Arola (eds.). Studia Fennica Folkloristica 4. Helsinki: Suomalaisen Kirjallisuuden Seura/FLS. Pp. 63–91.
Ariès, Philippe 1987. *The Hour of Our Death*. London: Penguin Books.
Bossuyt, Stijn 2005. The Liturgical Use of Space in Thirteenth-Century Flanders. In *Defining the Holy. Sacred Space in Medieval and Early Modern Europe*. Andrew Spicer & Sarah Hamilton (eds.). Aldershot, Burlington: Ashgate. Pp. 187–206.
Christiansen, Reidar 1958. *The Migratory Legends. A Proposed List of Types with a Systematic Catalogue of the Norwegian Variants*. Folklore Fellows' Communications 175. Helsinki: Academia Scientiarum Fennica.
Devlin, Judith 1987. *The Superstitious Mind. French Peasants and the Supernatural in the Nineteenth Century*. New Haven, London: Yale University Press.
Eilola, Jari 2004. Rajojen noituus ja taikuus. In *Paholainen, noituus ja magia – kristinuskon kääntöpuoli. Pahuuden kuvasto vanhassa maailmassa*. Sari Katajala-Peltomaa & Raisa Maria Toivo (eds.). Helsinki: Suomalaisen Kirjallisuuden Seura.
FSF 1931 = *Finlands Svenska Folkdiktning II Sägner 3. Mytiska sägner 2. Sägner till typförteckningen*. Utgivna av V.E.V. Wessman. Helsingfors: Svenska Litteratursällskapet i Finland.
Geiger, Paul 1937. Totengottesdienst. In *Handwörterbuch des deutschen Aberglaubens*. Band 8. Hanns Bächtold-Stäubli & Eduard Hoffmann-Krayer (eds.). Berlin, Leipzig: Walter de Gruyter. P. 1067.
Hamilton, Sarah & Andrew Spicer 2005. Defining the Holy. The Delineation of Sacred Space. In *Defining the Holy. Sacred Space in Medieval and Early Modern Europe*. Andrew Spicer & Sarah Hamilton (eds.). Aldershot, Burlington: Ashgate. Pp. 1–23.

Hiekkanen, Markus 2007. *Suomen keskiajan kivikirkot*. Helsinki: Suomalaisen Kirjallisuuden Seura.

Hurmerinta, Markku 1982. *Jumalanpalveluksen viettoon liittyvä tapakulttuuri kansanperinteen valossa n. 1890–1940*. Suomen kirkkohistorian pro gradu -tutkielma. Helsingin yliopisto.

Isaiasz, Vera 2012. Early Modern Lutheran Churches: Redefining the Boundaries of the Holy and the Profane. In *Lutheran Churches in Early Modern Europe*. Andrew Spicer (ed.). Farnham: Ashgate. Pp. 17–37.

Issakainen, Tenka 2012. *Tavallista taikuutta. Tulkinta suomalaisten taikojen merkityksistä Mikko Koljosen osaamisen valossa*. Doctoral thesis. University of Turku. Available at http://urn.fi/URN:ISBN:978-951-29-5158-1 [Accessed July 10, 2015]

Jauhiainen, Marjatta 1998. *The Type and Motif Index of Finnish Belief Legends and Memorates. Revised and Enlarged Edition of Lauri Simonsuuri's Typen- und Motivverzeichnis der finnischen mythischen Sagen*. Folklore Fellows' Communications 267. Helsinki: Academia Scientiarum Fennica.

Johansson, Kerstin Louise 1991. *De dödas julotta*. Bergen: Forlaget Folkekultur.

Juva, Mikko 1956. Suomen kansan uskonnollisuus 1600- ja 1700-luvulla. Eräitä kehityslinjoja. In *Suomen kirkkohistoriallisen seuran vuosikirja 43–44 (1953–1954)*. Helsinki: Suomen Kirkkohistoriallinen Seura. Pp. 32–47.

Kircko-laki ja ordningi 1686 = *Kircko-laki ja ordningi 1686. Näköispainos ja uudelleen ladottu laitos vuoden 1686 kirkkolain suomennoksesta*. 1986. Lahja-Irene Hellemaa, Anja Jussila & Martti Parvio (eds.). Helsinki: Suomalaisen Kirjallisuuden Seura.

af Klintberg, Bengt 2010. *The Types of the Swedish Folk Legend*. Folklore Fellows' Communications 300. Helsinki: Academia Scientiarum Fennica.

Köhler, Ines 1987. Geistermesse. In *Enzyklopädie des Märchens. Handwörterbuch zur historischen und vergleichenden Erzählsforschung*. Band 5. Berlin: Walter de Gruyter. Pp. 933–939.

Koski, Kaarina 2003. "Outoa tuntematonta väkeä". Näkökulmia väkeen tuonpuoleisen edustajana. *Elore* 10(1). Available at http://www.elore.fi/arkisto/1_03/kos103a.html [Accessed July 10, 2015]

Koski, Kaarina 2007. Narratiivisuus uskomusperinteessä. *Elore* 14(1): 1–21. Available at http://www.elore.fi/arkisto/1_07/kos1_07.pdf [Accessed July 10, 2015]

Koski, Kaarina 2008. Conceptual Analysis and Variation in Belief Tradition: A Case of Death-related Beings. *Folklore: Electronic Journal of Folklore* 38: 46–66. Available at http://www.folklore.ee/folklore/vol38/koski.pdf [Accessed July 10, 2015]

Koski, Kaarina 2011a. *Kuoleman voimat. Kirkonväki suomalaisessa uskomusperinteessä*. Helsinki: Suomalaisen Kirjallisuuden Seura.

Koski, Kaarina 2011b. Uskomusperinne ja kristillinen kasvatus 1800-luvulla. *Kasvatus ja aika* 5(4): 9–24.

Koski, Kaarina 2014. Folk belief and the Lutheran Church in Nineteenth-Century Finland. *Cosmos* 30: 65–92.

Koski, Kaarina & Pasi Enges 2010. "Mi en ossaas sanoa mitem mie näin." Erikoisten aistihavaintojen tulkinta uskomusperinteen pohjalta. *Elore* 17(1): 17–40. Available at http://www.elore.fi/arkisto/1_10/art_koski_enges_1_10.pdf [Accessed July 10, 2015]

Koudounaris, Paul 2013. *Heavenly Bodies. Cult Treasures & Spectacular Saints From the Catacombs*. London: Thames & Hudson.

Kouri, E.I. 1995. The Early Reformation in Sweden and Finland, c. 1520–1560. In *The Scandinavian Reformation. From Evangelical Movement to Institutionalization of Reform*. Ole Peter Grell (ed.). Cambridge: Cambridge University Press. Pp. 42–69.

Kropej, Monika 2008. Slovene Midwinter Deities and Personifications of Days in the Yearly, Work, and Life Cycles. In *Space and Time in Europe: East and West, Past and Present*. Mirjam Mencej (ed.). Ljubljana: Univerza v Ljubljani, Filozofska fakulteta. Pp. 181–197.

Kuha, Miia 2016. *Pyhäpäivien vietto varhaismodernin ajan Savossa (vuoteen 1710)*. Jyväskylä studies in humanities 286. Jyväskylä: University of Jyväskylä.

Kuujo, Anja 1954. Kirkonhaltia suomalaisessa kansanperinteessä. Esitelmä suomalaisen ja vertailevan kansanrunoudentutkimuksen lisensiaattiseminaarissa. S-sidos 44. Helsingin yliopisto.

Kuuliala, Viljo-Kustaa 1939. *Vanhoilta kirkoilta ja kirkkoteiltä. Kansanelämän kuvauksia.* Jyväskylä, Helsinki: K. J. Gummerus osakeyhtiö.

Laasonen, Pentti 1967. *Pohjois-Karjalan luterilainen kirkollinen kansankulttuuri Ruotsin vallan aikana.* Helsinki: Suomen Kirkkohistoriallinen Seura.

Laasonen, Pentti 1991. *Suomen kirkon historia 2. Vuodet 1593–1808.* Porvoo, Helsinki, Juva: WSOY.

Laine, Esko M. 2002. Pelottava ja kauhistava lukeminen. In *ABC: Lukeminen esivallan palveluksessa. ABC: Läsandet i överhetens tjänst.* Esko M. Laine (ed.). Helsinki: Helsingin yliopiston kirjasto. Pp. 11–31.

Lehtonen, Aleksi 1931. *Kirkon pyhät toimitukset.* Porvoo: WSOY.

Lempiäinen, Pentti 1990. Hautausmaaperinteen rikkaus. In *Viimeiset leposijamme. Hautausmaat ja hautamuistomerkit.* Pentti Lempiäinen & Brita Nickels (eds.). Imatra: SLEY Kirjat.

Manninen, Ilmari 1917. *Liperin seurakunnan historia Ruotsin vallan aikana.* Helsinki: Suomen Kirkkohistoriallinen Seura.

Milner, Murray 1994. Status and Sacredness: Worship and Salvation as Forms of Status Transformation. *Journal of the Scientific Study of Religion* 33(2): 99–109.

Nyman, Magnus 2009. *Hävinneiden historia. Katolista elämää Ruotsi-Suomessa Kustaa Vaasasta kuningatar Kristiinaan.* Helsinki: Katolinen tiedotuskeskus.

Olli, Soili-Maria 2004. "Paholainen on minun veljeni". Kirkon ja kansan paholaiskuva uuden ajan alussa. In *Paholainen, noituus ja magia – kristinuskon kääntöpuoli. Pahuuden kuvasto vanhassa maailmassa.* Sari Katajala-Peltomaa & Raisa Maria Toivo (eds.). Helsinki: Suomalaisen Kirjallisuuden Seura. Pp. 116–135.

Paden, William E. 1996. Sacrality as Integrity: "Sacred Order" as a Model for Describing Religious Worlds. In *The Sacred & its Scholars. Comparative Methodologies for the Study of Primary Religious Data.* Thomas A. Idinopulos & Edward A. Yonan (eds.). Leiden: E. J. Brill. Pp. 3–18.

Pleijel, Hilding 1970. *Hustavlans värld. Kyrkligt folkliv i äldre tiders Sverige.* Stockholm: Tryckmans.

Pócs, Éva 1989. *Fairies and Witches at the Boundary of South-Eastern and Central Europe.* Folklore Fellows' Communications 243. Helsinki: Academia Scientiarum Fennica.

Rimpiläinen, Olavi 1971. *Läntisen perinteen mukainen hautauskäytäntö Suomessa ennen isoavihaa.* Helsinki: Suomen Kirkkohistoriallinen Seura.

Ruutu, Antti 2004. Liivinmaan reformaation kuvainraastot. *Suomen kirkkohistoriallisen seuran vuosikirja* 94: 42–75.

Sarmela, Matti 1994. *Suomen perinneatlas. Suomen kansankulttuurin kartasto 2. Folklore.* Helsinki: Suomalaisen Kirjallisuuden Seura.

Scribner, Robert W. 1993. The Reformation, Popular Magic, and the "Disenchantment of the World". *The Journal of Interdisciplinary History* 23(2): 475–494.

Sheldrake, Philip 2001. *Spaces for the Sacred. Place, Memory and Identity.* The Hulsean Lectures 2000. London: SCM Press.

Shils, Edward 1975. *Center and Periphery. Essays in Macrosociology.* Chicago, London: The University of Chicago Press.

Siikala, Anna-Leena 2002. *Mythic Images and Shamanism. A Perspective on Kalevala Poetry.* Folklore Fellows' Communications 280. Helsinki: Academia Scientiarum Fennica.

Spicer, Andrew 2005. 'God Will Have a House': Defining Sacred Space and Rites of Consecration in Early Seventeenth-Century England. In *Defining the Holy. Sacred Space in Medieval and Early Modern Europe*. Andrew Spicer & Sarah Hamilton (eds.). Aldershot: Ashgate. Pp. 207–230.

Stark-Arola, Laura 1997. Lempi, Fire, and Female *väki*. An Exploration into Dynamistic Relationships in Finnish-Karelian Magic and Folk Belief. In *Elektroloristi* 1. *Amor, Genus & Familia. Kirjoituksia suullisen perinteen ja kansankulttuurin alalta.* Anna-Leena Siikala & Jyrki Pöysä (eds.). Available at http://www.elore.fi/arkisto/1_97/sta197.html [Accessed July 10, 2015]

Stark-Arola, Laura 2002a. The Dynamistic Body in Traditional Finnish-Karelian Thought. *Väki, vihat, nenä* and *luonto*. In *Myth and Mentality. Studies in Folklore and Popular Thought*. Anna-Leena Siikala (ed.). Studia Fennica Folkloristica 8. Helsinki: Suomalaisen Kirjallisuuden Seura/FLS. Pp. 67–103.

Stark, Laura 2002b. *Peasants, Pilgrims and Sacred Promises. Ritual and the Supernatural in Orthodox Karelian Folk Religion*. Studia Fennica Folkloristica 11. Helsinki: Suomalaisen Kirjallisuuden Seura/FLS.

Tarkka, Lotte 1998. Sense of the Forest: Nature and Gender in Karelian Oral Poetry. In *Gender and Folklore. Perspectives on Finnish and Karelian Culture*. Satu Apo, Aili Nenola & Laura Stark-Arola (eds.). Studia Fennica Folkloristica 4. Helsinki: Suomalaisen Kirjallisuuden Seura/FLS. Pp. 92–142.

Thomas, Keith 1971. *Religion and the Decline of Magic*. New York: Charles Schribner's Sons.

Turner, Harold W. 1967. *From Temple to Meeting House. The Phenomenology and Theology of Places of Worship*. The Hague: Mouton Publishers.

Uotila, Jarmo 1982. Kirkkomatka suomalaisessa kansanelämässä kansanperinteen mukaan n. 1890–1940. Suomen kirkkohistorian pro gradu -tutkielma. Helsinki: Helsingin yliopisto.

Uther, Hans-Jörg 2004. *The Types of International Folktales. A Classification and Bibliography*. I–III. Folklore Fellows' Communications 284–286. Helsinki: Academia Scientiarum Fennica.

Varonen, Matti 1891. *Suomen kansan muinaisia taikoja I. Metsästys-taikoja*. Helsinki: Suomalaisen Kirjallisuuden Seura.

Wirkkala, Ilmari 1945. *Suomen hautausmaiden historia*. Porvoo, Helsinki: WSOY.

Sandis Laime

The Place Valence Approach in Folk Narrative Research: The "Church Sinks Underground" Motif in Latvian Folklore

One of the key sources for the research of (belief in) supernatural places is place-related narrative. In folkloristic research, attention is usually paid to narratives and their performance, while places related to them are considered to a far lesser extent, although the two-part term 'place-related narrative (legend, story)' equally contains the notion of place and the oral tradition related to it. Place-related narrative is an inseparable notion, therefore to gain full understanding of the narrative, one should also know the place linked to it.

In my research, I have introduced and employed the so-called 'place valence approach', with the goal of finding the reasons why specific motifs and types of narratives are attached to specific landscape objects. The answer to this question often allows extra contextual information to be gained in order for us to understand the functions of such narratives, the chronology of the tradition, etc.

In the title of place valence approach, two notions have been combined: 'place' means a certain element of the landscape, the boundaries of which depend on the existing tradition, and 'valence' is a term borrowed from linguistics and chemistry that signifies the ability of one element to attract another. In the context of the approach under discussion, 'valence' denotes the capacity of a place to attract certain narrative motifs. It depends on various qualities of the place that encourage linking this place to motifs and types of narratives familiar in the respective area. The capacity of a place to attract a corresponding narrative is either realised or not realised by the tradition bearers. The approach is based on the assumption that specific motifs and types of narratives are attached to certain places if the place possesses a minimal set of features that establish a direct link to essential episodes of the particular narrative. By exploring several supernatural places linked to a single narrative motif or type and by looking for similarities between them, one gains the opportunity to find the most important common features in the characteristics of these places (i.e. the valence of such places), which, in turn, enables to capture more precisely the narrative functions and other issues. These common features are not necessarily mentioned in the narrative, therefore if one analyses only the oral tradition related to the place, it is possible to neglect them. At the same time, it must be noted that the link between a legend and a specific place is not always based on the characteristics of a place.

Awareness of specific place qualities may be one of the most significant components of the frame of reference in the moment of actualising supernatural experience. Juha Pentikäinen notes that when individuals' supernatural experiences are analysed, a psychological question arises: how is it possible that people see, hear or feel something that does not objectively exist. To address this problem, the notion of 'frame of reference' has been borrowed from perceptual and social psychology (Pentikäinen 1968: 114–115). It is a set of beliefs, views and values through which a person or a community perceives and evaluates information that determines communication and regulates behaviour. In the context of memorate research, it is a set of images in the human mind at the moment of supernatural experience that sums up topical subjective and memory-based beliefs (including the knowledge of a specific place), which activates the frame of reference (primary stimuli) and objectively perceivable phenomena in the surrounding environment (releasing stimuli). The actualisation of the frame of reference takes a crucial role at this point, the beliefs existing in a subconscious state become an element of consciousness that starts driving human perception and actions (Honko 1962: 96–99; Pentikäinen 1968: 114–115; see also Honko 1965). For example, the possibility that a person after observing unusual visual or acoustic phenomena will interpret this experience as supernatural and that subsequently it will be retold is far more likely if the experiencer is aware that he or she is located, for instance, in the territory of an abandoned graveyard. For a researcher, however, knowledge about the historical significance of a certain place can help understanding the reasons of the creation of memorates.

The current article will focus on historically and naturally determined place valence. First, historically determined place valence is linked to the significance of a place in a certain historical event or to its (prolonged) use for a specific purpose in prehistoric or historic times. Primary sources revealing the significance of such places in the prehistoric period are the archaeological ones, whereas in a historical period, both archaeological and written sources can be employed. By correlating data from these sources with the oral tradition, it is possible to establish the reasons that had once encouraged the linking of a certain place to specific types of narratives, as well as to find out the changes in the collective memory related to the historical event – the objective historical significance of a certain place does not change, whereas folk interpretations related to it can change over the course of time. This kind of analysis can also provide a considerable insight into issues related to the history, chronology and transformation processes of some (belief) tradition.

Second, naturally determined place valence is characteristic of geographically, geologically or otherwise unusual natural objects that have attracted the attention of local people by motivating them to relate such places to the religious beliefs and narrative plots widespread in their particular area.

Functions of legends can change depending on the kind of objects they are attached to. In order to illustrate this statement, motif F941.2 "Church Sinks Underground" from Stith Thompson's *Motif-Index of Folk-Literature* (Thompson 1955–1958) has been selected for analysis. Place valence analysis indicates at least four kinds of sunken church locations, the valence of which is determined both historically and naturally. Although in all four cases, the places are linked to a single legend motif, after uncovering the reasons for linking this motif with the specific objects, it becomes evident that in each case the legend has had a different function in drawing attention to different rules and taboos.

Former Catholic Churches and Chapels

The link between the "Church Sinks Underground" legend motif and specific objects in the landscape is mostly historically determined. However, in this case, at least three kinds of such place can be distinguished. It seems that in the majority of cases, legends about sunken churches concern sites where Catholic chapels and churches were situated prior to the Reformation. In the Middle Ages and during the period of Polish rule (the end of the 16th to beginning of the 17th century), the establishment of burial places around chapels was allowed and they were sanctioned as parish, manor or village cemeteries (Muižnieks 2003: 17).[1] As is still the case today in Catholic Latgale,[2] a central chapel or a crucifix is usually an integral part of the cemetery (Figures 1 and 2). After Reformation, the attitude of the Lutheran church to chapels built during the Catholic period was inconsistent – a number of them were legalised and restored, thus also sanctioning burial of the dead around them, but nevertheless the usage of a far larger number of chapels and cemeteries was forbidden (Muižnieks 2003: 17).

A typical example of this kind of place is the Lanti Kapu kalns ('grave hill') – a medieval cemetery in Burtnieki parish, northern Latvia. Written sources indicate that there used to be a chapel or a church in this cemetery, as well as two stone plates with crosses – evidently, gravestones (Kurtz 1924: 94; B 44).

In the legends about the Lanti medieval cemetery and chapel, the disappearance of the chapel has been mostly described realistically, for example, indicating that in the old days, there had been a church[3] on the hill, which was destroyed by the Swedes[4] (LFK 23, 11326)[5]; that there had been a church on the hill that had collapsed after a long time and a cemetery that had been grassed over (LFK 116, 3681); and that in the Swedish times, there had been a monastery (LFK 1771, 6819) etc.

Legends related to the Lanti Kapu kalns illustrate that by losing the link to real historical events, as they gradually fade away from the collective memory of people living in the vicinity, the disappearance of the church as a historical fact has gradually turned into a supernatural fact. This is evident from the historically specific experience being replaced by the "Church Sinks Underground" motif or its variation the "Church Bell Sinks Underground/ in a Spring":

Fig. 1. Wooden chapel in Dziervīne cemetery, Baltinava parish. Photo: S. Laime, 2006.

Fig. 2. Crucifix in Viduči cemetery, Medņeva parish. Photo: S. Laime, 2006.

> "Legend of the sinking of a church"
> In the old days, people said that in Kapkalns, a church had sunk and a large
> rettery nearby is now covered with moss. When the church was sinking into the
> ground, the church bell had fallen in that rettery. Old people say that on Jāņi
> night [Midsummer's eve], at eleven o'clock, one must go there and listen – that's
> when the bell is ringing. (LFK 1978, 2671.)

This and many similar legends are linked to places where three to four
centuries ago Christian chapels or small churches had been situated, thus
the valence of such places is clearly historically determined.

Pre-Christian Sacred Sites

Archaeologist Juris Urtāns (2004: 63–68) notes that in eastern Latgale, the
"Church Sinks Underground" motif is often related to hillforts and that in
these legends there is probably no reference to former Christian chapels. As
illustrated by the following legend about Silova hillfort in Ņukši parish the
content of these legends does not differ greatly from legends on places of
type 1:

> "About the Church"
> People say, a church had been on Greizais kalns [Crooked hill] in Silova. During
> a mass, it has, as if, sunk into underground with the priest and all the people
> inside (old people say this, I don't know if it's correct), the ground had spread and
> it sunk into underground. The old say that the bell had even rung during mass,
> but it doesn't ring anymore. (LFK 1940, 7362.)

In line with a study by Urtāns, 28 out of the 130 (21.54%) hillforts in
Latgale are linked to legends about churches that have sunk in them. A
larger number of such hillforts are situated in eastern Latgale – close to
the border of Russia and Belarus. Although the motif is sometimes linked
to hillforts elsewhere in Latvia, the number of such cases is small (four in
Kurzeme, one in Zemgale, four in Augšzeme and three in the Vidzeme
region). Urtāns assumes that in the past, there might have been pagan cult
places in these hillforts, especially taking into account that such cult places
have also been found in other territories inhabited by Baltic peoples. The
closest similarities to the hillforts of eastern Latgale have been found in
neighbouring territories – in the upper course of Dnieper River and in the
middle part of the drainage basin of the Daugava River, inhabited by bearers
of the Tusheml-Bancerov archaeological culture in the 5th/6th to 8th centuries.
For example, in Tusheml, Gorodok and Prudki hillforts holes have been
found in highest place or in corners where idolatry posts had been dug in.
This shows that representatives of this culture had the custom of developing
sanctuaries specifically in hillforts. Since the aforementioned hillforts of
Latgale, judging by the scarce evidence found, had been inhabited around
the same time, it is possible that the custom of establishing sanctuaries in
hillforts was also a common practice in the eastern part of Latgale. (Urtāns
2004.)

Many hills (but not hillforts) situated elsewhere in Latvia, in which pre-Christian cult places have been found in archaeological excavations, are also called Baznīcas kalns (Church hill). For example, during excavations in Strazde Baznīckalns, located in Kurzeme, ten funnel-shaped pits were found ribbed with basketwork and containing charcoal, calcined human bones and broken 11th to 14th century bronze jewellery. Since Baznīckalns is situated near the Strazde hillfort, most probably the sanctuary of people living in the hillfort was situated in Baznīcalns (Šturms 1938: 119–124).

The above examples indicate that also in this case, the valence of places linked to the "Church Sinks Underground" motif is historically determined; however, these legends contain a reference not to Christian churches, but to sanctuaries of the pre-Christian time. In other words, the fact of the existence of pre-Christian sanctuaries has been preserved in the collective memory of local people by recoding it in Christian terminology and attracting a corresponding motif from among migratory legends.

Stone Graves

Another kind of archaeological place that is sometimes linked to the "Church Sinks Underground" legend motif is that of stone graves, or so-called *tarand*-graves, common in northern Latvia, Estonia and southern Finland. These are considered to be the burial places of Baltic Finns. The earliest stone graves in the territory of Latvia are dated with the 2nd to 3rd centuries BC; however, they were more used in early and mid Iron Age (1st to 9th centuries AD). In this type of grave, the dead were buried in quadrangular chambers, or *tarand*s, with stone chamber walls being up to ten metres wide. When one *tarand* was 'full', another was made next to it. Thus, as time went by, long stone structures were made out of numerous chambers (Figure 3). In the territory of Latvia, around 80 such burial places have been found dated to the period up to the 5th century, whereas afterwards, the dead were buried in the old stone chambers and new chambers were no longer made (Vasks 2001: 224–225).

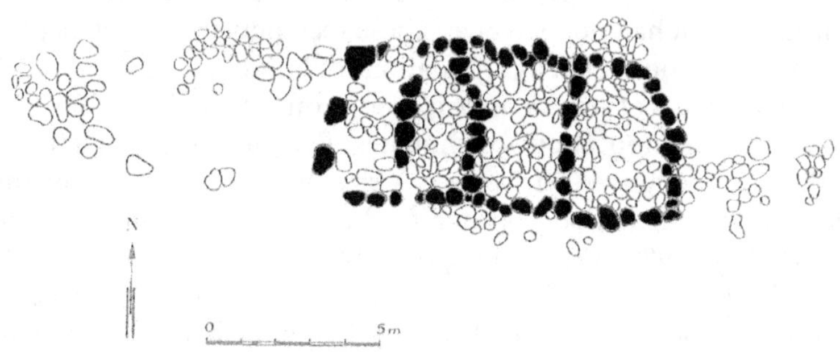

Fig. 3. Stone structures of Auciems stone grave, Raiskums parish. After: Latvijas PSR arheoloģija: fig. 47.

85

After the change in the ethnicity of inhabitants in the stone grave territory, the arriving Indo-Europeans did not usually consider the stone structures as being burial places. Nevertheless, as these places were easy to notice in the landscape, they acquired a new interpretation in oral tradition. In addition, one has to take into account the considerable amount of time that has passed since the graves were last used. Various legend motifs are employed to explain the origins of the stone graves, the most popular of them being A977.3 "Devil Drops Stones". Stone graves have also been sometimes linked to the legend motif F941.2 "Church Sinks Underground". Urtāns (1989: 13) assumes that the link between ancient stone graves and legends of sunken churches might have been established in relation to the secondary use of these places, namely, stone graves were often used as cult places for house spirits up until the 19th century.

Another explanation of the link between legend motif F941.2 and stone graves is possible. I came across it during field research in 2004 in Kārķi parish, northern Vidzeme. Near Kārķi village, there is a place called Velna klēpis ('Devil's lap'), which is a frequent name for stone graves in Vidzeme. According to what I was told by local forest guard Edgars Sproģis (born 1927), "in the times of the ancient Latvians", there had been an inn and near the inn a furnace. The place of the furnace was some four square metres large, made out of head-sized stones. The informant had removed the stones from the field, as it had been hard to do agricultural work around them. Answering the question of why he thought there had been an inn at this place, the informant said that he thought so judging by the size of the building's foundations. In addition, he had found fragments of clay mugs, but in the building near the inn, or "the furnace", there had been charcoal and ashes. (Laime 2006: 146.)

It can be concluded from the place name and the description provided by the informant that, probably, in this location there had been a stone grave with several stone *tarand*s (the sites of the 'inn' and the 'furnace'). It is also evident from the fragments of clay vessels he had found because it was characteristic to put clay vessels in stone graves in the Vidzeme region (Vasks 2001: 226). This is also evident from the fact that the informant had found charcoal and ashes on the site, since the people buried in Vidzeme's stone graves were usually cremated (Vasks 2001: 224). Regarding the topic discussed in this article, the key fact in this case is that for a number of reasons, the informant had not perceived these rectangular stone structures as an ancient burial ground, but as foundations of buildings.

Perhaps, on the basis of similar associations, stone graves have elsewhere been considered ancient locations of churches. For example, people living near the Aišēni stone graves, in western Vidzeme, have said that in this ancient site, a church had stood on one of the stone graves and a chapel on another (Urtāns 1989: 13). Although in this case the "Church Sinks Underground" motif is also related to archaeological places, the valence of these places can only to an extent be considered as being historically-determined, since no reference to the initial historical significance of these places can be found in legends. In this case, the respective legend motif is one of a series of motifs, using which people have attempted to reinterpret the emergence of prehistoric stone structures.

Natural Hollows in the Terrain

The fourth kind of places linked to the F941.2 legend motif differs greatly from the first two, but to a certain extent it corresponds to the third kind of place. In this case, legends are attached to more or less distinct naturally-formed hollows in the terrain that are considered to be the sites of sunken churches. An especially large number of such places are located in northern Latgale (Figures 4 and 5); however, there are similar sites elsewhere in Latvia, for example, Augstais kalns ('High hill') in Kārķi parish, northern Vidzeme. Augstais kalns is a 300-metre-long and 100-metre-wide lone hill that stands some 14 metres above the surrounding swampy meadows. In the middle part of the hill surface, there is an 11-metre-deep, 60–70-metre-long and 35-metre-wide lowered surface that has been considered the site of a sunken church (Laime 2005):

> On the way to Kārķi, you have to cross Zemā sila kalns ['Low forest hill']. It is said that an enchanted church lies under it. There, one could hear something like people talking underground. A church has once stood there. A river has flowed around the hill, except there is a road crossing one side of it. But in the middle of the hill, there is a large hollow, where a church has stood in the past.
>
> Once, a service was held in the church. The priest had stepped into the pulpit and had begun speaking. Meanwhile, a coachman was waiting outside at the door for the priest to end the sermon and come outside so he could drive him home. Suddenly, a cart had come up the road and a wizard sat inside it. The wizard was angry with the priest and now he wanted to pay him back. He stopped his cart at the church and begun conjuring. A song could be heard from inside the church, and it begun sinking. It sank, sank, and fully sank underground. People have long heard a sort of a silent drone there. (LFK 116, 14150.)

In legends regarding places of type 4, several reasons for the churches sinking have been mentioned. In other legend variants on Kārķi Augstais kalns, it is said that the church had sunk while a sister was being married to her brother, who had not recognised his sister after returning from a long war (LFK 116, 23467); or while the owner of a rich farmstead was being married to a maid who loved another man (Pētersone 1993: 9–10). In legends on similar places elsewhere in Latvia, it is noted that a church sank because of drunkards disturbing a service, because of peasants swearing in church, etc.

The valence of the fourth kind of places is naturally determined, as legends are attached to them due to their natural characteristics. In this case, various lowered surfaces, pits and craters – seen by locals as places of sunken churches – have had the potential to attract legends with this motif.

Fig. 4. Brieksīnes kalns ('Brieksīne hill') and cemetery in Baltinava parish – place of a sunken church. Photo: S. Laime, 2006.

Fig. 5. Balkanu kalni ('Balkani hills') in Šķilbēni parish – place of a sunken church, nowadays a tourist spot. Photo: S. Laime, 2006.

Conclusions

Analysis of the "Church Sinks Underground" legend motif according to a place valence approach allows one to draw some conclusions regarding the functions of these legends. It was noted before that place-related legends can be attached to specific places if these places correspond to certain criteria. As regards the "Church Sinks Underground" motif, the valence of these places is both historically and naturally determined:

1) a church or chapel historically existed in this place;

2) a prehistoric pre-Christian sanctuary was situated there;

3) the place is a prehistoric stone grave, with a structure similar to the foundations of buildings, including churches;

4) in the terrain of this place, a special lowered surface, such as a pit or a crater can be distinguished that might be associated with the site of a sunken church.

In order to uncover the possible functions of the "Church Sinks Underground" legend, information about what kind of places it is attached to might well be useful, as a legend's functions vary depending upon the type of object. Thus, for example, in the case of the first and the second kind, legends refer to a former Christian or pre-Christian sacred place. Especially in the first case, where Catholic chapels were often situated in the territory of a graveyard, these legends might have had a warning function, i.e., by telling these legends, areas were labelled in the landscape, in which human behaviour was firmly regulated to protect ancient sacred places and burial grounds. In order to emphasise the warning effect of a legend, the "Church Sinks Underground" motif was used together with other legend types and motifs that contain the (supernatural) experience of people who broke the rules of behaviour and were consequently punished.

The explanatory, or etiological, function prevails in the third and the fourth cases which explain how the mysterious prehistoric stone structures (type 3) or peculiar forms of terrain (type 4) have originated. In legends on the places of type 4, that have not been linked to former churches, emphasis is sometimes put on the causes of the sinking of churches. Thus the didactic function is included in narratives reminding the listener of some ethical, social, religious and other rules, the disregard of which can lead to consequences as dramatic as the sinking of a church. Certainly, in each specific case, a legend may have other functions as well. The place valence approach has proved its usefulness in cases where quantitative material is analysed, and therefore the results obtained by employing this approach can point out certain trends and interconnections.

The clarification of the causes that have encouraged people to attach a certain legend motif to particular place, makes it possible to gain a broader view of causes for the spread of particular legend motifs in a specific region. In the case of the "Church Sinks Underground" motif, it is evident that its distribution over the territory of Latvia is not even. Valence analysis shows that in cases where a legend is attached to a certain type of archaeological object (stone graves in northern Vidzeme and hillforts in eastern Latgale), the distribution of a legend is directly linked to the area of distribution of these objects. Since the legends attached to the above-mentioned places do not differ much, this common feature cannot be distinguished by textual analysis only.

The link between the "Church Sinks Underground" motif and places with naturally-determined valence is, by comparison, more flexible, as it is not linked to historical places of regional limitation. This is acknowledged by the fact that a modified variation of this motif ("Sauna Sinks Underground") has been recorded even in a village of Latvian settlers in Krasnoyarsk Krai, Siberia. In the vicinity of Sukinava village (formerly – Sibīrijas Marienburga), villagers said that there is a lowered surface in the terrain, where a sauna has once sunk: in a significant celebration, a farmer heated up his sauna, and by doing so he committed a great sin. When people went to the sauna to wash themselves, they saw that only a pit was left where the sauna had stood – "God had burnt it" (Laime 2007: 152–153).

If the "Church Sinks Underground" legend motif was only attached to places with historically-determined valence (for example sites of old churches and chapels), linking this legend to a place in the Siberian landscape most probably would not be productive since the knowledge of settlers on the local history was very poor. However, since this motif has also been linked to specific places on the basis of other features (in this case the unusual topography, which is not rare in the mountainous area of Sukinava), the relocation of the legend from Latvia to Siberia could happen successfully.

This article focused only on one aspect of place valence analysis and indicated that the functions of legends can change depending on the type of place it is attached to. The potential of this approach, however, has not been exhausted. It can be employed, for example, to trace the chronological development of some belief tradition or narrative plot. Analysis of the link between *ragana*[6] legends and places they are attached to established that these legends are linked to burial sites, which are all pre-18th century. This conclusion coincides with the fact that in the oral tradition of the late 19th and 20th centuries, *raganas* were not considered spirits of the dead, although the etymology of the word and the connection of *ragana* places with the burial grounds of Medieval and early Modern times indicate the opposite. This fact is significant, as very limited information is available regarding the process and chronology of transformation of this supernatural being. In this case, place valence analysis points to the 18th century as the time of substantial changes in *ragana* beliefs in Northern Vidzeme (Laime 2013: 297–300).

Another interesting aspect of place valence analysis is the impact of the landscape and peculiar places on the narrative plot. Awareness of the local landscape and the peculiarity of specific places can stimulate the narrator to modify a traditional legend plot to adapt it to the local landscape. For example, among the many Latvian variations of the widespread "Combat between Thundergod and Devil" legend motif (A162.3), encounters between Thunder and the Devil that prove lethal to the latter occur comparatively rarely. Interestingly, in numerous cases this variation of A162.3 has been influenced by the fact that these legends are attached to coffin-shaped stones, therefore it can be concluded that, to a certain extent, the plot of a legend has

90

been influenced by unusual features in the surrounding landscape.

Marjatta Jauhiainen (1998: 19) notes that the formation of legends is affected by age, gender, occupation, residence, religious orientation and the ethical perspective of narrators and audiences. In case of place-related legends, it is also the landscape with its historical, natural and supernatural places which implicitly assists in the process of legend creation.

Notes

1   Heiki Valk indicates that judging by folklore sources, in southern Estonia – the region adjacent to northern Latvia – chapels were situated in 224 out of 785 (28.5%) 13th–17th century cemeteries (Valk 1995: 502–503).
2   Latgale is a traditionally Catholic region in eastern Latvia.
3   In the oral tradition it is not common to distinguish churches and chapels. *Baznīca*, 'a church', is generally used to denote both kinds of religious buildings.
4   Evidently, the legend contains a reference to the so-called 'Swedish times', as after the Polish-Swedish War (1600–1629), the Vidzeme region, or so-called 'Swedish Livonia', was ruled by Sweden.
5   References to the collections of the Archives of Latvian Folklore (LFK) in Riga.
6   The word *ragana* in Latvian originally designated the souls of the dead or 'restless souls'. In the Middle Ages and Early Modern Era *raganas* were partially integrated into the belief system of witchcraft, humanized and turned into witches.

Sources

Honko, Lauri 1962. *Geisterglaube in Ingermanland* 1. Folklore Fellows' Communications 185. Helsinki: Academia Scientiarum Fennica.

Honko, Lauri 1965. On the Functional Analysis of Folk-beliefs and Narratives about Empirical Supernatural Beings. In *Laographia* 22. *IV International Congress for Folk-Narrative Research (1–6 September 1964, Athens). Lectures and Reports.* Georgios A. Megas (ed.). Pp. 168–173.

Jauhiainen, Marjatta 1998. *The Type and Motif Index of Finnish Belief Legends and Memorates. Revised and Enlarged Edition of Lauri Simonsuuri's Typen- und Motivverzeichnis der finnischen mythischen Sagen.* Folklore Fellows' Communications 267. Helsinki: Academia Scientiarum Fennica.

Kurtz, Edith 1924. Verzeichnis alter Kultstätten in Lettland. *Mitteilungen aus der livländischen Geschichte* 22(2): 47–117.

Laime, Sandis 2005. Kārķu Augstajā kalnā nogrimusī baznīca. In *Daba un vēsture 2006.* Zaiga Kipere (ed.). Rīga: Zinātne. Pp. 135–138.

Laime, Sandis 2006. Kārķu pagasta svētvietas un to folklora. In *Kultūras krustpunkti 2.* Juris Urtāns (ed.). Rīga: Mantojums. Pp. 138–149.

Laime, Sandis 2007. Ekspedīcija no Tomskas līdz Krasnojarskai. Atskats uz Latviešu folkloras krātuves 2005. gada Sibīrijas ekspedīciju. In *Meklējumi un atradumi 2007.* Baiba Krogzeme-Mosgorda (ed.). Rīga: Zinātne. Pp. 140–155.

Laime, Sandis 2013. Witches in Latvian Folk Belief: Night Witches. Summary. In *Raganu priekšstati Latvijā: Nakts raganas.* Rīga: Latvijas Universitātes Literatūras, folkloras un mākslas institūts. Pp. 275–302.

Latvijas PSR arheoloģija 1974. Rīga: Zinātne.

Muižnieks, Vitolds 2003. Baznīcas apbedīšanas vietas Rietumvidzemē 13.–18. gadsimtā. *Latvijas Zinātņu Akadēmijas Vēstis* 57(5/6): 10–34.

Pentikäinen, Juha 1968. *The Nordic Dead-Child Tradition. Nordic Dead-Child Beings. A Study in Comparative Religion.* Folklore Fellows' Communications 202. Helsinki: Academia Scientiarum Fennica.

Pētersone, Ilze 1993. *Kārķu novada vēsture.* Valka: Valkas tipogrāfija.

Šturms, Eduards 1938. Baltische Alkhügel. In *Conventus primus historicorum Balticorum Rigae, 16.–20. VIII 1937. Acta et relata.* Rīga: Latvijas Vēstures institūts. Pp. 116–132.

Thompson, Stith 1955–1958. *Motif-Index of Folk-Literature: a Classification of Narrative Elements in Folktales, Ballads, Myths, Fables, Medieval Romances, Exempla, Fabliaux, Jest-Books, and Local Legends.* Revised and enlarged edition. Bloomington: Indiana University Press.

Urtāns, Juris 1989. Aišēnu akmenskrāvuma senkapi. *Lauku Dzīve* 6: 12–13.

Urtāns, Juris 2004. Par Latgales pilskalniem – Baznīcklaniem. In *Skudra pie kalna. Arheologa stāsti.* Rīga: Nordik. Pp. 63–68.

Valk, Heiki 1995. The 13th–17th Century Village Cemeteries of South Estonia in Folk-Tradition and Beliefs. In *Folk Belief Today.* Mare Kõiva & Kai Vassiljeva (eds.). Tartu: Estonian Academy of Sciences, Institute of the Estonian Language and the Estonian Museum of Literature. Pp. 501–509.

Vasks, Andrejs 2001. Agrais dzelzs laikmets. In *Latvijas senākā vēsture. 9. g. t. pr. Kr.– 1200. g.* Ēvalds Mugurēvičs & Andrejs Vasks (eds.). Rīga: Latvijas vēstures institūta apgāds. Pp. 186–231.

Ülo Valk

Ontological Liminality of Ghosts:
The Case of a Haunted Hospital[*]

Ghosts Today

Contrary to the expectations of many scholars, who predicted the decline of the supernatural in the modern age of rationalism, stories about ghosts and the re-appearance of the dead – often grounded in personal experience – thrive in contemporary Europe. Even in cultures, where the dominant mind-set is sceptical or bound in materialist thought, the hauntings continue and ghosts have adjusted themselves to the secular environment. Paul Cowdell (2011: 1) has noted: "Ghosts are a stubborn presence in British culture, despite historically conditioned expectations that belief in them belongs to the past, and the presentation of local ghostlore as something that predates, and is threatened by, contemporary social change". In a comprehensive study of ghosts in North American folk tradition and popular culture, Diane E. Goldstein, Sylvia A. Grider and Jeannie B. Thomas (2007) have shown their active presence in supernatural narratives, told by people with diverse educational, ethnic and social backgrounds. Elizabeth Tucker (2007) has discussed lively traditions of ghost stories, including personal experience narratives among college students in America today and has drawn attention to their psychological and social functions, such as that of initiating students into a new community. María Inés Palleiro (2012) has pointed out that Argentinian ghost lore expresses both intimate contacts with the otherworld and collective experiences of historical traumas that appear in a fictionalised form. While examining ghost narratives in recent Latvian folklore, Guntis Pakalns (1995) has noted that they display surprising stability. Thus, it should not surprise us that ghosts in contemporary Estonia do not belong to the extinct or endangered species of vernacular demonology; instead, they appear in multiple discursive contexts and take on new guises. Tragic accidents on roads have generated legends about sinister ghostly cars that suddenly appear and vanish near certain inauspicious places, scaring lonely drivers at night. Phantom trains have been seen zipping by in the darkness along abandoned railways. (Kaldur 2008.) Ghost narratives belong to the repertoire of tourist guides and are told about many historical buildings, such as Kolga manor in North Estonia (Reha 2008). A couple of years ago I had a long conversation with a real estate agent in Tallinn who told me about ghosts in several buildings of the old town. It appeared that her willingness to share this knowledge with the clients depended on their mindset. For some people a ghost might add extra value to an old apartment, for others such an invisible companion might put a stop to any interest they may have had in purchasing or renting the place. Some years ago my daughter worked as a waitress in the historical café Werner in Tartu. She told me about the ghost-lore among the waitresses, who worked late and were the last ones to leave the building at night. Several of them had heard footsteps, seen mysterious lights and sensed the eerie presence of somebody in the empty building but the identity of the implied ghost remained unclear. It seemed to be the emergent, and probably ephemeral, ghost-lore of a group of young people who were adjusting to a new work environment and developing a sense of community.

Ghost narratives often appear in contemporary Estonian tabloid media and as such they are published on the internet, where they receive multiple comments from a variety of viewpoints, ranging from disdain and irony to explicit approval, sometimes backed up by references to personal experiences of the supernatural (see Valk 2012). There are internet forums in Estonia specializing in supernatural topics that include thousands of postings about ghosts and spirits (see Para-Web). Since 2001, a periodical *Secrets: Mystical Stories* (*Saladused: Müstilised Lood*) has been published, mainly consisting of stories, which the editors claim to be personal experience narratives, recorded and sent by the readers about their encounters with the supernatural. Some of the typical titles in the journal read: "We Gave up Our Summer Home and Left It for the Departed Mistress", "We Lived in Our New Home together with a Ghost", "How to Divorce from an Invisible Wife?", "Lehte Thinks It is Natural to Talk with the Dead", "The Dead Boyfriend Showed Me the Truth", "The Dead Girl Came after Her Property", "I Shared My Home in Annelinn with a Ghost", "My (Dead) Husband Rests in the Wrong Place", "Always There Is a Third One in Our Bed". On the one hand, such titles manifest intimate relationships, anxieties about broken family bonds, passionate conflicts and alienation from beloved people as leitmotifs. On the other hand, these stories express an uncomfortable sense of demonic presence and ghostly hauntings as something alien, disturbing and even inappropriate within the context of the modern rational world. A sense of displacement, of finding oneself in a 'wrong' environment – in a haunted apartment or in a newly bought summer house with otherworldly owners who still control their property – also express anxieties of social stress in Estonia. Some of these ghost narratives can be interpreted metaphorically, as symbols of current social conflicts and tensions, and as psychological reactions to them. However, sometimes ghosts seem to make no sense at all as they pop up in most unexpected situations and conversations.

In autumn 2008 I was attending an interdisciplinary workshop in Belgium and at the dinner table I was sitting next to a professor of political sciences from one of the leading British universities. He asked me about my topic of research and I answered that I was studying contemporary ghost narratives. Contrary to my expectations he took serious interest in my somewhat unusual academic pursuits and told me that he had experienced something himself. His ghostly encounters had been extraordinary and somehow out of place, so that he had found it difficult to share these memories with others. It turned out that his grandmother had been a medium and had held regular séances to communicate with spirits. My conversation partner said that once as a small boy he had opened the door of the séance room and was taken aback by a frightening scene. He saw a motionless group of people sitting in candle light around the table with raised hands and there was a plate under their palms floating in the air. He was scared and immediately closed the door. Now, as an adult man he had kept the manuscripts of her grandmother with the messages that she had channelled from the otherworld by means of automatic writing. From his grandmother he had inherited the ability to read palms and predict the future, such as a sad case of miscarriage that he had foreseen. He also said that he had encountered a ghost in his bathroom in his apartment in London – a woman with light curly hair whose dress was covered with bloodstains. When the ghost appeared for a second and third time, he recognised it as the same person. He said that these experiences had not been scary – he had just witnessed how the ghost appeared and disappeared after a while. My conversation partner had also maintained contact with his dead grandmother. As he said, sometimes while being alone at home he felt a cool breathe and a caressing touch, and he knew that this must have been his grandmother who signalled her presence.

I have told about this dinner-table conversation to my friends in Estonia and used it as an example of contemporary ghost narratives while teaching classes on legends and demonology at the University of Tartu. When stories are translated and retold in new contexts, culturally and geographically distant experiences are transmitted to new narrative environments. As ghosts are deeply embedded in international belief traditions, this kind of translocation can happen smoothly – differently from more culture-specific and regional belief narratives, such as those about bigfoot or chupacabra. The common core of ghost narratives in pan-European and global traditions has enabled their invasion by international popular culture, esoteric books and media. However, instead of attracting positive attention and becoming a topic of discussion, ghosts tend to be repelled from public discourse, which is dominated by scientific rationalism. They are banished to the cultural periphery and are discursively marginalized. In spite of his amazing first-hand experiences of the supernatural the professor from the U.K. had not been eager to share his memories with other people. As he said, witnessing the ghost in his bathroom had made no sense to him and it seemed irrelevant to talk about this apparition with anybody. Kirsten M. Raahauge has noted the same about people's supernatural experiences in contemporary Denmark. As the Danes generally do not believe in ghosts, they are bewildered by their encounters and find it difficult to mediate them through narratives. "Ghost" has become a residual category with unstable meanings, indicating something vague – a notion, which "is contested in all possible ways, by the person sensing it, by the people hearing about it, and by the narrative used to mediate the experience and fit it into everyday life" (Raahauge 2016: 105).

According to Kaarina Koski who has studied discourses about the supernatural in Finland today, the science-oriented reasoning tends

Fig. 1. The former hospital building on Toome Hill in Tartu. Having undergone renovation, it now houses the Faculty of Social Sciences of the University of Tartu. Photo: Ü. Valk, 2016.

to dominate in the society, and people who believe in the supernatural often suffer from stigmatisation. Handling the supernatural as fiction or entertainment, or explaining it scientifically sounds more acceptable than claiming the existence of spiritual reality. (Koski 2016.) Belief narratives about ghosts in contemporary Estonia have a similar kind of marginalised status, as they seldom appear in 'serious' discursive contexts, such as mainstream media, historical memoirs or documentary writings. If one admits having supernatural experiences, such as seeing a ghost, it seems to throw doubt upon one's status as a sane and rational individual. On the one hand supernatural experiences have been pathologized in public discourse, on the other hand ghosts have been subjected to fictionalization and become characters in genres of popular culture, such as films and esoteric books.[1] In the same way that encountering ghosts in everyday life is extraordinary, it is unusual when they suddenly appear in the 'wrong' discursive context, such as the mainstream news media. This happened in April 2008 when the weekly newspaper of the University of Tartu *Universitas Tartuensis* published an article "The Benevolent Ghost of the Women's Hospital is Afraid of Being Abandoned" (Merisalu 2008). The article addressed an event in the university history as the old hospital on Toome Hill in Tartu was about to close its doors and continue its work in new premises (Figure 1). The journalist reported about the strange experiences of the medical faculty in the haunted hospital and published them together with the comments of a few employees. The article expressed a variety of points of view on the hauntings, addressing the bigger question – how to make sense of these strange experiences and the concomitant narratives that are hard to explain in a culture where ghosts are not expected to appear. Whereas it is problematic to explicate the ontological reality of ghosts from a scientific perspective today, they have a firm and meaningful place in vernacular discourses that are not bound by the strict frames of scientific argumentation. Charles Briggs (2008: 101) has called these metadiscourses *"practices of vernacular theorizing"* and has emphasized the need to trace the intersections and exchanges that take place between *"vernacular theorizing* and *theorizing the vernacular".* The current article is an attempt to use these affluent folkloric resources for taking ghosts seriously and for giving credence to them within scholarly discourse. The variety of controversial views about ghosts delineates a state of existence that could be characterised as ontological liminality. A similar status for the ghostly is formed in narrative genres as the realm between shared, social reality and extraordinary experiences with a personal and imaginary flavour.

The Haunted Hospital and its Representation in Media

In 1802 the *Kaiserliche Universität zu Dorpat* was opened in Tartu as a successor of the *Academia Gustaviana*, the university that was established in 1632. In 1806 the maternity clinic of the university was brought to life thanks to the activities by professor Christian Friedrich von Deutsch (1768–1843) who was teaching obstetrics, pediatrics and veterinary for the students of medicine (Tamm 1943b: 581–587). The clinic was open to all women and its first rule read: "Every pregnant woman, either married or unmarried, local or a foreigner, religious or not, may be admitted to the clinic" (Tamm 1943b: 582). Although the clinic offered free food and accommodation and organized the baptism of new-born babies free of charge, its popularity only grew slowly. In the period 1806–1833, there were 608 childbirths in the hospital, i.e. on the average 22 births per year. In 1843 the clinic moved to a newly constructed building on Toome Hill, and starting from this year it might be appropriate to call it a hospital. In 1860 an anonymous article appeared in the Estonian newspaper *Perno Postimees* (1860), which advertised it all over Estonia. It is likely that the initiative to publish this article was taken by the medical faculty of the clinic to gain more publicity:

> We would like to remind the dear Estonian folk [*maarahvas*] that in Tartu there is a women's clinic [*naeste klinik*] standing on Toome Hill. Every loving husband may take his suffering wife to this house when the hour of delivery has come close or bring her even two or three weeks in advance. The wife will stay in a nice room and the required food will be given to her, and help and medicine and good care will be provided. When the child is born, an Estonian pastor [*maarahva õpetaja*] will be called to baptize the child, so that the heart of the mother will find peace about the blessing of the soul [*hingeõnnistus*] of the baby. (Perno Postimees 1860: 14.)

In 1861 the hospital had 16 beds, including 8 beds for gynaecological patients, and in 1888 the number of beds had grown to 40. In 1898 some living rooms were built on the top floor to accommodate students of the school of midwifery. (Kalnin 1982: 369.) The morbidity rate of patients and new-born babies remained quite high throughout the 19th century: during

1806–1852 it was 2.7% for mothers and 16.7% for babies; during 1855–1880 – 4.2% for mothers and 13.9% for babies; and during 1888–1893 – 1.6% for mothers and 10.5% for babies (Tamm 1943a: 501, 503, 507). In 1912 another floor was added to the two-storeyed building and the construction was expanded to make room for one hundred beds. During the First World War the building was looted but the women's hospital continued, working together with the University of Tartu and went through major reforms, such as the introduction of Estonian as language of tuition. During the Estonian war of independence against Bolshevik Russia (1918–1920), a Red Cross hospital was opened on its second floor. (Tamm 1943b: 597–598.)

Active and constantly growing, the hospital went through all the basic political turns and administrative changes at the University of Tartu. Until the last decade of the 19th century *Kaiserliche Universität zu Dorpat* was a German-speaking university. Then a short period of Russification followed and German doctors were replaced with Russian speaking medical faculty. In 1918, when Estonia had declared herself independent, Professor Jaan Miländer (1866–1940) – an ethnic Estonian – became the director of the hospital. Then the Second World War followed and Estonia was turned into a Soviet Socialist Republic, ruled from Moscow. In 1991 the Republic of Estonia regained her independence. Certainly, the history of the hospital also reflects the development of medicine and changing views about giving birth – a practice which is always culturally determined (see Keinänen 2003). Originally belonging to the domestic sphere, birth giving was transferred to the sterile environment of a hospital and increasingly medicalised, a process which probably reached its climax in the Soviet period, when it was subject to strict rules. Young mothers were separated from the newborn babies and it was forbidden for fathers and family members to visit them until they were released from their hospital rooms and could go home. The situation changed in the 1990s when several of these restrictions were lifted. The first family room was opened in 1993, and from 1994 fathers were allowed (and later encouraged) to attend the deliveries.

Judith Richardson (2003: 25) has noted that a lack of historical continuity tends to be an essential factor in the development of mysterious and ghostly views of the past. The multi-layered history of Estonia with its 20th century traumas might help to explain, at least partially, why the personnel of the hospital was prone to develop a vital tradition of ghost-lore. Secondly, the environment itself – the history of 165 years in the same building with changing generations of medical faculty and other workers, an emotionally charged everyday round of remarkably happy and sad events – might generate ghost-lore – just as long night watches in the old building must have predisposed people for eerie experiences, and for sharing them in conversations with their colleagues.[2]

It seems impossible to discover who were the first hospital workers to experience the haunting and when the affiliated storytelling tradition emerged, but most probably it happened long back in history. However, there is a date, when the ghost-lore suddenly made a visible presence in Estonian media. We have now reached April 11th, 2008, when the following article was published in the weekly newspaper of the University of Tartu, *Universitas Tartuensis:*

The Benevolent Ghost [vaim] of the Women's Hospital is Afraid of Being Abandoned

The former inhabitant of the Women's Hospital on Toome Hill who has been around for decades has recently started to signal its presence more actively. Midwife HV[3] cannot say exactly, why the ghost [*vaim*] of the building has become more and more active. "The reason might be that we have many new staff members or that we are going to move out soon and he feels that we are about to abandon him," she said.

Is it a man or a woman?

Actually it is not entirely certain whether there is a ghost [*kummitus*] in the hospital, and, if there is, how many there may be. Several stories about strange sounds and sightings have been circulating for a long time. According to UK, a senior doctor and professor of obstetrics and gynaecology, it is mainly younger employees who tell ghost stories [*tondijutt*]; she herself has neither seen nor heard the ghost. There is a legend circulating in the town, which relates that the ghost of the women's hospital is a male doctor who worked in the hospital and died there while living there in his old age. It is said that he walks on the stone floors of the house in his leather slippers, making a shuffling sound. Once, the old gentleman even shook a young male doctor who was resting. According to another story the ghost is a former senior nurse of gynaecology who had also lived and worked in the same building. The nurse had been an old maid who had received an apartment in the building of the women's hospital. She had been seen most frequently moving around. During the renovation she had walked around with a candle and had rattled at the doors. There are some extraordinary accounts of witnessing her at the fridge, where she was taking some food.

A rumour or wind?

KÜ, a senior doctor and professor of obstetrics and gynaecology considers all the legends to be just rumours. She has never encountered any night visitors nor heard any supernatural creatures in action. NH, the chaplain of the hospital does not even remember when he had heard stories about the ghost. "It could have been five years ago but who knows exactly," he recollects. As he says, he is not afraid of ghosts. Midwife HV has heard footsteps and strange noises but these could as well have been tricks of the old house. "Thinking logically, here are several laundry chutes and other places where wind can blow and probably these cause the sounds," HV told. At the time she admitted that if women in the lying-in department, who know nothing about the ghost legends, refer to something strange, this makes one wonder. "I am one of those who would like to see him, I have no fear but the ghost does not appear to me," HV smiled and added that if there is someone supernatural living in the building, he tends to be benevolent. The new employees may be slightly scared but the old workers are used to it. (Merisalu 2008.)

The short article expresses a variety of vernacular perspectives towards the haunting. The most striking assumption about the cause of the disturbed atmosphere has been formulated in the title. Is the ghost afraid of big changes and of being left behind by the personnel? The article gives no clue about the modality of the statement in the title, which can be read either as a factual report of the state of affairs, a humorous comment, or even a slightly ironic remark. Or is it a symbolic statement about the feelings of the personnel of the hospital before final farewell to the old building? In any event, the article includes motifs and narratives that express belief in ghosts. It appears that supernatural haunting is real and that the ghost is responsive to social changes – reacting either to the coming of new employees or the planned move of the hospital. The aggressive assault of male ghost on the young doctor has been reported as a real event. The article also reports another episode of a female ghost who had been witnessed taking food from the fridge. Thus, the text reflects upon the narrative tradition in the hospital but also testifies to its actuality as a set of factual accounts. However, the author shows that not everybody takes the ghost-lore seriously, as stories about the supernatural experiences are reduced to rumours or fantasies, and alternative rational explanations are offered, such as explaining the mysterious noises as the sound of the wind. The article is not dominated by a sceptical viewpoint; it appears instead that there is some reason to doubt rational theories and the reduction of the ghostly presence to mere storytelling. How can one explain the fact that patients who have never heard the local ghost-lore have had similar eerie experiences? Nothing is certain, but it seems likely that something strange is indeed going on in the old hospital.

In December 2008 another short article appeared in the local newspaper, *Tartu Postimees*, by another journalist, also reporting supernatural events in the hospital. A special issue of the newspaper was dedicated to the oral history of the hospital, which was about to move. 19 short articles, or "stories" as they were called, based on readers' letters and interviews, were published by the journalist Aime Jõgi (Jõgi 2008). The 18th of them was entitled "A Study with Signs of the Cross and a Lab with Runic Signs". Whereas the article in *Universitas Tartuensis* reflected different perspectives among the workers and left room for scepticism, Jõgi's article reports events, as they had been witnessed. First, it discusses the experiences of a senior nurse who had been disturbed by the rappings of the ghost, and mentions that a clergyman was called to read the prayer for the dead (*hingepalve*), which pacified the ghost. The article continues:

> On the second, intermediate floor[4] there is a lab with runic signs above its door. Workers of the lab RR, AA and TP tell plenty of stories about strange events, sending chills up my spine. Once a man was seen entering these rooms, but on examination the rooms turned out to be empty. The tinkling sound of the counting of test-tubes had been heard in the empty room next door, and the physical presence of somebody was felt behind one's back. Scissors have flown in the lab with an unnatural trajectory, somebody on night-shift has been pulled by the legs, and a man had been seen on the window, waving behind another person – a man who was not there.
>
> "We are not insane," AA laughs. "This is our life. After installing the runic signs it has become a little easier here." But now, right before moving the workers feel that "they" are again a bit more disturbed than usual. RR says, "They are probably worried about what is now going to happen to them." (Jõgi 2008: 8.)

A photo was added to the text, depicting the runic sign on the door of room 444. Its caption reads: "On the door of the lab of the women's hospital there is a runic sign to ward off ghosts [*vaimud*]" (Jõgi 2008). The article is a rare case where the mainstream media, which usually remains sceptical, presumes the reality of the supernatural events. Its tone is similar to the article in *Universitas Tartuensis*, as the ghostly activities are interpreted as precognition of the great and final move.

December 17th, 2008, was the day, when the last mothers together with their newborn babies checked out of the old building and the hospital ceased working. On the evening of December 19th, 2008, the farewell Christmas party of the workers was held in the hospital, and included speeches, thanksgivings, songs, dances and performances. The young doctors had produced a comical film about the historical move and it was screened during the party. Events depicted in the film included chasing the ghost and catching it with the purpose of transporting it to the new medical centre. Also a show about the history of the hospital from 1843 until 2008 was staged, and the ghost appeared here as well, performing a dance to Andrew Lloyd Webber's music from *The Phantom of the Opera* (Viimane vaatus 2009). Such a vivid participation of the ghost in the farewell party reveals that it had an important role to play in creating the sense of community. We could interpret the ghost as a personification of the shared knowledge, of joint memories and a growing sense of nostalgia – as a symbol of the old hospital. Although such a metaphoric interpretation seems relevant, it certainly does not exhaust the supernatural tradition, which appears far more complex if we look more deeply.

Making Sense of Ghosts: Vernacular Perspectives in Interviews

Narratives about ghosts and hauntings in contemporary Estonian traditions are diverse, and can hardly be said to form a uniform class of supernatural legends. Likewise, the related ideas and perspectives are too dispersed and incongruent for us to talk about an organised system of beliefs or a standard framework of vernacular theorising. The rational worldview of (semi-)scientific materialism leaves no space for ghosts and from the more traditional point of view of Lutheran Christianity they are problematic as well. The former diabolising interpretation of spirits and revenants as manifestations of the Devil does not work as there is no longer a firm place for the Devil in contemporary Estonian folk religion. Variety of religions, such as Catholicism, Orthodoxy, Buddhism, Hinduism, anthroposophy, new shamanism, neopaganism, spiritualism, and others that have to a greater or smaller extent affected the mindsets of Estonians have generated a hybrid and controversial assemblage of afterlife beliefs lacking any clear focus or comprehensive doctrine of post-mortal fate. Hence, making sense of ghost narratives is problematic both for the people who share them and take related beliefs seriously – and for those who have had personal experience with hauntings. Ghosts have been equally problematic for me in my attempts to offer some unified scholarly interpretation for their overwhelming presence in the social environment, which has been de-enchanted by scientific materialism and rationalism.

In the course of 2014 and 2015 I contacted some members of the former personnel of the hospital and asked them if they would agree to give interviews and reflect upon their memories of the ghost-lore of the hospital. Some people never responded to my emails, and some people with whom I talked politely turned down longer interviews. One of them said that she had worked in the other wing of the building and knew too little about the ghosts as the hauntings had occurred at the opposite end of the hospital. Somewhat surprised I later found out that indeed, the hauntings had been mainly localised in two areas – the rooms of the lab in half landing between the first and second floors and some areas of the third floor, its corridor, smoking room and the attic. The hospital rooms on the third floor had been constructed under the mansard roof as late as 1995 and 1996. According to the opinion of senior nurse Vaike, who had initiated this reconstruction, the haunting must have started because of this change. She said that "obviously, this construction disturbed the inhabitants of the place" and "therefore, they came to signal their presence". She described the place and her experience as follows:

> Vaike: There was space under the roof and a side room, where nurses, midwives and doctors used to smoke. There were stairs going to the attic, there was ventilation panel and I always heard the knocking from there. On the other side of the wall was my corner with medicine, I used to work there and I heard knocking every morning. [...] It signalled its presence when I went to work. It was always around 8 o'clock. Then, as was written in the article [V. refers to the article, published in *Tartu Postimees*], I went to the smoking-room to check if somebody was there. The cause could have been the mutter of conversation or something else... There was nothing, only silence.
> Ülo: Did the rapping last long? Were there rhythmic or only a few knocks?
> V: Yes, they were rhythmic. I was never annoyed by it. For some reason I was scared perhaps, I don't know. And I asked it not to disturb me.

Vaike never saw the ghost (*vaim*) but often sensed its presence in the gust of wind in the corridor, which was sometimes so strong that it moved the curtains in the room. Frequently she and her colleagues heard the sound of shuffling slippers (*susside sahin*) in the corridor, sometimes accompanied by a gust of wind. From the mysterious events she remembered the case when a patient who was alone in the room had complained that somebody had repeatedly pulled the blanket off her. Before the final departure, when Vaike was the last person working in her department on the third floor, preparing for the hospital's move, the atmosphere became very disturbed, and she was quite scared.

Unlike Vaike, who had had regular experience with the ghost, the midwife Heli had not witnessed anything clearly supernatural. However, she would have welcomed such an encounter:

> H: I have worked here only for a relatively short time but I have always been interested in these stories. In reality, I have not heard or seen anything. But it was simply so interesting! And when I was there on night watch, I was always expecting that something might happen now, that I too could hear or see something. In fact, all I know is based on the stories of others. I haven't had any contact myself. Or I don't know, maybe... There were some sounds, but it was an

old house and we came up with logical explanations for why the empty elevators should be moving, and so on…

Ü: … the elevators started to move by themselves?

H: Yes, the elevators moved when nobody was there. Under the roof on the third floor were the post-natal hospital rooms. Next to it was the Department of Gynaecology, where abortions and other such procedures were made. There was a chilly corner, people went to smoke there, so there was a smoking booth under the roof and pigeons lived there under the roof. Of course, they too can make sounds. As if something was happening under the roof constantly. But the older midwives made all these concrete connections. They knew more of the history and that way back some members of staff had lived in the hospital, as there had been some apartments there. There were stories about an old man [*vanapapi*], who had walked around in his leather slippers and who shuffled his feet. The sound of shuffling and dragging was heard all the time. It seemed that this old man was the angriest character [*kõige tigedam tegelane*]. He was heard in only one part of the house. This was meant to be the lab, where all blood tests were made, where his room or apartment had been. In this place he was very angry. They even made some signs on the doors and walls. I don't know exactly about the things that happened there. […] People who worked there were really disturbed, they even invited somebody who would help to expel the ghost [*vaim*].

We can see that Heli refers to the storytelling tradition and the elderly personnel as experts of oral history. She also linked the hauntings to the same places in the hospital as Vaike had done – the fourth floor, the lab and rooms next to it. She continued the interview, reflecting upon a scary event that had happened one night when she had been on duty:

H: Just next to the lab there was the doctor's common room. At night, when all was quiet, the doctors slept there. There was a young male doctor who came to work here and had quite an experience in that room. While he was sleeping, someone came and gripped his feet. He was a Russian doctor and gave a very lively and colourful description of it. He had the feeling of being suffocated, as if somebody had been pressing on his chest. As if somebody had seized his feet, so he could not run away. He was so scared, and never would go back to sleep in that room.

Ü: Did he tell you this or did you hear it from somebody else?

H: He told me himself. I was there on the same night watch. When he came in, early in the morning, he was very upset and quite frightened, and he described what happened vividly.

Ü: Did he connect this with the stories about ghosts?

H: Yes, he had heard the stories, and his father had worked in the same building for years. Some people laughed at him, but those who believed [in ghosts] took him seriously.

Remarkably, Heli again refers to the storytelling tradition that links different generations in the old hospital – in this case, a father and his son. The sleep paralysis that has been discussed by David Hufford as empirical foundation of some supernatural beliefs (1982) here perfectly fits in the ghost-lore of the hospital, localised in the lab and the adjacent rooms. In the interview Heli drew attention to the fact that stories about the haunting mainly spread among those workers who were regularly on night duty such as the nurses and midwifes, but not so much among the doctors. She described the conversation situations of the personnel, and how the haunting was discussed:

> Now and then we sat in the common room and it often happened that we talked about this topic. Jokes were made whenever we heard a weird sound in the evenings – yes, it must be the old man walking around! Things were turned into jokes. But, in fact, the elevators were often moving, this happened all the time. Why should they travel in elevators? [Laughs.]

A humorous modality, scepticism and eerie feelings about the supernatural were often expressed together. There had been too many witnesses to consider the ghosts to be a mere piece of narrative folklore. Heli remembered several personal experience stories of her elder colleagues:

> H: There was a midwife, who has now unfortunately passed away. She told us about some kind of a woman in a dressing-gown who had been seen walking on the stairs that led to the cellar. There was an elevator in one wing of the house and another in the other wing, most people preferred to walk on the stairs. But there were also some stairs that were used by the personnel only, not by the patients. The midwife described a situation one night when she had gone out to smoke. When she went upstairs, she saw that somebody was walking down to the cellar where no rooms were open to the public. She saw a night-gown and guessed that this must be a patient. She followed her, but said that she had found nobody. A couple of other nurses have said the same. [...] She described this at one gathering when we were talking about the ghosts [*kummitused*] of the women's hospital.
>
> Let me think of some other vivid stories. Once the post-natal department was being renovated and it was completely empty. Construction was going on, work was going on, and then a candle-light or a little lamp was seen in the rooms. Nothing concrete was seen, but it was just as if a light had been moving. There was a midwife who went to check what was going on and who was there. As a rule, the house is locked at night and nobody can get in. As I remember, when the light and shadow were seen was at the same time that food disappeared from the refrigerator of the personnel. People thought that perhaps there was a hungry visitor from outside who stole the food, but the doors had been locked and nobody could really come in.
>
> Ü: Did people make fun of this too?
>
> H: Yes, this seemed funny to many people, it was not taken seriously. However, those who had heard something themselves were a bit scared to move in the empty house. I had no fear, on the contrary it seemed exciting to me. I was waiting for something to happen, I wanted to see and hear something. I saw no reason why this should cause fear. I did not think that they want to do harm. But after the case with the male doctor I was a bit scared. I can remember that when we moved out of the building, we had a final party in the completely empty property, and we walked through all the nooks and corners, and I thought that what will probably happen is that they will stay behind, they won't follow us to the new building.

Interest, curiosity and a readiness to have a supernatural experience characterised Heli's attitude towards the ghost-lore. This positive interest was quite different from the views of the personnel in the medical lab – Anne, Kristi, Riina, Saima and Terje, who formed a close collegial circle. Four of them had had different kind of supernatural experiences when alone on nightshift (only Saima said that she had not witnessed anything supernatural). In the interview situation, all of them came together and shared with me not only their memories, but also the sense of the creepy atmosphere present when they had been working alone in the rooms of the lab, which was somewhat isolated in the huge building. Most of them began to work there at the same period, and started their night shifts in 1993 and 1994. The interview revealed that they had heard about the ghosts from older workers, who carried memories of the years when the rooms of the lab had been used as staff-apartments. There were stories about an old woman, who had died there, about a student who had hanged himself in these rooms and another suicide who had taken poison, and passed away on the fourth floor – the second most disturbed area in the hospital. However, it turned out that in the early years it had not been common to talk about the hauntings openly in the hospital because of the prevailing rationalism and the fear of making a fool of oneself. The young medical staff of the lab were more outspoken, they were bound by a similar "sensitive energetics", as they remarked, and they started to share their frightening nightly experiences with each other. Mirjam Mencej has shown that channelling the supernatural experiences and the related fears to storytelling and to prophylactic action brings them from personal to shared knowledge and thus helps to cope with them (2015). In the following narrative Kristi's personal dreamlike encounter becomes a shared experience when physical evidence is discovered that confirms its reality:

> My most terrifying experience came once during a night shift. It was a hard night as we had to make a blood transfer and I had to match blood types – something which demands great accuracy. I heard a scrabble here and there and I said, "You know, go to one corner," – next to the old thermostat, "You all stay there! Don't disturb me!" Suddenly, all was silent. Later I woke up, because a nightmare [*luupainaja*] had attacked me. I was conscious, but could not move, and I had the feeling that a panel of two tonnes was lying on me. I had inexplicable, hazy and turbid feeling of a great fear – fear of death. And then I saw strange creature who looked like a crooked, scrawny old women with curly dark grey hair. In the morning we found a piece of hair on the sofa – it was long and grey and it did not belong to anyone [of us]. Thus it was I got my punishment – you should not insult them.

The old man who was characterised by midwife Heli as an angry ghost and associated by her with the medical lab, also featured in the interview, as Riina had witnessed him in a dream-like experience. First, she heard the shuffling footsteps, then she saw how the locked door was opened and a man in black slippers entered. Riina gave a vivid description of an old man with grey hair who was wearing black trousers with grey stripes and creases, and a white shirt with pink and red dots and a knitted red vest. She said that he looked like a former resident of the place, but rather than seeming aggressive he looked kind and benevolent. When I said that several people in the other part of the hospital had described a similar ghost, Riina replied: "Oh, did they? Perhaps he was the one, indeed! Oh my..." It seemed as if she had not heard about the old man in slippers, who had been mentioned by several members of staff from other departments. This seems stunning, but as I listen to the recorded interview, Riina's utterance does not express so much surprise; it sounds more like a minor observation. The factuality of the hauntings had been so self-evident that there was no need to place any extra emphasis on the evidence.

As the ghostly presence was disturbing, the workers of the lab tried to find effective methods to control it. Kristi seemed most inventive about finding ways to appease or repel the ghosts. She said: "They liked singing a lot. There was a time when I carried my guitar along and sang for them in the evening and at night. Then they were more peaceful and tame." Together with her colleagues she had tried the traditional methods of warding off evil by burning a branch of a juniper tree and by spilling salt on the floor. In addition, they had applied various Christian means of protection, such as holy water and frankincense from the Catholic Church. Such experiments led to the conclusion that making runic signs above the door was the most effective means of defence, but they had to be replaced frequently. Kristi said that Hungarian runic signs from the Internet had been the most powerful ghost-deterrents (*tonditõrjuja*). Also, high-frequency vibration worked effectively as a repellent – that's why the TV-set was turned on the whole night.

Another major topic, besides that of controlling the ghosts, was the big question of what had caused the haunting and why it occurred in its specific forms. One of the interviewees had worked earlier in the oncology hospital, where many people had died, but had experienced no ghosts. This controversy triggered the following dialogue:

Anne: You see, in oncology majority of people are dying. Their souls go away somewhere but in the obstetrics clinic there are comers, and there are other souls as well.
Riina: Yes, indeed, and there are many of those who cannot understand. Let's say, the souls of abortions cannot understand what is going on. But those [encountered in dreams] did not belong to them. Did they take the appearance of previous life? We saw these images. Concretely, there was an elderly lady, and then there were figures of men. What did an adult man have to do in an obstetrics hospital? These days, he had nothing to do. Consequently, the soul had taken the form of a previous life. A phantom?
A: And it did not find a body to enter.
R: Exactly, may-be it tried to enter us... [Everybody laughs.]
A: ...and we did not want to. We had souls.

The long interview is rich in personal experience stories and different interpretations with almost no space for scepticism. A close circle of colleagues had gathered and the discussion involved both well-polished stories, obviously told many times before, and spontaneous comments about the lab as a place with "bad energetics". One of the most striking explanations for why the lab had been disturbed was formulated by Kristi:

> Maybe the activity in the lab is so high because of blood. The blood of unbaptised children comes to us. The very first blood that is taken from babies – the blood and its products come to us – which is used to make a deal with the Devil.

I was astonished to hear the hint of traditional beliefs about the Devil and the blood contract with him – which seem to emerge from oblivion – from another age of obsolete demonology of the 19th century. Although the New Spirituality with its beliefs in subtle energetics offer the main cultural resources for interpreting haunting, these frames obviously remain too narrow for vernacular exegetics.

We have one more perspective on the hauntings in the interview with Nestor, the chaplain of the hospital who had worked there since 1994. He said that he had had no experience himself, but that he had heard ghost stories from many people – mainly from those who had been on duty at night – about lights turning on, about hearing footsteps or having an uncanny feeling. Below is a part of our conversation:

> N: If I remember correctly, these stories mainly concerned the department of gynaecology – on the second and third floor under the roof. Every now and then, somebody came and said that once again something had happened last night. They couldn't sleep at all because they had heard these sounds. This kind of stories…
>
> Ü: So people were quite distressed when they told such things?
>
> N: Yes, people were quite distressed and disturbed. Several people who had been on night duty together had had the same experience at the same time. According to their accounts, several people heard, simultaneously, footsteps or the shuffle of slippers of somebody walking along the corridor. As they looked into the corridor, nobody was there. I can remember these kinds of stories.
>
> Once I went to the department of gynaecology at the request of the senior nurse Vaike to bless a room, or let's say the whole department. A small ritual was performed. A woman had just died there in the course of some medical procedure. Afterwards it became very disturbed in the department and on the whole floor. The patients, too, heard something and could not sleep. And then, fine, as something like this had happened, as a clergyman of course I can do what I can. So I performed the ritual of blessing the department and such disturbing things stopped, so they claimed.

Nestor said that as he had been working as a clergyman, people had addressed him with similar requests before, usually concerning somebody's home that had become disturbed after a family member had passed away and a secular funeral had been arranged. In this case a Lutheran funeral ceremony had to be conducted on the grave or the blessing ritual had to be performed at home. There had also been a couple of cases that were not linked with anybody's recent death, but a house had become disturbed because of former violent events like murder – people complained that lights went on at night, sounds and footsteps were heard and doors were opened. Nestor indicated that the ritual of blessing of an apartment or a house is included in the *Agenda Book* of the Lutheran Church. It starts "In the Name of Father, Son and Holy Ghost", includes relevant readings from the Bible, a short sermon and a prayer, which ends with the Lord's Prayer and the words of blessing (Agenda 1994). In traditional Estonian legends it is often the clergyman who serves as a mediator between the living and the otherworld and who deals with the supernatural, and we can see that this role has remained relevant up to today. The ritual performed in the hospital puts the local ghost-lore in the broader context of folk religion, where the Lutheran Church has played a notable role. Nestor also said that when people with religious background had contacted him because they were scared by their ghostly experiences, he had advised them to read the Lord's Prayer to lift the fear.

When I asked Nestor a general question about how people interpreted or explained the haunting, he replied:

> Yes, of course... It was because all kind of events had happened in the house. Even the crying of children was heard and other things like that. [...] The usual explanation was that many sad events had occurred in the hospital. Earlier it was not uncommon that women died here. The women's hospital has quite a long history. [...] Medicine was different in those early days. Probably there were more accidents and cases of death before. Sometimes babies die during birth giving even today but obviously this happened more frequently in olden days. Hence, the explanations concerned sad events in the building, and the souls or spirits [*hingekesed või vaimud*] that were related to these cases. [...]

We can see that afterlife beliefs provide a recurring framework for interpreting both the personal experiences of ghosts and the stories about them. The former inhabitants of the building and those who have died there are considered to be the cause of haunting. Fragmentary memories from the forgotten history of the hospital appear in the stories of three interviewees, several of which correspond to the characteristics of legends as a folklore genre. Legends have been characterised as stories that generate debate about belief, evoke contrary opinions (Dégh 2001: 97), and invoke the rhetoric of truth (Oring 2008: 159). However, ghost-lore of the hospital does not seem to address the fundamental existential questions of whether ghosts exist or not. Rather, the stories confirm the observation of Lauri Honko (1989 [1964]: 103) that "Belief in spirits is not founded on speculation but on concrete personal experiences, reinforced by sensory perceptions". The same perspective is held by David Hufford (1995: 28) who has shown that the belief that spirits and a spiritual domain exist are grounded in distinctive experiences that occur "independently of a subject's prior beliefs, knowledge, or intention". Perhaps it should not surprise us that the reality of uncanny experiences in the hospital is not questioned in the interviews, but accepted as simple fact, even if the modality is humorous. Purposeful arguments to verify the reality of ghosts are rare, vernacular theorising rather addresses the question of why the hospital is haunted, and looks for the answers in its history.

Ontological Liminality of Ghosts

Our conversation with Nestor took place in his office in the huge building of the new medical centre in Tartu. He said that the exchange of information and storytelling situations had totally changed after the hospital moved:

> You might ask if somebody knows such stories in the new house, but I, at least, have not heard them. I must say that now there is much less communication than before. There are many things I don't know. Earlier on, contact was good because we all were pressed quite close together in a [narrow] space. People spoke with each other then. Now I read in my emails about what should be done and who among the patients I should visit. Earlier it was natural that somebody stepped by and told me about the patients or suggest that I visited the doctors' room.

Indeed, it would be difficult to imagine lively ghost-lore without close communication at an inter-personal level. Ghosts need small groups with a sense of community. David Yamane (2000) has drawn attention to the fact that we cannot study religious experiencing in real time and its constituents, but have to analyse its representations in retrospective accounts. It is through language and primarily through narratives that people make sense of and convey their experiences (Yamane 2000: 173, 176). The same holds of uncanny experiences in a haunted building – they remain void of meaning until the visual, auditive or other perception is finalized in a verbal account that addresses the tradition. Supernatural experience turns into ghost-lore if it is verbalised and intertextually linked to the interpretive framework of former conversations and storytellings. Sometimes the old building itself turns into an agent or a living body that is controlled and personified by a spiritual entity. Metaphoric approaches which see ghosts as narrative characters symbolizing social tensions or distress also make sense. Even in vernacular theorising questions emerged, why the ghost and the related lore became activated just before moving to the new building? Did the poor ghost express anxiety about being left alone? Or was it about the community who was reluctant to move and expressed its distress through the stories about haunting, a wishful return to the past? The question about the possible feelings of the ghost belongs to vernacular discourse and the question about the symbolic meaning of narratives is part of folkloristic theorising. They seem to represent two opposite points of view, two different ontologies. Is there a way to reconcile these seemingly conflicting views? After all, how can we make sense of ghosts?

Certainly, a hospital like the one that stood on Toome Hill represents a social space that is far from ordinary. Birth-giving and dying – both ultimate and awe-inspiring domains of human existence – together generate the sense of an extraordinary environment, a place that is marked off from the surrounding secular urban sphere. Generations of staff, mothers and patients who have passed through the hospital create a sense of history, which is still present and is materialised in the walls of the old house. Strong attachment to the old building among the personnel was obvious. As ghost-lore addresses the metaphysical dimensions of life, it can create strong, personal and powerful sense of place (Thomas 2007: 45). Bearing in mind this exceptional environment, it might be possible to offer some answers to the existential questions posed above. Namely, ghosts appear in the spectral zone between physical existence and imagination. This means that the lack of substance on the one hand defines their existence and essentializes them, on the other hand dissolves them into the inscrutable realm of shadows. Empty lifts moving at night, the sound of footsteps, rappings, anthropomorphic apparitions, and other expressions of human activity – without any human presence and not involving any human agency – are all typical ghostly manifestations. It has also been noted that ghost gravitate towards marginal zones of residential spaces, appearing in attics, cellars, staircases – in no-go areas or places that are betwixt-and-between (Bennett 1999: 44; Grider 2007: 152; Tucker 2007: 36–39). Ambiguous as they are, ghosts reside in liminal spaces between memory and oblivion, present and past, belonging and unrootedness, life and death, existence and non-existence. As beings without physical bodies ghosts are not like us, humans, and yet they manifest human characteristics. In their post-mortal existence they are nothing but dead, although as restless dead they are active agents who haunt the liminal zone where verbal genres and physical reality coalesce. On one hand, ghosts are summoned and brought to life by storytelling and thus belong to the narrative world. On the other hand, words only document and perpetuate them. Ghosts manifest the ontological liminality between the storyworld and live experience.

Epilogue

After a thorough renovation the hospital building on Toome Hill was opened again on February 8, 2012 to house the Faculty of Social Sciences and Education of the University of Tartu. I have questioned the faculty and staff members and some students but have heard nothing about any hauntings.

However, there is some evidence that after all the ghosts followed the personnel to the new building. Medical staff of the laboratory told me that before moving out, they had left a box opened at night and asked the ghosts to join them in the new place. Something similar had happened in some other departments of the hospital and it is difficult to say if this was done only jokingly or not. Senior nurse Vaike told me about mysterious events in the Outpatients Department (the same department where Vaike had worked in the old building). She had retired a few months after the move but visited the new department and talked with the senior nurse. She had told Vaike that several times the roll of drying paper next to the sink had mysteriously unwound itself. In addition, the tap did not function properly and the water kept running. Workmen came to fix these problems repeatedly, but without success. The senior nurse of the new hospital had mentioned that "perhaps the ghost [*kummitus*] had come along". In addition, staff from the former lab spoke about dark shadows and spectral figures seen at night and doors that were mysteriously opened. Saima, who had not witnessed anything supernatural in the old hospital, had started to have strange experiences in the new place. She said that while spending time on night-watch, she had sometimes heard the familiar clicking sound – as if somebody had placed a blood count on the hatch. When she went to check it, nothing was there.

Notes

* I am deeply grateful to my eight informants, personnel of the hospital for taking their time to meet me for interviews and for providing me with insiders' insights to the life and lore of the old hospital. Without the valuable contribution of these people writing this article would not have been possible. However, even though they all have given me their kind permission to publish their names along with the passages from interviews, I have decided not to disclose their full names here, but use pseudonyms instead. I am also thankful to Ms Merilyn Merisalu for her kind permission to translate and publish her article, originally published in the weekly newspaper *Universitas Tartuensis*, and to Dr Jonathan Roper for language editing. The research has been supported by the European Union through the European Regional Development Fund (Centre of Excellence, CECT) and by the Estonian Ministry of Education and Research (Institutional Research Project IUT2–43).

1 About fictionalization as a process of inter-cultural translation of supernatural genres into decontextualised stories with little relevance to social reality and belief, see Valk 2015.
2 Eda Kalmre has studied legends about the Lilac Lady who haunts the building of the Estonian Literary Museum in Tartu. She has also noted that the psychological experience of night-watches in a large dark house are an essential factor in keeping the legend alive (Kalmre 2001: 102). The same has been observed by Mirjam Mencej who has explored the ghost-lore of security guards in a haunted university building in Ljubljana (2015).
3 I have changed the full names of the interviewees to their initials in the English translation of the article (and in the passage quoted below from another article).
4 A part of the old building has been constructed as a wing onto the rest of the house. The entrance to these rooms is on the half landing of the stairs between first and second floors.

Sources

Interviews

March 24, 2014: with the chaplain of the hospital Nestor
March 27, 2014: with midwife Heli
January 26, 2015: with senior nurse Vaike
April 15, 2015: with the staff of the medical laboratory – Anne, Kristi, Riina, Saima, and Terje

Literature

Agenda 1994 = *Eesti Evangeeliumi Luteri Usu Kiriku Agenda*. Tallinn: EELK Konsistoorium. Available at http://www.eelk.ee/~kvonnu/agenda.html [Accessed January 21, 2015]

Bennett, Gillian 1999. *"Alas, Poor Ghost!" Traditions of Belief in Story and Discourse*. Logan, UT: Utah State University Press.

Briggs, Charles L. 2008. Disciplining Folkloristics. *Journal of Folklore Research. Special Issue: Grand Theory* 45(1): 91–105.

Cowdell, Paul 2011. *Belief in Ghosts in Post-War England*. Submitted to the University of Hertfordshire in partial fulfilment of the requirements of the degree of Ph.D. Available at http://uhra.herts.ac.uk/handle/2299/7184 [Accessed January 21, 2015]

Dégh, Linda 2001. *Legend and Belief. Dialectics of a Folklore Genre*. Bloomington, Indianapolis: Indiana University Press.

Goldstein, Diane E., Sylvia Ann Grider & Jeannie Banks Thomas 2007. *Haunting Experiences. Ghosts in Contemporary Folklore*. Logan, UT: Utah State University Press.

Grider, Silvia Ann 2007. Haunted Houses. In *Haunting Experiences. Ghosts in Contemporary Folklore*. Diane E. Goldstein, Sylvia Ann Grider & Jeannie Banks Thomas (eds.). Logan, UT: Utah State University Press. Pp. 143–170.

Honko, Lauri 1989 [1964]. Memorates and the Study of Folk Belief. In *Nordic Folklore. Recent Studies*. Reimund Kvideland & Henning K. Sehmsdorf (eds.). Bloomington: Indiana University Press. Pp. 100–109.

Hufford, David J. 1982. *The Terror that Comes in the Night. An Experience-Centered Study of Supernatural Assault Traditions*. Philadelphia: University of Pennsylvania Press.

Hufford, David J. 1995. Beings without Bodies. An Experience-Centered Theory of the Belief in Spirits. In *Out of the Ordinary. Folklore and the Supernatural*. Barbara Walker (ed.). Logan, Utah: Utah State University Press. Pp. 11–45.

Jõgi, Aime 2008. Tartu sünnitusmaja lood. *Tartu Postimees*, 11.12.2008: 5–8.

Kaldur, Marko 2008. *Salapärane Eesti ehk moodsaid linnalegende, kaasaegseid muistendeid, vandenõuteooriaid, ajaloolugusid, külajutte tänapäeva Eestist*. Tallinn: Olion.

Kalmre, Eda 2001. The Lilac Lady. A Collective Belief-Legend as a Homogeneous Entity. In *Folklore als Tatsachenbericht*. Jürgen Beyer & Reet Hiiemäe (eds.). Tartu: Sektion für Folkloristik des Estnischen Literaturmuseums. Pp. 85–105.

Kalnin, V. 1982. Arstiteadused. In *Tartu Riikliku Ülikooli ajalugu II* (1798–1918). Karl Siilivask (ed.). Tallinn: Eesti Raamat. Pp. 360–372.

Keinänen, Marja-Liisa 2003. *Creating Bodies. Childbirth Practices in Pre-Modern Karelia*. Stockholm: Stockholm University.

Koski, Kaarina 2016. Discussing the Supernatural in Contemporary Finland: Discourses, Genres, and Forums. *Folklore: Electronic Journal of Folklore* 65: 11–36. https://www.folklore.ee/folklore/vol65/koski.pdf [Accessed January 19, 2017]

Mencej, Mirjam 2015. Security Guards as Participants in and Mediators of a Ghost Tradition. *Fabula* 56(1/2): 40–66.

Merisalu, Merilyn 2008. Naistekliiniku heatahtlik vaim kardab mahajätmist. *Universitas Tartuensis* 13(2338), 11.04.2008: 4.

Oring, Elliott 2008. Legendry and the Rhetoric of Truth. *Journal of American Folklore* 121: 127–166.

Pakalns, Guntis 1995. Ghost Narratives in Latvia – Changes During Recent Years. *Foaftale News: Newsletter of the International Society for Contemporary Legend Research* 37, June 1995. Available at http://www.folklore.ee/FOAFtale/ftn37.htm#Latvia [Accessed January 21, 2015]

Palleiro, María Inés 2012. Haunted Houses and Haunting Girls: Life and Death in Contemporary Argentinian Folk Narrative. In *Vernacular Religion in Everyday Life. Expressions of Belief*. Marion Bowman & Ülo Valk (eds.). Sheffield, Bristol, CT: Equinox. Pp. 211–229.

Para-Web. Available at http://www.para-web.org/index.php [Accessed January 21, 2015]

Perno Postimees 1860. Terwisse hoidmissest ja leidmissest. Wötke abbi, kui abbi pakkutakse. *Perno Postimees* 2, 13.01.1860: 14–15.

Raahauge, Kirsten Marie 2016. Ghosts, Troubles, Difficulties, and Challenges: Narratives about Unexplainable Phenomena in Contemporary Denmark. *Folklore: Electronic Journal of Folklore* 65: 89–110. https://www.folklore.ee/folklore/vol65/raahauge.pdf [Accessed January 19, 2017]

Reha, Liis 2008. *Kolga mõisa kummituslood Ulvi Meieri jutuvaramus: bakalaureusetöö.* Tartu: TÜ eesti ja võrdleva rahvaluule osakond. Available at http://dspace.utlib.ee/dspace/handle/10062/26399 [Accessed January 21, 2015]

Richardson, Judith 2003. *Possessions. The History and Uses of Haunting in the Hudson Valley.* Cambridge, MA, London: Harvard University Press.

Tamm, Arkadius 1943a. Tartu Ülikooli Naistekliiniku teaduslik tegevus 1806–1942. *Eesti Arst* XXII(10): 497–530.

Tamm, Arkadius 1943b. Tartu Ülikooli Naistekliiniku asutamine, juhatajad ja meditsiiniline koosseis. *Eesti Arst* XXII(11): 581–608.

Thomas, Jeannie Banks 2007. The Usefulness of Ghost Stories. In *Haunting Experiences. Ghosts in Contemporary Folklore.* Diane E. Goldstein, Sylvia Ann Grider & Jeannie Banks Thomas (eds.). Logan, UT: Utah State University Press. Pp. 25–59.

Tucker, Elizabeth 2007. *Haunted Halls. Ghostlore of American College Campuses.* Jackson, MS: University Press of Mississippi.

Valk, Ülo 2012. Belief as Generic Practice and Vernacular Theory in Contemporary Estonia. In *Vernacular Religion in Everyday Life. Expressions of Belief.* Marion Bowman & Ülo Valk (eds.). Sheffield, Bristol, CT: Equinox. Pp. 350–368.

Valk, Ülo 2015. Discursive Shifts in Legends from Demonization to Fictionalization. *Narrative Culture* 2(1): 141–165.

Viimane vaatus vanas majas 2009. = Farewell party of the Women's Hospital of the University of Tartu. Tartu: TÜ IT Multimeedia talitus. Filmed by Toomas Petersell, Enno Kaasik, Juho Jalviste on December 19, 2008. [Video recording in the Music Department of the Library of the University of Tartu.]

Yamane, David 2000. Narrative and Religious Experience. *Sociology of Religion* 61(2): 171–189.

Kristel Kivari

Webs of Lines and Webs of Stories in the Making of Supernatural Places[*]

Methodological advice. The main purpose of the lecture must be to show that unusual and frightening natural phenomena have scientific explanations, that they occur under the circumstances of the rules of nature and as such there is no evidence to attribute these phenomena to supernatural powers (spirits and gods). The lecturer must convince the audience that 'wonders' do not exist, or if we use the term for rare and seemingly inexplicable phenomena, it can be explained by scientific methods too. (Müürisepp 1960. Auxiliary material for the Scientific Explanation for Unusual Natural Phenomena lecture. Tallinn, Estonian SSR, Society for Dissemination of Political and Scientific Knowledge.)

Science appears as the powerful 'other' in religious and vernacular thinking: it is the grounds for contest and allegiance. As the paragraph above shows, pertinent to its context of publication, it is the same in reverse: the empathetic attribution of the supernatural to religion draws its borders in contrast to scientific inquiry. The author of the paragraph above reflects the understanding of religion as complete trust in and appropriation of natural forces to supernatural agents at a time of scientific optimism that formed part of Soviet political ideology under the name of 'Scientific Materialism'. The author, Estonian natural scientist Karl Müürisepp, was working in the area of geology. In this, the realms of the supernatural and the scientific are not so easily identifiable, as the supernatural accommodates active vernacular and alternative thinking about powers that are beyond human control. At the time he wrote, there were in the close vicinity of his academic surroundings, groups and institutions at work with experiments on bioenergy, biophysics and the connections between mind and matter. These experiments were not connected in any way with spiritual or religious meanings, however the researchers themselves were often walking a tightrope of complete restriction of their academic careers because of their personal curiosity and involvement with spirituality. "These were institutions that did not exist and they performed research on phenomena that did not exist", said one of my informants, giving comments upon the involvement of the institutions with the research into different 'anomalies' in the Soviet Union. Enthusiasm to find the X-factor in the environment or in the human psyche that could bridge the split between science/technology and the possibilities that are known from the dowsing tradition has guided experiments in fringe areas of scientific work.

This article gives an insight into dowsing with the help of two conceptual lines. Although the research material comes from contemporary Estonia, the first part of the article introduces dowsing practice as found in the history of geology in Central Europe. It touches the formation of rationalist and scientific discourse which has been referred to by Max Weber as the disenchantment of the intellectual sphere. The second line addresses the title of the current volume. The supernatural places in the discussions of contemporary dowsers are articulated through webs of associations between different stories, as well as between different places.

The supernatural is problematic to define as a distinct category, as it involves the border between material and cultural reality. Particularly, the vernacular discussion emerges from the split between these two. The search for concealed forces in nature, the explanation of various experiences and folkloric motifs, and the overall notion that there is something beyond, is what establishes the framework for perceiving the supernatural. The supernatural places in dowsing theories are the 'knots' of the webs: the invisible web of energy-lines as well as stories connected to them. These knots enable access to the cognition and culture that are an alternative to the materialistic worldview. Dowsers consider the unknown power or system of existence. The search for it, for the principle or the spiritual entities that might be involved in this, is the ground for different activities and ideas within Estonian Geopathic Association (*Eesti Geopaatia Selts*), the discussions that I use as research material in current analysis.

Dowsing as a vernacular practice is very much influenced by its position within wider social and economic contexts. Modernisation, which relies on scientific and institutional authority, has stigmatised the historical practice of miners as well as the popular scene that includes contact with the supernatural (energies, spirits, ghosts, visions of the past times etc.). Despite this, contemporary dowsing enthusiasts follow both: they apply a scientific approach to traditional motifs that were familiar to the miners of early modern Saxony and are still well known today as evidence of underground streams or the crossings of energy lines. Although the movement of rods in human hands has remained an unsolved problem in terms of contemporary physics, the motifs that are described in early modern period are still part of dowsing knowledge. The following look at early geology is here to show the explanation of natural markers (such as fissures, all sorts of emanations, also mystical lights) within the theories of generation of minerals and meteorology. The same natural markers, as well the geological profile of the particular place is incorporated into search for the web between the places which would give explanatory connections between different stories as well function as a bridge between science and religion.

Prelude: Dowsing and Early Geology

Since early modern times, dowsing as a practice has been offensive to people who advocate a reliance on experimental, rationalist and thus 'scientific' knowledge. The concerns of the critics have been wider: it touches on the orders of modern society, the position of professionals and the hierarchy of knowledge production.

The problem with dowsing has emerged together with scientific and capitalist entrepreneurship, which values ambition for universalist rules, with professional guarantees instead of local and subjective knowledge. Dowsing, as part of divinatory magic, appears in the writings on early Earth science for two reasons. As Martin Rudwick (2005: 32) notes, writing on the history of geology: "Local experts were of particular importance in the sciences of the Earth, for their specific experience: the phenomena and physical features of scientific interest were intrinsically local in character, and those living in a particular region could often acquire an intimate knowledge of them."

The second reason for the discussion over dowsing was the literature on mining within emerging theoretical thought. Warren Dym (2011: 86) notes that the general 'mining book' (*Bergbuch*) held heterogenous content. Thus, literature on mining from the period of the 16th to 18th centuries in Saxony included several types of texts: tables of extraction figures, shareholder lists, mining customs and laws, minting manuals, assaying manuals, manuals on the measuring and charting of veins, glossaries of mining and metalworking terms, chronicles, general overviews of the administration and procedures of mining and metallurgy, etc. The material also consisted of Johann Mathesius's printed collection of mining sermons which functioned as a practical mining book in Saxon mining too (Dym 2011: 86). Thus the textual format and the position of the writers set the practice in its specific contexts of writers and publishers. Relying on Dym, the (dis)continuation of local practices, esoteric knowledge or alchemical theories, esotericism and metaphysical content could have been also influenced by the demands of the audience.

The dowsing rod, *Rute* or *Wünchelrute*, found a place in modernist pursuit of progressive knowledge against the local background of treasure-hunting tales and habits. If considered as legends about finding a treasure or mineral vein (silver, for example) these stories circulated in the professional tradition of miners, popular books, calendars and aforementioned variety of literature on mining (Besterman 1926; Dym 2011: 90).

The explanation given for the movement of the rods was in accordance with the various theories about generation of mineral ores. According to these theories, the rod is supposed to react either to the mineral fumes or to fissures in the ground. By the mineral exhalation theory, minerals were seen as growing, bearing fruits and decaying beneath the surface. Although the theory of the subterranean winds and vapours goes back to pre-Socratic philosophers, and the theory of mineral genesis from exhalations appears to have been an idea of Aristotle's (Norris 2006: 44), the mineral exhalation theory was later combined with the ideas about sulphurous seed refining itself by a complicated process under the influence of particular location, chemicals and temperature as well as astral powers. (Norris 2006: 55.)

Connection between stars and metals was reflected in the choosing of the right material for the rod. The influential mining theorist from Saxony, Georgius Agricola (1912 [1556]: 39), reflected the idea in his main book *De Re Metallica*, saying "others use a different kind of twig for each metal, when they are seeking to discover the veins, for they employ hazel twigs for veins of silver; ash twigs for copper; pitch pine for lead and especially tin, and rods made of iron and steel for gold".

Different theories about, and approaches to, the nascent science of geology circulated side by side up to the 18th century. The emergence of aqueous theory was more connected with practical mining (Norris 2007: 89). According to this view the generation of metals was seen as connected to underground water or proto-mineral liquid that formed and moved through the underground fissures. Summarising Agricola's approach to the generation of metals, John Norris (2007: 73) asserts that "the three principal aspects of Agricola's observations involve the presence of underground fissures, the copious water encountered in mining operations, and mineral depositions such as encrustations and dripstones. Agricola organised these observations into a self-consistent system of subterranean processes, in which he linked mineral deposits to the creation of the types of fissures that they occupy, both operations depending on the action of underground water".

Apart from fissures and fumes, a distinctive phenomenon called *Witterungen* was incorporated into the early miners' knowledge. *Witterungen* ('weathers') referred to various natural indications of an underground mineral vein such as fogs, fumes, smell, heat, and sparks, all of which could also be viewed in the shafts and on the ground. Agricola (1912 [1556]: 38) refers to *Witterungen* as the reason behind various phenomena in nature: "therefore in places where the grass has a dampness that is not congealed into frost, there is a vein beneath; also if the exhalation be excessively hot, the soil will produce only small and pale-coloured plants". Thus, direct observations of nature can reveal the existence of mineral veins. According to the *Naturphilosophie* of the Renaissance, the Earth was seen as a living body that performed the functions of inhalation and exhalations and which also bore fruit (that could decay). The dowsing rod reacted to these inhalations and exhalations and other inner processes of the Earth's body (Dym 2011: 74). Hot air, flames and glowing were part of the various ideas in *Bergbuch* [mining book] that were noted as natural markers, god-given signs or, in contrast, temptations of the devil. As Dym (2011: 85) says in summary, "*Bergwissenschaft* ['mining science'] was a more synthetic body of theory and practice [...] it included tales of discovery, biblical stories, alchemical and astrological theories, dowsing theory, as well as knowledge of the mining compass (*Grubenkompass*), the mathematics of mine surveying (*Marckscheidekunde*), and the craft of mine construction".

Authors, writing on ideas of Earth and mining practices during the early-modern period, are far from being in agreement on the ethos of the miner and successful or unreasonable practices of prospecting, digging and safety. Dowsing as incidental knowledge was more prevalent in practice and was incorporated into the skills and knowledge of local experts with limited reflection on thorough theoretical or theological discussion. Relying on Dym, dowsing occupied its (controversial) position within mining science up to the invention of contemporary prospecting techniques. However, during the 18th century, the political and economic changes augmented vernacular, experience-based thinking with new standards of systematisation and professionalism (Dym 2011: 78).

Despite being bound in local legends and practices, the art of dowsing during the early-modern period reveals the core ideas of the practice today. As then, so today the practice exists side-by-side with wider divination magic. Agricola (1912 [1556]: 42) draws up the position of dowsing in vernacular practice saying, "the wizards, who also make use of rings, mirrors and crystals, seek for veins with a divining rod shaped like a fork; but its shape makes no difference in the matter, it might be straight or of some other form, for it is not the form of the twig that matters, but the wizard's incantations which it would not become me to repeat, neither do I wish to do so".

Today in the context of the wider New Age scene, the popularisation of the use of pendulums sets the art of dowsing in its traditional context: while being a tool for progressive inquiry into the unknown, the theme finds a niche in the wider esoteric context of individual authority. Dowsing seems to exist today in the same position of approval and disapproval; it creates curiosity and provides fertile ground for experience stories and wider social debate. It looks at the everyday environment with unconventional eyes and introduces ideas that are outside the dominant forms of knowledge production, spreading through questions, doubts and experiences, the tradition of liminal areas of knowledge and practice. Stemming from this people ask questions about health and general wellbeing, the natural history of a particular location and the bond between natural and supernatural reality and the human body in a particular place. As well as finding water, underground pipes and cables, and aiding in decisions relating to house and garden planning, the dowsing methods and their results have value for the dowser in the form of visions and physical effects that act as the source of additional knowledge and values. As a tradition, dowsing offers a reflexive framework for debate. In this the search for underground water streams, fissures in the ground, the colour and shape of nature and the hardly identifiable connection between the human body and the environment will echo through any enquiry into supernatural reality in the form of powers, energies and emanations.

Disenchantment as an Intellectual Problem

The position of dowsing during the period of intensive development of capitalist entrepreneurship and natural sciences created a conflict between domains of authority. The conditions for the formulation of reliable and legitimate knowledge were connected with different hierarchies.

This process not only created the method for scientific inquiry but also influenced professional standards. Those modernistic standards were based on the principle of rationalisation of the intellectual (which includes also the political and the economical) sphere. The term "disenchantment" [*Enzauberung*], devised by Weber, has been used to describe the process of Enlightenment, and denotes the split between sources of authority, stating "that principally there are no mysterious incalculable forces that come into play, but rather that one can, in principle, master all things by calculation. This means that the world is disenchanted." (Weber 1946: 139.) Although the enlightened ideal was to free science from magic, supersitions and "childish fairy tales" (Dym 2008: 833), the historians of science have seen the period as being much more diverse, and the processes involved as far slower and less uniform (Fara 2008; Dym 2011). Modern conditions, that were based in different epistemic attitudes, created a changed set of problems to those experienced by the earlier natural philosophers and traditional miners.

Egil Asprem (2013) has researched the contact between science and esotericism in the first quarter of the 20th century. He reconceptualises Weber's disenchantment thesis as an intellectual problem rather than a socio-historical process. The emphasis on the problem "provides an alternative to process-oriented narratives of the development of 'Western culture', 'Western science', and 'Western philosophy', emphasising the conflicting responses of individual historical actors rather than the idea of an unstoppable march of abstract 'processes'" (Asprem 2013: 555). The history of geology in relation to the question of dowsing is a good example of the intellectual sacrifice made in subordinating individual tradition-bound authority to the discourse of scientific and rational method of knowledge making.

Asprem summarised the principal questions of the problem of disenchantment as follows: are there incalculable forces in nature? How far do the boundaries of our knowledge extend? Is there or can there be any basis for morality, value, and meaning in nature? (Asprem 2013: 32.) The questions are philosophical generalisations of formulations found in individual situations, although in the context of dowsing they are sometimes phrased surprisingly similarly. The particular stream of vernacular thinking regarding the enquiry of dowsers addresses the discursive position of their activity with the term 'alternative'.

Contemporary vernacular thinking usually employs discourses and hierarchies of knowledge that are dominated by secular-scientific education and ideology. However, in the context of democracy and the free market, the values of individual choices give voice to the 'problems of disenchantment'. This is totally illegitimate from the disenchanted viewpoint, but finds support in concepts such as tradition and innovation, referring to subjective experience, identity and belonging. The interest in dowsing is usually wider and involves curiosity in different themes circulating under the heading "alternative". People refer to their interests as hard to define. The phrases "I am interested in these things" or "I am involved in these things"[1] includes areas of interest designated with the same title "alternative", "paranormal phenomena", etc., which contain different themes and sources and are often guided by inner cultural criticism of the modernistic worldview.

"These things" (*need asjad*) refers to the circle of disparate stories that supports some focused ideas but which otherwise remains debatable, forming a referential network for unique situations. Despite relative obscurity, the interest usually addresses the cosmological constitution of the universe or society and takes into account the role of the personal and individual. Despite these frames, which touch on issues of power, knowledge of nature and authority, the worldview, using Linda Dégh's (1995: 133) words, "is not an abstraction but part of an active and persuasive elaboration of the traditional material, the framing of the folklore text by its *ad hoc* formulator, who fits in into the cultural-conceptual system of its audience". Thus the expressions of individual dowsing experiences are related in the context of contemporary theoretical thought. The encounter with the supernatural in the current case is experienced according to research into the paranormal, which inherently addresses the problem of disenchantment in order to weave together the natural and supernatural.

Societies in the Study of the 'Alternative'

Although this article reflects discussions among dowsers in the Estonian Geopathic Society, the background of this contemporary material involves various activities in the larger spiritual scene, which is influenced by various New Age trends.

Thus, two aspects dominate contemporary dowsing practice. Dowsing is performed for many purposes: to find underground water, and to find suitable locations to plant a tree, building a house, or setting up a work room or bedroom. People carry pendulums with them in their handbag or pocket in order to measure the energy of the water or food that they drink and eat. The intimacy of the practice is reflected in the fact that although the dowsing rods and pendulum are often thought of as tools, people do not usually lend their tools to strangers.

However, the private part of the practice does not exist without the social part. There are public courses that teach people how to use dowsing rods or pendulums, trainers who take people into nature to teach them how to find and perceive the energies of a particular location, printed and web materials, discussion groups and popular media create a voice of authority within the wider vernacular debate. The word 'energy' as a marker of various emotions, impressions and impulses links different spheres of life with a broad spectrum of interpretations.

In the case of dowsing, interpretations follow the pattern of inquiry of the enthusiasts in clubs and societies. The mission of such activities is to create a network for the discussions of the supernatural, with themes varying from health issues to politics and history. The supernatural in these themes involves recognition of concealed power that has the ability to influence the living in various ways. In their regular discussions, the societies bear the attempt to create unified knowledge within various folkloric ideas, experiences, reports and rumours. The label 'alternative' takes off from the conflict between the discourses perceived by members. Thus, it indicates border knowledge that does not quite suit the frames of publicly accepted knowledge and which does not form a unified body of principles, methods or institutional authority.

Three clubs in Estonia, which share similar interests and also have members in common, have formulated their objectives as regards study and research. For example, the Estonian Society for Research into Ancient Knowledge (*Eesti Muinasteaduste Selts*) concentrates on a broader spectrum of themes. Their society is "a circle for the people who think by themselves and can apprehend the world in its diverse aspects and life as a whole. Contemporary science (both from the military and civil side) is only focused on the material and physical forms of life. Ancient Knowledge looks at life as a whole, as was done in ancient times. It is a process of investigating alternative knowledge (not discarding the achievements of science) and its application to our daily situations." (EMS, translation by the author.) Apart from web discussion groups, these circles attempt to produce empirical data in their training and field trips in order to contribute to the advancement of public knowledge through theories, practices or techniques relating to the unknown.

A group with similar interests, Energo-club (*Energo Klubi*), has a list of questions which unite its activity on their web page: "What impact does the environment have on modern man? How does the Earth radiation influence human health? How does one find healthy food in an urbanised society? What cosmological developments occur in the Solar system and beyond?" (*Energo Klubi*, translation by the author.) The club stresses the practical side of the education they seek in order to benefit the individual's life.

The Estonian Geopathic Society (*Eesti Geopaatia Selts*), which is the focus of this article, bases itself on inquiry into traditional geology-bound dowsing. The main activities, as laid down in the association's charter, are:

- To study Earth fields and their influence on our body.
- To study and describe the physical and psychic reactions of organisms to Earth fields.
- To find possibilities to use Earth fields and related phenomena in order to heal the body. (EGS.)

The Estonian Geopathic Society was formed as a research group at the Institute of Geology under the Estonian Academy of Sciences at the end of 1980s (due to the easing of the political climate) with the intention of creating a uniting network that included sympathisers from other Baltic research institutes and universities. Within this cooperation, 16 "Earth Fields and their Influence on Organisms" conferences have taken place in Estonia, Latvia, and Lithuania. For each meeting, a volume of abstracts and articles is published and the collection of them forms a body of various ideas relating to environmental 'anomalies' that are reasoned to be special points of energy, fields and networks of lines (see Kivari 2015). Thus, the study of Earth fields within the research group has brought together a network of academics – from the fields of geology, medicine, physics, agriculture and psychology – to link their frontiers and move towards the promising theory that, apart from having a practical outcome, dowsing could possibly also have metaphysical significance. The first printed volume of articles, from the seminar in Salaspils, Latvia in 1990, was dedicated to ecology and the mutual relationship between human and the environment. The articles proposed mathematical models from the signals obtained by dowsing methods used when investigating water veins or other "anomalous zones", descriptions of "phon fields" and the "psycho-physiology" of the dowser. The practice of dowsing was given centre stage; the motivation was the challenge to establish systems, models and relevant descriptions of supernatural contact between man and nature. The attempt to build up an interdisciplinary network for the study of the dowsing phenomena was based on the recognition of the complexity of human experience as well as the endeavour to bridge the disparate nature of scientific inquiry into a "holistic" whole.

However, at the end of the 1990s academic and experimental dowsing was replaced with some resignation of interest and change of focus among leading thinkers. In 2003 the Society was officially registered on an independent basis. This is not only a technical detail but also reflects the fact that interest in dowsing changed within this society and on the wider scene due to the various influences of the new millennium, particularly the emergence of distinct New Age professionals and the commercialisation of the sphere.

Thus the questions of such clubs address directly to the "problem of disenchantment". Apart from attempting to gain knowledge about nature – are questions that touch directly on the split between the discourses where individual experience is used as an argument. The alternative stream of thinking works in two ways. Firstly it provides a unifying approach to the bits and pieces of knowledge from general education. In this case the creativity of vernacular thinking moves towards a secure intellectually and experientially apprehensible worldview. However, from another viewpoint the alternative theories challenge the security of the dominant discourses of education, medicine, economics and politics. A speaker at a Geopathic Society gathering, an academic physicist by profession, illustrated the discussions of different groups in society with a parallel to the annual Soviet parades. Talking about legitimate 'official' knowledge and education, he said that, "it is like a march in front of the tribunes, after which a small frozen company stays behind in the corner for a shot of vodka and to talk about the things *as they are*" (FM 4, stress in original). With these two directions, the subjective and the personal, the non-normative aspect of culture is shared.

Supernatural Places: Geology, Hartmann's Net, Ley Lines and Beyond

Generally, the movements of dowsing rods, twigs or pendulums have been associated with surface geology, meaning that the power that deflects the rods and twists the twig is reasoned to be an emanation (in the form of some kind of radiation) from the geological forms of the ground. Such natural forms as faults or caves in the bedrock or underground water streams have sometimes been associated with, and at other times separated from, concepts of networks that cause similar features: peculiar forms in nature, the colour and shape of trees and plants, the impact of the environment on buildings and technology. In line with the continuous dematerialisation of understanding of nature, physics and physical fields, the explanations have been changed from magnetism, standing waves or just radiation to subtle energy, fields of information or accumulations of vital force.

German physician Ernst Hartmann (1915–1992) developed the idea of the network of invisible lines or walls in the environment via his interest in radiesthesy. Apart from initiating a research group for geobiology, he spread his ideas in various publications in the 1950s and 1960s, of which *Krankheit als Standortproblem* (1954) has been central. According to his theory these magnetic-like lines form a regular grid around the Earth along compass lines at a distance of approximately 2 metres; the negative effect they exert on living in a particular place is the reason for a higher rate of mortality in that place. The evidence of the Hartmann's net is seen on nature in the form of weak or dead trees in hedges, and cracks in the asphalt and in buildings. These harmful influences are concentrated in a Hartmann's knot, where two lines of radiation are said to cross. According to various printed and oral material, sleeping or working at a Hartmann's knot causes problems with health and technology and could even lead to fatal results. Although the network is often referred to as a theoretical concept, it is used as a dynamic reference for various vernacular interpretations.

Ley lines, as a relatively new concept in Estonia, integrate the boundaries of the material and immaterial worlds through the idea that the living world is influenced by the imperceptible flow of life-giving energy, which is in a dynamic relationship with material and social reality. The idea is reflected in the overall position that the history of a place is recorded at an imperceptible level. The history is mainly constituted of intense human emotions like joy, suffering, devotion, etc. Although the places under interpretation exist separately and each in its original history and particular physical form, the concept of the lines gives them a full spiritual meaning as being in relation with other such places, the cosmos, and people who are mediums. British antiquarian and photographer Alfred Watkins, to whom the term ley lines is attributed, sought the correlations between significant places. He wrote in the foreword of his famous 1922 publication *Early British Trackways*, "I had no theory when, out of what appeared to be a tangle, I got hold of the one right end of this string of facts, and found to my amazement that it unwound in orderly fashion and complete logical sequence" (Watkins 2004 [1922]: 5). He used a special angle which he placed on the map to find significant places from the Roman age that were connected by hill tracks and which explained the geographical patterns of culture. Thus, again, it is the connection and context that gave full meaning to the particular places.

Ley lines in the contemporary spiritual scene are related to the role of the mediums, people who can apprehend and 'read' these flows and who hold authority with global significance. Ley lines represent vital functions like water, population, politics, but also sacrality and the values of spiritual interrelatedness. Globalism is reflected in the importance of maps as well the networks of psychics, channellers and Earth healers.

The places which are connected with the lines, and the lines which give attention to special places give the framework to perception and explanation of the supernatural. However, the category of supernatural can be used in this case only as an analytical abstraction of various vernacular motifs: distinctive shapes of natural objects, visions and feelings which provide proof of transcendental forces, or existence outside of the dominant materialistic understanding of reality. These places and motifs fill the category of supernatural with experiences and stories as well as inspiration for further seeking. Hartmann's net and ley lines integrate the material and natural with the spiritual and cultural. The authority of the individual interpreter together with bodily experience binds the immediate with the ultimate frameworks of knowledge about the world. If one compares 'academic' dowsing, which still echoes in the charter of the Estonian Geopathic Society, with the interest in dowsing from the second decade of this millennium, a change in framework can be noticed in the interpretations of the places.

Networks of Nature and Tradition: Dowsers' Stories

The analysis below employs field material from meetings of the Estonian Geopathic Society recorded in Tallinn during spring 2012 and autumn 2013. The regular meetings usually include one or two presentations and an open discussion. All the speakers whose voices I have used here have a common background of experimental interest in dowsing and research into different "anomalies" during the first half of the 1990s. One of them reports no longer using dowsing rods, while the others are active within the Society or use the method for their private needs, consultation in the planning of buildings or other technical work.

The change of interest among these people appeared in around 1995. It is important to note the word 'interest' in this context. The curiosity for new information and novelty in explanation has a definite impact on the formulation of what could be called the tradition of modern times. The novelty in this case is not so much connected with the values of consumption, but rather the potential for inspiration and creativity in developing a meaningful understanding that implicitly or explicitly addresses the frameworks of knowledge or wider social institutions. Deepening individual interest in the theme is closely connected with personal authority, thus speakers at the Society's meetings usually have some kind of authority in the form of experience of dowsing, in their career path or knowledge of technology or science.

One of the speakers, an experienced dowser, reasoned his withdrawal from the experimental work through a lack of new information and the exhaustion of the theories and interpretations.

Until the year 1995 I was engaged intensively with the rod, at my home and elsewhere, in nature. I gained a solid picture of the objective reality that is found there, if we can call it objective – it is disputable of course. It does not fit within any known physical field. To explain it with the electromagnetic field, standing waves, whatever is diffusing from the surface – these things just do not fit together. This structure that is figured out there is completely different.

> [...] There is equipment for everything! But I have a feeling that they [the impulses that various pieces of equipment are able to register] are secondary effects. Somehow, I gained an understanding that these features... streams of water, fissures..., [geological] structures... that the *thing* [in Estonian '*see asi*', the source of the impulse] locks itself into some kinds of crack. If there is a tiny crack in the ground, like water finds its way, this is not a reason but is a side-phenomenon. The fact is that you don't have, nor do I have, a trustworthy scientific explanation for this.
>
> But I can tell why I quit this enquiry in '95. It is somehow a funny reason. I was experimenting alone. And also, experienced in science, and you know..., the experiments do not always succeed. For different reasons. The power fails, something falls down, this kind of thing. But if you are experienced in experiments, then you have a special feeling when this happens just occasionally, or when somebody wants to screw you. And if I got that feeling that somebody spitefully interrupted my carefully designed experiments, I thought, it's better to end it. (FM 4.)[2]

Another speaker refers to a supernatural presence in the process of investigating dowsing. The limits of knowledge, sometimes as motivation, sometimes as warning, often appear in dowsers' accounts of their experiences.

> Perhaps there is a functioning, breathing system behind this. The system could be hidden from us, that's why the research is impeded. For some obscure reason... the worker dies, dying is very typical. If V. [a geologist interested in dowsing and other alternative theories] writes in his notebook after visiting the boulder in A. that "I came to understand what it is all about", and he is dead after four days... It means, we do not have to mystify all this, but I want to stress that we in our childish capability can move towards getting to know the complex natural system that we shouldn't touch and change. Because the knowledge could be relevant for us in a sense that we cannot yet predict. [...] I know a scientist who says that he does not start his experiments before thinking how it looks from the [supernatural] Other's point of view [*teiselt poolt*]. He is an experienced person already. Because if you are a hunter and go out and lay out your traps, you can catch a fox. But if it is a werefox? Who is laying traps then? [Laughs] That's why the people who show themselves off in the esoteric world are funny... (FM 3.)[3]

The researcher or dowser who stands at the border of the known and unknown worlds must be conscious and responsible about the consequences of the experiments and generalisations he or she is making. The distinction between 'Us' humans, and the 'Other' as the world of unknown powers and motivations is contested by powerful social frameworks and authorities. In different accounts of approaching 'supernatural places' – places that give rise to visions due to special energy, places with sacral meaning, connected with UFO sightings – the spiritual or professional ethos is often touched upon, as are career motives and knowledge.

> It was particularly interesting in the vicinity of Tuhala[4], where I was consulted about the plan for a new residential area. I was asked to set the future houses in the right places. I was looking around to see where the geological disturbances and good places were and my pendulum swung intensely in one place. Me: what

force [*jõud*] was that? I stepped back quietly and found that line of force [*jõujoone*]. And if I stepped off of that, the pendulum swung again: it showed me the place. It was three or four metres wide, very high-powered. Three or four houses were planned on that line of power; we set them aside. You cannot let people sleep there, only if you want some knowledge or wisdom, then, indeed, you can put your office on that line. (FM 1a.)[5]

Many dowsers do consult the planning of residential areas at the request of the developer or the owners of the property. The emergence of professional dowsing consultants in Estonia is closely connected with the activity of influential architect Rein Weber, who held the courses that introduced the use of pendulums. The courses gained extreme popularity in the period 1997–2005, and the inspired participants have since widened the dowsing scene with their business and hobby initiatives. Apart from introducing the pendulum as a tool for everyday practical use, Weber taught techniques for the elimination of existing negative radiation. The idea of radiation, and the possibilities of benefit to sleep or fruitful work offers a reflexive framework giving additional meaning to areas or buildings during construction. The conditions of intellectual or creative capability are sometimes associated with the conditions of sacrality or supernatural presence.

The idea of 'power' involves both the ability and dedication to intellectual work or religious devotion. Remaining at a particular location for a long time while sleeping or working is part of the concept of radiation. The influence, the 'geopathic stress', disturbs bodily functions, but creates the conditions for concentration.

For the dowser the context gives a particular interpretation: whether it is done for practical purposes or for personal interest. The technique of dowsing is often explained using the model of questions and answers. The dowser concentrates on water, the lost item, the person or time period and gets answers through the dowsing rods, pendulum or visions. For example, the speaker quoted last has different experiences in his work, although the discipline, geology, is behind his interpretation and binds the natural, geographic and individual into one vision.

[As well as different types of place] there are also so-called wormholes in spacetime. I was investigating the sacred grove of Kunda hill with some people, and travelled around in the region in Viru-Nigula. In front of the chapel ruins of Maarja-Magdaleena[6] I suddenly felt that I must purify myself from everything and forget my physical body. And about 2–3 metres before the entrance I saw that there was no chapel, nothing. I saw a big stone, there were 12 bonfires burning, men and women were dancing there dressed in canvas clothes, there were chickens, children running around. I somehow realised that this is 3000 years ago, that this Catholic chapel is built on an Estonian sacred site. (We were visiting the place with the Geopathic Society, and you are right, we measured the circle, the chapel is exactly inside the circle.)

I have seen the map of Estonian geological faults [*geoloogilised lõhed*] and the map of ancient forts: almost all [forts] are situated at the crossing points of faults. (FM 1a.)

The ruins of St. Mary's chapel in Viru-Nigula are dated as the oldest chapel in the northeast region of Estonia. The chapel, which was built at the beginning of the 13th century, has not been in use since the Reformation and is now a tourist sight and the destination for annual Catholic pilgrimage. Thus the sacrality is presented through remote history. The sacred places that are free of definite institutional affiliation are more easily used as the scene for individual religious expressions and interpretations.

The speaker refers to the popular idea that the continuation of sacred places from pre-Christian to contemporary times is the result of their location at special energy points. The division between negative and positive radiation explains the situation of the ultimate presence of sacrality in front of the altar or entrance to the building. Therefore church altars are placed at the positive energy column whereas the rest of the space is rather negative. By means of this division, dowsers explain the feeling of exaltation or relief in front of the altar. Energy as the marker of the mutual relationship between human and environment is reflected in the principle that people can "load" places with their social activity or religious devotion; and vice versa, places with the meaning and personal sacrality can become "stomped" if too many people visit them.

Although none of the speakers initially saw any direct relationship or correlation between such visionary experiences, geology and energies, they came to see this through dowsing. The theory of geological faults, energy lines crossing, the possibilities to apprehend remote places or times form the dynamic body of the dowsing tradition within which interested dowsers can produce the inspiration for further experiences. In this, visions of pre-Christian feasts have national-romantic colour, although they reflect the alternative to urbanised, global culture with a Christian background.

Another example refers to the story of many Estonian farmhouses: to the mass deportation of people to Siberia during the Stalinist regime.

> I got to know these things while dealing with geopathy. There were many times I visited old farms, old houses, so called sacred places, and... constantly the subjects come to me. This means, I see them. All this geopathic side has its influence, although I have not done any particular research to see how it may be connected. But I came to this through dowsing practice.
>
> As often happens, a farmer invites me – come and check my well, it's dry. I go and check the well, although I do not like dealing with wells. And apart from what I came to see – hey, did you know that there are friends [The speaker uses the word *tegelased* which could also be translated as protagonists, characters, used with an unceremonious tone of speech] living here! Where did you get that house, is it your family's house? – No, I bought it during the Soviet time! – But I see that the owners are still here, and they are angry at you. The owners were deported to Siberia and came back. So that's it! That's why there is such a mess. Luckily there are also farms that have gone from generation to generation within the same family, there are a real parade [of bygone generations]. If the young people are doing well, everything shines brightly. So in such cases in definite places different realities strike together in real time. It could have such consequences that we cannot estimate and of course everything is not equally measurable. (FM 2.)[7]

The continuation of ownership: the masters of the farms, villages or sacred groves often appear in such visions. Access to supernatural authority is possible through dowsing practice, the dowser's ethos and the medium's social approval.

Usually the visions reflect the specific location, continuity and national values. Although seemingly similar to the idea of a uniting network of energy lines, ley lines present the global viewpoint. As said previously, ley lines are associated with the practice of dowsing on maps, which is performed when identifying connections that could reveal the pattern of and therefore access to sacrality. The concept of ley lines is not very widely used in Estonia and distribution of the idea through the Internet and other international sources is evident. Despite this, a distinguished member of the Estonian Geopathic Society, a psychic, channeller and healer, presents herself with the ability to repair the lines. She is in contact with international sympathisers and receives and shares the messages of her visionary company about her mission to keep ley lines working in order to secure the flow of life-giving energy. Because of her strong orientation towards visionary prophetic experience, she has a controversial position in the society that reflects interest, sympathy as well as open negation and stigmatisation.

At the end of the society's meeting she often gives some news from her field. She reports that she is on a mission to take care of ley lines, which ensure that the global functions of world water, ecology, peace and population progress smoothly. The network of "line-keepers" shows the ultimate interconnectedness of the world and that ideas about ecology and the conflicts of big politics are increasing humankind's spiritual values.

> My first conscious work of reparation was in 1997 in Cyprus, I was invited there for a conference about the Earth's negative radiation. I had a presentation there and then a message was given to one Canadian woman that L. [the speaker] needs to go to an old church and repair the energy line. This was the line of Michael [*Miikaeli liin*], which passed that location. They had measured that location using their equipment and the energy was negative. When I had done my work, the line turned strongly positive. They asked, what will happen now, will there be peace between Israel and Palestine... There was no peace, but the peace negotiations started for the first time in history. Later I asked is this line broken or what, why is there still no peace. They said, you want things to be as you want, it is too soon. There are locks of time laid upon this, if these are removed, there will be peace and the line will then be working fully. (FM 1b.)[8]

A certain religiosity within globalism rests in the distribution of individual authority. People see personal responsibility within the wider system, which builds up and enhances their spiritual activity. The interconnectedness of the local and global, as well as different time periods, is an empowering issue for the medium. However exceptional within the Geopathic Society in Estonia, the channeller can also be associated with the global movement of Earth healers (see for example Bowman 2007: 308).

> What disrupts these ley lines? Ley lines are disrupted by negative energy: by wars, plundering, torture and so on. For example, lately I was sent to Pskov to fix the lines. It was said that I had to do it during this winter. I'm not familiar with Pskov, I don't know its places and history. Thus I looked at the map from Google and my hand immediately recognised the lines and crossings. I found the place, drove there and there was a monument with an inscription saying, "Here was a German concentration camp during 1941–1943 where 65,000 Russian soldiers were tortured and killed." I stood there and I saw dark grey, with a purple line in the grey. The marks of torture and killing are still visible at the line. And when I had done my deed I saw that the line rose up high, shining, golden energy starting to flow there. (FM 1b.)

The interconnectedness of history and politics, ecological and supernatural security are reflected in the different layers of the medium's position. The authority and subordination of his or her responsible position between global and local provide the fertile ground for new and emerging interpretations. Appropriation of sacredness links distant places in supernatural reality. This reality is determined by the flows of energy and information and the possibilities of access to this energy via the medium.

The lifecycle of the plot can be understood through the creative potential that they involve. Thus, vernacular theories, which are in connection with larger social systems of knowledge, provide ideas for further negotiation. Energy and information, as the powerful keyword of contemporary economy and politics, work as metaphors between material and immaterial reality. The possibility that reality is determined by subtle signals encoded with important aspects of principles that could bridge the spiritual and natural worlds touches again on the "problem of disenchantment". Visions, dreams, bodily impulses as well as vernacular practices related to the universal and natural seek a position for the individual, intimate and local.

> Post-war science was dealing with materials and energetics. At the same time, E. P. [influential military engineer during the Soviet period] noted that the keyword is still informatics, that we live in a transition period and are moving towards subtle signals and fields. This means that the period of tenderness [*lembesignaalide ajastu*] is approaching and the time of strong signals and energy is coming to an end. Sensitive, psychic or medium: does he catch electrons or protons? It could be so that the information is coded in the universe. The idea was favoured by Baltic Germans in the Estonian Metapsychic Society[9] during the interwar period. They were of the opinion that conifers and sedimentary rock can record subtle signals, thoughts or feelings because they contain resin and have a mineralised structure. It is hard to imagine the record of thoughts, but the recording of the emotions could be sensible. Tragedies, mass murders and collective misery could accumulate; this was their explanation for why ghosts appear in stone houses in old towns. (FM 1c.)[10]

The last paragraph reflects the efforts to find generalised knowledge, although the position he refers to is not the subject of mathematical logic from which a distinct rule can be deduced. As a vernacular idea that has links to ghost stories and understanding of the chemical structure of materials it provides the inspiration for further inquiry and interpretation. He stresses the importance of subtle signals, which explain the various folkloric reports of supernatural experiences. The phrase 'tenderness' reflects the tellers' position on dowsing practice and practitioners. The supernatural world, with these tender signals as signs of the new age, build up a new cosmology based on vernacular authority.

Conclusion

The article has brought together various periods from the history of the idea that people with dowsing rods or pendulums are able to apprehend what is in the ground and within the environment. Apart from the continuation of the very motives of dowsing practice, the principle of the Earth as a living body has found a continuation within vernacular thinking on the connecting lines that create supernatural reality through various associations.

Such concepts as energo-information, fields of information, biocommunication, etc., have broadened the interpretations within dowsing so that it has changed from a miners' lore to a wider investigation of the supernatural. Adrian Ivakhiv (2007: 277) has used the term 'conceptual glue' for the notion of energies as the bonding agent between different sources, ages and places. Applying the concept of uniting lines of subterranean water or the network of energy flows, the dowser creates sacral meaning in particular places through connections. By doing so these places become evidence of a supernatural reality, whereas the source of this quality is somewhat larger and drives the inquiry of enthusiasts towards various notions. Traditional place-lore is a highly valued source for those seeking patterns in the landscape, because the popular idea that people in ancient times had sensory abilities that have been lost in urbanised societies of modernity. Thus the presence of dowsing signal, 'energy', was more easily apprehensible and was more a part of everyday decisions. As an alternative to the mainstream rationalistic worldview, these connections often build up a new spiritual cosmology in which the position of the individual is at the same time threatened as well as empowered by the appearance of the supernatural.

The position of individual tradition-bound authority in parallel with the institutional 'scientific' system of knowledge illustrates explicitly the context for contemporary vernacular thinking. Asprem refers to the process of disenchantment as a projection that should be looked as though it is an emerging and continuous set of problems that exist between tradition, religious and scientific authorities. The dowser as a medium reveals the messages of supernatural reality while at the same time being a researcher into the unknown that touches on the cosmological position of the individual. In doing so, he or she formulates the principles of the otherworld, which somehow construct a new theology using plausible techniques, meanings and, most importantly, explicit ethics which stresses local, traditional, nonviolent and environmental values. The dynamics and interconnectedness of the local and global, religious and practical with the concept of Earth energies and ley lines outlines the very nature of the debate on a spiritual worldview where the positions of the natural and supernatural are discussed.

At the same time, the discussion touches the question of authority, which is measured by the validity of information. "The concept of vernacular authority is based on the idea that any claim to being supported by tradition asserts power because it seeks to garner trust from an audience by appealing to the aggregate volition of other individuals across space and through time. [...] Vernacular authority emerges when an individual makes appeals that rely on trust specifically *because* they are *not* institutional." (Howard 2013: 80–81.) The "alternatives" take the problems of disenchantment as a starting point and framework of orientation.

Writing about the constitution of nature as a folklorist, I have placed myself at the centre of the "problems of disenchantment". I favour the recognition of Barbara Walker who states that, "regardless of how conceptualisations are formed, they are formed by nature and are, at best and always, limiting, compromising, and accepting of a particular way of thinking. A leap of faith is necessary whenever we adhere to any system of thought, whether it means relying on pi or some other unknown". (Walker 1995: 2.)

Webs of lines enable to make webs of associations which do not necessarily follow the legitimate pattern of an officially approved worldview. Despite this, when doing research on the tradition a number of influential sources, such as history, politics and economics, which describe the official worldview from different angles, come into the discussion.

Notes

* This research has been supported by the European Union through the European Regional Development Fund (Centre of Excellence, CECT) and by the Estonian Ministry of Education and Research (Institutional Research Project IUT2–43).

1 A literal translation from the phrase in Estonian *Mind huvitavad need asjad; tegelen nende asjadega.*
2 The speaker was involved in the work of the Society during the 1990s. As a physicist by profession he was asked to give a lecture on the recent developments in physics that could have connections with phenomena relating to dowsing.
3 A member of the Society with the life-long interest of investigation of paranormal phenomena. Author of articles and books.
4 Tuhala is a region in North Estonia, which is famous for geological and archeological peculiarities. The area is under landscape protection due to its carst features, pre-Christian settlement is seen in numerous cultic stones, burials and in *Hiie*-toponyms which reflect the place or vicinity of sacred grove. The locals have also popularized the area as full of strong energy columns. (About the energies in Tuhala, see Kivari 2012.)
5 A dowser and author of presentations and articles on the Society's conference. He gives advice on planning as well as integration of knowledge of the energies with touristic routes at his home-region.
6 Although the speaker refers to the ruins as being dedicated to Mary Magdalene, historically the chapel is dedicated to St. Mary (*Viru Nigula Maarja kabel*).

7   The dowser, who has been involved with experiments on dowsing inside the farming buildings, cowsheds and storehouses. He was asked to speak about his various experience in dowsing.

8   A psychic and channeller who is engaged with the international web of "line-keepers". A healer and author of two books.

9   Estonian Metapsychic Society (*Eesti Metapsüühika Selts*) was an organisation which dedicated its activity to the investigation of psychic phenomena: magnetism, telepathy, clairvoyance during 1932–1940. The society held popular seances and lectures. (Abiline 2013: 56.)

10 The same speaker as indicated with FM 3 recorded on different meeting.

Sources

Fieldwork material

Material used in this article is part of my doctoral project exploring the concept of Earth energy, its different uses, personal stories and practices. I have been engaged in the work of Geopathic Association since the beginning of 2012. The meetings are held once in a month in Tallinn in addition to the various lectures and practical events that are organised on the wider esoteric and alternative culture scenes.

FM 1, recorded on 3.04.2012. The meeting was dedicated to the concept of ley lines. Three speakers were invited from among members of the Association. (FM 1a, FM 1b, FM 1c)

FM 2, recorded on 3.09.2013

FM 3, recorded on 8.10.2013

FM 4, recorded on 5.11.2013

Literature

Abiline, Toomas 2013. Uue vaimsuse eelkäijad: antroposoofia, teosoofia, vabamüürlus ja parapsühholoogia Eestis 1918–1940. In *Mitut usku Eesti* III. Marko Uibu (ed.). Tartu: Tartu Ülikooli Kirjastus. Pp. 37–78.

Agricola, Georgius 1912 [1556]. *De Re Metallica*. Herbert Clark Hoover, Lou Henry Hoover (transl.). London: The Mining Magazine.

Asprem, Egil 2013. *The Problem of Disenchantment. Scientific Naturalism and Esoteric Discourse 1900–1939*. Doctoral thesis. University of Amsterdam, Faculty of Humanitites.

Besterman, Theodore 1926. The Folklore of Dowsing. *Folklore* 37(2): 113–133.

Bowman, Marion 2007. Ancient Avalon, New Jerusalem, Heart Chakra of Planet Earth. The Local and the Global in Glastonbury. In *Handbook of New Age. Brill Handbooks of Contemporary Religion* 1. Daren Kemp & James R. Lewis (eds.). Leiden, Boston: Brill. Pp. 291–314.

Dégh, Linda 1995. *Narratives in Society. A Performer Centered Study of Narration.* Folklore Fellows Communications 255. Helsinki: Academia Scientiarum Fennica.

Dym, Warren Alexander 2008. Scholars and miners. Dowsing in the Freiberg Mining Academy. *Technology and Culture* 49(4): 833–859.

Dym, Warren Alexander 2011. *Divining Science. Treasure Hunting and Earth Science in Early Modern Germany*. Leiden, Boston: Brill.

EGS = Webpage of Estonian Geopathic Society (Eesti Geopaatia Selts). Avilable at http://geopaatia.ee/ [Accessed December 4, 2016]

EMS = Webpage of Society for Research into Ancient Knowledge (Eesti Muinasteaduste Selts). Available at http://ems.ee/avaleht/ [Accessed December 4, 2016]

Energo Klubi = Webpage of Energo Club (Energo Klubi). Available at http://klubi. energo.ee/ [Accessed December 4, 2016]

Fara, Patricia 2008. Marginalised practices. In *The Cambridge History of Science. Eighteenth Century Science* 4. Roy Porter (ed.). Cambridge: Cambridge University Press. Pp. 485–505.

Howard, Robert Glenn 2013. Vernacular Authority: Critically Engaging "Tradition". In *Tradition in the Twenty-First Century. Locating the Role of the Past in the Present.* Trevor J. Blank & Robert Glenn Howard (eds.). Colorado: Utah State University Press. Pp. 72–99.

Ivakhiv, Adrian 2007. Power Trips: Making Sacred Space through New Age Pilgrimage. In *Handbook of New Age. Brill Handbooks of Contemporary Religion* 1. Daren Kemp & James R. Lewis (eds.). Leiden, Boston: Brill. Pp. 263–286.

Kivari, Kristel 2012. Energy as the Mediator between Natural and Supernatural Realms. *Journal of Ethnology and Folkloristics* 6(2): 49–68. Available at https:// www.jef.ee/ index.php/journal/article/view/98 [Accessed April 16, 2018]

Kivari, Kristel 2015. The Theory of the Earth Energy: Academia and the Vernacular in Search of the Supernatural. *Implicit Religion* 18(3): 399–422.

Müürisepp, Karl 1960. *Ebatavaliste loodusnähtuste teaduslik seletamine. Annoteeritud loenguplaan koos vajaliku kirjanduse loeteluga.* Tallinn: Poliitiliste ja Teadusalaste Teadmiste Levitamise Ühing.

Norris, John 2006. The Mineral Exhalation Theory of Metallogenesis in Pre-Modern Mineral Science. *Ambix* 53(1): 43–65.

Norris, John 2007. Early Theories of Aqueous Mineral Genesis in the Sixteenth Century. *Ambix* 54 (1): 69–86.

Rudwick, Martin 2005. *Bursting the Limits of Time. The Reconstruction of Geohistory in the Age of Revolution.* Chicago, London: University of Chicago Press.

Walker, Barbara 1995. Introduction. In *Out of the Ordinary. Folklore and the Supernatural.* Barbara Walker (ed.). Logan, Utah: Utah State University Press. Pp. 1–7.

Watkins, Alfred 2004 [1922]. *Early British Trackways. Moats, Mounds, Camps and Sites.* Providence: Resurrection Press.

Weber, Max 1946. Science as a Vocation. In *From Max Weber: Essays in Sociology.* H. H. Gerth & C. Wright Mills (eds., transl.). New York: Oxford University Press. Pp. 129–158.

Regional Variation, Environment and Spatial Dimensions II

FROG

When Thunder Is Not Thunder; Or, Fits and Starts in the Evolution of Mythology[*]

Thunder is a sound, a resonance that can sweep across the sky and cause walls or even the very earth to tremble. It is an event that exceeds any natural human capacity. When it reaches us, like any sound, the sound of thunder is recognised as an outcome. However, the agent, act or circumstance that produces a sound of such magnitude and pervasive scope remains invisible in the atmosphere and can only be approached through the capacity of imagination. In modern Western cultures, we have become naturalised to thinking in abstractions. In other cultural environments, the abstract would be primarily rendered by and conceptualised through symbols: 'thunder' is correlated with an imaginal[1] image through which it becomes understandable rather than remaining an incomprehensible unknown. In historical cultures where thunder was an ecological reality, it emerges as a fundamental mythic image, which may be surprisingly concrete. This does not mean that there is no abstract conceptual model of 'thunder' in such cultures. Instead, the image provides a concrete and yet flexibly ambiguous signifying representation through which a conceptual model is communicated, manipulated and negotiated. Simply put, the image provides a way of thinking about thunder, talking about it, and situating it in relation to other things.

Mythic images become bound up with mythic motifs, cultural practices and traditional narratives. The constellations of relationships with one another that these form become characteristic of a mythology. Changes in cultural practices and dominant ideologies impact on images and motifs and how people interact with them, and these impacts may cascade through the constellations in which the elements of tradition participate and through the broader system of symbols in the mythology. In cultures of the Circum-Baltic area, for example, 'thunder' was conceived as a being, a god. The mythic image of this god and the relevance, social significance and relationships of thunder to other things in the world were dialectically constructed and construed through cultural practices. The image of the god was characterised as striking 'devils', 'trolls' or mythic agents considered malicious or hazardous to humans and human cultural order. These beings were equally imaginal mythic images characterised by, for example, fleeing before thunder, and they could be correlated with concrete symbols, such as the dog as an image of the devil (cf. Valk 2001: 112–113). Accordingly, it becomes only natural that thunder will strike dogs or that someone running during a thunderstorm might be mistaken for a devil and be struck dead. In 19th-century Estonia, the mythic image of thunder began to be reimagined as scientific thinking penetrated the discourse, but reimagining thunder did not (immediately) dissolve thunder's relationships with different images, motifs and narratives: imagining thunder as electricity could lead to reimagining dogs as magnetic with a continuity of the motif that thunder strikes dogs (Valk 2012: 55, cf. 53); imagining thunder as an atmospheric phenomenon could lead to reinterpreting taboos against running as related to causing movements in the air that attract thunder, with nothing to do with 'devils' (Valk 2012: 53, 58–59, cf. 52, 61). Numerous images and conceptions of thunder have held currency around the Baltic Sea over the centuries, from thunder as an innate power of a god to its identification with an object-attribute such as a chariot or shifting emphasis from thunder to the lightning-weapon in the form of an arrow, axe or hammer.

Mythic images, motifs and narratives are shaped and maintained through and in relation to social practices. The present article explores these patterns of adaptation and transformation through the case of a particular mythological plot type, the so-called Aarne–Thompson–Uther (ATU) tale type ATU 1148b, or "The Theft of the Thunder-Instrument" (labelled "Thunder's Instruments" in Uther 2004 II: 48–50). ATU 1148b is interesting in this regard because it appears to have been prominent in the multicultural Circum-Baltic arena and to have become established quite widely, although it initially took shape around an image of thunder as produced from some form of musical instrument. This underlying image of thunder is otherwise historically quite obscure and was superseded by alternative images in different cultures. The plot appears historically interfaced with conceptions of the relationship between thunder and mythic agents hazardous to cultural order (simply referred to as 'devils' hereafter). It also appears interfaced with relationships between thunder and rain and between thunder and fertility or life on earth. Nevertheless, the plot and its characteristic elements were also adapted to a broad range of other uses that made them current and relevant for contemporary cultural practice.

The present discussion of variation and adaptation builds on two earlier studies: a survey of sources for ATU 1148b that was concentrated on the question of historical relationships between them (Frog 2011) and a subsequent study concentrated on medieval Scandinavian evidence of the plot (Frog 2014). Here, focus turns to sustainability of the ATU 1148b tradition in changing cultural contexts. A structural approach to variation is applied to examine the development of the tradition in fits and starts of innovation as opposed to evolution on a more fluid continuum of historical change. Attention is given to exceptional examples of the narrative and will gradually turn to two cases in which the ATU 1148b tradition became attached to a local landscape and the implications of this for the narrative's sustainability. The Sámi identification of the narrative with a sacred site was briefly addressed in the initial survey (Frog 2011: 81). The Norwegian case of Thor's Road was not and will receive a more developed discussion here.

Terms and Concepts

Before introducing the tradition and discussing variation, it is first necessary to briefly review and formalise the terminology and concepts used here. This is essential to the structural aspect of the investigation because terms like 'motif' are frequently used flexibly or ambiguously; if terms are not formalised, distinctions made here will blur into one another.

Myth is here considered in a broad sense as "a form of *knowing*" (Doty 2000: 55–56, original emphasis) rather than as a narrative genre (cf. Doty 2000: 49). It is characterised by a quality of signification in social practice (cf. Barthes 1972 [1957]: 109; Lotman & Uspenskij 1976). Thus a myth may be symbolically centralised as a particular narrative or identity (for example, the story about the Crucifixion of Jesus; the identity of thunder as a masculine god with blazing eyes), but a myth may also be an abstract conceptual model interfaced with many traditions in different ways (for example, the conceptions that thunder strikes devils and that devils run from thunder). The quality of myth characterises symbols and structures that engage emotionally invested paradigms for thinking (cf. Doty 2000: 55–58) or social resources with which to think (Lévi-Strauss 1962: 128). The term *conceptual model* is here preferred for the social phenomenon often referred to as a 'belief'; belief is here regarded as an individual subjective engagement with the conceptual model, which may equally be contested (cf. Dégh & Vázsonyi 1976 [1971]: 109). The term *mythic* is used to qualify any element (image, motif, narrative pattern, etc.) that is socially characterised by engaging one or more myths. These mythic elements will here be regarded as symbols, observing that any unit of tradition that can be referred to and addressed as a whole can also be meaningful as a whole and thus act as a type of sign or symbol. This is no less true for a plot as complex as "The Theft of the Thunder Instrument" than for the identity of a god.

A symbolically *decentralised* mythic element engages a myth without social conventions of exclusivity – i.e. the particular symbol or complex of symbols is not socially equated with a particular story about a particular god or event. Decentralised mythic elements are associable with categories (GOD, HERO; small capitals indicate symbolic elements) or 'types' (cf. motif-types, tale-types) as well as what I call *symbolic partials* that carry connotations according to patterns of use in a culture or tradition although they do not appear independent of more complex images or motifs (for example, WINGS, HORNS, SUPERNATURAL SPEED). A symbolically *centralised* mythic element is socially characterised by exclusivity in engaging a myth: MONSTER may present a decentralised mythic image whereas a particular mythic monster such as the Christian DEVIL presents a centralised mythic image recognised as a unique identity. A centralised mythic element may present a specific exemplar of a broader, decentralised element and dialectically inform its significance. For example, THOR STRIKES GEIRRØDR is a centralised motif of Thor's defeat of a particular giant that functions as one manifestation of the broader decentralised motif THUNDER STRIKES DEVILS, of which it was also a prominent exemplar. Where no broader decentralised element is socially current, alternative use of a centralised motif will index its conventional context referentially (thus in modern cultures, a motif of crucifixion unavoidably indexes the motif or at least the image of the Crucifixion of Jesus). Certain roles and functions like THUNDER-GOD are structurally exclusive and both require a symbolically centralised element and simultaneously inform its identity. Such roles and functions may link symbolically centralised elements as equivalent across cultures, such as THOR, PERKUNAS and ST. ELIJAH being equivalent symbols for THUNDER-GOD in their respective linguistic-cultural and religious contexts. Structurally exclusive roles and functions should be distinguished when assessing variation across cultures or in relation to cultural change.

Mythology is here considered a socially maintained matrix of symbolic resources, through which myths are engaged, communicated and negotiated, and also the constellations, structures and conventions for combining those symbolic resources (see further Frog 2015). The term *mythological* (as opposed to 'mythic') is reserved for elements characterised by belongingness to imaginally constructed places and/or times beyond the present world order, although they may penetrate into the present world order. According to this approach, belief legends, taboos and so forth engage myths through mythology, but legends are differentiated from narratives traditionally referred to as 'myths' by their engagement with symbolically decentralised rather than centralised mythic symbols and by identification with the present world order (even if the present world may be penetrated by mythological elements such as the thunder-god).

Mythic symbols are socially constructed, associated with one or more areas of cultural competence, and emotionally invested with the quality of myth. Mythic images and motifs are here considered as minimal symbolic elements of mythology and approached according to a metaphor of language. A *mythic image* is static and corresponds to the category of a noun. It may be a complex, symbolically centralised mental representation (for example, THOR, HELL), although not all of its features will necessarily be realised in any single expression (see, for example, Siikala 2002: 47–56). However complex or simple, it will be qualified as a unit whole (systems of conventionally co-occurring images can be distinguished as *image systems*). A *motif* is dynamic, incorporating a correspondence to the category of a verb phrase. It can be approached as a type of construction (Goldberg 2006), which incorporates one or more images in a coherent relationship. The degree of flexibility of a conventional motif will vary on a spectrum from a highly crystallised prefabricated 'chunk' of narrative or a particular constellation of open-class items, which may also participate in an ontology of degrees of abstraction or centralisation, such as HERO SLAYS MONSTER → THUNDER STRIKES DEVIL WITH LIGHTNING-WEAPON → THOR STRIKES (GIANT1, GIANT2, GIANT3, GIANT*n*) WITH MJǪLLNIR (his hammer).

Less crystallised motifs can be described as having *open slots*, each of which can be filled by an appropriate *slot-filler*.[2] Open slots in a motif may be characterised by symbolic partials that complement the slot-filler(s) (for example, colour, images, object-attributes, etc.). The open slots are also fundamental to interfacing the motif with the context in which it appears. For example, the open slots in the motif HERO SLAYS MONSTER will be contextually

140

conditioned regarding who fills the HERO slot, whether the protagonist or someone else, and potentially also concerning the MONSTER slot. Although individual motifs may be more or less flexible with regard to the images that they relate to one another, it will nevertheless remain characterised as a conventionally atomic unit of significance like a formula in language (cf. Wray 2002). As such, mythic motifs in particular reciprocally characterise their slot-fillers (although changing conventions in and interpretations of the slot-fillers will eventually affect the meaningfulness and associations of the motif). Mythic images and motifs will, as a rule, conventionally interface with one or more conceptual models, even if the precise interfaces may be adapted over time (cf. the change in THUNDER from an agent to electricity that yields a reinterpretation of DOG above). Accordingly, the same motif may be realised in narrative and also be an *immanent motif* – imagined as something that can happen in the world because the motif is the symbolic realisation of an underlying conceptual model of how forces in the world work (for example, THUNDER STRIKES DOG or FLEEING DEVIL). As a consequence, the potential for the motif to happen can shape behaviours through taboos and so forth.

A *theme* is a system of conventionally associated images, motifs, constructions and/or sets of equivalence classes of these that provides a resource for realising a unit of action, description or other aspect of performance during narration (cf. Propp 1968 [1928]: 12–13; Arend 1933; Lord 1960: 68–98; Frye 1968). Whereas images and motifs are characterised as atomic meaningful units, a theme is characterised as an immediate constellation of meaningful units (or equivalent sets of such units) and strategies, structures and conventions for their combination (including, for example, the repetition of a motif with variation). Individual themes may vary in flexibility and crystallisation and be more or less centralised. Themes appear to take conventionalised shape in relation to structural units of narration in which they occur (cf. Lord 1960: 198). This reciprocally conditions the conventional size of a theme as a unit, which can be hypothesised not to conventionally exceed the scope of a scene, even if conservative conventions of reproduction link themes in a regular series. A *scene* is a structural unit at the level of narration comprised of one or more themes and/or complex(es) of images and motifs as well as the connecting tissue with which these are realised. Changes in scene in narration can be generally identified by changes in participating characters, setting or circumstances (Hymes 1981: 170–175). In the comparative study of a plot type, it is possible that a scene may be recognised and discussed abstractly through a characteristic theme, but the scene can still be distinguished as a unit of narration of the plot type as distinct from the theme as a resource for realising it. Within narration, a scene may be characterised by semantic or pragmatic functions that could potentially be realised through different themes. A *narrative pattern* is a constellation of elements (images, motifs, themes and/or equivalence sets of these), their organisation and interrelations, forming a coherent sequence, although not necessarily constituting a plot forming a narrative whole. An *act* is a unit of narration constituted of one or more scenes that forms a coherent sequence which constitutes a stage or episode in the development of the plot (cf. Hymes 1981: 175). An act of a conventional narrative will be characterised by a narrative pattern. A conventional *plot* or *plot type* is here an abstracted constellation of elements (images, motifs, themes and/or equivalence sets of these) along with their organisation and interrelations that characterise a complete narrative from complication to resolution.

When addressing specific examples and the forms taken by ATU 1148b, the term *variant* will be used for individual entextualised examples while *version* will refer to the form of the narrative being entextualized; where a distinct version has become socially established, the socially established version will be referred to as a *redaction* of the tradition (a term which has been controversial in scholarship, but remains practical and familiar).

When addressing variation, a final practical term and concept is *centrality*, used to describe the number and degrees of interfaces with and dependencies on a compositional element, conceptual model or some quality of these (cf. Converse 1964). Centrality may be primarily semantic, such as bravery in the identity representation of Thor as a mythic image (Schjødt 2013: 12–13), or pragmatic, such as the mythic image and conceptual model of the thunder-instrument in ATU 1148b. Centrality is a factor that affects the social establishment of adaptations and variations within a tradition. In the following discussion, attention will be given to the distinction between adaptations that appear to remain exceptional or unique and those which become socially established.

ATU 1148b: "The Theft of the Thunder Instrument"

Forms of ATU 1148b were found across both Uralic (Finno-Ugric) and Indo-European cultures, attested among Baltic, Finnic, North Germanic and Sámic linguistic-cultural groups in a Circum-Baltic isogloss (see Frog 2011; 2014). Neither the plot nor the underlying conceptual model of thunder can be attributed to either an Uralic or Indo-European linguistic-cultural heritage. The tradition thus spread cross-culturally and also established a new model for thunder in all these cultures. Historically, ATU 1148b was a symbolically centralised mythological plot about a particular adventure of the thunder-god, and its mythic quality was maintained through its adaptations for (remarkably diverse) aetiologies in all but branches of Scandinavian and Sámic traditions. An isolated Greek example was also recorded in ca. 500 A.D. Although not relevant to the present discussion per se, this example's historical and geographical remoteness from the Circum-Baltic traditions was significant for assessing the historical fundamentals of both the plot and conception of thunder underlying the various forms of ATU 1148b.

Earlier surveys and studies of this tradition were carried out using the Historical-Geographic Method, beginning from comparisons between Scandinavian and Estonian traditions (Olrik 1905: 140–146), followed almost immediately by comparisons with Sámic (Olrik 1906) and then North Finnic traditions (e.g. Krohn 1922: 202–207; see also Loorits 1932; de Vries 1933: 99–124; Anderson 1939). The medieval Scandinavian form in eddic verse, referred to as the 'Thor-bride redaction' below, was then considered a primary form which passed into other cultures during the Viking Age or later. During the Second World War, J. Balys (1939: 33–43, 206–209) introduced the Lithuanian traditions and single Latvian attestation. He considered the plot to have spread from a Scandinavian tradition, but its form in eddic verse to be derivative of an earlier form closer to that found in Finland and Karelia. However, Balys' work, written in Lithuanian, never penetrated discussion (cf. Bertell 2003: 185–190). Not long thereafter, Uku Masing (1944) identified an early Greek example, which paralleled the more complex form of the narrative found in Estonia, but this also failed to incite a critical reassessment of the historical primacy of the Scandinavian Thor-bride redaction (see e.g. Schröder 1965: 28). This comparative direction of study did not continue after the War, and the discussion remained largely dormant for about half a century (until, on the Greek example, Hansen 1995; 2002: 305–314; see also Masing 1977: 124–129). When the Scandinavian material was finally reassessed, medieval evidence of a Scandinavian ATU 1148b parallel to the Thor-bride redaction came to light (Frog 2011: 87–91; 2014: 135–142). A model for the history of ATU 1148b traditions was developed that is consistent with current understandings of how folklore and mythology spread and transform over time.

The plot of ATU 1148b initially had at least two acts: the first act concerns the theft of the god's 'instrument' used to make thunder; the second concerns the recovery of the stolen object and the defeat of the adversary. The following outline is based on forms of the narrative found in South Finnic (North Estonian, South Estonian and Seto), North Finnic (Finnish and Karelian) and evidence of the Scandinavian traditions as well as the Greek example; parentheses indicate elements not attested for all groups but that are probable for historically earlier forms of the tradition at least among Finnic and Scandinavian groups (on Sámic, Latvian and Lithuanian traditions, see further below):

Act I. *Scene 1:* A devil steals the sleeping thunder-god's musical, mechanical or symbolic instrument and conceals it in his realm or home. (There is no rain and everything in the world begins to die.) *Scene 2:* The god assumes the disguise and role of a servant, entering the service of a master (with whom he has a fishing adventure). (*Scene 3:* The master is invited to a wedding in the home of the devil.)

Act II. *Scene 1:* (The god and his master attend a wedding in the home of the devil.) The devil brings out the god's instrument. The devil (and/or guests) cannot play the instrument successfully (owing to insufficient strength). (A challenge is initiated by either the host or by the god through his master.) The host unwittingly provides the instrument to the god, expecting a positive return (entertainment). The god plays successfully, destroying the host, household and/or otherworld community (sparing his companion). *Epilogue:* (The god's master is returned home unharmed and) the god returns to his role of thunder-god in the sky.

The role of thunder-god can be considered structurally exclusive. It can be inferred that, in the process of cross-cultural transmission, the image of the vernacular thunder-god became identified with this role. This image was subsequently displaced by the vernacularised image of St. Elijah (*Ilja*) among the Seto, an Orthodox culture of southeast Estonia and adjacent Russia,[3] while the protagonist is ambiguously referred to as 'god' (*jumala*) in North Finnic examples (and in the Latvian example), which allowed a Christian interpretation. The plot interfaces the role of the adversary with social structures (with the hall and celebration) and predicates the image of the adversary with physical strength less than that of the god. The image filling this role nevertheless appears to have been informed by vernacular categories with no indication of a centralised mythic image of the adversary being transmitted cross-culturally. However, several aspects of a conceptual model of thunder are integrated into the plot:

1. Thunder is produced by an object-attribute that can be taken from the thunder-god and concealed while he sleeps.
2. The object will not sound or not sound correctly unless worked with sufficient strength.
3. The object can be literally or metaphorically 'played' as a musical instrument.
4. The object can be unwittingly presented to the god with expectations of positive entertainment.
5. Without the object, the god remains disempowered against his adversary.

In Greek, for example, this object is called an ὄργανον αὐτοβόητον ('self-playing instrument') (*Dionysica* I.432), which nevertheless does not sound correctly when played by Zeus' adversary, who is said to lack sufficient strength. The centrality of the model of thunder to the pragmatics of the plot's structure inhibits the range of mythic images that can fill that role without prompting an adaptation of the plot itself. It may be noted that lightning seems generally to have been conceptualised as being implicit in thunder or vice versa rather than thunder and lightning as being paired and complementary symbols. In other words, the god will normally *either* have a thunder-instrument *or* a lightning-weapon, but not both. Accordingly, aetiologies of lightning can be regarded as linked to implicit aetiologies of thunder.

South Finnic ATU 1148b Traditions

Only South Finnic traditions maintained a conventional aetiology of thunder from a blown instrument 'played' by the god.[4] There is an apparent correlation between the currency of this conceptual model and both the number and complexity of ATU 1148b variants that were recorded (see further Loorits 1932; Anderson 1939; Frog 2011: 82–83). Nevertheless, the image of thunder from a blown instrument was not the most culturally central model (see Loorits 1949–1957 II: 7–27), and the number of documented examples remains comparatively small when this plot-type was of such interest to folklore collectors (Loorits 1932: 95).

South Finnic variants of ATU 1148b exhibit distributions of historically established redactions by region as well as more localised innovations. In one variant, for example, the devil is envious of the god's instrument and steals it. Both the devil's characteristic fear of thunder and emphasis on hostility between thunder and the devil are absent. The narrative concludes abruptly following the successful theft as an aetiology of the devil's association with bagpipes. (Loorits 1932: 63–64.) This example presents formal continuities of the theme of the theft (including its images and motifs) that characterise Act I Scene 1 of ATU 1148b. However, the theme is resituated in relation to an alternative opening with different motivations of the devil and follows it with an alternative outcome. This resituates the material at the structural level of narration with the consequence that it should not be considered the same 'scene' in such a broad comparison. Moreover, the ambiguous mythic image of the thunder-instrument (normally simply *pill* ['instrument']) is reinterpreted and exchanged for a concrete conventional image of bagpipes (*torupill*). Although the example could be a humorous play on ATU 1148b, a mythic quality of the theme is still reflected through its use for an aetiological narrative. This version is unique in the corpus and never appears to have become socially established.

ATU 1148b also appears to be reflected in a potentially unique legend: after a great deal of flashing lightning, a devil was seen fleeing with a horn and hiding beneath a stone, after which the god followed the devil under the stone; the god returned with the horn, mentioned as having a broken edge and lightning blasted the stone (Loorits 1949–1957 II: 23–24). This legend manifests motifs of thunder hunting the devil and thunder striking a stone. Motifs and the sequence of movements between spheres or worlds drawn from ATU 1148b are presented as a fantastic happening observed by a shepherd, and thus they are collapsed into a rapid series of localized events as they would be seen from the perspective of that observer. The motif of the theft (Act I.1) must be inferred, although it is relevant to understanding the significance of the images. The description of the god following under the stone parallels the god travelling to the devil's realm and recovering the thunder-instrument before returning to the sky (Act II). However, there is no disguise (Act I.2) and presumably no hosted celebration (Act II.1). The blasting of the stone follows the god's return to the sky rather than occurring in the context of the recovery event itself (Act II.1), which allows it to be observed by the witness. It is not clear in this example whether the horn is the source of the lightning or only the sound of thunder; the informant concludes that the sound of thunder during the rest of the storm "rang just like a blast from an instrument with a broken edge" (Loorits 1949–1957 II: 23–24). The legend presents implicit evidence of the opening and concluding motifs of ATU 1148b and its series of movements between worlds, but these are collapsed into a simple theme that eliminates intermediate material of the plot. This use in a legend seems not to have become socially established.

Oskar Loorits (1949–1957 II: 18) similarly mentions a legend in which it thunders and lightning blasts severely between two springs, and when the storm has passed a black dog with a red rifle on its neck is seen running from one spring to the other. Loorits interprets the black dog as a devil and the red rifle as the thunder-instrument / lightning-weapon stolen from the thunder-god. His interpretation is reasonable, but it is dependent on recognizing the symbols BLACK DOG = DEVIL, RED RIFLE = THUNDER-/ LIGHTNING-ATTRIBUTE and the motif DEVIL POSSESSES THUNDER-ATTRIBUTE as necessarily an outcome of the motif DEVIL STEALS THUNDER-ATTRIBUTE within a broader theme and narrative pattern associated with ATU 1148b. In one respect, this and the preceding uses of this type may seem to blur the distinction between whether ATU 1148b was a centralised or decentralised plot. However, it might be best regarded as referential use of the centralised plot linked to mythic time which then provides a frame of reference for interpreting the events told in the legend. It may nevertheless be observed that the motif DEVIL POSSESSES THUNDER-ATTRIBUTE differs from the motif THUNDER STRIKES DEVIL in that the former is interfaced with a particular theme and narrative pattern whereas the latter is not, allowing greater flexibility in its range of uses and potential for manipulation.

North Finnic ATU 1148b

Evidence of Finno-Karelian traditions is in general more uniform than South Finnic ATU 1148b traditions, although it had already fallen almost completely out of current use (see Frog 2011: 82). Examples are oriented to humour and rarely mention the devil's fear of thunder while the theft is often implicit or stated as a sentence. The thunder-instrument is referred to by the obscure term *jyristimet* ('things which thunder'), which seems unique to this narrative. The mythic image remains rather ambiguous and conformed to the narrative structure. It could potentially be identified as a hand-mill (cf. Krohn 1922: 203; Frog 2011: 91–92) and should be regarded as an archaism. Acts I and II have been collapsed into a single sequence: the counter-role of the fisherman with whom the god enters service in Act I is identified with the counter-role of the host in Act II. The motif of the god taking a (disguised) role as a servant thereby accounts for the god's entry into the devil's household. This adaptation obviates the separate role of the fisherman, and the devil becomes the god's companion on the fishing adventure. It also obviates the invitation and the context of a celebration in the devil's home: the disguised god accomplishes a series of strength feats which conclude with working the *jyristimet*. The uniformity of the structure of this ATU 1148b tradition is striking because it suggests that an innovative adaptation produced a condensed form of ATU 1148b that became socially established and then spread, perhaps, if not probably, with Finnic language's spread during and since the Viking Age (on which, see Frog & Saarikivi 2015: 88–98).

The one exception to the uniformity of the Finno-Karelian tradition realises the socially more central mythic image of the thunder-wagon as the stolen thunder-attribute. Integrating this image seems to have motivated a restructuring of motifs and themes. This adaptation appears to have integrated the motif of the theft, otherwise not normally realised

146

as an independent scene, with the motif of the god entering the house of his adversary as a servant: the devil enters the house of God as a servant, inverting their roles. As in the aetiology of the devil's association with bagpipes above, the narrative does not continue with an Act II: the devil unleashes the destructive power of the wagon (rather than causing drought) and this is presented as an aetiology of God's hostility toward devils; the recovery of the stolen attribute is not mentioned. It is uncertain whether this version of ATU 1148b was ever socially established as a distinct redaction.

Medieval Scandinavian Branches of ATU 1148b

Scandinavian ATU 1148b traditions were predominantly documented in the medieval period, which leaves only vague reflections of the tradition in often problematic sources. I have discussed the two major branches of this tradition and its sources more fully elsewhere (Frog 2014). One branch of development (considered primary) appears to have associated ATU 1148b with the thunder god Thor's adversary Geirrøðr (for discussion, see Frog 2014: 135–142). However, the material is only clearly manifested in a mytho-heroic adventure of a human hero Thorsteinn *bœjarmagn* ('Thor-Stone Mansion-Might') in *Þorsteins þáttr bœjarmagns* ('The Tale of Thorsteinn *bœjarmagn*'). The hero obtains a magical weather-producing object (Guðni Jónsson & Bjarni Vihjálmsson 1943–1944 III: 400–402), which is associated with Thor's hammer through particular motifs, but this is never stolen. Act I of ATU 1148b is completely absent. Act II is preceded by an alternative theme that establishes Thorsteinn as the servant of a giant who has been invited as a guest to a celebratory event in the adversary's hall, which Thorsteinn then enters unrecognised. The absence of the theft obviates the recovery of the stolen object, but Act II is otherwise fully realised, and even includes a performance with the weather-producing object for the entertainment of the host described with the verb for 'playing' a musical instrument (Guðni Jónsson & Bjarni Vihjálmsson 1943–1944 III: 412–413). In this case, the mythic image of the weather-producing object appears to be rooted in yet another conceptual model and image of thunder (symbolically associated with fire-striking) that can be considered a curious archaism when ATU 1148b was adapted for this heroic adventure. The adaptation of Act II for the construction of an adventure of a human hero was one of several strategies in the narrative to correlate the image of Thorsteinn with the image of the god Thor through correspondence of their roles in mythic motifs.

The most famous branch of ATU 1148b is the Thor-bride redaction, familiar through the eddic poem *Þrymskviða* (see further Frog 2014: 142–154). This tradition manifests the basic motifs and structures of ATU 1148b but with radical variations. The image of the thunder-instrument has been displaced by the lightning-weapon, which is ransomed in exchange for the goddess Freyja. Introducing Freyja provides an essential condition for the thunder-god to be disguised as the bride at a celebration rather than as the servant of an invited guest. In contrast to other redactions of ATU 1148b, the disguise explicitly humiliates the god. Consistent with the

ATU 1148b tradition, the invited guest (or rather bride) is passive while an accompanying character disguised as his/her servant orchestrates the action. However, the roles have been exchanged so that Thor is passive and Loki, disguised as his servant, orchestrates the action. This redaction also exhibits marked inconsistencies with belief traditions. Most strikingly, the thief appears not to fear thunder: ransoming the lightning-weapon for the goddess suggests that the stolen object will be returned. Similarly, destructive thunder is produced by the god's chariot when he travels following the theft, which contrasts with the fundamental loss in ATU 1148b and its symbolic significance (connected to rain, fertility and the natural order of seasons). The mythic image of thunder is juxtaposed with the god's transvestite disguise *from the perspective of the poem's audience* while remaining unacknowledged by the giants. The Thor-bride redaction appears to engage the symbolic resources of ATU 1148b in the manner of parody, contesting myths about thunder as opposed to communicating and reinforcing them (potentially targeted precisely because of the archaic and obscure image of thunder and metaphor of 'playing'). This innovation carried the plot resource in a new direction that established it in a function of secular entertainment. This comical adaptation produced a form of ATU 1148b that was viable in a Christian milieu: it became the only known Scandinavian ballad to handle a mythological subject (Liestøl 1970: 15–18; cf. Jonsson et al. 1978: 252; Frog 2014: 146–147, 152–154). The secular functions of this resource in medieval and later Scandinavia enabled its sustainability. This same process affected the plot and its motifs, dislocating their mythic quality to the point that the protagonist was not necessarily a god at all.

The Lithuanian Tradition

At the southern periphery of the Circum-Baltic isogloss, examples of ATU 1148b were only recorded in the 20th century (see further Balys 1939: 33–43, 206–209; Frog 2011: 84–86, on the Latvian example, see Frog 2011: 84). The conceptual model of thunder produced by a musical instrument seems to have proven unsustainable and the plot seems to have broken down entirely without an alternative image adapted to the pragmatics of its structure. The motif of the theft appears in the production of legends especially about the origin of the thunder-god Perkūnas hostility toward devils. Although the object that the adversary steals from the god may symbolically correlate with the lightning-weapon or be identified as some other attribute of the god, Perkūnas retains the actual lightning-weapon and uses it to strike his adversary. For the purpose of the narrative, the stolen object therefore need not be recovered. The motif of ATU 1148b appears to have become a decentralised plot resource, although its mythic significance continued to be reflected in its use for aetiological narratives.

ATU 1148b in Sámic Traditions

At the northern periphery of the Circum-Baltic isogloss, evidence of Sámic ATU 1148b traditions is extremely limited. Relevant narrative material is only found where the god is called *Termes/Tiermas* ('Thunder') (cf. Rydving 2010: 97–98, 101–102). It seems to have been adapted to a conceptual model of thunder as an innate power of the god rather than a separable object-attribute (cf. Frog 2014: 126; cf. also Masing 1977). Only one example of the mythological narrative is known, recorded with sayings that correlate the image of the bound god with drought. The image of the god became identified as the object of the theft and the locking away of 'thunder', which produced a redaction with the god's capture and imprisonment, although this part of the narrative is not preserved (if it was ever significant). The god's activities following the 'theft' in Act I and Act II became pragmatically unviable. Act II maintains the recovery of 'Thunder' (liberating the god) accomplished by the role of a servant who has entered the house of the adversary. When 'thunder' is identified directly with the god ('Thunder'), rather than with a mechanical or musical object-image, the motif or theme of the servant being challenged to make the object function for the entertainment of the host cannot be realised. In its place, the core motif of Act I Scene 1, the theft of thunder while the possessor sleeps, has been integrated: the servant releases (steals back) 'Thunder' while the adversary sleeps. Thunder then punishes his adversary, who had desired drought, with seven weeks of rain and he returns fertility to the earth.

Although only one account of the mythological narrative is preserved, additional examples of the mythic image of imprisoned thunder and the motif of thunder's release by the servant of his mythic adversary support the earlier circulation of some form of this redaction of ATU 1148b. Skolt Sámi fairy tales integrate this theme into a tale about a servant of the devil who is forbidden to enter a single chamber (cf. tale-type ATU 312), in which the imprisoned god is revealed, and in exchange for his release, Thunder fills the role of a magic helper in a Magic Flight theme (ATU 313, see Frog 2011: 81). This mythic motif may also have been assimilated into South Sámic (legends associated with) shamanism, according to which the god is unbound to fill the role of a helping spirit (cf. Bertell 2006; Frog 2011: 81). Unlike the mythological narrative and sayings about 'bound thunder' recorded with it, these uses of the motif do not identify the god's imprisonment with a lack of rain. The Magic Flight theme, in which Thunder helps the servant flee his pursuing adversary, is also inconsistent with deep-rooted conceptual models of Thunder as a striker of devils (cf. Rydving 2010: 93–95). These uses of the liberation theme subordinate the god to human agency paralleling roles normally associated with different categories of being: this image of Thunder is not the same as the image of the god in the mythological narrative. They also dislocate the god from associations with rain, fertility and his role as striker of devils. They suggest that the mythological narrative no longer had widespread currency and presumably had not been current for some time.

The mythological narrative was told with reference to the sacred and sacrificial cave on Thunder's Island in Thunder's Lake, which is on the southern end of Lake Inari. This cave was identified as the location where the god was held captive. The identification of the narrative with a specific site in the landscape provided the plot-resource of ATU 1148b with an aetiological function, which encoded it in the landscape. It accounted for the sacredness of the cave, but the situation of this cave on an island in a lake connected to the huge Lake Inari would also almost certainly have been viewed in relation to the seven weeks of rain with which the god punished his adversary; the story made the landscape itself a manifestation of the god's power. Information about the capture of the god is not relevant to this function, which explains its absence from the documented source (if not from the tradition). The aetiological function appears to have given the narrative relevance and significance even to those who might not subscribe to its literal truth. The identification of the narrative with a site in the landscape appears directly connected to the maintenance of the plot as a mythological narrative.

Thor's Road

One of the legends of the loss and recovery of Thor's hammer accounts for the origin of a road cutting through a large scree called Urebøe near Lake Totak in Telemark, Norway.[5] This narrative has remained peripheral to discussions of ATU 1148b traditions (cf. Grimm 2012 [1880] I: 181 n.1), and it has been dismissed as a unique local curiosity (e.g. Christiansen 1958: 88). It is first attested in Engelbret Michaelsen Resen Mandt's 1777 manuscript *Historisk beskrivelse over øvre Tellemarken*. In this account, "Toer Trollebane" ('Thor Troll-Bane') is described as a troll who intrudes on a wedding celebration. His appetite for beer proves insatiable and the wedding party stops serving him, with the exception of one man who provides a keg of his own. Thor is angered by this hospitality. He takes the man to safety and smashes the mountain so that the village is buried in a landslide. Thor then digs out a farm for the man, but he struck so hard with his hammer that its head flew from its shaft. An agreement is made with the man that if 'he' (the man?) finds it again, 'he' (Thor?) will clear a road through the scree; the hammer is found and the road is cleared. (Mandt 1989 [1777]: 54–55.) Johann Michael Lund (1785: 186) describes the landslide covering a church and village, suggesting familiarity with some sort of local legend, and Wilhelm Maximilian Carpelan (1824a: 24–25 = 1824b: 227) mentions that Thor caused the landslide in anger, lost his hammer and created the road called "Thors Vei" ('Thor's Way') while searching for it, but there is no mention of the wedding scene or other cause of Thor's rage. A potentially idiomatic expression found in personal correspondence from the year 1824 may also refer to this tradition (Olsen 1955). A second version of the narrative, also including the toponym, was published by Andreas Faye in 1833. This version claims that there were two weddings. The "gud Thor" ('god Thor') was served with casks at the first and an ordinary bowl at the second. The bridal pair who served him with casks is taken to safety with their guests while everyone else is destroyed. The hammer is said to slip from the Thor's hand and the road is a by-product of his search for it. (Faye 1833: 3–6.) Faye's account appears to be independent of Mandt's and was affirmed by at least one reader according to the post-script in a later edition (Faye 1948: 5). However, Faye (1833: 5) clearly clearly edited his narrative according to his antiquarian interests, for example referring to Thor as "Asgards stærke gud" ('strong god of Ásgarðr') and situating him anachronistically in a pantheon. This contrasts with Mandt's account, where Thor is identified as a troll, opening the question of to what degree Faye may have edited other elements of the narrative.

Of the two acts in which the legend appears structured, the second act describes the loss and recovery of the head of the hammer (Mandt) or of the hammer itself (Carpelan, Faye), resulting in a road through the devastation of the landslide. The loss and recovery of the thunder-god's thunder-attribute is so exceptional in the Circum-Baltic area that it is improbable that this tradition is wholly independent of ATU 1148b, although the attribute is identified here with the lightning-weapon as in the Thor-bride redaction (and symbolically in Lithuanian versions). Its use in an aetiological legend is also consistent with adaptations of ATU 1148b in the other cultures discussed above. In this case, the narrative plot appears reduced to a simple theme perceived from the perspective of the human world (cf. the South Finnic legends). Framing it in the human world situates Thor as an otherworldly outsider while identifying the celebration event with the human in-group community. The change affected in the god's counter-role eliminates the mythic adversary and may be directly related to the adaptation of the theft motif to the accidental 'loss' of the object. The use of ATU 1148b material appears subordinated to the origin of the road, which the legend explains.

The first act describes the god (troll) visiting a wedding, destroying a wedding party, and producing a landscape feature. This follows a narrative pattern equivalent to Act II of ATU 1148b, perhaps with interference from a motif of an encounter with an uninvited otherworldly guest.[6] Variations appear attributable to the shift in perspective affected by adaptation to a legend and pragmatic outcomes of the absence of the motif of the theft as an instigating event. This eliminates the motivation for visiting the celebration (recovering the stolen object), and consequently eliminates the associated disguise and need to secure an invitation to the celebration, which may be a factor in meeting the companion at the event rather than arriving with him. The narrative pattern of Thor visiting an otherworld hall or celebration at which he is hosted badly, performs feats (including drinking, as in the Thor's Road legend) and destroys his host, is found in a number of mythological narratives (cf. McKinnell 1994: 57–86). This could therefore potentially have been adapted from other adventures of Thor, yet examples of the narrative pattern form a constellation interfaced with ATU 1148b, which may be at its foundations (Frog 2011: 87–91; 2014: 135–142). When this co-occurs with the theme of the loss and recovery of the thunder-attribute or lighting-weapon, the legend appears most reasonably explained as an adaptation of ATU 1148b. This adaptation appears to have developed in specific relation to a landscape aetiology that accounts for the destruction of a village and church by a landslide and a road and place for a farm in the otherwise devastated area.

The association of the legend of Thor's Road with ATU 1148b does not resolve whether it is an adaptation from the primary form of ATU 1148b or the Thor-bride redaction. The Thor-bride redaction spread throughout Scandinavia in the ballad tradition and was prominent in this region: seven of the fourteen Norwegian variants were recorded in Telemark. However, the ballads emphasise humour through the humiliation of the transvestite disguise, absent here. There is also a structural difference between the two branches of the Scandinavian tradition in the relationship between Thor and his companion: in the Thor-bride redaction, the companion accompanies Thor from among the divine in-group community; in the other branch, as in the South Finnic tradition, the companion is outside of that community and is an invited guest of the celebration (see Frog 2011: 87–91). Structurally, the theme of the companion as an invited participant in the celebration who is met there and then saved from the destruction of everyone else corresponds to the narrative pattern of ATU 1148b traditions other than the Thor-bride redaction. In the Thor-bride redaction, the god and his companion are paired figures forming a complementary unit on the basis of an established relationship in the mythology. In other ATU 1148b traditions, these engage first as a role and counter-role developing a new social relationship with an unequal power relation in which the god is superior. Without these factors, the Thor-bride redaction also lacks an explicit motif of distinguishing the companion as a friendly 'other' who should not be killed along with everyone else, a motif prominent in the Thor's Road legend. In addition, the Thor-bride redaction exhibits no evidence of engaging belief traditions. There is no reason to believe that the ballads would maintain the mythic quality of the motifs, themes and story-pattern of ATU 1148b, and this would normally seem to be a qualifying precondition of their adaptation to describe a mythic origin of something. Conversely, the motifs and their relationships align far more directly with evidence of the broader ATU 1148b tradition and with the account in *Þorsteins þáttr* in particular (even down to the thunder-attribute as a two-part object in Mandt's version). Nevertheless, the Norwegian legend was clearly considered comical when it was recorded (Faye 1833: 5), like the ballads and also like the medieval *Þorsteins þáttr*.[7] The most probable explanation for this legend is that it is a local ATU 1148b tradition that was not dependent on the Thor-bride redaction. This suggests that another version of ATU 1148b was current parallel to the Thor-bride ballads at the time when this legend took form. It also suggests that the attachment of the plot to a feature of the local landscape as a (potentially humorous) aetiology established a function that enabled its longer-term sustainability while the ATU 1148b tradition on which it was based disappeared.

Perspectives

The ambiguity of symbols associated with mythology seems to be fundamental to their long-term sustainability as valuable and interesting resources. The preceding review highlights that the multiformity of a tradition and the diversification of its conventional forms and uses facilitates its long-term sustainability (in some form). On the one hand, variability enables the potential for individuals to adapt a tradition to new circumstances where it is considered useful and interesting to do so. On the other hand, diversification enables the plot resource to be maintained in one or more social contexts or functions as it disappears from others. In the case of ATU 1148b, its history appears to have been characterised by transformations and adaptations that occurred in fits and starts. The narrative was adapted, reinterpreted and revised by individuals and negotiated its form and meaning within and across communities. The potential of this tradition to be an adaptable plot resource is attested by the number of its unique variations and the range of genres with which it became connected. Most variations never became socially established, advancing from a distinct version to a distinct redaction: it is not enough that one person is willing and able to adapt or revise the plot resource, updating it to social and cultural circumstances or using it in a new way. In order to become socially established, a variation or adaptation must be engaged *socially* and advance into circulation (cf. Converse 1964; Frog 2013a: 109–110).

If the long history of ATU 1148b in the Circum-Baltic is accepted, this means that the different conventionalised forms of the plot in different genres, regions and cultures are the result of precisely this sort social engagement on a repeated basis. Hence, the spread of innovations within communities and across networks of communities *diversified socially circulating forms of the tradition*, with the outcome that some of these *superseded and/or assimilated locally established alternative redactions* as a historical process. The uniformity of the one-act North Finnic traditions is most probably attributable to the spread of an alternative dominant form of the narrative (cf. Frog 2013b: 87–89), probably oriented more toward humour and adventure than belief traditions. Similarly, the use of the theft as a decentralised motif in the Lithuanian tradition appears to reflect the social spread of a generative strategy that enabled the plot resource to maintain interest and relevance. The preserved forms of these traditions are only outcomes of the long and labyrinthine history of ATU 1148b that must have had many historical strata of such transformations both within each culture and presumably across cultures as well.

Social changes and the rise of Christianity incited a recession and reassessment of mythological narrative plots. The diversification of ATU 1148b was key to its sustainability in those changing environments, although especially in a medieval Christian milieu these could not be wholly disentangled from the discourse on (and against) paganism. Adaptations of the plot which could be handled as purely secular proved to be sites of sustainability. This is exemplified by the Thor-bride parody spreading with the ballad through medieval Scandinavia from Iceland to Sweden to gradually become a dominant and even exclusive form of ATU 1148b in most cultural areas. ATU 1148b presents a peculiar story, and seems in several (Finnic and Scandinavian) cases to have maintained archaic images and conceptions of thunder. That peculiarity may have been a significant factor in its overall sustainability. The suspension of such mythic images suggests that the specific aetiology of thunder was secondary to functions of the narrative (for example, as a portrayal of the god's power, the significance of thunder to rain and life in the world, the relationship between thunder and devils). However, the peculiarity seems also to have made it interesting and entertaining as a resource. Evidence of ATU 1148b suggests that, in all of these different cultures of the Baltic Sea region, the threads that bound this plot resource up with belief traditions were rapidly fraying. Perhaps the greater number of the variants is concerned with its potential for humour and as an adventure story about the god. On the other hand, the archaic mythic images which are suspended in the narrative make it reasonable to wonder how long it may have been carried along on precisely such fraying threads, and whether the true blow to this tradition was the changing emphasis and centrality of narratives about the thunder-god in an increasingly Christian environment. Amid these processes, no doubt far more alternative adaptations and diversifications of this plot-resource emerged than we can perhaps even imagine – adaptations that just as quickly disappeared. However, attachment of the narrative to the landscape provided a distinct function that could be sustained even where stories of the thunder-god might otherwise be ideologically controversial. In the Sámi case, this may have been an identification of the events of the mythological narrative itself with a particular place, whereas in Norway it may have been a more extreme and comical adaptation. In both cases, the permanence of landscape features lent their endurance to the telling of these tales in a community, enabling a disappearing myth the possibility to survive.

NOTES

* This paper presents research developed in the project The Generation of Myth in a Confluence of Cultures, funded by the Kone Foundation and the Finnish Cultural Foundation, and completed within the framework of the Academy of Finland project Mythology, Verbal Art and Authority in Social Impact of Folklore Studies, University of Helsinki. I would like to thank Anna-Marie Wiersholm of the Norsk Folkeminnesamling and also Terry Gunnell for their assistance and support in investigating the Thor's Road legend. I would also like to thank Ülo Valk and Daniel Sävborg for their many comments that have greatly strengthened this article.

1 The term *imaginal* is used in this article as an adjective meaning 'engaging use of the imagination'. This differs slightly from conventional uses of the adjective *imaginary*, which customarily denotes 'a product of imagination; lacking empirical reality'. The distinction being made here has two significant features. First, the separate term helps avoid the implicit opposition between 'real' and 'imaginary'. Second, it places emphasis on the relationship to imagination as a process rather than as a product. Together, these features facilitate considering the 'imaginal' aspect of understandings irrespective of their relationship to modern scientific research. Put simply, the difference between understanding the world as flat or the world as round is not a difference between one being 'imaginary' and the other being 'real': both are imaginal images of the world that provide frames for thinking and understanding in the same way; the difference between them is how each of these images correlates with frameworks of scientific thinking.

2   This model is in some respects similar to the 'motifemic slots' and 'allomotifs' that
    fill them described by Alan Dundes (1962). Dundes' model is based on the same
    principles applied here, but it differs in three significant respects. First, Dundes'
    model was developed on the earlier ambiguous use of the term 'motif' within a plot
    type, which could be an image, motif or theme. His term 'allomotif' is thus formally
    ambiguous and becomes problematic in the current framework. Second, Dundes's
    model is descriptive at the level of a corpus rather than considering variation in
    practice, with the consequence that it does not differentiate between synchronic
    variation and variation between historically established redactions. Third,
    Dundes's model was intended only to account for slot-fillers that are traditional
    elements which can vary with one another. The present model is developed to
    distinguish units of different formal types and their relations to one another, and
    it accommodates slot-fillers that are not traditional (e.g. THUNDER STRIKES
    HIDING DEVIL [under this stone right here]; [I, my neighbour, someone at
    school, STRONG JOHN] SEES GHOST).

3   The exchange of a vernacular image for St. Elijah in the structurally exclusive role
    of thunder-god is commonly observed across Orthodox areas (cf. Loorits 1949–
    1957 II: 24). This phenomenon is also found in Orthodox Karelia, although not
    uniformly. See also Harvilahti 2013.

4   Loorits 1932: 109–111; 1949–1957 II: 22–23. This should be distinguished from the
    identification of the thunder-god as playing a drum in tale-type ATU 1165, where
    drumming does not produce thunder (cf. Loorits 1949–1957 II: 26–27; Uther 2004
    II: 57–58; Frog 2011: 86–87).

5   I am thankful to Mathias Nordvig (p.c.) for drawing this narrative to my attention
    at the "New Focus on Retrospective Methods" conference (Bergen, Norway, 13.–
    14.09.2010).

6   Cf. the common motif Q1 "Hospitality Rewarded – Opposite Punished" (Thompson
    1955–1958). Olav Bø et al. (1981: 265–266) observe a possible parallel in the story
    of Philemon and Baucis in Ovid's *Metaporphosis* VIII, in which disguised gods
    meet with bad hospitality from everyone but two old men who provide hospitality
    and then the gods remove the two men to a remote location while all other homes
    are destroyed and theirs is turned into a temple. The parallel is striking but is not
    necessary to pursue in the present context as it is complementary to rather than
    a potentially relevant source for the elements associable with ATU 1148b.

7   The loss of the head of the hammer into the earth would also index thunder-stone
    traditions – i.e. the correlation of lightning with the image of a stone weapon of
    the god striking the earth and remaining there. In conjunction with this, the loss
    of the hammer quite possibly (if not probably) also humorously parodied beliefs
    that Thor's hammer miraculously returned to the god whenever thrown (Faulkes
    1998: 42), which is also identified with the magical object in *Þorsteins þáttr* (Guðni
    Jónsson & Bjarni Vihjálmsson 1943–1944 III: 400–402).

Sources

Anderson, Walter 1939. *Zu dem Estnischen Märchen vom Gestohlenen Donnerinstrument.*
    Tartu: University of Tartu.

Arend, Walter 1933. *Die typischen Scenen bei Homer.* Berlin: Weidmannsche
    Buchhandlung.

Balys, J. 1939. *Griaustinis ir velnias baltoskandijos kraštų tautosakos studija.* Kaunas:
    Tautosakos Darbų.

Barthes, Roland 1972 [1957]. *Mythologies.* New York: Hill & Wang.

Bertell, Maths 2003. *Tor och den nordiska åskan: Föreställningar kring världsaxeln.* Stockholm: Stockholms Universitet.

Bertell, Maths 2006. Thoor-olmai – den samiske åskgudens medhjälpare: Källäge och möjliga vägar att gå vidare. In *Sápmi Y1K: Livet i samernas bosättningsområde för ett tusen år sedan.* Andrea Amft, Mikael Svonni (eds.). Umeå: Umeå Universitet. Pp. 29–42.

Bø, Olav, Ronald Grambo, Bjarne Hodne & Ørnulf Hodne (eds.) 1981. *Norske segner.* Oslo: Det Norske Samlaget.

Carpelan, W. M. 1824a. Et Besøg i Fjeldstuen, 1823. *Magazin for Naturvidenskaberne* 2(1): 1–27.

Carpelan, W. M. 1824b. Et Besøg i Fjeldstuen, 1823. *Hermoder* 6: 213–231.

Christiansen, Reidar Th. 1958. *The Migratory Legends: A Proposed List of Types with a Systematic Catalogue of the Norwegian Variants.* Folklore Fellows' Communications 175. Helsinki: Academia Scientiarum Fennica.

Converse, Philip 1964. The Nature of Belief Systems in Mass Publics. In *Ideology and Discontent.* D. Apter (ed.). London: Free Press. Pp. 206–261.

Dégh, Linda & Vázsonyi, Andrew 1976 [1971]. Legend and Belief. In *Folklore Genres.* Dan Ben-Amos (ed.). Austin: University of Texas Press. Pp. 93–123.

Doty, William G. 2000. *Mythography: The Study of Myths and Rituals.* 2nd edn. Tuscaloosa: University of Alabama Press.

Dundes, Alan 1962. From Etic to Emic Units in the Structural Study of Folktales. *Journal of American Folklore* 75(296): 95–105.

Faulkes, Anthony (ed.) 1998. *Snorri Sturluson, Edda: Skáldskaparmál.* London: Viking Society for Northern Research.

Faye, Andreas (ed.) 1833. Thor og Urebø-Urden. In *Norske Sagn.* Arendal: L. A. Krohn. Pp. 3–6.

Faye, Andreas (ed.) 1948. Thor og Urebø-Urden. In *Norske Folke-sagn.* 3rd edn. Oslo: Norsk Folkeminnelags Forlag. Pp. 3–5.

Frog 2011. Circum-Baltic Mythology? The Strange Case of the Theft of the Thunder-Instrument (ATU 1148b). *Archaeologia Baltica* 15: 78–98.

Frog 2013a. The Parallax Approach: Situating Traditions in Long-Term Perspective. In *Approaching Methodology.* 2nd rev. edn. Frog, Pauliina Latvala, with Helen F. Leslie (eds.). Helsinki: Academia Scientiarum Fennica. Pp. 99–129.

Frog 2013b. Shamans, Christians, and Things in between: From Finnic–Germanic Contacts to the Conversion of Karelia. In *Conversions: Looking for Ideological Change in the Early Middle Ages.* Leszek Słupecki, Rudolf Simek (eds.). Vienna: Fassbaender. Pp. 53–98.

Frog 2014. Germanic Traditions of the Theft of the Thunder-Instrument (ATU 1148b): An Approach to Þrymskviða and Þórr's Adventure with Geirrøðr in Circum-Baltic Perspective. In *New Focus on Retrospective Methods.* Eldar Heide, Karen Bek-Pedersen (eds.). Folklore Fellows' Communications 307. Helsinki: Academia Scientiarum Fennica. Pp. 120–162.

Frog 2015. Mythology in Cultural Practice: A Methodological Framework for Historical Analysis. *RMN Newsletter* 10: 33–57.

Frog & Janne Saarikivi 2015. De situ linguarum fennicarum aetatis ferreae, Pars I. *RMN Newsletter* 9: 64–115.

Fryc, Donald K. 1968. Old English Formulaic Themes and Type-Scenes. *Neophilologus* 52(1): 48–54.

Goldberg, A. E. 2006. *Constructions at Work: The Nature of Generalization in Language.* Oxford: Oxford University Press.

Guðni Jónsson & Bjarni Vihjálmsson 1943–1944. *Fornaldarsögur Norðurlanda* I–III. Reykjavik: Forni.

Grimm, Jacob 2012 [1880]. *Teutonic Mythology* I–VI. Cambridge: Cambridge University Press.

156

Hansen, William 1995. The Theft of the Thunderweapon: A Greek Myth in Its International Context. *Classica et Mediaevalia* 46: 5–24.

Hansen, William 2002. *Ariadne's Thread: A Guide to International Tales Found in Classical Literature*. Ithaca: Cornell University Press.

Harvilahti, Lauri 2013. Ethnocultural Knowledge and Mythical Models: The Making of St Olaf, the God of Thunder, and St Elijah during the First Centuries of the Christian Era in the Scandinavian and Baltic Regions. In *The Performance of Christian and Pagan Storyworlds: Non-Canonical Chapters of the History of Nordic Medieval Literature*. L. B. Mortensen, T. M. S. Lehtonen (eds.). Turnhout: Brepols. Pp. 199–219.

Hymes, Dell 1981. *"In Vain I Tried to Tell You": Essays in Native American Ethnopoetics*. Philadelphia: University of Pennsylvania Press.

Jonsson, Bengt R., Svale Solheim & Eva Danielson 1978. *The Types of the Scandinavian Medieval Ballad: A Descriptive Catalogue*. Stockholm: Svenskt Visarkiv.

Krohn, Kaarle 1922. *Skandinavisk mytologi*. Helsinki: Holger Schlidts.

Lévi-Strauss, Claude 1962. *Le totemisme aujourd'hui*. Paris: PUF.

Liestøl, Knut 1970. *Den norrøne arven*. Oslo: Universitetsforlaget.

Loorits, Oskar 1932. *Das Märchen vom gestohlenen Donner-instrument bei den Esten*. Tartu: Gelehrte estnische Gesellschaft.

Loorits, Oskar 1949–1957. *Grundzüge des estnischen Volksglaubens*. I–III. Lund: Lundequist.

Lord, Albert B. 1960. *The Singer of Tales*. Cambridge: Harvard University Press.

Lotman, Jurij M. & Boris A. Uspenskij 1976. Myth – Name – Culture. In *Semiotics and Structuralism: Readings from the Soviet Union*. Henryk Baran (ed.). White Planes: International Arts and Sciences Press. Pp. 3–32.

Lund, Johann Michael 1785. *Forsøg til Beskrivelse over Øvre-Tellemarken i Norge*. Kiøbenhavn: Joh. Rud. Thiele.

Mandt, Engelbret Michaelsen Resen 1989 [1777]. *Historisk beskrivelse over øvre Tellemarken*. Olav Solberg (ed.). Espa: Lokalhistorisk Forlag.

Masing, Uku 1944. Die Entstehung des Märchens vom gestohlenen Donnerinstrument (Aarne-Thompson 1148b). *Zeitschrift für deutschen Altertum und Literatur* 81: 23–31.

Masing, Uku 1977. Kõuelind ja veesarvik (AaTh 1148B). In *Studia orientalia et antiqua* II. Tartu: University of Tartu. Pp. 117–169.

McKinnell, John 1994. *Both One and Many*. Roma: Il Calamo.

Olrik, Axel 1905. Tordenguden og hans Dreng. *Danske Studier* 1905: 129–146.

Olrik, Axel 1906. Tordenguden og hans Dreng i Lappernes Myteverden. *Danske Studier* 1906: 65–69.

Olsen, Magnus 1955. 'Tor i Ura'. *Maal og Minne* 1955: 121–123.

Propp, Vladimir 1968 [1928]. *Morphology of the Folktale*. Austin: University of Texas Press.

Rydving, Håkan 2010. *Tracing Sami Traditions: In Search of the Indigenous Religion among the Western Sami during the 17th and 18th Centuries*. Oslo: Institute for Comparative Research in Human Culture.

Schjødt, Jens Peter 2013. The Notions of Model, Discourse, and Semantic Center as Tools for the (Re)Construction of Old Norse Religion. *RMN Newsletter* 6: 6–15.

Schröder, Franz Rolf 1965. Thors Hammerholung. *Beiträge zur Geschichte der deutschen Sprache und Literatur* 87: 3–42.

Siikala, Anna-Leena 2002. *Mythic Images and Shamanism: A Perspective on Kalevala Poetry*. Folklore Fellows' Communications 280. Helsinki: Academia Scientiarum Fennica.

Thompson, Stith 1955–1958. *Motif-Index of Folk-Literature: A Classification of Narrative Elements in Folktales, Ballads, Myths, Fables, Mediaeval Romances,*

Exempla, Fabliaux, Jest-Books and Local Legends. I–VI. Revised and expanded edition. Copenhagen: Rosenkilde & Bagger.

Uther, Hans-Jörg 2004. *The Types of International Folktales: A Classification and Bibliography*. I–III. Folklore Fellows' Communications 284–286. Helsinki: Academia Scientiarum Fennica.

Valk, Ülo 2001. *The Black Gentleman: Manifestations of the Devil in Estonian Folk Religion*. Folklore Fellows' Communications 276. Helsinki: Academia Scientiarum Fennica.

Valk, Ülo 2012. Thunder and Lightning in Estonian Folklore in the Light of Vernacular Theories. In *Mythic Discourses: Studies in Uralic Traditions*. Frog, Anna-Leena Siikala, Eila Stepanova (eds.). Studia Fennica Folkloristica 20. Helsinki: Finnish Literature Society. Pp. 40–67.

de Vries, Jan 1933. *The Problem of Loki*. Folklore Fellows' Communications 110. Helsinki: Academia Scientiarum Fennica.

Wray, Alison 2002. *Formulaic Language and the Lexicon*. Cambridge: Cambridge University Press.

Madis Arukask

Sorcery, Holiness, the Third Sex – The Role of Herdsman in Finnic and North Russian Folk Culture[*]

Introduction

The present article focuses on the role of the herdsman and the beliefs and practices related to his activities in the Vepsian culture area (and comparatively, based on parallel material, the whole North Russian culture area) in the 20th century, taking as its point of departure material collected by the author mainly in 2009–2011, and later. The herdsman's role has clearly been special here, lending a distinct character to the relevant folk descriptions that sets them apart from other material. The subject has been discussed previously, by Russian researchers in particular, many of whose treatments are referred to in the present article. Certainly, however, the beliefs associated with the herdsman in different places and through different experiential prisms cannot be reduced to a single unified explanation, although it may be possible to move towards something of that kind, with some degree of probability. Yet regional differences remain, and above all the fact that the relevant material collected at different times and under different circumstances can never be sufficiently embracing, while the angles of approach taken and aims set by various scholars have obviously not been identical. The corpus of material on Vepsian herdsman magic is certainly not complete enough to allow for an exhaustive discussion of the topic. In addition, the traditional reality that forms the vital background of this subject is, in one way or another, necessarily alien to us as modern researchers.

The subject is sensitive and partially tabooed, meaning that the popular explanatory repertoire will necessarily be diffuse, conjectural or even deliberately distorted. At the same time the subject is inspiring due to its extraordinary nature and the fact that the herdsman's role has combined several important spheres and activities dominant in the culture of the temperate forest and burn-beat agriculture zone: above all, of course, animal husbandry as one of the central means of livelihood over the centuries, but also the forest and human society in their opposition and cooperation, animist partnership, the supernatural, and many others, up to gender-related topics.

The Herdsman's Activities as Seen by the Informants

In order to learn something about a phenomenon of popular belief that has sunk into relative obscurity today, it is crucial to have some knowledge of the subject matter before the interview in order to direct the conversation and to obtain specific details. Herdsman magic is definitely not among the first themes to emerge in a fieldwork situation. The problem is complex. There is no question that each middle-aged or older Vepsian/North Russian informant is aware of the extraordinariness of the herdsman – if not of his traditional role, then at least as personified in a particular individual – as they have observed it in the past. Quite predictably, the herdsman is known for his main occupation – no one has any difficulties in giving a general description of herding activities, if called on. Some may speak about the herdsman's rituals in connection with the practices of St. George's Day, such as the encircling ritual around the herd (in Vepsian *ümbardus*, in Karelian *kierokšet, kierros*, in Russian *obhod, otpusk, spusk*, etc.), which they have had occasion to witness. At this point, the uninformed researcher may find that the flow of information stops, so that his or her material remains on the level of mere ethnographic description. In that case, the herdsman merely forms part of a means of livelihood, instead of being the pivotal point of an independent complex of folklore and popular belief.

The informants' way of remembering and memorising can be compared to a honeycomb-like structure (cf. also Raudalainen 2001: 66), where separate pieces of knowledge lie contiguous to each other like cells in a honeycomb. Yet one piece of knowledge need not automatically lead to another, contiguous one; the pieces of information may remain isolated from each other if the interviewer is ignorant or careless enough and does not lead the informant to bridge the cells. With some luck, the informant may keep moving along the 'gold vein' of his own accord, but even if he does, the movement may remain limited – if the researcher, unable to sense and recognise the value of the material being unfolded, should cut the topic short because of his or her own limited knowledge.

Sometimes one can also hear accidental descriptions of the herdsman's activities – for instance during fieldwork concerning traditional village feasts, including St. George's Day. A typical description will portray the herdsman with his magical objects, such as an icon, a bladed tool of some sort, and so on, placed in a sieve, walking around the herd at the edge of the village – carrying out the encircling ritual (cf. Guljaeva 1986: 180; Fišman 1986: 192; Vinokurova 1994: 75; 1988: 14 ff.; Moroz 2001: 247–248, and others). Or one may be told about the mistress of the house performing the same ceremony before sending her animals out with the village herd – especially if the informant herself has done it. Generally, this is also the end of the story, since the ordinary community member's gaze usually does not follow the herdsman further and has no inside knowledge of his activities. The information gleaned from the perspective of the ordinary community member is usually fragmentary. Things may be different if the informant himself is descended from a herdsman's family. In that case, we can see the parents' peculiar position in a characteristic situation through the observant eyes of a child; but even such closer awareness of the situation may remain relatively limited or one-sided.

As far as the art of traditional narrating is concerned, it is usually female informants who stand out more conspicuously, being themselves equally interested in communicating with the stranger (the researcher). Thus, the information may remain somewhat one-sided as to gender aspects, or the researcher may be inclined to see the whole communal traditional culture as woman-centred or even exclusively feminine (cf. Heikkinen 1994: 164–166). Thus the picture that emerges may prove one-sided – or even lopsided. The same problem goes for discussions of herdsman magic, due to the inherent importance of culturally constructed gender associated with it. Certainly the views of male informants on this subject differ from those of women, since in the second half of the 20th century representatives of the 'stronger sex' in Soviet society were either dismissive of, or openly negative about, issues relating to folk belief. Thus one of my long-term informants, A. P., former chief engineer of the local state farm, from Nemž village in Leningrad Oblast, was happy to speak about former life on the farm and how it was abolished, as well as about his family history with its repeated theme of the people repressed as *kulaks* before the war. Yet he refrained from speaking about the magic aspects of animal husbandry and herding as unworthy subjects, although he must have been aware that even the collective and state farm herdsmen of the region kept practising traditional magic in the 20th century and were highly valued for it.

The herdsman himself, who will generally keep the silence imposed on him by the rules of magic, must obviously hold a completely different view. In an interview given in 2010, V. V., a herdsman of 27 years' service and a descendant of a family of herdsmen living in Ladv village, repeatedly emphasised that the herdsman had to "keep mum". He also metaphorically said that upon becoming herdsman, one is "born again". The man who had performed his last ritual walk around his herd as recently as 1993, also described (with resort to gestures) the punishment of the Forest Master (Veps. *mecižand*, the animistic guardian spirit of forest and wild beast) – who is said to weigh the agreement-breaking herdsman down with the handle of his own dropped whip across the victim's neck, which he breaks by applying pressure to the handle.

Thus in trying to open up herdsman magic, we can generally approach it from two opposing perspectives: that of the ordinary member of the community (usually a woman), in which the herdsman will in fact remain elusive; and that of the herdsman himself (the performer of the ritual, the magical mediator or secret keeper). A rare text written directly from a herdsman himself can be found in the collection of Vepsian texts edited by Marija Zajceva and Marija Mullonen (1969: 228–232), where a (female) cattle-herder describes a magic encircling of the cattle performed in 1964, with the charm read not by herself, but a male seer (in Vepsian *tedai*, in Karelian *tietäjä*, 'one-who-knows') who also participated in the ritual:

I made *ümbardus* around all the animals. How do you do the *ümbardus*? We take hairs, and keys with the lock, and an egg, and a bit of candle. We tie this *ümbardus*,[1] egg and candle and all into a towel. We place the axe, tie an icon up onto the plank over the gate, and then walk around the animals three times. I hold the axe with the blade upwards. I come behind, the other man reads ('cause I don't know the words): "from all predators, and those that crawl on the earth..."; three times we walk around the animals, then we open the gate and let the whole herd together. People are not allowed there. The *ümbardus* is done at home or in the fields. The one that walks, that gives the *ümbardus*, says: don't curse there or swear or do any bad deed, and then your cows will stay together in the forest and come back home.

Behind the different perspectives of the herdsman and the lay-person we can discern different modes of religious experience with their corresponding modes of representation. Using Harvey Whitehouse's (2008: 41–44) *imagistic–doctrinal* model of distinction in order to analyse and articulate religious experience, the opposition becomes obvious. In the first (*imagistic*) case, a powerful personal (traumatic, ecstatic) experience prevails, providing the foundation for highly articulated personal knowledge based on conscious reflection, as well as for religious innovation. In the second (*doctrinal*) case we witness the influence of doctrinal learning and ritual repetition, in which the experiential aspect has a more modest role. This perspective tends to create a system, a religious ordering of phenomena. As part of folk religion, herdsman magic and rituals constitute a subject that, quite predictably, leaves space for both of these views.

From the ordinary community member's perspective, the herdsman's activities are stereotypical, limited, thus distinctly visualisable and in a way, commonplace. Clearly the herdsman's activities on St. George's Day (as well as on other occasions related to the ritual calendar) have been observed on a yearly basis, without the observer occupying any central role in the proceedings. This has given him or her an orderly and systematized knowledge of the herdsman and his activities, which can easily be communicated in a few sentences or narrative passages. From this viewpoint, the herdsman as such with all his activities may appear no more than a weird, marginal figure driven to the fringes of society, expected merely to ply his trade according to society's demands and needs. The mental image of him has been formed through witnessing his yearly repeated rituals, without ever trying or being able to adopt any other vantage point. When working with such one-sided source information, the folk religion researcher may easily find his or her material impoverished. He will occupy as a matter of course the position of an ordinary community member, combining diluted religious experience with interpretative common sense. The quasi-social scientific arguments derived from this point of view are more often than not rather irrelevant and uninteresting.

The experiential, imagistic perspective, represented in our case naturally by the herdsman's own viewpoint, offers the extraordinary vision of the insider – the reverse of the same coin. As the herdsman frequently had the opportunity of holding negotiations with representatives of the supernatural (the forest), or at least of accompanying the seer to such negotiations, we can imagine the extraordinary intensity and peculiarity of his experiences which he generally was unable to share directly with anyone. A report from Nemž describes how, on one occasion, upon the summons of the seer as representative of the humans "a grey-headed being emerged out of the earth, growing taller than the trees under the eyes of the people present" (Trifoev 2013: 60–61; see also descriptions in Guljaeva 1986: 179; Moroz 2001: 255–256).

The herdsman was enclosed in his own magic knowledge, forced to uphold it with his whole essence and behaviour. This underscores the inherently extraordinary (and reclusive) nature of his role. It seems that in general, the herdsman had no use for the community's opinions or ideas of his task; from his viewpoint, these were no more than profane gossip or nonsense. In contrast to the unifying tendency of the community-centred perspective the perspective of each separate herdsman, as indicated by various regional descriptions, was dominated by an experiential and ritual uniqueness expressed, in the real world, by the individuality of each *ümbardus* as a compact, as well as by the variation of the terms and conditions of the compact depending on the individual who concluded it.

The herdsman's customary reticence and isolation have inevitably given rise to stereotypes concerning him, which may, however, be contradictory in their details. In the broader North Russian cultural space there seems to be no clear agreement as to whether the herdsman had to be physically abnormal, unfit for other work or, on the contrary, robust and seemingly cut out for communicating with the supernatural (Mišurinskaja 2000: 59; also Fišman 1986: 194–196). Apparently the dominant stereotype identifying the herdsman was not physical, but cultural. The herdsman had to be someone excluded, culturally marginalised by the society, and the features that marked him out – or allowed him to be recognised – as such could be quite diverse.

Yuri Lotman and Boris Uspenskij (1982) have discussed this socio-psychological type as "the accepted Other" – a role that awakens unease while also commanding respect, one that is definitely needed yet at the same time also held at a distance by the community unwilling to identify with it. The same characteristic features also mark the herdsman's role in North Russian (including Vepsian) cultural space. The herdsman is not unambiguously ostracised or disparaged there, as he may be towards the south (cf. also Zelenin 1991: 87). On the contrary: the herdsman knows and feels the responsibility of his role with its obligations and restrictions; he is respected, but the respect has not been unambiguously positive or glorifying. In the contradictory figure of the herdsman as a culturally marginalised person we can see pre-cultural features, as it were – features that cannot be subjected to such simplifying (occidental) dichotomies as good versus evil, etc. In a South Vepsian folktale, the herdsman is represented as opposed to the priest whose animals he must herd (see Kettunen 1925: 41–43). Finding himself in conflict with the priest, the herdsman asserts his magic powers by playing music that has a destructive effect on human society – he makes both animals and humans dance until they drop down exhausted. These examples lead us to the issue of the cultural genesis of the herdsman's role as such – the issue of from what religious role and cultural type his archetype might derive. In view of the culturally and ethnogenetically mosaic nature of the North Russian cultural space, the question is anything but unfounded or irrelevant.

Activities Preceding the Encircling Ritual

In the sample text given above, the encircling ritual was already cursorily touched upon. The ordinary community members could usually observe the herdsman's ritual activities on the day the cattle were let out, which generally fell on St. George's Day, but occasionally, and depending on the weather, might fall on some other date, for instance around St. Nicholas' Day (cf. Guljaeva 1986: 173–174; Moroz 2001: 233; concerning the Vepsians, Vinokurova 1988: 6, 14–19; 1994: 69–70, 73–75). That will have been the day appointed for the encircling ritual around the cattle. However, the period that preceded it also involved important activities for the herdsman, such as preparations for the ritual, obtaining the objects and means necessary both for the ritual and for herding itself, but above all, concluding the magic agreement and negotiating its conditions.

In order to conclude the magic agreement with the forest, the herdsman had to hold negotiations, either in person or with the help of someone more knowledgeable than himself, either the community seer or some more knowledgeable herdsman (cf. Bobrov & Finčenko 1986: 155–157; Stepanov 2006: 257–258, and others). Here we can already observe a division of roles. There have obviously been seer-herdsmen able to take full responsibility for both the magic aspects of the ritual and for the practical herding work, acting simultaneously as agent subjects and in the sense also as objects of the agreement. Here the division of the whole herding complex into a dynamic and a static aspect is visible, particularly from the herdsman's perspective. Dynamicity can be observed in the period before St. George's Day and the encircling ritual when the herdsman (or seer standing in for him) is a negotiator, passer across the boundary that separates human community from the forest, a magically active party in brokering a partnership. After the conditions have been agreed on and the compact has come into force, the herdsman must be understood as a static character whose main task consists of keeping the agreements and taboos necessary to fulfil the obligations (and doing the job) required by his community.

Here it must be noted that all this is relevant only for that kind of compact in which the second party to the compact was the animistic sphere of the forest, with the Forest Master at its head. This meant that the communal herd was entrusted to the safekeeping of the forest, for the forest to guard. The forest as an animistic sphere was seen as the caretaker of the herd, personified for the ordinary community members by the herdsman. Thus the forest was seen simultaneously to endanger the herd and to guarantee its protection; and insofar as, from the human perspective, the greatest responsibility thereby lay with the herdsman, it secured him the peculiar respect of the community. At the same time, the herdsman also bore the

164

brunt of the pressure, from concluding the agreement to maintaining the taboos afterwards. Yet provided he could handle the pressure and the commitments, his actual toil would have been rather negligible – both *de jure* and *de facto* it would not have been the herdsman who guarded the cattle, but the animistic forest/Forest Master, leaving the herdsman with only the duty of leading the herd into the forest in the morning and bringing or calling them back in the evening.

Side by side with the so-called 'wild' agreement there was also a 'divine' version under which heavenly powers in the form of saints were regarded as the actual guardians of the herd (cf. especially Moroz 2001: 235–240; also Fišman 1986: 193–194; Durasov 1988: 103–104; 1989: 276). In that case, no compact was made with the forest, although the encircling ritual was performed in the same manner. The mechanism in operation here was clearly predictable for a Christian (that is, more Christianity-centred) folk culture; in any case, it excluded the magic compact with the forest, which has even been called "terrible" (Moroz 2001: 238) among Russians or "devilish" among the Karelians of Tver (Fišman 1986: 193). Under such a compact, the herdsman's toil would probably have been harder, although from the belief perspective, it is still magic that we are dealing with since the herdsman was helped by saints to whom he addressed the relevant invocations. As for the religious and ideological mode, we of course see two completely different ways of herding, at least from the perspective of a dualistic worldview. The two kinds of partnership, one with the forest, the other with divine powers, obviously refer to traditionally and ecologically different types of belief, as well as to the historical impact of natural forces and different ways of livelihood. The third type that could be pointed out, a completely mechanical herding without any direct resort to magic or special knowledge, has been less common in the Finnic and North Russian area we are looking at. It is in the third type that the herdsman can be regarded as an entirely insignificant, despicable marginal figure for whom the ordinary community members felt nothing but contempt. This is also how he has been described in the Slavic tradition in general (Zelenin 1991: 87; Moroz 2001: 249).

In folk narrative, the difference between wild and divine herding need not have emerged as of primary (or any) importance.[2] Perhaps people were neither really aware of the herdsman's magic backing and partners, nor of the corresponding arsenal of magic devices. Indeed it would have been impossible for them to display such interest in a special professional; instead, on tacit agreement, they left all his special professional knowledge alone, consciously keeping their distance. This in turn increased the general anomaly of the herdsman's role. In narratives, the difference between the two separate modes of herding is discernible only in a few details. Yet narratives include many characteristic and colourful details about herdsmen that seem to refer (albeit perhaps not exclusively) to herding under the wild/ forest compact. The actual *ümbardus* ceremonies (both as compacts and as rituals) performed by herdsmen have always been individual, gaining a level of generalisation only in folk narrative.

In the dynamic phase before St. George's Day, the herdsman could engage in such activities as might be forbidden or impossible for him to carry out later in the herding period. During this time he could carve for himself the herdsman's staff or horn, a task involving axe- or knife-work (later on, cutting trees or plants would be forbidden), as well as go around the byres collecting hairs from his future herd to be (Durasov 1989: 267) in order to use them later in protective magic. Such seemingly unauthorised entrance into byres in itself indicates how extraordinary the herdsman's role was, especially in view of the fact that in traditional society, the byre has rather been a sphere off-limits for all strangers, managed by the family (especially the mistress) of the house in cooperation with the Barn Master (Veps. *tanazižand*, the animistic guardian spirit of barn and domestic animals in it). The herdsman's inroads into the mistress's sphere can also be seen as carrying sexual connotations or intrigue – a subject that we shall return to later.

As pointed out above, the time before the letting out of cattle involves a period of legitimate crossing (or trespassing) of boundaries, when among other things, anthills have been brought from the forest and scattered onto the cattle path. According to analogic magic, ants and anthills have been related to the herds staying compact and keeping together, a belief reflected in the corresponding charm formulae. Tree branches blessed in a church or chapel on Palm Sunday have also been put to magic use upon the letting out of cattle (cf. Vinokurova 1994: 75; 1988: 18, and many others). Perhaps this, too, can be regarded as an example of how elements deriving from the wilderness are transferred into the human community and put to good service.

Another process that had to take place under the wild compact was negotiating its terms and conditions. Some reports refer to a 'usual' situation in the forest or liminal area in which the herdsman (seer) meets the Forest Master and negotiates or even fights with him – an encounter that often involves supernatural experiences (cf. e.g. Fišman 1986: 196–197; Guljaeva 1986: 179). It is characteristic of such encounters that the herdsman often wears woollen mittens (see also Kriničnaja 1986: 184). Folklore texts record awe-inspiring phenomena – a strong wind, trees bent to the ground (Salve 1995: 427–428) – taking place upon the arrival of the Forest Master, which require extraordinary presence of mind from the representative of the human community.

Herdsmen who had not, for some reason, been able to make the magic agreement on their own, had to enlist the help of a seer. On such occasions, the agreement with the forest was concluded by a seer whose professional tasks already involved being in contact with the forest (for instance finding lost people or animals, etc.). Through these negotiations the herdsman probably also received his set of specific obligations and prohibitions, to be observed under the agreement during the current herding season. The phrase "to take the *ümbardus*" indicates on the one hand that *ümbardus* is granted by someone (the Forest Master; the seer), while on the other it allows for some activity or agency on the part of the herdsman. Thus, since the magic competence that herdsmen were most prized for was also obtainable for a certain fee, the herdsmen who lacked it themselves made purposeful visits to seers before St. George's Day. *Ümbardus* can in such a case be understood as a magic formula, either acquired/obtained by study or existing in material form – e.g. words read onto something by the seer (cf. also Bobrov & Finčenko 1986: 154).

Primarily under the terms of the divine compact, the herdsman may perhaps have owned or obtained his *ümbardus* in written form. These would have been longer collections of incantations resembling instruction manuals, which may have come in the form of small handwritten books. Such writings could be purchased from other herdsmen and they served as proof of the herdsman's competence and magic potency. Such written texts circulated mainly in North Russian areas, and some of them have come into the hands of researchers (see esp. Bobrov & Finčenko 1986; Morozov 2001). Several of their aspects (including stylistic ones) point to a Christian or church-related origin (Fedosova 2010: 132 ff.), enabling us to associate them primarily with divine agreements. It has been conjectured that they may have first appeared in the areas inhabited by Old Believers (Bobrov & Finčenko 1986: 164), with their higher levels of literacy. Since historically, they have mainly been written in Russian,[3] it is questionable how much they could have been used among Vepsians and other Finnic peoples whose knowledge of Russian was rather poor up to the 20th century. The aforementioned herdsman, V. V., from Ladv village in Leningrad Oblast, said that, "the text was written in Russian, but read in Vepsian". Here we must take into account that the written *ümbardus* could also be used as an artefact – it was enough just to own it; or perhaps it may have been read out during the ritual by some literate person.

Thus we can see that, as befits magic, all kinds of replacements have been possible in the preparatory (dynamic) phase of the herdsman's activities. It was not the direct agency of the particular person that mattered, but the fact that some important activities had been performed on his behalf in good time, after which the herdsman could begin to perform his main seasonal duties. Understandably, all this would again have added to the mysteriousness of the herdsman's role in the eyes of the ordinary people.

The Herdsman's Behaviour, Taboos, and the Community's Obligations to Him

The intermediacy of the herdsman's role was also expressed in his behaviour, in the demands and prohibitions he was subjected to under the compact, as well as in his appearance and his characteristic morality. In the traditional societies' social role gallery, the herdsman-type, as we saw above, is best accommodated by the figure of "the accepted Other" (cf. Lotman & Uspenskij 1982), a categorisation justified both by social expectations and stereotypes and, from the folk belief perspective, by the details of the magic compact that to which he is subject. Speaking about this figure in the Russian cultural context, Lotman and Uspenskij have noted his frequent foreign extraction: the herdsman is either from more distant place, or at least from outside the community. The same can be said about the herdsman's origins all over the Finnic and North Russian cultural space. Herdsmen hailing from outside are valued more highly, and in some parts certain peoples or regions of origin have been acclaimed as sources of especially potent and famous herdsmen. Thus, the Vagans and Cherepans (i.e., Russians from the region of the Vaga River and Cherepovets, cf. Vinokurova 1988: 24–25) have been esteemed among the Vepsians of various regions; the Votians have highly esteemed the Izhorian herdsmen of the Soikkola peninsula (Adler 1968: 135; Talve 1981: 54–55); the Karelians of Tver have prized herdsmen from the Arkhangelskaya Guberniya (Virtaranta 1967: 103), etc. In the absence of such foreign herdsmen, however, the community obviously had to make do with some local marginal figure. In recordings, the attitude of "but once we had here one...", referring directly to some kind of exclusion, with its view of the herdsman as somehow uncommon, is also found in narratives concerning herdsmen of local origin.

Since each agreement was a detailed individual contract, it is impossible to compile a universal list of the various requirements that herdsmen had to meet according to folk belief. In addition to the individual nature of each case, the type of the agreement – whether it was divine or wild – certainly also made a difference. Especially in the latter case, strict asceticism has been stressed. The herdsman was initiated, as it were, into something strenuous and at the same time, very mysterious. In the prohibitions he was subject to (see Guljaeva 1986: 178; Ščepanskaja 1986; Vinokurova 1988: 21–22; Durasov 1988: 102–103; 1989: 274–275; Moroz 2001: 240–241; Mišurinskaja 2000, and many others) we can discern traits confirming the following magic principles: the importance of the herd and its integrity; the duty of preserving the earth and nature together with the herd, as the latter was given into nature's safekeeping; the respect that the people owed to the herdsman and his herd; and the requirements that the herdsman himself was subject to in order not to deviate from or fail in his magic agreements, which also concerned his sexuality and religion. Since the herdsman could be characterised as a mediator between human culture and the forest/wilderness, tasked with keeping them in equilibrium, much of his behaviour can be understood in precisely these terms because, since the balance between the two spheres depended on the herdsman's own psycho-physiological condition, the latter was to suffer no damage either mentally or physically. This was secured both by the herdsman's immunity (which in turn increased his marginalisation and anomality) and his self-discipline.

A main imperative here was *stasis* as opposed to *ekstasis*, serenity as opposed to agitation. The herdsman was not allowed to get angry with anybody or anything. The farmer's family was required to keep a reasonable distance in their relations with the herdsman and to refrain from (at least expressly displaying) any ill feelings towards him. This requirement was buttressed by various prescriptions as to their everyday behaviour. Over the herding season, the several farmsteads concerned took turns in accommodating him. He was provided with bedding and food (including provisions for his day in the forest), which as a rule could not be worse than those enjoyed by the other members of the household. In addition to the wages previously agreed with the community, each household also had to provide him with clothes on the day he stayed with them – in the morning he went out with his herd, wearing the clothes given to him from the farm; in the evening he changed into his own clothes, and next day moved on to the next farmstead (cf. Guljaeva 1986: 174, and many others). The fact that he went into the forest wearing the clothes provided by his host farm can be interpreted as a link between the village and the forest that involves the herdsman's physical body.

At the same time, physical contact with the herdsman has been described as taboo. The herdsman never shook hands with anybody (Ščepanskaja 1986: 168; Durasov 1988: 102), nor could he accept anything directly from anyone's hands. The things offered to him could be placed on the ground, from where he then picked them up (Moroz 2001: 243). The fact that special tableware may have been reserved for his exclusive use while on the farm, and that he may have taken his meals as well as used the sauna separately from other household members, again indicates that he was kept at a distance from ordinary people. According to other reports, he was forbidden to step into anybody else's footprints (Fišman 1986: 195). The physical taboos seem to indicate that the herdsman was peculiarly charged, thus becoming dangerous to other people and/or the magic agreement. Let us recall that it was the herdsman's business, as bearer of the magic agreement, to protect *ümbardus* in its material form from lay people (that is, everybody else). Apparently the magic agreement was extended, to a greater or lesser degree, to the herdsman's own body, which helps us to understand his physical sacredness (or sacred pollutedness) in his contacts with other people.

There are no reports of the herdsman storing or transmitting positive energy. He is not known to have given blessings, nor are there any reports of any item related to him having been used in beneficial magic. In this connection it is interesting to note that according to some reports, the herdsman has been forbidden from going to the church (Fišman 1986: 195). If his compact was of the 'wild' type he was not allowed contact with (high-religious?) Christianity as a 'human' thing. At the same time, according to other reports, he had to stay away from the dead or death-related things, so whenever there was a death in the village, he had to stay away from it (Moroz 2001: 240). At the same time, however, dirt brought from the cemetery could be used to perform the *ümbardus* (cf. Guljaeva 1986: 178); but this ceremony fell into the dynamic phase preceding the herding season, when the use of diverse powers was relevant and perhaps could even increase the efficiency of the agreement. Later on, as we can see from the taboos and customs governing the herdsman, all alien powers (i.e., other than those of the forest) were excluded, at least under the wild agreement.

The ban on cursing and quarrelling might be regarded as yet another measure intended to avoid upsetting the herdsman's equilibrium. The herdsman had to avoid all kinds of conflict and steer clear of problems unrelated to his immediate job. His duty of avoiding entertainments and sexual relations could also be classified under the same category. It has been stressed that he was not to participate in roundelays, the entertainment of the village youth; nor to sleep with women – yet marriage was not prohibited to him, since except for the spring and summer herding season governed by the magic agreement, he was allowed to lead an ordinary life, beget children, hunt, and so on. Blood-related taboos were of at least equal, if not greater, importance for the herdsman as the ones concerning quarrelling and anger. The herdsman was not to shed anyone's blood (cf. the prohibition on hitting his animals), nor to hurt himself so as to cause any bleeding. By shedding the blood of himself or his animals (as immediate parties to the agreement), the herdsman would obviously violate an important article of the agreement. By shedding another person's blood, however, he could soil his own purity under the agreement – that is, become unfit, polluted in the eyes of his agreement partner.

Again, obviously in case of the wild agreement, the herdsman was forbidden to damage his integrity by shaving or cutting his hair, acquiring, as a result, a completely 'wild' appearance himself. Thus he became discernible in the village not only for his activities, but also by his appearance, his habitus. The prohibition of injury meant that he could not use (metal) tools. More precisely, all work that could have caused injury to himself or others was forbidden for him. This prohibition, however, concerned not only other people, but all living (i.e. wild) nature and its creatures, in general. The herdsman was not allowed to break or cut branches in the forest nor, apparently, to cut hay. He was forbidden to eat berries (under the wild agreement, as some reports state, black-coloured berries) in the forest. Each kind of work was wrought with the danger of unwittingly causing harm to living creatures (albeit perhaps only to insects) – something strictly ruled out for the herdsman. There are reports of cases where the herdsman was even prohibited from killing gnats, in which respect he might be compared to the Jainist monk with his prohibitions intended to help him preserve the integrity of all life forms. The taboos governing the herdsman turn up in the following text sample; in a more general manner, they are set out and arranged into clusters in the table below.

The herdsman, you see, mustn't... he goes into the forest and sees berries; but he mustn't pick berries. Father took us, me and my little sister, into the forest; we went and picked blueberries and brambles. But father must not pick. And he must not cut trees, not at all. Nothing... If you walk, then just walk. The whip, the whip is what all herdsmen guard, what they keep by their side. The whip is most important to him, like an amulet. And when he takes it... the *ümbardus*, he takes it and goes..., and does no work at all. Nothing. Only herding. And... it may harm his herd, or the bear comes, the wolf takes, or a cow just gets lost, and, you see, earlier too, some cows lost milk, then the herdsman promised it to the Forest Master so nothing should happen; he let him take the milk away, this is how it was, you see. But otherwise, too, he could do nothing (no work). If you touch anything, do any work, this may harm you and then farmers' wives will not hire you any more.

What else was prohibited for the herdsman?

Well, now, he mustn't drink vodka, yes, mustn't be drunk or anything; mustn't quarrel over who takes what; now I don't know whether he might live with a woman or not, perhaps he might..., but otherwise he is, all things in the summer..., like this..., like, I know, the eunuchs live like that, like they do

Table 1. Prohibitions governing the herdsman

Related to nature	Related to physical integrity and mental equilibrium	Related to sexuality	Related to the magic agreement/ incantation	Related to other spheres/ rituals
• harming animals, birds, insects (all work forbidden) • harming trees or shrubs • picking and eating the berries in the forest	• cutting hair, shaving • shedding his own or other creatures' blood • cursing and quarrelling	• having sexual intercourse with woman • seeing the menstrual blood of a woman (the mistress of the house), her bare feet, her uncovered head • participating in entertainment	• climbing through a fence gap • giving up the objects that held the *ümbardus* (his staff, belt or some other item)	• attending funerals • going to church

nothing... I do nothing, then I am a holy person, it's the same way... like that..., as they say..., the angels and..., and that..., and now, I do nothing bad. Nothing. In order that I can do nothing bad, I'll rather do nothing at all. He didn't split wood, didn't saw; he does nothing. What would happen if he worked and did something to some animal, or perhaps killed a gnat or a fly – I don't know..., what promise he had made, what... words.
(V. L., Vidl, Leningrad Oblast, 2010.)

The ban on human objects could be expressed by the prohibition on pulling up turnips or plucking ears of corn (things obviously unrelated to wild nature) from the field. Climbing through fence gaps was emphatically forbidden for the herdsman. This can be associated with the symbolics of the (metal) fence surrounding the herd that is often mentioned in protective spells. By climbing through a fence gap, the herdsman would have seemed to indicate that the fence protecting his herd was penetrable, thus violating his agreement. Here we have come to the central concept of the ritual. *Ümbardus, obhod*, etc., together with the magic activities that signified them, are based on a protective surrounding of the herd which, on the one hand, makes the cattle invisible and uncatchable, while at the same time it is based on an agreement, maintaining the precarious balance of which is the herdsman most important task.

Culturally Constructed Gender and Sexuality in Herdsman Magic

Several aspects of the herding-related customs invite us to study the importance of culturally constructed gender within this complex of phenomena. Since during the herding season, i.e. the static phase of the magic agreement, the herdsman was subject to various prescriptions circumscribing or altering his daily human existence, it cannot be a mere accidental 'moral norm'.[4] On the other hand, a broader symbolic sexuality can hardly be alien to any system of belief, where the intercourse of divine beings, for instance, was seen to have direct influence on the human world order, and so on. Thirdly, we must keep in mind that in traditional cultures, all beliefs concerning fertility and growth tend to be implicitly related to sexuality and even the orgiastic.

Elements of the latter are also observable in the customs related to herding, especially as performed by the community/women. According to some reports (Zelenin 1991: 90), upon letting her cattle out the mistress of the house may have brushed the animals' backs with a shirt she had worn during sexual intercourse. This can be taken as a direct reference to sexuality transferred through contact, in order that the animals reproduce well (cf. also Tarkka 1998: 121). The focus here is on women's clothes and the implications of wearing them, casting into relief the strong relationship between the mistress (i.e. the female) and the herd, at least (understandably and predictably) in the domestic/human sphere. The communal and the forest-related seem to enter into competition here, in which the herdsman had to function as a mediator, but above all take care that the human sphere should not come to dominate over the other party to the agreement – the forest.

The latter conjecture is held up by some examples: if upon letting out the cattle, the women's skirt hems were lifted, for instance by the wind, it was thought that the animals would race around all summer long, tails raised high. The herdsman of course saw this as an ill omen. If women and girls jumped and sprang upon letting out the herd, it was thought the cattle would be brisk and productive in the summer (Zelenin 1991: 89). Based on Karelian materials, it has been pointed out that female sexuality and fertility were most immediately associated with the herd – both symbolically and as mediated by the relevant contact and rituality. Laura Stark has distinguished between the positive and negative influence of female sexuality, discussing the ritual or situation known as *harakoiminen*, where the animals going out of the byre pass between the spread legs of a woman standing by the door, or when a woman happens to step over a thing or object, thereby exercising a specific influence on it (Stark-Arola 1998a: 47–50; 1998b: 166–168, 224 ff.). In the domestic sphere (i.e. the woman's world), the influence was positive and protective, but not elsewhere. A clear distinction was made between cows and horses, the latter clearly belonging to the men's sphere (cf. Vinokurova 2006: 290, 320–322). The mistress's relationship with her animals (primarily cows) was sensual (Tarkka 1998: 121).

Thus it is obvious that women exercised some magic influence over the herd, which the herdsman had to control or avert. The herdsman had to check the mistress's attire when she was near the herd (she was prohibited to go barefoot or with her head uncovered), calling her to order even with the help of his whip, if necessary. The herdsman's relation to the herd was, on the contrary, calming and soothing. It was his task to tame the feminine sexuality inherent in the herd. The use of cemetery soil for *ümbardus* mentioned above must surely have served the same purpose. On the one hand, women were seen as belonging to the domestic sphere, and in general they did not cross over the boundary into the wilderness as much as men did. At the same time, they were associated with nature and the elemental powers due to their fertility (cf. Tarkka 1998: 116–117). Thus, the herdsman's role was oddly in-between – he had to function as a buffer between the human and the elemental spheres, whenever confrontation arose. It is in this role that the herdsman's knowledge and control of the extra-human elemental powers (the forest) and the elemental power within human society (femininity) and his ability to neutralise their tensions seem to have played a crucial part.

Direct reference to feminine fertility or fertilizability has obviously posed as great danger to the herdsman as seeing or tolerating the mistress's inappropriate attire. Therefore he was banned from participating in girls' roundelays. The herdsman was forbidden to see menstrual blood on the mistress's clothes (Ščepanskaja 1986: 169); if the mistress had had intercourse with her husband, she usually had to wash herself and change clothes before going to let the cattle out (Stepanova 2000: 31). This can also be related to the general ban on blood among the herdsman's taboos; yet the sexual aspect certainly also plays a role. As we saw above, sexual intercourse with women, including his own wife, used to be a general taboo for herdsmen. What we are witnessing here is the cultural construction of a kind of 'third sex', the temporary or permanent alteration of the sexual orientation of a person of definite biological gender, mainly in the interests of society. Similar examples of temporary change can be brought from shamanic rituals, where gender is altered in order to efficiently communicate with the opposite sex and for the benefit of the community. Permanent (lifelong) 'third sex' can be found in various social situations in several corners of the world (India, Thailand, Albania,[5] etc.).

The herdsman obviously belongs under the first case, a periodic or temporary shift of sexual orientation. In order to accomplish his task, he must not behave as an active, masculine agent in his relations with the supernatural (the forest); instead, he must adopt a sexually passive, almost 'sexless' or 'third-sex' position. The comparison of the herdsman with the eunuch or monk seems most appropriate, in this sense. More broadly, the same is confirmed by the herdsman's work prohibition. It is precisely through different types of work that gender roles have been defined in traditional societies (men's work versus women's work). The herdsman was not allowed to demonstrate his masculine vigour, which would have manifested itself in work. Similarly, it was forbidden for him to use sharp-bladed tools, another attribute signifying masculine activity, during the herding period. He was to be the passive border-guard, as it were, safeguarding the boundaries, not actively penetrating them. This reflects the ban on harming the earth and nature – an act identifiable with sexual violation, penetration of femininity.

In this respect, the herdsman's role during the herding season has been opposite to the other role related to the forest and magic – that of the hunter. Although the hunter was likewise obliged to acknowledge and express respect for the forest and the Forest Master as the master of animals, and may have observed some sexual taboos (sexual intercourse before going to hunt, keeping women and the feminine power of fertility away from his hunting implements), his relation to the forest was entirely different. Unlike the herdsman and his herds, the hunter did not move along the boundaries but was a real trespasser – penetrating the forest with the aim of temporarily upsetting the balance (by catching, killing his prey), and having later to restore it by means of relevant rites. Both the hunter's activities and the relevant terminology are rife with sexual connotations. In a similarly way to love magic, the hunter is the cunning one, the coaxer, the 'stalker'; the symbolic language of a hunting trip is identifiable with that of wooing or marrying (also Ilomäki 1986: 59, 126–130; Tarkka 1994: 253–254; 1998: 99–109). Hunting is characterised by periodic transgression of boundaries. It is a regular invasion of an alien sphere, an emphatically masculine activity.

The social function of the third sex always involves increasing coherence. The role implies (self-)sacrifice, apparently devoid of human passions. The emotional mode of hunting can be characterised by greed for prey and later ritual repentance, but also by the desirability of tactfulness while striving towards one's aim. The same is characteristic of masculine sexuality, or sexuality in general. The personal passions and instincts quite conspicuous in ordinary sexuality are repressed in the cultural third sex – both the practical and the magic tasks of this role are rooted in collective interests. The report recorded by Nina Hagen-Torn in the first half of the 20th century, stating that the herdsman was allowed to attend the orgiastic St. George's Day feast of an exclusive group of Izhorian married women where ordinary behavioural norms were violated (see Pančenko 1998: 103), also indicates that during the period covered by his taboos the herdsman is not an 'ordinary male' but something else. Thus, the herdsman had to sacrifice his ordinary male sexuality in order to accomplish, in the interests of society, the task of maintaining a more general and vital equilibrium. This is also the reason why in some places, the herdsman could be a boy or old man, that is someone not in his fertile stage (cf. Tarkka 1998: 122).

Concluding Remarks

Examining the herdsman culture in the Finnic and North Russian cultural space, we encounter a number of questions. In my view, the most interesting problems relate to two main areas – the genesis of the role of seer-herdsman who stands in an agreement relationship with the forest, and issues related to the history of the cultural contacts between Finnic peoples and Slavs.

The first problem seems to turn on the issue of the herdsman's culturally constructed gender with its possible background and roots and its seemingly rather diverse parallels. The herdsman's taboos – above all, the prohibition of talking about certain subjects, and the ban on harming living nature – are also present in many other cultures. A good example of respect for the realm of insects and all other living creatures is provided by the above-mentioned religions where monks and nuns must not cause harm to any living thing, either deliberately or unwittingly, and where the exercises may involve things like letting gnats suck your blood (e.g. in Jainism). The herdsman's taboos also included the prohibition of killing or brushing off insects congregating on his body.

The parallel with Jainism is, of course, illustrative here, and not a reference to any genetic link. The request for silence, however, can be encountered much closer – in Hinduism, but more relevantly, in Orthodox monastic culture, where it governs monks practising particularly strict asceticism. Orthodox high culture's connections to the herdsman tradition are obvious in the encircling ritual as a whole – regionally or occasionally, the herd has been blessed by Orthodox priests, who naturally have performed the blessing with Orthodox prayers. The divine *obhod* emerging together with literate culture provides an example of the symbiosis of Orthodoxy with folk culture, or perhaps even of the transfer of elements of high religion – or even a whole ritual structure – from Orthodox high religion into folk culture. In this case, the herdsman's anomaly or 'saintliness' could be explained by a straightforward copy of Orthodoxy which has acquired the shape of a strange travesty in folk culture.

Another noteworthy issue is the herdsman's sexuality and culturally constructed gender. In our given case, it clearly constitutes a temporary cross-gender move or alteration of sexual orientation for the duration of the seasonal herding period, that is the 'static' phase of the herdsman's role. Here, too, we might see parallels with the Orthodox monk's status, which involves taking the relevant oaths and then (either temporarily or permanently) turning away from worldly life, with all the attendant consequences. Along these lines, the herdsman's asceticism would again look like an odd loan or copy from Orthodox high culture, side by side with the charms tradition with its Christian (including apocryphal) elements.

Obviously, the herdsman's 'third-sex' role is not to be seen as a permanent cultural gender shift turning him into a eunuch or transforming him into the opposite sex for ever. On the contrary: in the herdsman's sexual taboos concerning the female sex we can notice the correlation of earth/nature with the feminine. It is worth repeating that together with sexual intercourse, the damaging of the earth/nature is prohibited for the herdsman. Something of a similar nature is also observable in the Finnic celebration of the vernal Ascension Thursday (in Votian called *maaentšäüz* – 'earth's breathing day'), when any kind of work related to the soil, as well as any manner of damaging the earth and, in some places, also sexual intimacy with women were prohibited (the latter constituting damage done to the woman's integrity). This is illustrated by a report from Põlva parish in South Estonia: "on Ascension Thursday it was forbidden to sleep with a man, otherwise all flax growing in the fields would flatten like rye in stacks" (Hiiemäe 1984: 182). The whole complex is probably associated with the feminisation of the earth characteristic of agricultural societies, contrasted by the masculinity of the sky. The rules that bound ordinary men on only a few days remained in force for the herdsman throughout the herding season in order to secure the integrity and inviolability of the border between the two parties to the compact. Thus the herdsman as guarantor of the magic agreement seems to have inhabited the sacred sphere all the time – the whole herding period is, for him, a holy time and situation. At the same time it is uncertain whether the origins of this holiness can be reduced simply to Orthodoxy.

Moreover, the Vepsians and Karelians (as well as, substratally, the North Russians) are forest peoples whose culture was dominated by burn-beat (and not sedentary) agriculture, and whose relations with the forest and the supernatural were based not only on opposition, but also on partnership.

Here the question arises of the non-Christian genesis of the role of herdsman in general and the seer-herdsman, who performs the wild *ümbardus*, in particular. In the relations governed by the wild agreement, we perceive most clearly the partnership with the forest; the forest/Forest Master acts as trustee keeping the herd safe (from his own predators) for a fee and on conditions agreed upon beforehand. Yuri Lotman (1993: 346 ff.) has pointed out that any kind of contractuality is regarded as pagan, anomalous and marginal in Orthodox Russian culture, yet it is clear that Finnic herdsman magic is not a loan from Western Europe with its Roman law rooted in paganism, but an original cultural phenomenon. This, however, refers to the second possible cultural root of the herdsman's role, traceable to pre-Christian folk culture.

Cross-gender moves in ritual situations are characteristic of shamanism, where the shaman must undergo temporary (cultural) gender shifts in order to communicate adequately (cf. holy marriage) with his supernatural guardian spirits. Such cross-dressing is not uncommon in shamanism, and the diversity of gender roles (as well as tolerance of them) seems generally to be greater and more widespread in shamanistic (pre-Christian) cultures. It seems certainly the case that at some point, the shamanistic culture type together with its fondness for trance and the supernatural, has been supplanted by the seer-centred culture in which the spheres of the supernatural and holy are located in a physically more easily perceivable proximity and communication with them does not depend so heavily on an altered state of consciousness and the techniques for achieving it. The seer using recitative incantations instead of shamanic songs was himself the bearer of magic knowledge and thus unburdened by the task of going into trance to obtain it (cf. Siikala 2002: 345–346).

Nevertheless, some conspicuous features of herdsman magic come across as indirect references to shamanism. I mean primarily the above-mentioned temporary alteration of gender orientation, but also the support of the forest as a helpful animistic sphere in general, as well as the magic impact of the herdsman's instruments (the horn, the whip, the drum made from fir, etc.) on reality. The herdsman as 'the accepted Other' is not culture-centred in the modern sense, but someone who comes from beyond the borders and is 'located' beyond them throughout his period of work. His relationship with everyday reality and quotidian human society is one of control and endorsement. Yet no one in Finnic or North Russian culture questions his authority or necessity; he is respected as someone special and people try to please him. Instead of (or side by side with) the features characteristic of agricultural society, we have here a communication with the supernatural that does not take its bearings from the Christian religious scene but persists in using earlier schemes and devices. The following table displays some more important differences in culture type, the herdsman as a role, and the corresponding magic.

176

Table 2. The differences between tradition-ecological[6] culture types based on herdsman magic.

Burn-beat agriculturists and cattle breeders	Southern large-scale corn cultivators
Partnership between nature and human culture	Competition between nature and human culture
Orality	Partial literacy
'Wild' encircling ritual	'Divine' encircling ritual
Seer-herdsman	Herdsman as social marginal
Herdsman as safeguarder of boundaries	Herdsman as violator of boundaries
Herdsman as periodically belonging to the 'third sex'	Herdsman as a failed man

To what extent does the herdsman culture we have been examining characterise historical interethnic relations between the Finnic peoples and the Slavs? Since the special status of the herdsman is mainly recognised in the forested regions, among peoples with a Finno-Ugric substratum, and is quite unknown in the more southerly regions of Russia or Ukraine, we can safely presume it is of Finnic origin. This would mean that the culture of agricultural Slavs has later combined with the culture of forest herding, superimposing on it elements borrowed from high religion and literary culture.

In all probability, herding took root in the forested eastern reaches of North Europe over the last several millennia, predating both large-scale corn cultivation agriculture and the arrival of Christianity. Thus we should conclude that herdsman magic is of Finno-Ugric origin and includes several original elements that have later been partially combined with or supplanted by Slavic and Orthodox ones. Such syncretic vitality indicates that it has been important and persistent in the Finnic and North Russian cultural area for a very long time. The herdsman as a social role has quite predictably preserved and combined various elements from an evidently very diverse gallery of roles, both via genetic evolution and due to contiguities.

Notes

* This research has been supported by the Alfred Kordelin Foundation, by the European Union through the European Regional Development Fund (Centre of Excellence, CECT) and by the Estonian Ministry of Education and Research (Institutional Research Project IUT2–43 and Research Grant ETF9271).

1 The Vepsian *ümbardus* refers here specifically to the magic objects used in the ritual. More broadly, *ümbardus* (Rus. *obhod*) signifies a number of seemingly different things which nevertheless conceptually characterise one and the same at the meta-level. The name can stand for the encircling ritual itself; the agreement between the community and the forest; the material object carrying or embodying the incantation/compact (the wax ball with animal hairs, the lock, the signalling instrument, etc.) that had to be kept secret or hidden from the uninitiated; perhaps also an acoustic signal known only to the herdsman and used for calling the animals. As party to the agreement, the herdsman himself has also been, in a way, part of the *ümbardus* – his person was quite mechanically and inseparably tied to it all.

2   In a short article, Andrej Moroz has emphasised that herdsmen have frequently confused the wild and the divine agreements and their elements in their narratives. In principle, he distinguishes the common encircling ritual as part of the wild *obhod*, and goes on to doubt whether the wild *obhod* is performed as a ritual at all (cf. Moroz 2003).

3   At the same time, there are also relatively old written incantations in Vepsian (the earliest of them from the 17th century; cf. Toporkov 2010: 107–110, 132–133, 137–139; also Vinokurova 1988: 20–21).

4   Tatjana Ščepanskaja (2001: 85 ff.) has referred to this as "reproductive taboo", while in men's magic, power has been preserved via "anticreative" behaviour.

5   On the institution of *virgjereshe*, the sworn virgins fulfilling the role of men, still extant in Albania, see e.g. Novik 2012.

6   Here I refer and resort to the types of religion among the Finno-Ugrians, as presented by Lauri Honko (see 1994: 66–69). According to him, animistic perception and more diverse communication with nature spirits is particularly characteristic of burn-beat agriculture practitioners, while among large-scale corn cultivators it evolves into a dualistic opposition.

Sources

Adler, Elna 1968. *Vadjalaste endisajast I. Idavadja murdetekste.* Tallinn: Eesti NSV Teaduste Akadeemia.

Bobrov & Finčenko 1986 = Бобров, А. Г. & А. Е. Финченко 1986. Рукописный отпуск в пастушеской обрядности Русского Севера (конец XVIII – начало XX вв). In *Русский Север: проблемы этнокультурной истории, этнографии и фольклористики.* Т. А. Бернштам & К. В. Чистов (eds.). Ленинград: Наука. Pp. 135–164.

Durasov 1988 = Дурасов, Г. П. 1988. Обряды, связанные с домашним скотоводством на Каргополье, в конце XIX – начале XX в. In *Культура Русского Севера.* К. В. Чистов (ed.). Ленинград: Наука. Pp. 99–107.

Durasov 1989 = Дурасов, Г. П. 1989. Обряды, связанные с обиходом скота в сельской общине Каргополья в XIX – начале XX в. In *Русские: семейный и общественный быт.* Москва: Наука. Pp. 265–282.

Fedosova 2010 = Федосова, К. А. 2010. Слово и действие в пастушьих отпусках: устное бытование рукописного текста. In *Фольклор: текст и контекст.* Москва: Государственный республиканский центр русского фольклора. Pp. 131–142.

Fišman 1986 = Фишман, О. М. 1986. Связь пастушеской и свадебной обрядности у карел. In *Русский Север: проблемы этнокультурной истории, этнографии и фольклористики.* Т. А. Бернштам & К. В. Чистов (eds.). Ленинград: Наука. Pp. 190–205.

Guljaeva 1986 = Гуляева, Л. П. 1986. Пастушеская обрядность на реке Паше (традиция и современность). In *Русский Север: проблемы этнокультурной истории, этнографии и фольклористики.* Т. А. Бернштам & К. В. Чистов (eds.). Ленинград: Наука. Pp. 172–180.

Heikkinen, Kaija 1994. Havaintoja magian käytöstä vepsäläisissä kylissä. In *Vepsäläiset tutuiksi.* Kaija Heikkinen & Irma Mullonen (eds.). Karjalan tutkimuslaitoksen julkaisuja 108. Joensuu: Joensuun Yliopisto. Pp. 145–168.

Hiiemäe, Mall 1984. *Eesti rahvakalender* III. Tallinn: Eesti Raamat.

Honko, Lauri 1994. Belief and Ritual: The Phenomenological Context. In *The Great Bear. A Thematic Anthology of Oral Poetry in the Finno-Ugrian Languages.* Lauri

Honko, Senni Timonen & Michael Branch, poems transl. Keith Bosley. New York: Oxford University Press, Finnish Literature Society. Pp. 63–77.

Ilomäki, Henni 1986. *Eläinten nimittäminen ja luontosuhde. Petojen roolit pohjois-ja rajakarjalaisissa kalevalamittaisissa runoissa.* Folkloristiikan julkaisematon lisensiaatintutkielma. Helsinki: Helsingin yliopisto.

Kettunen, Lauri 1925. *Näytteitä etelävepsästä* II. Helsinki: Suomalaisen Kirjallisuuden Seura.

Kriničnaja 1986 = Криничная, Н. А. 1986. О сакральной функции пастушьей трубы (по материалам северных пастушеских обрядов). In *Русский Север: проблемы этнокультурной истории, этнографии и фольклористики.* Т. А. Бернштам & К. В. Чистов (eds.). Ленинград: Наука. Pp. 181–189.

Lotman 1993 = Лотман, Ю. М. 1993. Договор и вручение себя как две модели культуры. In *Избранные статьи в трех томах* 3. Таллинн: Александра. Pp. 345–355.

Lotman & Uspenskij 1982 = Лотман, Ю. М. & Б. А. Успенский 1982. "Изгой" и "изгойничество" как социально-психологическая позиция в русской культуре преимущественно допетровского периода. In *Труды по знаковым системам XV. Типология культуры. Взаимное воздействие культур.* TRÜ toimetised 576. Tartu: Tartu Ülikool. Pp. 110–121.

Mišurinskaja 2000 = Мишуринская, О. В. 2000. Пастушеская обрядность (Тихвинский и Лодейнопольский районы). In *V региональная научная конференция молодых ученых "Этнографическое изучение Северо-Запада России". Краткое содержание докладов.* Санкт-Петербург: Издательство Санкт-Петербургского университета. Pp. 56–59. Available at: http://www.ethnology.ru/doc/conferences/Tesis-2000.rtf [Accessed June 27, 2015]

Moroz 2001 = Мороз, Андрей Борисович 2001. Севернорусские пастушеские отпуска и магия первого выгона скота у славян. In *Восточнославянский этнолингвистический сборник.* Москва: Индрик. Pp. 232–258.

Moroz 2003 = Мороз, Андрей Борисович 2003. "Лесной отпуск". Тайное знание севернорусского пастуха и его репрезентация в крестьянской общине. In *Локальные традиции в народной культуре Русского Севера. Материалы IV международной конференции "Рябининские чтения-2003".* Петрозаводск: Музей-заповедник Кижи. Pp. 206–208.

Morozov 2001 = Морозов, И. А. 2001. "Отпуск" пастуха из Каргопольского района Архангельской области. Подготовка к публикации И. А. Морозова. In *Мужской сборник. Выпуск 1. Мужчина в традиционной культуре.* Москва: Лабиринт. Pp. 120–124.

Novik 2012 = Новик, А. А. 2012. *Виргьереши* – девственницы Северо-Албанских Альп как феномен социальной структуры традиционного общества. In *Феномен социализации в этнической культуре. Материалы XI Санкт-Петербургских этнографических чтений.* Санкт-Петербург. Pp. 72–79.

Pančenko 1998 = Панченко, А. А. 1998. *Исследования в области народного православия. Деревенские святыни Северо-Запада России.* Санкт-Петербург: Алетейя.

Raudalainen, Taisto Kalevi 2001. Traditsioonisidus elulooline jutustamine: mäluainese etnopoeetiline tekstualiseerimine. In *Kultuur ja mälu.* Terje Anepaio & Ene Kõresaar (eds.). Studia Ethnologica Tartuensia 4. Tartu: Tartu Ülikooli Kirjastus. Pp. 59–78.

Salve, Kristi 1995. Forest Fairies in the Vepsian Folk Tradition. In *Folk Belief Today.* Mare Kõiva & Kai Vassiljeva (eds.). Tartu: Estonian Academy of Sciences, Institute of the Estonian Language and the Estonian Museum of Literature. Pp. 413–434.

Siikala, Anna-Leena 2002. *Mythic Images and Shamanism: A Perspective on Kalevala Poetry.* Folklore Fellows' Communications 280. Helsinki: Academia Scientarum Fennica.

Stark-Arola, Laura 1998a. Gender, Magic and Social Order. Pairing, Boundaries, and the Female Body in Finnish-Karelian Folklore. In *Gender and Folklore. Perspectives on Finnish and Karelian Culture.* Satu Apo, Aili Nenola & Laura Stark-Arola (eds.). Studia Fennica Folkloristica 4. Helsinki: Finnish Literature Society. Pp. 31–62.

Stark-Arola, Laura 1998b. *Magic, Body and Social Order: The Construction of Gender Through Women's Private Rituals in Traditional Finland.* Studia Fennica Folkloristica 5. Helsinki: Finnish Literature Society.

Stepanov 2006 = Степанов, А. В. 2006. Некоторые аспекты животноводческой магии на Русском Севере. In *Морфология праздника.* Санкт-Петербург: Издательство Санкт-Петербургского университета. Pp. 254–266.

Stepanova 2000 = Степанова, А. С. *Устная поэзия тунгудских карел.* Петрозаводск: Периодика.

Ščepanskaja 1986 = Щепанская, Т. Б. 1986. "Знание" пастуха в связи с его статусом. In *Русский Север: проблемы этнокультурной истории, этнографии и фольклористики.* Т. А. Бернштам & К. В. Чистов (eds.). Ленинград: Наука. Pp. 165–171.

Ščepanskaja 2001 = Щепанская, Т. Б. 2001. Сила (коммуникативные и репродуктивные аспекты мужской магии). In *Мужской сборник. Выпуск 1. Мужчина в традиционной культуре.* Москва: Лабиринт. Pp. 71–94.

Talve, Ilmar 1981. *Vatjalaista kansankulttuuria.* Suomalais-ugrilaisen seuran toimituksia 179. Helsinki: Suomalais-Ugrilainen Seura.

Tarkka, Lotte 1994. Other Worlds – Symbolism, Dialogue and Gender in Karelian Oral Poetry. In *Songs Beyond the Kalevala. Transformations of Oral Poetry.* Anna-Leena Siikala & Sinikka Vakimo (eds.). Studia Fennica Folkloristica 2. Helsinki: Finnish Literature Society. Pp. 250–298.

Tarkka, Lotte 1998. Sense of the Forest: Nature and Gender in Karelian Oral Poetry. In *Gender and Folklore: Perspectives on Finnish and Karelian Culture.* Satu Apo, Aili Nenola & Laura Stark-Arola (eds.). Studia Fennica Folkloristica 4. Helsinki: Finnish Literature Society. Pp. 92–142.

Toporkov 2010 = Топорков, А. Л. 2010. *Русские заговоры из рукописных источников XVII – первой половины XIX в.* Москва: Индрик. Available at: http://verbalcharms.ru/books/Toporkov1.pdf [Accessed June 27, 2015]

Trifoev 2013 = Трифоев, В. П. 2013. *Сказание о Немже.* Санкт-Петербург.

Vinokurova 1988 = Винокурова, И. Ю. 1988. Ритуал первого выгона скота на пастбище у вепсов. In *Обряды и верования народов Карелии.* Петрозаводск: Карельский филиал АН СССР. Pp. 4–26.

Vinokurova 1994 = Винокурова, И. Ю. 1994. *Календарные обычаи, обряды и праздники вепсов (конец XIX – начало XX в.).* Санкт-Петербург: Наука.

Vinokurova 2006 = Винокурова, И. Ю. 2006. *Животные в традиционных верованиях вепсов.* Петрозаводск: Издательство Петрозаводского государственного университета.

Virtaranta, Pertti 1967. *Lähisukukielten lukemisto.* Suomalaisen Kirjallisuuden Seuran toimituksia 280. Helsinki: Suomalaisen Kirjallisuuden Seura.

Whitehouse, Harvey 2008. Cognitive Evolution and Religion; Cognition and Religious Evolution. *Issues in Ethnology and Anthropology* (3): 35–47. Available at http://www.anthroserbia.org/content/pdf/articles/whitehouse_cognitive_revolution_and_religion.pdf [Accessed June 27, 2015]

Zajceva & Mullonen 1969 = Зайцева, Мария Ивановна & Муллонен, Мария Ивановна 1969. *Образцы вепсской речи.* Ленинград: Наука.

Zelenin 1991 = Зеленин, Д. К. 1991. *Восточнославянская этнография.* Москва: Наука.

Bengt af Klintberg

The Wonders of Midsummer Night: Magical Bracken

The study of supernatural places is of great importance to legend research, since the localisation to a certain place is a characteristic trait in many legends. The supernatural place is sometimes combined with a certain time of the year, most often one of the major holidays. This is the case with the topic I have chosen to talk about, the belief that bracken casts its seeds or blooms during Midsummer night or the night of St. John the Baptist. This night, the shortest of the whole year, when the sun was believed to turn, was according to European folklore a time when many wonders occur: hidden treasures in the ground come up to the surface, the water in springs and rivers turns into wine (af Klintberg 2010: B121), dreams and visions predict what will happen in the future. These supernatural events are often enacted in places in nature that are far from human settlement, places that thus become temporarily supernatural.

An account of the legend complex which has developed around the bracken requires not only a folkloristic but also some botanical expertise. I cannot boast of being an expert on botany, but I have tried to find out which of the possible ferns are connected with the wonders of Midsummer night. First we can establish that those cryptogamic herbs which are called *fern* in English, *Farn* in German and *ormbunkar* in Swedish make one of the most common families in the vegetable kingdom with about 90,000 known species around the world. The unifying feature of these herbs is that they do not propagate by means of flowers and seeds but by means of spores, which are often to be found underneath the leaves and which fall to the ground as a fine powder. Propagation can also take place through root suckers.

Those plants, which most people associate with the word *fern* are those which are also called *bracken* in English and *bräken* in Swedish. They are often found as undergrowth in forests where the ground is humid. They make but a minor part of all ferns, in Sweden around thirty five species (Mossberg & Stenberg 2003: 42–59). The legends about blooming bracken at Midsummer are seldom specific with reference to species, but I have got the impression that the storytellers have been thinking of the most common bigger species.

In many cases the legends seem to be about that bracken which is called *Pteridium aquilinum* in Latin and whose English name is *common bracken*.

The German and Swedish names, *Adlerfarn* and *örnbräken*, are, like the Latin name, explained by the fact that the stalk, when cut off, has a form reminiscent of an eagle with its wings spread out. Another interpretation of the section surface is that it shows a letter, which has resulted in the herb being used for predictions, for example about the initial of the name of a future spouse (Opie & Tatem 1996 [1989]: 148). It has a straight, thin stalk, around 50 centimetres long, supporting large horizontal leaves. Specimens of the common bracken often form a dense carpet in the landscape. Another large species of bracken consists of several tall leaves which grow up directly from the root. Its Latin name is *Dryopteris filix-mas* and it is called *male fern* in English, *Wurmfarn* in German and *träjon* in Swedish. A closely related species is *Athyrium filix-femina*, in English *common lady-fern*, in German *Wald-Frauenfarn*, in Swedish *majbräken*, in Estonian *naistesõnajalg*. An English record from 1660 which presumably refers to fern seed talks about "the female fern", that is *Athyrium filix-femina* (Vickery 1995: 44), and one also finds it in Estonian legends (Rantasalo 1959: 53).

Bracken is green, but the ball-shaped spore sacs are often yellow, sometimes reddish yellow, and in many cases form long rows. When the spores fall to the ground in the autumn, this cannot be observed with the eye, since the male and female cells are microscopically small. The belief about the seeds of the bracken must have arisen because the spore sacs look as if they might contain little round seeds. However, since there were never any seeds to be seen on the ground under the bracken leaves, the explanation emerged that they fell at a very special point of time, at the magical time when so many other wonders took place in nature, the summer solstice or the night of St. John.

Legends about Bracken and their Vernacular Categorisation

In this paper I want to give an overview of the legend tradition about the wondrous transformation of bracken during the short Midsummer night. Most of my examples will be from Sweden, but there will also be parallels from different parts of Europe. The basic contents in this legend complex are very similar in the whole distribution area: it has been said that the bracken casts its seeds, but this happens only during a short period of time on Midsummer night, the night which in most European languages bears the name of St. John the Baptist. The belief in a flower that blooms in the middle of the night seems to be of later origin than the belief in the magical seeds. There are a few records from various parts of Europe where the rarity of the event is further stressed when it is said that the bracken blooms only once every hundred years. When the seeds fall to the ground they do so with such a force that they can penetrate a metal bowl (e.g. Brøndegaard 1987: 47). A common motif is that one should put several cloths or as many as nine or twelve sheets of paper underneath the plant. The seeds are then said to penetrate all layers except the one at the bottom. If one happens to be present when the wonder takes place and succeeds in collecting the seeds or the flower, fantastic possibilities open up: one may find treasure, one becomes omniscient, one has luck in all enterprises, and – if one has a seed somewhere in one's clothes – one becomes invisible. It is especially the last idea that has triggered people's imagination and led to the creation of legends.

Even if the basic features are the same all over Europe, one finds several minor differences among the legends. The reason for this is that they have integrated motifs from other, related legend complexes, and these are not the same all over Europe but differ in various parts of the continent. What makes an analysis of the entire material interesting from a theoretical perspective is that the texts permit us to see what has caused these combinations. A close reading of the texts reveals that there are points of connection which have made the storytellers bring certain traditions together as parts of the same category. My paper will thus illustrate what could be called vernacular or emic categorisations among those who have told and listened to the legends.

I have followed the habit among folklorists of starting my investigation by consulting Stith Thompson's *Motif-Index of Folk-Literature* (1955–1958) to get a general overview of the source material. I found the motif of a magic fern or bracken under two numbers. The first is motif D965.14, "Magic Fern Blossom. May Be Obtained on St. John's Eve", and the second is motif D1361.5.1: "Magic Fernseed Renders Invisible." After the former motif there is a reference to a Lithuanian source, after the latter some few references to German, English, Scottish and Irish sources. This gives, however, only a hint of the total distribution. The tradition has, as a matter of fact, been well known in almost all of Europe, which becomes evident from the articles under the entry "Farn" in *Handwörterbuch des deutschen Aberglaubens* (Marzell 1930) and *Enzyklopädie des Märchens* (Meinel 1984). Of these two articles the one in *Handwörterbuch* by the prominent German ethnobotanist Heinrich Marzell is especially rewarding. There is also a special study by the Finnish folklorist Aukusti Vilho Rantasalo, *Das 'blühende' Farnkraut* (Rantasalo 1959: 50–72). His rich exemplification reveals that folklore about ferns is abundant in Finland and even more so in Estonia. In 1989 the Hungarian ethnologist Béla Gunda published an article on the blooming fern (Svanberg & Luczaj 2014), while Mall Hiiemäe has discussed the topic in Estonian folklore (Hiiemäe 2007 [1987]: 245–249).

Before I give an account of regional variations within legend tradition, a brief historical survey is appropriate. There is no evidence from classical antiquity that the belief in bracken seeds or flowers appearing at a certain night existed at that time (Marzell 1930: 1216). The oldest instances are from the high Middle Ages, and they deal exclusively with the seeds and their wonderful qualities. A poem by the 13th century poet Konrad von Würzburg contains the following lines (my translation): "If I had seeds of fern, I would rather throw them to be swallowed by catfish than I failed to be faithful to her", written to the lady celebrated in his poem (Marzell 1930: 1223). A plausible interpretation of the words is that fern seeds were considered so precious that one would be very reluctant to give them away.

There are several literary instances from 16th and 17th century England of the widespread belief at that time, that fern seeds could make you invisible. In Shakespeare's *Henry the Fourth* (1596) one finds the following line: "We have the receit of Fernseede, we walke invisible" (II,1). His contemporary colleague Ben Jonson has one of the characters in his play *New Inn* exclaim: "I had – No medicine, sir, to go invisible – No fernseed in my pocket." (Marzell 1930: 1224). A third example is found in a poem by Andrew Marvell, *Daphnis and Chloe* from 1681 (verses 81–84):

> The witch that midnight wakes
> For the fern, whose magic weed
> In one minute casts the seed,
> And invisible him makes. (Opie & Tatem 1996 [1989]: 147.)

In witchcraft trials and literature on magic from the 17th century one encounters information that can hardly be interpreted otherwise than as evidence of a trade in seeds, alleged to be fernseeds. In Erfurt a townsman was executed by sword in 1601 because he had hidden fern seeds in his armpit to make himself invulnerable (Marzell 1930: 1218). In a book of magic, printed in 1674 in Basel, one finds the information that a young man, an acquaintance of the author, had mixed gunpowder and fernseed to become a 'freeshooter' who killed all game he aimed at (Marzell 1930: 1218). In Austria in 1648 a young man was questioned, accused of having sold seven fernseeds that he had himself picked and which had the power to protect their owner during a journey and give him success in his enterprises. Marzell assumes that the specimens which were here called seeds could have been spore sacs from the leaves of ferns.

The Swedish tradition is on the whole homogenous, even if some legends are about bracken seeds while others are about its flower. A representative example is this unprinted record, made in 1932 in the province of Västergötland:

> The *giske* plants, which have big, tall leaves which are pointed at the top, bloom during Midsummer night between twelve and one o'clock. They bloom and ripen in one hour and the seeds fall off. If you take your chance then and hold twelve sheets of paper under them, the seeds run through eleven sheets but remain lying on the twelfth, but it is not worthwhile to talk or laugh while doing this, because then they disappear.
>
> There was a farmhand who was to take seeds of the *giske* during a Midsummer night. He watched the seeds carefully, and when they fell he held the papers under them. And they remained on the twelfth sheet, but at the same moment a hen appeared pulling a load of straw, and it whimpered over and over: "I'm going to Jönköping, I'm going to Jönköping" [a town]. "That's not very likely" the farmhand said grinning. At the same moment both the seeds and the paper sheets and the *giske* plant went away. The farmhand felt ashamed that he had broken his silence, because he would have been able to make himself invisible and many other things if he had managed to take the seeds.
>
> A maid in [the parish of] Åsle, who was out during a Midsummer night and took a nap near a *giske* plant, got seeds of the fern in her shoes. When she came home to her master and mistress in the morning, they couldn't see her, but they heard how she walked forth and back on the floor, but when she took off her shoes she became visible to them again. (ULMA 3933 pp. 2–5.)

The dialect word used for the fern, *giske*, usually designates brackens in general, but according to one note it refers to *Dryopteris filix mas*, male bracken (DFU, 'geske'). If we take a closer look at the record, we will find that it consists of three sections. The first contains beliefs about bracken in a generalised form, after which two legends are told. The first of these is a very well known treasure legend in Swedish tradition (af Klintberg 2010: V62). The only difference between the bracken version and hundreds of other records is that the hen does not appear when the treasure hunter is about to grab a treasure chest but when he wants to take the fern seeds on the sheet of paper. The second legend is a concise version of the legend about the magical bracken which has been most widespread in European tradition, a legend about a person who becomes invisible when a bracken seed by chance slips into his clothes (af Klintberg 2010: R171).

The reason why legends about bracken seeds can be categorised as belonging to treasure legends is of course due to the wonderful qualities of the seeds, which makes them as valuable as any treasure. There are, however, other explanations as well. Most important is that the seeds may only be obtained during Midsummer night, which according to the legends is also the optimum time for treasure hunting. A common trait in treasure legends is that hidden treasures rise to the surface of the ground on Midsummer night. Often they give off a light like that from a flame which leads the treasure hunter to the treasure. This is also a recurring trait in Swedish records describing what happens to the bracken in the midnight hour. In his ground-breaking work *Wärend och wirdarne*, the doyen of Swedish folklore research, Gunnar Olof Hyltén-Cavallius, writes:

> A person who goes to take the bracken flower is met on his way by hideous snakes and dragons, who try to scare him away. The flower itself looks like the pupil of an eye, but shines like a candle or a little bright burning star. The one who has the bracken flower is lucky in everything and can also make himself invisible. A farmhand, who crossed a field on Midsummer night, happened to get a bracken flower in his shoe. When he later came to other people and talked to them, nobody could see him until he undressed; then the bracken bloom fell out of his shoe. (Hyltén-Cavallius 1868, appendix, p. xxi.)

A common trait in Swedish treasure legends is that the treasure hunter meets with optical illusions that prevent him from taking the treasure. They might be frightening, when they appear as snakes, dragons or flayed bulls, or comical. In the latter case it is often a lame hen that is seen pulling a hay wain (af Klintberg 2010: V61) or a lame hen or old woman asking the treasure hunter if he thinks that she will reach a distant town before dawn (af Klintberg 2010: V62). The vision makes the treasure hunter break his or her silence, and at the same moment the treasure disappears.

In the first of the texts quoted, the legend from Västergötland about the *giske* seeds, we have an example of the latter form, a comical optical illusion. In the second text, the one taken from Hyltén-Cavallius' *Wärend och wirdarne*, the visions are frightening. A third example, recorded in the province of Uppland, contains both alternatives:

> Once there was a young man, who went away one Midsummer night to pick this flower. At 12 o'clock he saw an immense mass of snakes and around them colossal oxen with huge horns and other monsters. He became afraid, to be sure, but he still remained silent. However, the flower sprouted, but before it was quite complete, he happened to see a lame hen coming pulling a big hay wain. This seemed so ridiculous to him that he burst out laughing, and at once the flower disappeared and with it all the other visions. (Grip 1917: 73.)

Treasure legends are thus a category to which the legends of the bracken seeds and bracken flower are assigned in Sweden and several other countries. If we widen the geographical perspective we will, however, find another vernacular category of even greater importance: the Devil legends. The legends about somebody who obtains the magical bracken have often intermingled with other legends about people who become owners of a valuable witchcraft tool through a compact with the Devil. They may become 'freeshooters', or acquire a book of black magic, a spiritus familiaris or a purse from which money never goes missing. These legends differ from most treasure legends in that the acquisition of the flower or the seeds are part of a transaction. The person who wants to get them must in exchange leave three drops of blood or in some other way establish contact with the Devil. Some of the oldest descriptions of how to obtain bracken seeds belong to this category.

In treasure legends documented in the Slavic and Baltic countries the bracken flower is often an important ingredient. It is a prerequisite for finding the treasure, which is guarded by the Devil or some evil spirit in the Devil's crew (Rantasalo 1959: 59). As a consequence they often contain traits typical of Devil legends.

A well-known literary example is Nikolai Gogol's short story "St. John's Eve" ("The night of Ivan Kupala" in Russian), published for the first time in 1830 and inspired by legends that Gogol heard during his childhood in Ukraine. The young poor farmhand Petro falls in love with the beautiful daughter of his master but is driven away from the farm after having given her a kiss under the very eyes of her father. A strange man, by many believed to be the Devil, promises to help him to win the girl back. He is told that on St. John's eve he should go to a certain place where the bracken blooms at midnight and pluck the flower. He follows the advice, and a witch appears who hands him a spade. He finds the treasure with the spade but is told that the lid cannot be opened until human blood has been shed over it. The demonic influence of the witch makes him lose control of himself so that he kills his sweetheart's little brother. After this terrible crime he becomes increasingly insane, and at the end of the story he is carried away by the Devil. All that remains is a pile of ashes where he once stood, and the gold has turned into pieces of broken pottery. (Gogol 1961.)

Even if Gogol has embroidered the plot into a lengthy romantic narrative in the fashion of his time, there is no doubt that the main features are based upon a folk legend, something that Gogol affirms. This legend seems to have been very well known in Russian and Ukranian folk tradition. In her book *Russian Folk Belief* Linda J. Ivanits (1992: 11) writes: "Very widespread was the belief that in the forest on this day [Kupalo's Day, that is St. John's Day] a miraculous fern bloomed with fiery brilliance, indicating the location of buried treasure". In Slavic tradition the bracken flower is described as belonging to the sphere of the Devil, and Ivanits has also published a legend about this flower under the title "Devils". The difference between the Slavic and the Scandinavian treasure legends is that the latter do not describe the search for treasure as a sinful act where success implies a compact with the Devil.

The plots in those European legends which have been categorised as belonging to the legends about the Devil have developed in two different ways. One is that a prerequisite for a successful acquisition of the bracken seeds or bracken flower is a compact with the Devil. Another one is that the protagonist of the legend protects himself with Christian symbols and therefore succeeds in taking them from the Devil. One example is a Portuguese legend based on the belief that the Devil shakes the bracken on St. John's night so that invisible seeds fall. A man succeeds in taking them because he has laid a cloth with silver coins in each corner under the bracken. Then he escapes from the place making crosses on the ground with his sword. The sign of the cross protects him against the Devil who wants to tear him to pieces. (Rantasalo 1959: 67.)

Similar legends, in which a person succeeds in obtaining the bracken flower with the aid of protective Christian symbols, have also been told in Estonia. In several legends this protection comes from the hymnbook, in others from the fact that the cloth under the bracken has been blessed by the parish parson (Rantasalo 1959: 56).

When studying the legends about bracken and the magic of St. John's night, one discerns a third vernacular category which might be called ethnobotanical. Bracken is just one of several wild herbs which have been associated with concepts of magic and witchcraft, and it is not surprising that these traditions have sometimes intermingled. The supernatural time which plays such a central role in the legend complex about the bracken, St. John's night, is also mentioned in connection with other herbs with alleged supernatural qualities. A plant that already in classical antiquity had an aura of nocturnal terror is the *Mandragora officinarum* or mandrake, in Swedish *alruna*, which was believed to grow under gallows from the sperm of hanged criminals and whose fleshy root could be made into a little human-like figure with the power of drawing money to its owner (Schlosser 1912; Norlind 1918: 23 ff.; Köhler-Zülch 1997).

Another magic herb has in several languages a name in which the first element is 'iron', for example German *Eisenkraut* and Swedish *järnört*. It was among other things believed to make iron explode: horseshoes that trod on it and sickles that happened to cut it burst into pieces, or the iron blade came loose from the handle. The folk beliefs about this iron plant have been especially rich in Slavic folklore, but they are also documented in the countries east of the Baltic. If a person had it in his hand, he acquired supernatural strength (Rantasalo 1959: 36 ff.; cf. Norlind 1918: 20). A species which has in many places been said to have these magical qualities is *vervain* in English, *Verbena officinalis*.

Neither of these two plants has, however, become mixed up with the blooming bracken of St. John's night as often as a plant that, like bracken, belongs to the ferns, *Botrychium lunaria*. In English it is called moonwort, in German *Springwurzel* and in Swedish *låsbräken* or *låsgräs* (cf. Svanberg 1998: 209). The Swedish first element *lås* means 'lock', and the name bears witness to a belief that existed in classical antiquity, namely that the owner of the herb could open any lock. The belief seems to go back to sympathetic magic: parts of the plant have in people's eyes been reminiscent of a key or a lock (e.g. Dybeck 1849: 16).

The most widespread description of how one may obtain the magic moonwort carries the advice that one should utilise the woodpecker's ability of finding this herb, which is considerably smaller than the brackens we have met previously and therefore difficult to catch sight of. In Sweden this belief was recorded in no less than three versions by an industrious collector from the early 19th century, Leonhard Fredrik Rääf. One of them goes as follows:

> Stuff a big plug into the hole of the nest of a black woodpecker; the bird, which cannot peck it out, will fly away for a moonwort and blow on the plug, which will jump out, after which it will leave hold of the herb. If you pick it up and keep it in your mouth while blowing on whatever you like, it will immediately open. (Rääf 1957: 280.)

The belief complex about a magic herb which opens all locks is not very widespread in Swedish tradition and often has the character of secret knowledge transmitted in handwritten form in books of black magic. It was known in classical antiquity as is attested by a description in *Historia naturalis* by Pliny the Elder (cf. Rantasalo 1959: 43 ff.). In his survey of folklore about magic herbs, Rantasalo gives several examples of the widespread belief that one should take the opportunity when the young of the woodpecker have hatched and the bird has momentarily left its nest. It is to save the shut-in young that the woodpecker flies away and finds a moonwort (Rantasalo 1959: 40 ff.).

In Estonian folk tradition one encounters a special version of this concept: a hedgehog manages to find a moonwort after it has been blocked from its nest and separated from its young by a wooden fence (Rantasalo 1959: 45).

A comparison of the sources clearly shows that the traditions about the seeds and flower of bracken and those about the moonwort that opens up all locks have often been brought together to the same vernacular category of magical herbs, which has resulted in the two traditions having often been mixed up. The bracken flower is thus said not only to make one invisible and lead to treasure but also to make locks open. Moonwort is likewise said not only to open locks but also to make its bearer invisible and help him or her find hidden treasure (Rantasalo 1959: 59). About both herbs, it is said that the enterprise of seizing them requires careful preparation in the form of one or several pieces of cloth or several sheets of paper put on the ground (cf. Rantasalo 1959: 53).

Unintentional Acquisition of Bracken Seed or the Bracken Flower

If we look at the folklore which describes intentional attempts to seize bracken seeds or flowers during St. John's night, we find that form might differ. This folklore might have the form of a legend reporting a single course of events, but it can also consist of a description of how to proceed and what might happen, that is, folk beliefs in a generalised form. Those records that describe unintentional contacts with the magic of the bracken seeds or its flower have on the other hand practically always legend form. They are narratives about people who happen to be in a forest during St. John's night and without noticing it pick up a bracken seed or flower in a shoe or a bootleg. This leads to consequences that surprise both the protagonist and the people in his or her village.

The most frequent motif in these legends is that the protagonist becomes invisible. One legend type which has been especially widespread in German-speaking areas is about a farmer who has walked into the forest on St. John's eve to search for a runaway domestic animal and happens to get a bracken seed in one of his shoes. This makes him invisible, and when he enters his farmhouse all the people are very surprised when they hear him speaking but cannot see him. The farmer takes off his shoes, the seed falls out, and he becomes visible again. Most of the records come from northern and eastern Germany: Westphalia, Mecklenburg, Saxony (Marzell 1930: 1221). This legend has reached as far west as the Aran Islands off the west coast of Ireland. In the 1880s Oliver J. Burke recorded a version on one of the South Isles of Aran in which a farmer walked out to search for a foal that had strayed:

> After a wearisome and fruitless search during the night he returned [...] He was amazed to see that neither wife nor children welcomed him home. [...] At length, breaking silence, he said, "I haven't found the foal." [...] They all sprang to their feet, and his wife called him by name to give over that nonsense, and to come out from his hiding-place [...] then he remembered that he had, on the previous night, crossed a meadow loaded with ferns, an that some of the seed might have got into his shoes, and that he was therefore invisible. (Burke 1887: 99–100.)

The detail of the person being out in the forest looking for a stray domestic animal, a cow, a calf or a foal, reflects an everyday reality in European peasant society. There were not many causes for farm people to go out into the forest after darkness had fallen. However, during the summer it happened now and then that an animal that had been grazing in the forest during the day was missing when the herd returned to the farm in the evening. Then the farmer was forced to go out and look for it. It is easy to imagine that many people might have been filled with uneasy feelings during the search while the dark shadows deepened around them.

A similar legend has been told in Russia and the Baltic countries. It begins as a story about a farmer who goes out to search for a runaway domestic animal, but the plot then develops into a treasure legend, not unexpected considering the fact that east European folklore about the bracken flower is so closely connected to treasure. In a Russian record from the late 19th century we meet a peasant who has gone into a forest to look for his horses. He wanders about until dark without finding them and at last turns to go back. Walking along a dark road he sees a horse-drawn wagon coming in full speed and hears a voice shouting: "Get out of the way!" The peasant turns off the road and removes his cap, thinking that gentlemen are out driving. But the wagon stops in front of him, and someone says: "Take your shoes off, otherwise you'll be in trouble!" The peasant removes his shoes, and at the same moment the wagon and the man have all disappeared. The man understands that a bracken flower must have accidentally been caught in his shoe when he walked about in the forest, and that the drivers of the wagon must have been demonic spirits that guarded a nearby treasure. When the peasant took off his shoe, the flower fell out, and the spirits could grab it. (Ivanits 1992: 168.)

The same legend type has been documented in the district of Pärnu in Estonia. A boy, who is out on St. John's night and has been running over a field covered with brackens, happens to get the magic bracken flower in one of his birch-bark shoes. This is observed by a Devil who is guarding his treasure, and he threatens to take the boy, if he does not give him the bracken flower. The boy had not noticed what had happened, but when he takes off his shoe, the flower falls out and he is saved. (Rantasalo 1959: 59.)

In Denmark legends about the unintentional acquisition of bracken seeds have a special context since the motif has been connected with the beliefs and legends about witches. The explanation for this is that the time for the annual assembly of the witches is, according to many Danish legends, St. John's night (Kristensen 1901: 101 ff.). The Danish folklore collector Evald Tang Kristensen recorded several legends on this theme. One is about a farmhand who met his sweetheart on a Saturday evening, which happened to be St. John's eve, and on his way home he walked over a heath. On the Sunday he went to church together with his master and mistress. On their way home he could not help laughing when he looked at his mistress. The farmer got angry and asked why he laughed. The farmhand answered that he had seen a cream cask on her head when she was sitting in the church. When the farm mistress heard this, she took off the shoes of the farmhand and turned them upside down, and a bracken seed fell out. Now the farmer and the farmhand understood that the mistress of the farm was a witch who stole cream from her neighbours by means of magic. (Kristensen 1900: 425.) This is a widespread Scandinavian legend, but in most variants the events take place during an Easter sermon, and the connection with the folklore of St. John's eve and hence the motif of the bracken seed is missing (cf. af Klintberg 2010: N40).

One may ask why unintentional acquisition has to such an extent inspired creation of legends. My answer is that the motif is dramatically and sometimes also comically rewarding, since it contains an element of surprise. But even more important is that the listeners have been able to identify themselves with the protagonist of the legend. Many who have heard stories about attempts to obtain bracken seeds or the bracken flower on St. John's night have probably dissociated themselves from such an action, since it has been conceived as forbidden black magic. But all, even those who repudiated such godless behaviour, had experiences of walks in forests among thick fields of bracken.

Knowledge about Wild Herbs Obtained from Spirits in Nature

The traditions about bracken seeds and flowers belong, as we have seen, to the realm of folk beliefs and legends. In conclusion I would like to linger over another legend tradition which is connected with the real use of bracken, above all in folk medical contexts. It is especially the roots of some brackens that have been made use of; several recipes are to be found in medieval herbals. In southeastern Sweden a legend has been told in which the message is that the spirits of nature possess a knowledge of wild herbs that humans do not. In Kristianopel in the province of Blekinge, on the Baltic coast, the following legend was told as late as in the 20th century:

> Once the men were out fishing with seine nets, and they got the daughter of the merwoman in their seines. When they came home, they emptied the fish on the floor of their cottage. Then a creature ran in under a bed. Soon after the merwoman entered the house shouting: "Whatever you suffer, and whatever you whine, Tonguebill, you must not say what the bracken root is useful for!"
>
> And still today no man knows what that root is good for. Bracken is indeed a plant that has big roots, but no one knows if they are good enough to be of any use. (Af Klintberg 1972: no. 34.)

In a variant of the same legend type (af Klintberg 2010: F6) from the same Swedish province it is a female forest spirit who has a love affair with a man. The man wants to get rid of her and is just about to shoot her when she says: "If you spare me, I will tell you that the bracken is the most useful of all herbs, and I will let you know all its secret qualities." She is, however, killed, and therefore still today no one knows the hidden qualities of the bracken. (Wigström 1952: 175.) The legend type has also been documented in Hessen in Germany, but there the herb with unknown qualities is wild sage, belonging to the salvia family (Petzoldt 1970: no. 312b).

What makes this legend so interesting are the implications that there is secret knowledge among the spirits of nature that man has not yet acquired. There are several other Scandinavian legends in which spirits of nature teach humans how to use wild herbs. In one of them a woman is advised to use mugwort when she is brewing (af Klintberg 2010: K7), in another a forest spirit tells a wife about the protective qualities of daphne and valerian (af Klintberg 2010: E30).

Conclusions

One conclusion which might be drawn is that there is a difference between the legends and beliefs about the bracken in most parts of Europe and those in the northern fringe area. In most parts of Europe bracken seed and flowers have become diabolised as a consequence of the medieval condemnation of them as belonging to the Devil. In parts of northern Europe, however, the belief in elves and other nature spirits never became as closely associated with the Devil as further south. Therefore Swedish legends can describe attempts to acquire bracken seeds and flowers, where the Devil is not mentioned but where the resistance comes from spirits of nature.

To sum up: the legends about magical bracken and its seeds and flowers seem to have originated in the Middle Ages and were very widespread all over Europe in the 16th and 17th centuries, as witnessed from herbals, court reports and literary evidence. The belief in the seeds is older than the belief in the glowing bracken flower. The latter especially belongs to Slavic folklore in the east and Baltic and Scandinavian folklore in the north and shows a close affinity with the belief in fires as marking treasure.

The core of the legend complex is very simple, but it has been combined with related legend complexes such as treasure legends, Devil and witch legends and legends about other magical plants. These combinations provide interesting information as to how storytellers have categorised their traditions.

Sources

Unprinted

DFU = Dialekt- och folkminnesarkivet, Uppsala: Thomas Larsson, Dimbo, Västergötland, "Om giskefrö och jordagods" (ULMA 3933, pp. 2–5).

Literature

Brøndegaard, V. J. 1987. *Folk og flora* 1. København: Rosenkilde og Bagger.
Burke, Oliver J. 1887. *South Isles of Aran*. London: Kegan Paul, Trench & Co.
Dybeck, Richard 1849. *Runa. Läsning för fäderneslandets fornvänner*. Stockholm: J. L. Brudins förlag.
Gogol, Nikolaj 1961. *Ukrainska noveller*. Stockholm: Forum.
Grip, Elias 1917. *Några bidrag till kännedom om svenskt allmogeliv*. Stockholm: Magn. Bergvalls Förlag.
Hiiemae, Mall 2007 [1987]. Sõnajalg õitseb jaaniööl. In *Sõnajalg jaaniööl*. Eesti Mõttelugu 73. Tartu: Ilmamaa. Pp. 245–249.
Hyltén-Cavallius, Gunnar Olof 1868. *Wärend och wirdarne* 2. Stockholm: P. A. Norstedt & Söner.
Ivanits, Linda J. 1992. *Russian Folk Belief*. New York, London: M. E. Sharpe, Inc.
af Klintberg, Bengt 1972. *Svenska folksägner*. Stockholm: Norstedt.
af Klintberg, Bengt 2010. *The Types of the Swedish Folk Legend*. Folklore Fellows' Communications 300. Helsinki: Academia Scientiarum Fennica.

Köhler-Zülch, Ines 1997. Mandragora. In *Enzyklopädie des Märchens* 9. Berlin: Walter de Gruyter. Pp. 112–118.

Kristensen, Evald Tang 1900–1901. *Danske sagn* VI–VII. Århus. Facsimile edn. 1980, København: Nyt Nordisk Forlag Arnold Busck.

Marzell, Heinrich 1930. Farn. In *Handwörterbuch des deutschen Aberglaubens* 2. Berlin, Leipzig: Walter de Gruyter. Facsimile edn. 1987, Berlin, New York: Walter de Gruyter. Pp. 1215–1229.

Meinel, Gertraud 1984. Farn. In *Enzyklopädie des Märchens* 4. Berlin: Walter de Gruyter. Pp. 860–866.

Mossberg, Bo, & Lennart Stenberg 2003. *Den nya nordiska floran.* Stockholm: Bonnier.

Norlind, Tobias 1918. *Skattsägner.* Lund, Leipzig: Gleerup.

Opie, Iona & Moira Tatem 1996 [1989]. *A Dictionary of Superstitions.* Oxford, New York: Oxford University Press.

Petzoldt, Leander 1970. *Deutsche Volkssagen.* München: C. H. Beck.

Rääf, Leonhard Fredrik 1957. *Svenska skrock och signerier.* Stockholm: Almqvist & Wiksell.

Rantasalo, Aukusti Vilho 1959. *Einige Zaubersteine und Zauberpflanzen im Volksaberglauben der Finnen.* Folklore Fellows' Communications 176. Helsinki: Academia Scientiarum Fennica.

Schlosser, Alfred 1912. *Die Sage vom Galgenmännlein im Volksglauben und in der Literatur.* Münster: Theissingsche Buchhandlung.

Svanberg, Ingvar 1998. *Människor och växter. Svensk folklig botanik från "ag" till "örtbad".* Stockholm: Arena.

Svanberg, Ingvar & Lukasz Luczaj (eds.) 2014. *Pioneers in European Ethnobiology.* Uppsala: Elanders Sverige AB.

Thompson, Stith 1955–1958. *Motif-Index of Folk-Literature: A Classification of Narrative Elements in Folktales, Ballads, Myths, Fables, Mediaeval Romances, Exempla, Fabliaux, Jest-Books and Local Legends.* I–VI. Revised and expanded edition. Copenhagen: Rosenkilde & Bagger.

Vickery, Roy 1995. *A Dictionary of Plant-Lore.* Oxford, New York: Oxford University Press.

Wigström, Eva 1952. *Folktro och sägner från skilda landskap.* Svenska sagor och sägner 11. Uppsala: Lundequistska Bokhandeln; København: Ejnar Munksgaard.

Daniel Sävborg

The Icelander and the Trolls
– The Importance of Place

The aim of this article is to discuss some problems in saga studies that scholars have for a long time examined through traditional philological methods, which has meant that both the questions and the answers have been governed by these methods and this discipline. This article rather attempts to actualise some folkloristic concepts and perspectives and, while still focusing on the saga texts, tries to solve the problems in another way.[1]

The Icelandic family sagas are most famous for down-to-earth stories about farmers and their quite trivial conflicts which lead to local feuds. This characteristic is a part of their well-known 'realistic' character. But there are in fact also many of meetings with the Otherworld, the Supernatural in a broad sense. One example is found in *Njáls saga*, where a certain Hildiglúmr is presented:

> On the Sunday night twelve weeks before winter, Hildiglum was outside the house; then he heard a tremendous crash, and the earth and sky seemed to quiver. He looked to the west, and thought he saw a ring of fire with a man on a grey horse inside the circle, riding furiously. He rushed past Hildiglum with a blazing firebrand held aloft, so close that Hildiglum could see him distinctly; he was as black as pitch, and Hildiglum heard him roaring out [...]. Before Hildiglum's eyes, it seemed, the rider hurled the firebrand east towards the mountains; a vast fire erupted, blotting the mountains from sight. The rider rode east towards the flames and vanished into them. Hildiglum returned to the house and went to his bed, where he fainted and lay unconscious for a long time. When he recovered he could remember every detail of the apparition he had seen, and told his father about it. His father asked him to tell it to Hjalti Skeggjason. Hildiglum went to Hjalti and told him. Hjalti said, 'You have seen the witch-ride, and that is always a portent of disaster.' (Transl. Magnusson & Pálsson in *Njáls saga* 1960: 260–261.)

There are some remarkable features in this description. A crash is heard, and the earth and the heaven shake exactly when the supernatural rider is seen. All the time a distance is kept between Hildiglúmr and the rider: they never speak to each other, and there is no interaction between them. Hildiglúmr's unconsciousness afterwards marks the meeting with the supernatural as an extreme experience. The fact that Hildiglúmr's father does not understand the event but sends him to an authority also marks the non-normality of

194

the event. All these features mark the experience as something un-natural, abnormal and rare. They mean that the episode nevertheless works quite well in a realistic context with down-to-earth conflicts that dominate this saga.

But there are more saga types in Old Norse literature than the family sagas. There are saga types that are famous for the opposite of down-to-earth stories and realism. *Egils saga einhenda*, for example, tells of adventures in the very distant past (it is unclear when) in Russia, Hun-land, Gautland, Denmark, Giantland, the so-called Underworld and several lands with fantasy names. The main heroes go out to search for two princesses who have been abducted by a grotesque flying monster. In a distant land they suddenly meet somebody:

> They saw a monster up among the rocks, broader than it was high. It spoke in a shrill, bell-like voice and asked who was so bold that he dared steal one of the queen's goats.
>
> "Who are you, oh beautiful, bed-worthy lady? Where's your queen's country?"
>
> "My name's Skin-Beak," she said, "I'm the daughter of Queen Eagle-Beak who rules over Jotunheim. Her residence isn't very far from here, and you'd better go and see her before you start stealing things."
>
> "You're absolutely right", said Asmund, and gave her a gold ring. (Transl. Pálsson & Edwards in *Egils saga einhenda* 1985: 233.)

The "monster" is a troll-woman. Here we may also speak about a meeting with an Otherworld being, a supernatural being in a broad sense. However, in this case there is no crash and earthquake, and no distance. On the contrary, an easy, unproblematic conversation and interaction is described. There is no unconsciousness, no shock, no lack of understanding of what has happened, no surprise of any kind. Everything here is obvious, described as pure fact. In short, the episode is very different from the story about Hildiglúmr's meeting with the fire-rider in *Njáls saga*.

This difference is not necessarily surprising. *Egils saga einhenda* belongs to a different saga genre, the so-called *fornaldarsögur*, 'sagas of ancient times'. *Fornaldarsögur* are never about down-to-earth conflicts among farmers in Viking Age Iceland, as the family sagas are, but take place in a distant past and in distant lands, and meetings with monsters are common. The family sagas – at least most of them – clearly claim historicity. In contrast, the *fornaldarsögur* and the so-called *riddarasögur* ('sagas of knights') do not generally make that claim. Some of them are clearly intended as pure fiction. Both the *riddarasögur* and a sub-group of the *fornaldarsögur* have sometime been called *Märchensagas* by German scholars (for example, Schier 1992: 600–601).

When the word *Märchen* is mentioned, folkloristic theory seems to be of relevance. The fundamental distinction between *Sage* and *Märchen* comes to mind.[2] A short, and admittedly simplified, recapitulation clarifies what parts of the distinction I am interested in.

The *Sage* has some pretension of talking about the truth, or at least a possible truth, while the *Märchen* has not. Both *Sage* and *Märchen* often depict encounters with otherworldly beings, but they depict these meetings in fundamentally different ways. Here I follow Max Lüthi's (1986 [1982]: 10) description: "in the folktale these actors stand side by side and freely interact with one another. Everyday folktale characters do not feel that an encounter with an otherworld being is an encounter with an alien dimension." The folktale hero "is not astonished, and he is not afraid. He lacks all sense of the extraordinary" (Lüthi 1986 [1982]: 7). In another work Lüthi (1976: 46) claims: "The real fairy-tale hero is not astonished by miracles and magic; he accepts them as if they were a matter of course. Supernatural figures endowed with magical powers appear, to oppose or help him, not to bear witness for a completely different, supernatural world which makes us shudder in horror or ecstasy." This is contrasted with such encounters in the *Sage*: "Fear, curiosity, or a sense of transgressing limits grips the person who comes across the trace of an otherworld being" (Lüthi 1986 [1982]: 5). The *Sage* "revolves around the inexplicable intrusion of a completely different world" (Lüthi 1976: 44). Generally, and as a summary of this, Lüthi ascribes the *Märchen* a basic "one-dimensionality" (1986 [1982]: 10), while the *Sage*, in contrast, can be described as two-dimensional (although Lüthi does not use this word).

We recognise a lot of these contrastive features in the two episodes from *Njáls saga* and *Egils saga einhenda*. In the meeting with the troll-woman in *Egils saga einhenda* most of the features Lüthi described as fundamental for the *Märchen* are found: "these actors stand side by side and freely interact with one another". The heroes "do not feel that an encounter with an otherworld being is an encounter with an alien dimension"; no "wonder", no "astonishment", no "sense of the extraordinary"; during the meeting with the giants Egill reacts "as if they were a matter of course". We clearly have to do with signs of "one-dimensionality" in the *Egils saga einhenda* episode.

In contrast, in the description of Hildiglúmr's meeting with the fire-rider in *Njáls saga* we may clearly talk about "fear, curiosity, or a sense of transgressing limits grips the person who comes across the trace of an otherworld being", a story that "revolves around the inexplicable intrusion of a completely different world". All the elements I listed earlier in the *Njáls saga* episode can be called 'markers of two-dimensionality'.

I find these distinctions between *Sage* and *Märchen* useful in the analysis of encounters with the Otherworld in Old Norse literature. This of course does not mean that different Icelandic sagas could be called *Sagen* and *Märchen*. The Icelandic sagas are all long elaborate literary works and differ in many ways from the much shorter oral single-episodic *Sagen*. But it does seem possible to use Lüthi's basic distinction of one-dimensionality vs. two-dimensionality as a model to understand and explain the encounters with the Otherworld in the Icelandic sagas, and, most important, the differences between different episodes in the sagas.

The idea to point out such differences between *fornaldarsögur* and family sagas in their depiction of encounters with the supernatural is not entirely new. Old Norse scholars such as Aðalheiður Guðmundsdóttir, Stephen Mitchell and Else Mundal have all described a sense of borderline between the human world and the Supernatural that we find in the family sagas but not in the *fornaldarsögur* and *riddarasögur*.[3] John Lindow

(1986: 277, 280) has pointed out that the 'marvellous' is taken for granted in the *fornaldarsögur* and 'romances' (*riddarasögur*) but not in the family sagas. He also notes that people in the *fornaldarsögur* and 'romances' meet the supernatural anywhere and anytime, but in the family sagas mainly during darkness or conditions of bad weather.

Here I will search for some patterns and develop some of these themes. But chiefly I will use the distinction between one-dimensionality and two-dimensionality to solve some scholarly problems concerning the family sagas.

*

So far the issue seems to be about a difference between two saga genres, the family sagas (such as *Njáls saga*) on one hand and the *fornaldarsögur/* romances (such as *Egils saga einhenda*) on the other. This is also the main contrast given by the scholars mentioned above.

However, it is not that simple. All encounters with the Otherworld in the family sagas are not depicted in the way of the *Njáls saga* episode about Hildiglúmr's meeting with the fire-rider.

In the family saga *Gunnars saga Keldugnúpsfífls*, the protagonist Gunnarr meets two female trolls during a journey to an unidentified arctic land far to the west. They talk, they fight and Gunnarr kills one of the trolls and befriends the other (pp. 358–359, 360–363). There is close contact and interaction all the time. Neither Gunnarr nor the narrator describes anything about this as remarkable. In short: we have no signs of two-dimensionality here. The tendency is the same as in the *fornaldarsaga Egils saga einhenda* and the opposite of the Hildiglúmr episode in *Njáls saga*, although both *Gunnars saga* and *Njáls saga* are family sagas.

This means that in the one genre of family saga we have two contrasting tendencies in the descriptions of meetings with the Otherworld: the one-dimensional of the *Märchen* type on one hand, and the two-dimensional of the *Sage* type on the other. How should we interpret these two tendencies within the same genre?

The only answer so far is given – partly indirectly – by scholars who want to explain the occasional occurrence of supernatural motifs in the supposedly realistic family sagas. Most leading scholars want to defend the traditional description of the family sagas such as *Njáls saga* as fundamentally realistic. But in the same time they admit that there are certain examples of Otherworld encounters in exactly *Njáls saga* and several other family sagas. The way to explain this supposed contradiction has been to point out some features that resemble the ones I mentioned earlier.

In another scene in *Njáls saga* one of the protagonists is seen after his violent death, sitting in his grave mound, which has magically opened, reciting stanzas about revenge (pp. 192–194). In his attempt to reconcile this description with the characterisation of *Njáls saga* as realistic, Vésteinn Ólason (2007: 15) has pointed to certain features in the description: there is a physical distance between the people who witness the event and the un-dead man, and there is no interaction between them. These are elements that are also found in the Hildiglúmr episode in the same saga. And we may actually add another feature in the episode that is also a reminder of the Hildiglúmr scene: those who hear about the event at the grave mound doubt it and discuss whether it can be true. All these elements are markers of two-dimensionality.

I agree with Vésteinn Ólason that such features give a scene a 'realistic' character – it seems to be a story that claims to be true, in the same way as *Sagen* claim to be true. The presence of the trolls in *Gunnars saga Keldugnúpsfífls* is a different case for Vésteinn Ólason. Since this family saga has a lot of Otherworld encounters, but none of these 'realistic' markers, Vésteinn has to explain the contradiction of the description of the 'realistic' family saga in a different way. The solution is to declare *Gunnars saga*, and many of other family sagas that have Otherworld encounters, as 'post-classical' and not really genuine family sagas (pp. 14–16). It would then be much later than the 'classical' family sagas such as *Njáls saga*, and it would thus be natural that it differed from them and lacked their typical features.

These post-classical family sagas are claimed to be different from the classical ones in many respects. Above all, they are ascribed a more fantastic character than the classical ones; they are claimed to be full of magic and monsters, trolls, giants, dragons, etc.[4] But they are also ascribed other pretensions regarding reality and history than the classical sagas. While the classical family sagas are supposed to pretend to tell stories of real, historical events, the post-classical ones, on the other hand, are supposed to have – at least to a high degree – been intended and perceived as pure fiction.[5] In this way, they would then resemble the *fornaldarsögur* and the *riddarasögur*: the post-classical family sagas are usually claimed to have emerged as a phenomenon under the influence of these genres.[6]

Thus, in the classical/post-classical dichotomy we have a possible explanation for the two opposite tendencies to depict encounters with the Otherworld in the family sagas. This explanation could be broken down into three points:

1. It is a matter of the time of composition. The early sagas use two-dimensional depiction, while the late sagas use one-dimensional depiction.
2. It is a matter of influence from other genres. The genuine (classical) family sagas use two-dimensional depiction, while the sagas influenced by the *fornaldarsögur* use one-dimensional depiction.
3. It is a matter of a claim to reality vs. fiction. The sagas that pass themselves of as historically true use two-dimensional depiction, while the sagas that present themselves as fiction use one-dimensional depiction.

But is this explanation correct? Or is it even the only possible one?

*

In the classical family sagas we have several cases of encounters with Otherworld beings that certainly seem to confirm this explanation. I will give one example.

One famous episode in *Eyrbyggja saga* tells of the haunting at Fróðá. We meet many revenants, a flying moon indoors, a seal coming up from the fireplace, blood rain, etc. But the longest single story in the episode concerns a strange supernatural being. One evening people hear sounds from the dry-fish store. It sounds like the fish is torn out from its skin. People look in the store, but nothing is seen. Later they hear more and more that the dry-fish is torn; they look again, and a short-haired tail is seen. Some men pull the tail, which seems dead, but nothing happens. Suddenly the tail is drawn through their hands and disappears and is never seen again. Later they take out the fish, finding that every fish has been torn out of its skin. Nothing is found alive in the store. (Pp. 147–150.)

In this episode we have a lot of markers of two-dimensionality. People are scared and surprised at the meeting with the supernatural. For a long time the Otherworld being is invisible; people only hear it, and do not see it. When it is seen, it is only seen briefly, and only a very small part of it; in fact, it is so small that it is not clear what creature it is. No interaction takes place between humans and the supernatural being. It disappears totally; it has not come to the dry-fish store through our world, and disappears without going through the store.

There are several other episodes of a similar kind in the classical family sagas. In these episodes two-dimensionality is marked in the depiction of the encounter with the Otherworld. This is the same tendency as in the two *Njáls saga* episodes mentioned earlier, and it is a tendency opposite to the one found in the *fornaldarsaga Egils saga einhenda* and the post-classical family saga *Gunnars saga Keldugnúpsfífls*.

*

So far the solution given by Vésteinn Ólason seems to be confirmed. The two-dimensionality of the *Sage* kind in supernatural encounters does indeed seem to be typical for the classical family saga. But what about the post-classical sagas? Do they all have the one-dimensionality of *Gunnars saga Keldugnúpsfífls* in encounters with the Otherworld?

The post-classical sagas are full of encounters with Otherworld beings and there are certainly many cases that are characterised by the one-dimensional tendency. For example in *Jǫkuls þáttr Búasonar* (pp. 48–55), *Þorsteins þáttr uxafóts* (pp. 359–369) and *Orms þáttr Stórólfssonar* (pp. 409–417) heroes encounter several trolls in Greenland and Norway. This surprises neither the hero nor the narrator, and the hero interacts naturally with the trolls, fights some of them and befriends others. In *Þorskfirðinga saga* the hero Þórir visits a cave in Norway, fights some dragons and takes their treasure (pp. 187–189). In all these cases the encounter with these beings is depicted with full one-dimensionality.

Again, this is clearly in accordance with the picture given by Vésteinn Ólason. One-dimensionality of a *Märchen* kind does indeed seem to be typical for the post-classical family saga. Vésteinn's idea that the difference between one-dimensionality and two-dimensionality corresponds with the classical-postclassical dichotomy seems to be confirmed once more.

*

However, there are problems with this solution. Let us at first go to some more cases in the classical sagas.

Bjarnar saga Hítdœlakappa is a classical family saga, and in most ways a very typical one. It is mainly concerned with trivial down-to-earth conflicts between neighbouring farmers. But in one episode we are told about the hero's journey on the Atlantic.

> It happened, when Bjorn was accompanying the king, and sailing with his company in southern seas, that a dragon flew over the king's company and attacked them and tried to snatch one of the men. Bjorn was standing nearby and covered the man with his shield, but the dragon clawed almost through the shield. Then Bjorn gripped the dragon's tail with one hand, while with the other he struck behind the wings, and the dragon was severed, and fell down dead. The king gave Bjorn a large sum of money and a fine long-ship; with this he sailed to Denmark. (Transl. Alison Finlay in *Bjarnar saga Hítdœlakappa* 2000: 15.)

Here we have no surprise from either the narrator or the hero, no fear, no curiosity, and no sense of transgressing the limits. Instead we have unproblematic close contact and interaction. This is exactly the same one-dimensionality as in the *Märchen*, as in the *fornaldarsaga Egils saga einhenda* and as in the post-classical sagas I have mentioned. But here, in this case, we find this tendency in a classical family saga.

And the same is true in some other classical sagas too, which describe encounters with Otherworld beings. As for example in *Kormáks saga*, where the hero is killed in a fight with a giant (*Kormáks saga* 1939: 299), or in a short episode in *Njáls saga* about the hero Þorkell, who travelled to Estonia and Finland and killed a dragon and a centaur (*Njáls saga* 1954: 302–303). In these cases we have full interaction all the time, no wonder, surprise, etc. There are several similar episodes in the classical sagas. They are as one-dimensional as a *Märchen*.

This means that Vésteinn Ólason's solution – his attempt to defend the 'realism' of the classical family sagas – is not so obvious after all. The two-dimensional tendency is not the sole tendency in the classical family saga stories about encounters with the Otherworld.

So what about the post-classical sagas? Are all their Otherworld encounters really characterised by the one-dimensionality of the *Märchen* type?

Bergbúa þáttr is the post-classical saga that is most consequently concerned with the theme of Otherworld encounter: the whole saga is about a meeting with a mountain-elf. The story can be summarised as follows: the protagonist and his servant escape a storm and hide in a cave, where they hear sounds; after a while they see something glow which they interpret as eyes; then they hear a voice recite a poem, in which the reciter identifies himself as a giant and mountain-elf; the day after the two men continue their journey (pp. 442–450).

Here we may note that there is always a distance kept; there is no interaction or conversation; the men only hear the being, but do not see him, just (perhaps) a small part of him (the eyes). This is comparable with the creature in the dry-fish store in *Eyrbyggja saga*, which people could also only hear, and, finally only saw a small part of. Thus, in the post-classical saga *Bergbúa þáttr*, we have a lot of markers of two-dimensionality.

I mentioned *Þorskfirðinga saga* earlier, in which the hero fights dragons in Norway. At the end of that saga a dragon is mentioned again. It is said that there was a rumour that Þórir, the protagonist, was transformed into a dragon, and that people thought they had seen a dragon flying in the mountains (p. 226). There is thus a remarkable distance to the monster, and there is no interaction. There seems to be doubt in that the dragon is presented as merely a rumour.

In short, in these post-classical sagas we find markers of two-dimensionality of the typical *Sage* kind, of the kind we have met a lot in the classical family sagas. We have already seen that there were several cases where classical sagas depicted the encounters with the Otherworld with a one-dimensional tendency of a *Märchen* kind. Regarding the depiction of the encounter with the Otherworld there does not seem to be a clear difference between the alleged groups of classical and post-classical family sagas. The solution of Vésteinn Ólason is thus refuted.

However, we still have to interpret the results. The question from the beginning of the article remains: why are some Otherworld stories in the family sagas depicted as one-dimensional and others as two-dimensional?

*

One possible explanation could be that the choice has to do with the narrative function of the encounter with the Otherworld. It is a remarkable fact that in several of the episodes characterised by two-dimensionality, the Supernatural being had the function of 1) premonition – as the fire-rider in *Njáls saga*, whose function is to foreshadow violent deeds; or the function of 2) causing sickness or accidents – as with the mysterious dry-fish monster in *Eyrbyggja saga*, who appears shortly before the death by drowning of most of the men in the farm, or the mountain-elf in *Bergbúa þáttr*, since this saga concludes with the information that the servant died one year after the event. On the other hand most of the episodes characterised by one-dimensionality are adventure stories about heroes searching for great deeds and treasures and encountering trolls, giants and dragons as part of that. This is true for the episodes in *Gunnars saga* and *Bjarnar saga*, and for the *Njáls saga* story about the monster fight in Estonia, etc.

This does indeed seem to be a possible explanation of the difference, although it does not explain everything, and in fact is more a description than an explanation. And for example the concluding dragon story in *Þorskfirðinga saga* has nothing to do with premonition or causing death – yet it is two-dimensional. We have to search for other explanations too.

*

In fact, there *does* seem to be a pattern in when the encounters are depicted as two-dimensional and one-dimensional. Specifically, those episodes I have mentioned *without* markers of two-dimensionality take place *outside*

Iceland, something that holds true for both classical and post-classical sagas. The dragon in *Bjarnar saga* attacks the hero in the south, in the Atlantic, during the hero's journey around England. Kormákr is killed by the giant in Scotland. The trolls in *Gunnars saga Keldugnúpsfífls, Jǫkuls þáttr, Þorsteins þáttr*, etc. are found in Greenland and Norway. The dragons in *Þorskfirðinga saga* are found in Norway. And in contrast most of the stories with markers of two-dimensionality take place *in Iceland*. It is in Iceland that people are scared by the monster in the dry-fish store. It is in Iceland the fire-rider frightens Hildiglúmr. It is in Iceland the undead man recites stanzas in his open mound. It is in Iceland the two men in *Bergbúa þáttr* hear and sense the mountain-elf in the cave.

In some cases we have met both the opposite tendencies in the same saga. And it is worth noting that *Njáls saga* depicts the fire-rider in Iceland *with* markers of two-dimensionality, but the dragon encounter in Estonia *without* them, and that *Þorskfirðinga saga* depicts the dragon in Iceland *with* markers of two-dimensionality, but the dragons in Norway *without* them. This underscores the connection between these tendencies and the geographical setting.

It is not a new idea that there is a connection between the geographical setting and the occurrence of Otherworld beings. Else Mundal (2006: 720) has, for instance, written: "It is no doubt true that fantastic – and supernatural – elements are much more frequent in texts which tell about events that happened long ago and far away than in stories from the author's own time and environment."[7] This may be true when we look at the Old Norse literature in general, comparing all genres, but it does not say very much about the family sagas. As we have seen there are a lot of Otherworld beings *in Iceland* in these sagas: trolls, giants, dragons and other monsters – such beings are certainly not only far away in distant lands. What really has a clear connection with the geographical setting is something else, specifically the way of *narrating* these episodes, the way of *describing* these encounters with monsters, with the supernatural; that is, with or without what I have called markers of two-dimensionality. I thus think that the geographical setting is the clue.

*

The task of interpreting – explaining – this connection with the setting still remains. The easiest interpretation is of course to return to where I began: the distinction between *Sage* and *Märchen* and Lüthi's description of their respective distinctive features. We could then, as a hypothetical interpretation, regard episodes of Otherworld encounters *with* markers of two-dimensionality as *Sagen*, legends, and thus as stories considered to be basically true, historical, and correspondingly, we could regard episodes *without* these markers as one-dimensional *Märchen*, and thus as stories considered to be non-historical, fictitious.

The connection with the setting would actually be well consistent with this view. Lüthi (1986 [1982]: 7–8) notes that the Otherworld beings in the *Sagen*, even though they are marked to belong to another dimension, are "physically close to human beings. They dwell in his house, in his fields, or in the nearby woods, stream, mountain, or lake." In the *Märchen* the opposite is true; even though they seem to belong to the same world as the humans they dwell far away from them: "Rarely does the hero meet them in his house or village. He comes across them only when he wanders far and wide" (Lüthi 1986 [1982]: 8).

I believe that it is correct to describe a lot of the stories about supernatural encounters in the sagas as *Sagen*, legends connected with specific places in Iceland. But there are some problems with the hypothetical explanation I gave. Specifically it is a fact that encounters with Otherworld beings outside Iceland *generally* in Icelandic literature are depicted without any markers of two-dimensionality. This holds true for the kings' sagas too, which we know were regarded as basically historical, true.

King Olav's encounter with a sea monster in *The Legendary Olav Saga* (p. 58) is depicted with typical one-dimensional tendency, and so is King Harald's encounter with a dragon in *Morkinskinna* (pp. 80–82) and the encounter with trolls in the earliest *Olav Tryggvason saga* (*Saga Óláfs Tryggvasonar* 1932: 175–177). However, these sagas are certainly not *Märchen* in the sense that they would have been regarded as fiction. They were history for the contemporary audience. Nevertheless they have the same one-dimensional tendency as the *Märchen*. But in these cases, as in the family sagas, the most important thing is that these encounters take place outside Iceland – in these cases in the Mediterranean, Constantinople and Norway respectively.

I think there is a somewhat different explanation for the difference between two-dimensional and one-dimensional depiction in the family sagas and for the connection with the geographical setting. I wish to claim that the closer to the vicinity of the narrator/author, the greater need there was to mark two-dimensionality. Meetings with trolls were not normal in the author's own environment, even though he certainly believed they existed there. Thus it was necessary to mark the non-normal, the unnatural. But in foreign lands, on the other hand, it was different. There such beings could, from an Icelander's perspective, very well be quite normal, natural; they were not more surprising than many other foreign things in foreign lands – such as castles, cities, or elephants, which did not occur in Iceland but certainly did not belong to another dimension. Strange beings were also described as natural in the foreign lands in the learned literature that was available in Iceland.

The conclusion is that the supernatural beings *in Iceland* in the family sagas can clearly be said to belong to the realm of *Sage*, the legend. These beings were considered real, but fundamentally different from us, belonging to what could be called another dimension. The trolls, dragons and giants in Greenland, Scotland, the Atlantic and Norway did not belong as clearly to the realm of *Sage* – but neither did they to the realm of *Märchen*, of fiction, of fantasy. They also belonged to a possible reality for the contemporary audience. They belonged to one and the same world as other strange things in these foreign lands.

The issue is after all not a matter of *Sage* vs. *Märchen*, neither of presenting a truth vs. presenting a fiction. It is rather a matter of stories about events in the vicinity vs. events abroad.

Notes

1 Many of the matters discussed here are analyzed in a broader context in Sävborg 2009: 323–249. Some aspects are mentioned also in Sävborg 2014: 74–86.
2 For a general definition of *Sage*, as opposed to *Märchen*, see Lüthi 1961: 23–24.
3 See Aðalheiður Guðmundsdóttir 2006: 33; Mitchell 2006: 702; Mundal 2006: 724.
4 See for example Vésteinn Ólason 2007 and 1998: 186.
5 See for example Einar Ólafur Sveinsson 1958: 126; Clover 1984: 618; Vésteinn Ólason 1998: 20–21.
6 See for example Sigurður Nordal 1953: 261; de Vries 1967: 529; Einar Ólafur Sveinsson 1958: 124–125; Jónas Kristjánsson 1997: 285.
7 Cf. also, for example, Ásdís Egilsdóttir (2006: 64): "Fantasy is associated with the past and remote places."

Sources

Aðalheiður Guðmundsdóttir 2006. On Supernatural Motifs in the Fornaldarsögur. In *The Fantastic in Old Norse/Icelandic Literature. Sagas and the British Isles. Preprint Papers of The Thirteenth International Saga Conference, Durham and York 6th–12th August, 2006.* John McKinnnell, David Ashurst & Donata Kick (eds.). Durham: Centre for Medieval and Renaissance Studies, Durham University. Pp. 33–41.

Ásdís Egilsdóttir 2006. The Fantastic Reality: Hagiography, Miracles and Fantasy. In *The Fantastic in Old Norse/Icelandic Literature. Sagas and the British Isles. Preprint Papers of The Thirteenth International Saga Conference, Durham and York 6th–12th August, 2006.* John McKinnnell, David Ashurst & Donata Kick (eds.). Durham: Centre for Medieval and Renaissance Studies, Durham University. Pp. 63–70.

Bergbúa þáttr. In *Harðar saga*, etc.

Bjarnar saga Hítdœlakappa 1938. In *Íslenzk fornrit III: Borgfirðinga sǫgur.* Sigurður Nordal & Guðni Jónsson (eds.). Reykjavík: Hið íslenzka fornritafélag.

Bjarnar saga Hítdœlakappa 2000. In *The Saga of Bjorn, Champion of the Men of Hitardale.* Alison Finlay (transl.). London: Hisarlik Press.

Clover, Carol J. 1984. Family Sagas, Icelandic. In *Dictionary of the Middle Ages* 4. Joseph Stayer (ed.). New York: Charles Scribner's Sons. Pp. 612–619.

Egils saga einhenda 1954. In *Fornaldar sögur Norðurlanda* 3. Guðni Jónsson (ed.). Reykjavík: Íslendingasagnaútgáfan.

Egils saga einhenda 1985. In *Seven Viking Romances.* Hermann Pálsson & Paul Edwards (transl.). London: Penguin.

Einar Ólafur Sveinsson 1958. *Dating the Icelandic Sagas. An Essay in Method.* London: University College London.

Eyrbyggja saga 1935. In *Íslenzk fornrit IV.* Einar Ól. Sveinsson & Matthías Þórðarson (eds.). Reykjavík: Hið íslenzka fornritafélag.

Gunnars saga Keldugnúpsfifls 1959. In *Íslenzk fornrit XIV: Kjalnesinga saga.* Jóhannes Halldórsson (ed.). Reykjavík: Hið íslenzka fornritafélag.

Harðar saga, etc. 1991. In *Íslenzk fornrit XIII.* Þórhallur Vilmundarson and Bjarni Vilhjálmsson (eds.). Reykjavík: Hið íslenzka fornritafélag.

Jónas Kristjánsson 1997. *Eddas and Sagas. Iceland's Medieval Literature.* 3rd edn. Peter Foote (transl.). Reykjavík: Hið íslenska bókmenntafélag.

Jǫkuls þáttr Búasonar 1959. In *Íslenzk fornrit XIV: Kjalnesinga saga.* Jóhannes Halldórsson (ed.). Reykjavík: Hið íslenzka fornritafélag.

Kormáks saga 1939. In *Íslenzk fornrit VIII: Vatnsdœla saga.* Einar Ól. Sveinsson (ed.). Reykjavík: Hið íslenzka fornritafélag.

The Legendary Olav Saga 1982. In *Olafs saga hins Helga. Die „Legendarische saga" über Olaf den heiligen (Hs. Delagard. saml. 8 II)*. Anne Heinrichs, Doris Janshen, Elke Radicke & Hartmut Röhn (eds., transl.). Heidelberg: Winter.

Lindow, John 1986. *Þorsteins þáttr skelks* and the Verisimilitude of Supernatural Experience in Saga Literature. In *Structure and Meaning in Old Norse Literature. New Approaches to Textual Analysis and Literary Criticism. The Viking Collection 3.* John Lindow, Lars Lönnroth & Gerd W. Weber (eds.). Odense: Odense University Press. Pp. 264–280.

Lüthi, Max 1961. *Volksmärchen und Volkssage. Zwei Grundformen erzählender Dichtung.* Bern: Franke Verlag.

Lüthi, Max 1976. *Once Upon a Time. On the Nature of Fairy Tales.* Lee Chadeayne and Paul Gottwald (transl.). Bloomington: Indiana University Press.

Lüthi, Max 1986 [1982]. *The European Folktale. Form and Nature.* John D. Niles (transl.). Bloomington, Indianapolis: Indiana University Press.

Mitchell, Stephen 2006. The Supernatural and other Elements of the Fantastic in the *fornaldarsögur*. In *The Fantastic in Old Norse/Icelandic Literature. Sagas and the British Isles. Preprint Papers of The Thirteenth International Saga Conference, Durham and York 6ᵗʰ–12ᵗʰ August, 2006.* John McKinnnell, David Ashurst & Donata Kick (eds.). Durham: Centre for Medieval and Renaissance Studies, Durham University. Pp. 699–706.

Morkinskinna 1932. STUAGNL 53. Finnur Jónsson (ed.). Copenhagen: J. Jorgensen.

Mundal, Else 2006. The Treatment of the Supernatural and the Fantastic in Different Saga Genres. In *The Fantastic in Old Norse/Icelandic Literature. Sagas and the British Isles. Preprint Papers of The Thirteenth International Saga Conference, Durham and York 6ᵗʰ–12ᵗʰ August, 2006.* John McKinnnell, David Ashurst & Donata Kick (eds.). Durham: Centre for Medieval and Renaissance Studies, Durham University. Pp. 718–726.

Njáls saga 1954. In *Íslenzk fornrit XII: Brennu-Njáls saga.* Einar Ól. Sveinsson (ed.). Reykjavík: Hið íslenzka fornritafélag.

Njáls saga 1960. Magnus Magnusson & Hermann Pálsson (eds., transl.). Baltimore, Maryland: Penguin books.

Orms þáttr Stórólfssonar. In *Harðar saga,* etc.

Saga Óláfs Tryggvasonar af Oddr Snorrason munk 1932. Finnur Jónsson (ed.). Copenhagen: Gad.

Sävborg, Daniel 2009. Avstånd, gräns och förundran: Möten med de övernaturliga i islänningasagan. In *Greppaminni: Rit til heiðurs Vésteini Ólasyni sjötugum.* Margrét Eggertsdóttir, Árni Sigurjónsson, Guðrún Ása Grímsdóttir, Guðrún Nordal, Guðvarður Már Gunnlaugsson (eds.). Reykjavík: Hið íslenska bókmenntafélag. Pp. 323–349.

Sävborg, Daniel 2014. Scandinavian Folk Legends and Post-Classical Sagas. In *New Focus on Retrospective Methods.* Eldar Heide, Karen Bek-Pedersen (eds.). Folklore Fellows' Communications 307. Helsinki: Academia Scientiarum Fennica. Pp. 74–86.

Schier, Kurt 1992. Fornaldarsögur. In *Kindler neues Literatur Lexikon.* Walter Jens (ed.). München: Kindler. Pp. 598–602.

Sigurður Nordal 1953. Sagalitteraturen. In *Litteraturhistorie B. Norge og Island.* Nordisk kultur 8. Stockholm: Bonnier, Oslo: Aschehoug, Copenhagen: Schultz. Pp. 180–273.

Vésteinn Ólason 1998. *Dialogues with the Viking Age. Narration and Representation in the Sagas of the Icelanders.* Reykjavík: Heimskringla.

Vésteinn Ólason 2007. The Fantastic Element in Fourteenth Century *Íslendingasögur*. A Survey. *Gripla* 18: 7–22.

de Vries, Jan 1967. *Altnordische Literaturgeschichte 2.* 2ⁿᵈ edn. Berlin: de Gruyter.

Þorskfirðinga saga. In *Harðar saga,* etc.

Þorsteins þáttr uxafóts. In *Harðar saga,* etc.

MART KULDKEPP
http://orcid.org/0000-0002-0942-717X

A Study in Distance: Travel and Holiness in *Eiríks saga rauða* and *Eireks saga víðförla*

The aim of this article is to propose an analysis of some conceptual convergences in two Old Norse travelogues: *Eireks saga víðförla* (*The Saga of Eirek the Far-Travelled*), and the episode of Leif Eiriksson's discovery of Vinland in *Eiríks saga rauða* (*The Saga of Eirik the Red*). I will refer to these respectively as *Eirek's saga* and *Eirik's saga*, in order to avoid confusion between the names.[1]

The term holiness, used throughout this article, should be understood as a shorthand for the complex Christian idea of 'closeness to the divine/ related to God'. Just as 'travel', the notion is used here for a heuristic purpose. I therefore refrain from an extensive discussion about the historical uses and meanings of the word, either in the Middle Ages or later,[2] and I do not intend to claim anything about holiness in general – beyond it being a broadly relevant notion for my analysis of the two sagas mentioned above. What is important, however, is to note that I understand holiness as a Christian subcategory of the more general notion of the supernatural.

By considering how the themes of travel and holiness are related in these texts, I attempt to outline a more general hypothesis about how the notion of distance might be useful in analysing the category of the supernatural. Even though the following is intended solely as a short pilot study, the implications it raises probably have relevance beyond these particular texts. In future, they can hopefully be tested on more extensive material.

Introduction

At first sight, there is little beyond the title to bring together the two texts under consideration. *Eiríks saga rauða* (henceforth *Eirik's saga*), undoubtedly the better known of the two, is counted among the so-called sagas of the Icelanders: it has Icelandic characters and is set at least initially in Iceland. It has the particular distinction of being one of the two sagas that tell the story of the Norse discovery of North America around the year 1000. This means that it has attracted much scholarly attention, and is treated nearly always together with the other such saga, *Grœnlendinga þáttr* (*The Saga of the Greenlanders*).

Eireks saga víðförla (henceforth *Eirek's saga*) is a much more obscure work: a narrative of a Norwegian prince's search for Earthly Paradise, which he eventually finds beyond India. The text has somewhat uneasily been included under the genre moniker of *fornaldarsögur norðurlanda* (sagas of the ancient times of the north), meaning sagas that have non-Icelandic (but Nordic) main characters and are set somewhere in northern Europe before the settlement of Iceland (see Kleivane 2009: 38–39). Indeed, *Eirek's saga* shares many features with other works in this genre, including the theme of a journey to some supernatural place, and it is clear that it is modelled closely on other similar texts with little or no Christian content. Rosemary Power (1985: 157–159) has listed the plot elements found in a typical *fornaldarsaga* about a journey to the otherworld, and *Eirek's saga* conforms to most of them. However, it also includes at least one very uncharacteristic trait: the explicitly Christian moral.[3]

It is unlikely that these two sagas have previously been compared to each other. In addition to the traditional differences in genre classification, this can be attributed to the fact that the similarity of their plots, although readily apparent, is on first sight rather trivial. It might be summarised as follows: both texts tell the story of a journey to a far-away place, which in one case lies to the west, and in the other to the east. The heroes, both of them youths from prestigious families, must overcome some hardships, but are eventually able to complete the journey and return home, adding greatly to their honour.

Similar stories are found in many other works of Old Norse literature, as well as in Scandinavian folklore,[4] and this general parallelism alone would not draw any special attention to these two particular texts. But I would argue that if we take into account some further nuances of the narratives, a comparative analysis would nevertheless be useful – not because I presume the two works to be textually related, but, on the contrary, because they seem to independently express some characteristic features of either Old Icelandic collective mentality, literary convention, or both. I would rather leave aside the issue of whether it is the one or the other, but it can be presumed that there is always an interplay between the two.

Synopsis of the Text: The Leif Eiriksson Episode of Eirik's Saga

The short episode of Leif Eiriksson's discovery in *Eirik's saga* (*Eiríks saga rauða* 1985: 209–214; *Eirik's saga* 1965: 84–88) commences with Leif, the promising son of Eirik the Red, starting his journey to Norway in order to stay there with king Olaf Tryggvason. After a short intermission on the Hebrides, he indeed reaches Norway, joins the king's court and has many honours bestowed upon him. The following summer, he expresses a wish to return home, which the king approves on the condition that Leif takes on the mission of Christianising Greenland. Leif thinks it would be difficult to accomplish, but the king assures him that he is best fitted for it:

[The king said:] '[A]nd your good luck will see you through'.
'That will only be', replied Leif, 'if I have the benefit of yours too'. (*Eirik's saga* 1965: 85.)

The story then continues with a very elliptical account of Leif setting sail, running into prolonged difficulties at sea and finally discovering some lands (Vinland) whose existence he had not suspected. The lands are described as particularly bountiful:

> There were fields of wild wheat growing there, and vines, and among trees there were maples. They took some samples of all these things. (*Eirik's saga* 1965: 86.)

On the way back, he rescues some shipwrecked seamen and takes them home with him, showing them much hospitality. He also preaches the new religion. Because of all this, his status is greatly increased in the community:

> He showed his great magnanimity and goodness by bringing Christianity to the country and by rescuing these men; he was known as Leif the Lucky. (*Eirik's saga* 1965: 86.)

The narrative goes on with an account of the reluctance of his father Eirik the Red to convert, which leads to a strife with his wife, Thjodhild. There is also much talk of undertaking a new voyage to the lands that Leif had discovered. For that purpose, people approach Eirik, who had a reputation for good luck and foresight. First he is reluctant, but eventually agrees to make the trip.

Eirik's journey, however, is riddled with misfortune. Before leaving, he hides a treasure of gold and silver and is immediately punished by falling from his horse and injuring himself, so that he has to ask his wife to remove the treasure.[5] On the journey itself, he runs into prolonged difficulties and is unable to reach the seas he is looking for, as the ship is thrown back and forth across the ocean. Eventually, he and his men have to return home "worn out by exposure and toil" (*Eirik's saga* 1965: 87).

Synopsis of the Text: Eirek's Saga

Eirek's saga begins with Eirek, the promising son of king Thrand of Thrandheim, making a vow to "travel the whole world" to find the Earthly Paradise or "The Land of the Living".[6] He sets out and initially reaches Denmark, where he befriends a Danish prince, also called Eirek. Together, they continue next year to Miklagard (Constantinople) where they enter the service of the King of Greeks (the Byzantine Emperor) and prove themselves worthy in all ways.

One day, Eirek of Norway and the king have a conversation and Eirek asks many questions about the creation of the world, God, heaven, hell, and eternal life, as well as the location of the Earthly Paradise. When the king says that it is located "east of furthest India", Eirek asks for his help getting there, which the king agrees to on the condition of Eirek's baptism:

> The king says, "Stay the next three years here with us and then go, since you're in need of my help, and you must heed all my warnings. Be baptised and I will assist you." (*The Tale of Eirek the Traveller* 2005.)

Subsequently, Eirek and his men are baptised and the three years pass.

When they continue with their journey, they travel through many strange and wonderful lands without difficulty, as they are protected by the letter and seal of the king and the patriarch of Miklagard. Eventually, they reach a great river with a bridge of stone over it, and see a land on the other side:

> On the far bank of the river they saw a beautiful country with tall flowers and plenty of honey, and from it they smelt a sweet scent. That direction was bright to look at. They saw neither hill nor height nor mountain in that country. Eirek realises these must be the lands the Greek king spoke of. (*The Tale of Eirek the Traveller* 2005.)

On the bridge lies a dragon with gaping jaws. Eirek the Dane does not dare to go towards it, but Eirek the Norwegian rushes together with one of his companions into the beast's mouth. Thinking his friend is dead, Eirek the Dane turns back home and tells the story, so that Eirek the Norwegian becomes famous for his travels.

But Eirek and his companion do not die. They are initially blinded by smoke, but when it disperses, they find themselves in the beautiful land of abundance: "lush and bright as satin, with sweet scents and tall flowers, and streams of honey ran all over the land, in every direction". They find a strange column suspended in the air, with a ladder by its side. They enter it and see a luxurious interior with plenty of good food and drink. After eating, drinking and praising God, they fall asleep and Eirek is in a dream visited by an angel who informs him that thanks to God, he had found the Earthly Paradise, which, however, "is like wilderness compared to [real] Paradise". The angel asks whether Eirek wants to stay or return to his own country and Eirek replies that he wants to go back to tell his people "about these glorious demonstrations of God's power". He then receives the angel's blessing for this mission in the northern lands. After six days, he and his companion set out again and go through the whole journey in reverse, once more staying for three years with the king of the Greeks. Then they return to Norway and Eirek stays there for ten years.

> And in the eleventh winter, there was one day he went early to pray. Then the Spirit of God took him, and they looked for Eirek but he wasn't found. Eirek had told his dream to his companion, the one that he dreamt in the tower, and this man passed it on, and he believed that the angel of God must have taken Eirek and kept him safe. This Eirek was called Eirek the Traveller. (*The Tale of Eirek the Traveller* 2005.)

The saga ends with an epilogue, which argues that "though heathen men may get great fame by their deeds and feats of valour", they receive merely human praise for their courage, whereas those "who have loved God and put all their faith in Him and acted according to the spirit of holy Christianity" receive both more earthly praise, as well as everlasting life with Almighty God, just as Eirek did.

This epilogue is probably a later interpolation and could stem from the hand of one of the scribes of *Flateyjarbók*, Jón Þórðarson (see Kleivane 2009: 43–44). But even if not a sign of original authorial intention, it nevertheless clearly points out that the text could be interpreted in that way.

Leif and Eirek as Earthly and Spiritual Travellers: A Comparison and Analysis of the Texts

The very short episode of Leif the Lucky and the longer (but still rather short) tale of Eirek the Traveller are obviously equals in neither form nor content, even though they can be claimed to be broadly similar. However, I would argue that there are some further striking similarities between them, which I will now point out:

1. The journeys of both heroes have the character of a spiritual quest that subsequently transforms into a holy mission. Leif's first goal is to become a retainer of the Christian king Olaf Tryggvason, and later, to act as a missionary in Greenland. Eirek is first going to find the Land of the Living/the Earthly Paradise (with somewhat unclear motivation), and, later, to inform the northern peoples about the glory of God.

2. In both stories, the hero receives crucial help from his patron, a Christian king. In the case of Leif, it is Olaf Tryggvason who provides him with his own missionary luck (in addition to Leif's own). In the case of Eirek, it is the King of the Greeks and his wisdom that enables him to find the Earthly Paradise.

3. Both heroes travel to (from an Icelandic point of view) geographically very remote lands: one to the west (Vinland), another to the east (the Earthly Paradise). Both lands, when reached, are described in language suggesting mythical abundance; and, at least in the case of Eirek, also explicit Christian holiness.

4. Both heroes, after spending some time in the holy land they had found, continue with missions to their home countries, and preach Christianity there. They both become very highly regarded as result and are given new names that reflect this increase in status: Leif the Lucky (*Leifr inn heppni*) and Eirek the Far-Travelled (*Eirekr víðförli*).

5. In both texts, the protagonist's "Christian" success is in some way contrasted against heathen – i.e. purely earthly – fame and glory. In the case of Leif, this exemplary heathen is his also very famous and previously successful father Eirik the Red, who proves reluctant to convert. Eirik attempts to undertake a similar journey to Vinland, ending with total failure. In the case of Eirek, the added epilogue

explicitly emphasizes the superiority of Christian fame and glory over those which can be acquired by heathen men. Unlike in *Eirik's saga*, however, where the superiority of Christianity is proven by Eirik's failure, *Eireks saga* does not illustrate the argument with a story, but simply makes a distinction between two different types of praise, one of which is more desirable than the other.

Most of these points have indeed been recognised before, even if not in the same comparative framework. In the case of *Eirek's saga*, the theme of Christian spirituality is more or less obvious, but the same has also been pointed out in the case Vinland voyages, which, regardless of their historical truth-value, seem to function as primarily spiritual/allegorical literary devices modelled on biblical archetypes.[7] Walter Baumgartner (1993: 23) has gone as far as to argue that "it [Vinland] is simply based on the idea of the biblical Paradise, and that fall and salvation are played out there" while William Sayers (1993: 9) has claimed that "[t]aken together, the voyages to North America are a series of *exempla*: each is different, each makes a statement about its chief agents. [...] The advancing narrative [of the Vinland sagas] reflects the Christian view of history as linear progression towards judgment and salvation for the deserving."

There has also been some attention paid to the theme of the tension between Christianity and paganism in both sagas. For example, Geraldine Barnes (2001: 6–7) points out the episode of Eirik the Red injuring himself as "a signal that the pagan *heill* which attended his settlement in Greenland has been weakened" whereas "Christian Leifr Eiríksson, by contrast, is endowed with a form of luck free from pagan associations when he gains the epithet *inn heppni* ('the lucky') after rescuing fifteen people stranded on a reef off Greenland [...]" so that "Eiríkr [...] becomes the focus of Christian–pagan opposition".[8]

In the case of *Eirek's saga*, the tension has been seen as centring on Eirek himself. John Douglas Shafer notes that "[t]hough the exploration in *Eireks saga* is as explicitly connected with piety as in *Yngvars saga*, here the central character is not spreading the Christian faith but seeking it" (Shafer 2010: 176) and "[i]t is reasonable to conclude that both heathen custom and the guiding power of the Christian god conspire here to motivate Eirekr's journeys to distant lands" (Shafer 2010: 24). The edifying function of the epilogue, comparing heathen and Christian travellers, does not, however, seem to have been fully appreciated.

We can conclude that both texts seem to follow a similar rhetorical pattern, with the ultimate aim of demonstrating the superiority of Christianity over heathenism. This is accomplished by harnessing the well-known saga motif of the hero acquiring glory and fame when travelling to remote lands. This stereotype, referring to the Vinland sagas, is nicely summarised by Sayers (1993: 8–9): "Possible demographic pressure or the prospect of economic advantage are de-emphasized as motivation [for travel] in favour of the explorers' curiosity and social pressure to pursue the fame to be won from a successful voyage." This can surely be generalised to other saga journeys to remote places. Also Kristel Zilmer (2005: 75) notes "we do also find certain distinctive features about foreign travels that set them apart from the more customary-natured inland mobility. These longer journeys are in a very specific way connected to the idea of manhood and honour, which includes gaining wealth, renown and high status – that is to say, travelling abroad signals accomplishments on a more distinguished level exactly for the reason that it takes place outside one's usual environment and allows one to achieve something out of the ordinary."

This time, however, the journeys are invested with spiritual significance and thus raised above their mere 'earthly' counterparts: undertaking a long and perilous journey to a far-away land leads to success in spiritual development and missionary activity, not merely earthly fame and glory.

This rhetorical structure suggests a convergence between two discourses of travel: the Christian tradition of pilgrimage, and the indigenous tradition of winning earthly glory through sea voyages, stemming perhaps already from the Viking age. An important point is that these, respectively spiritual and earthly ways of acquiring something through travel, are not depicted as incompatible. Rather, the Christian traveller is simply more successful than the heathen traveller: he reaps all the earthly benefits of the latter, but also receives the even more important spiritual benefits, especially the afterlife in heaven. This is exemplified in Leif Eiriksson proving to be more lucky in both earthly and spiritual affairs than his unconverted father Eirik the Red, and in the suggestion that Eirek the Far-Travelled is superior to others (others glorified with the epithet *víðförli*) because he received both more earthly glory than they, as well as eternal life with Almighty God.

Dealing with the lack of apparent religious motivation in the beginning of *Eirek's saga*, Shafer (2010: 187) writes that "whether the Norwegian Eirekr also desires this world-renown, or whether this desire for fame forms a part of Eirekr's initial motivation in making the solemn vow to reach the Deathless plain we can only guess." As far as the saga's edifying purpose is concerned, however, Eirek's own desires are less important than his eventual rewards, which explicitly include both worldly and heavenly glory. Furthermore, an additional contrast can be seen between him and his friend Eirek the Dane, who, although in everything alike with his namesake, nevertheless is afraid to follow him into the mouth of the dragon. Therefore, Eirek the Dane must remain mostly (not wholly, since he too is baptised) an 'earthly' traveller, whereas Eirek the Norwegian becomes a mostly spiritual one.

A further point that can be derived from the previous one about convergence is that both stories are conversion narratives in a general sense: the hero is shown as having undergone a positive change as a result of his successful journey. This change is firstly a social one, expressed in statements about the heroes' increased fame and honour after they had returned, and symbolised by the community giving heroes new names (or rather epithets commemorating their achievements): Leif the Lucky and Eirek the Far-Travelled.[9]

Kristel Zilmer (2005: 81) notes that "wanting to go abroad and make oneself a name is not always enough; a man also has to have certain pre-qualifications. He has to have what it takes to become a real traveller." Whereas Leif and Eirek certainly possessed these qualifications from the outset – they are both referred to as promising youths –, the baptism and guidance of the king can be seen as a sort of a second-level qualification. In other words, the hero's social improvement is also paralleled by his spiritual improvement, the first stage of which is baptism. Leif undergoes this while staying with Olaf Tryggvason, and Eirek with the King of the Greeks. Baptism and guidance from a king function as necessary prerequisites for the heroes to reach the holy land. Their stay in the holy land, the second stage of their conversion, is the culmination of the narrative and sets Leif and Eirek apart from other Christians, making them worthy missionaries.

Both kinds of improvement – social and spiritual – are at the same time intimately connected to the heroes' travels: their advancement in the physical sense equates to their advancement in other ways. Sverrir Jakobsson (2006: 942) has argued in connection to journeys to the East (i.e. in the story of Eirek and other *víðförli*-sagas) that the 'Eastern road' meant not only a progress towards a geographical goal, but also led to social and spiritual advancement – not least by gaining instruction in Christianity: "[i]n this sense, the journey toward Paradise takes place on many levels." The same can certainly be said about Leif's voyage to Vinland.

This narrative convergence of the (indigenous tradition of) social improvement and the (Christian means of) religious improvement through travel makes the texts ambiguous, allowing for a multitude of allegorical readings. Most importantly, this includes the striking imagery used in the depiction of Vinland, identifying it with something Paradise-like. But it also includes the eating and drinking or sampling of resources both heroes engage in in the land they reach (Eirek even while staying inside the strange church-like column), analogous to the Holy Communion: partaking in the holiness in a literal sense. Additionally, Leif rescuing shipwrecked seamen, while not a religious act *per se*, might be regarded as an earthly foreboding of him spiritually 'rescuing' his fellow Greenlanders. Furthermore, the whole career of Eirek seems to point him out as a predecessor of the real Christianisation of the North that was to come in the days of Leif.[10]

It can be conjectured that the question "how could heathen men have done such great deeds in the past?" must have been a debated one in Medieval Iceland, in light of the strong indigenous tradition relating the achievements of various ancient heroes. *Eirek's saga* and the Leif Eiriksson episode of *Eirik's saga* can, whatever their other aims, be possibly interpreted as contributions to that discourse, attempting to demonstrate that while the deeds of heathen men in the past were great, the deeds of Christian men in the past were even greater – because they were Christian, even if equal in other good qualities.

Holy Lands and the Acquisition of Holiness

To recap, the spiritual and missionary success of the heroes is parallel to their earthly success as travellers. It is their journeys – first to Norway and Miklagard, then to far-away holy lands – that make both heroes become more holy. The first stage of their conversion is baptism, which enables them to find the places they are looking for, and the second stage is the visit to the holy place itself, which allows them to become missionaries. This gives a certain geographical dimension to their social and spiritual journeys. The next step would be to consider what this reading implies about the sagas' concept of holy places. Where are they? How can they be found? How do they function?

The answer to the first question seems to be straightforward: they are located respectively in North America and beyond "the farthest of Indias", which are both very remote places. The reason for remoteness might seem natural: holy places must be imagined as situated outside the geography of everyday experience in the same way that holiness itself is an exceptional quality. Conversely, exceptional qualities, such as holiness, are most naturally associated with places that are unusual, not least by the virtue of being unreachable unless in very exceptional circumstances. Therefore, it would be natural to assume that the heroes' second stage of conversion should happen in a place that is more or less completely otherworldly, even further removed (and consequently even more holy) than the somewhat geographically remote place of their baptism. As also argued by Baumgartner (1993: 29): "the 'transition' or the symbolic transformation from the Viking spirit to a 'modern' Christian, ethical and political mentality has to happen in the text in a distant, mythical place."

However, at the same time, this point must be modified, because the places in question are depicted as not only distant from the everyday reality in an abstract sense, but also in a real sense, relating to the geography of the known world. Vinland and the land beyond India might have been very remote from Icelandic point of view, but there is no suggestion in the two sagas that they somehow belong to a different sphere of existence. They are reachable by normal means of movement, and they can be returned from, even if only in certain circumstances – in this case, only by exemplary Christians, invested with the luck or knowledge of a Christian king.

The reality of these places could thus be called liminal: if put on a scale of reality, they would be situated between tangible, everyday places, accessible to everyone, and transcendent places, totally unreachable for mortals. The latter also exist. In Eirek's dream, the angel points out that there is also a different 'real Paradise', which probably cannot be reached the same way.[11] Thus, the distance with the 'real' supernatural persists even when the plot moves to the holy land itself. On a different level, this is also demonstrated by the fact that the angel has to appear in a dream – a state one step removed from reality.[12]

Liminal places function as gateways between the natural and the supernatural, allowing the hero, who still belongs to the natural world, to have particularly close contact with the supernatural. As argued by Eldar Heide (2011: 64) in a slightly different context: "[h]oly islands, however, are still in this world and may be freely visited by mortals; thus they have an intermediate position, are liminal places, ideal as points of contact with the Otherworld." This also holds true about Vinland and the Earthly Paradise – they function as interfaces with the real Paradise, places where holiness can be acquired.

The same argument can to a lesser degree be made about Norway and Miklagard, which function as places of acquisition of first-stage holiness. There, the heroes receive their baptism and guidance for further travels from the Christian king, enabling the second stage of their conversion.

It might be said that the holiness of the places in the two narratives is thus an 'analogue' kind of otherness, not based on a binary opposition between two variants (holy/non-holy), but allowing for degrees of holiness.[13] Perhaps it would also be justified to speak of a scale of liminality that increases proportionally to the geographical remoteness of the place.

To this, there are probable parallels in the Medieval pilgrimage tradition. A journey to Jerusalem must have been regarded the same way, its geographical remoteness and the difficulty of the journey contributing to its holiness. The same point has been made by Shafer (2010: 271): "The closest far-travel comes to being an end unto itself is in pilgrimage; [...] pilgrimages are at least partially validated by the distance travelled and difficulties endured to achieve them."

At the same time, the places have to be (if only liminally) real, in order to be able to be reached by mortal heroes. This means that the crossing of the boundary to them is not miraculous and instant, but takes the form of a long journey. It is important to note that the emphasis on the success of the hero can render the journey both more and less perilous. Sverrir Jakobsson (2006: 941) argues concerning Eirek's journey from Miklagard to the Earthly Paradise that "[t]he East seems very safe and civilized, and no heathen armies make the journey to Paradise hazardous for the protagonist and his fellowship." In the case of the equally successful Leif, however, there is a mention of hardships on the sea, but as Zilmer (2005: 84) notes: "[t]o a certain degree the shift between favourable/unfavourable travel conditions may even depend on whether we are dealing with positive or negative missions. However, the main characters may also experience such hardships, the purpose of which is rather to highlight their outstanding skills and strength."

Covering the distances, whether full of additional hardships or not, requires physical prowess and skills, as well as Christian luck or Christian knowledge. It is the latter that raises Leif and Eirek above their heathen counterparts; but as argued above, it is a difference in degree, not in kind.

In this way, the earthly/spiritual ambiguity characteristic of the depiction of heroes' accomplishments is also current in the sagas' depiction of holy places themselves. In both cases, there is symbolic convergence between two kinds of distance: the real and physical distance in space, and the spiritual distance between heathenism and Christian holiness. By covering the former, the hero also covers the latter: by travelling physically, he also travels spiritually; and a place that is further away is (relatively) more holy than the place that is closer.

A Hypothesis of Distance

Through a comparative analysis of the two narratives, I have tried to point out the connections between the themes of travel and the acquisition of holiness. In short, it seems that they are interconnected to an inseparable degree. However, I would still argue that geographical distance is a primary feature through which another kind of distance, holiness (as a Christian subcategory to the supernatural), is being constructed. Geographic remoteness can be expected to relate more directly to the everyday experience of people than holiness would, and the underlying conceptual metaphor seems to be REMOTENESS IS HOLY, rather than HOLINESS IS REMOTE.[14]

Geographical remoteness can probably also be regarded as a quantitative marker of otherness more generally, enabling all sorts of phenomena in narratives that would be quite literally out of place in one's homestead. Although the supernatural places depicted in the two sagas function in a clearly Christian framework, there is little specifically Christian about this principle. There have been other investigations into the construction of foreign otherness in sagas (Barraclough 2009; 2012; Aalto 2005; 2006, to name a few), which seem to agree that otherness is a deictic phenomenon strongly connected to the perceived geographical distance from the Old Norse world (especially Iceland). See for example Eleanor Rosamund Barraclough's (2009: 100) description of the Medieval Icelanders' 'mental map' of the territories west of Iceland: "an east-to-west geographical axis emerges, moving from cultural familiarity to exotic western wildernesses. This is true externally, in terms of the relationship between the various lands of the North Atlantic (as a rule, Iceland is more stable than Greenland, which in turn is more familiar than Vínland, which is less strange than lands such as Einfætingaland and Hvítramannaland as mentioned in *Eiríks saga*)."

This idea should obviously be tested on more material, but I would suggest that different kinds of 'supernatural' could in Old Norse literature and probably in other traditions be fruitfully analysed as functions of distance, which in its basic form is geographical. The geographic distance covered by travel – movement away from some point of locality, presence, normalcy and stasis – might be seen as underlying reality, be it imaginative or historical, that is easily converted into other kinds of distance (otherness). These include the spiritual distance, but also temporal distance (far-away lands might be associated with ancientness, i.e. with dragons, giants and humans with supernatural strength), and social distance (people living in remote areas depicted as lowly and backwards, or, on the contrary, more noble than usual). Barraclough (2009: 101) suggests that "[i]n part, the literary descriptions must reflect some degree of the geographical and meteorological reality, with the 'cultural memory' and realistic oral traditions concerning the region's weather and living conditions being transferred in some form into the written texts that emerged."

Different kinds of distance easily converge, indicating a lack of interest in the specifics. For example, there seems to have been little difference between ethnic and supernatural otherness in Old Norse imagination. As John Lindow (1995: 16) has pointed out "[w]hat is striking about these emblems

216

of contrast assigned to other groups and to strangers in Nordic tradition is how closely they resemble attributes of supernatural beings." Therefore, although different kinds of otherness can be used as analytical categories, their commonalities are much more remarkable.

Finally, the connection of the idea of supernatural with the idea of distance makes it possible to view encounters with places, people or objects that appear to be supernatural without geographical distance (occasional gravemounds, holy groves, churches, witches, foreigners, berserks, swords, gold rings, etc.) playing a role in some way in some way as shortcuts (in time, space or social order) that lead outside the conventional reality much the same way as a journey over the sea would. Daniel Sävborg (2009: 346) has pointed out that encounters with the supernatural that take place in Iceland are in Sagas of Icelanders almost always described with the help of "distance markers" (the encounter takes place in a dream, there is no close contact with the viewer, the story is told in a way that creates doubt in its veracity, etc.), whereas encounters taking place in foreign lands are usually told without such markers. This indicates that in the latter cases, the geographical distance already functions as the necessary othering strategy, requiring no other such devices.

The work of developing further and testing out this hypothesis remains to be done. However, as I think is suggested by the two texts analysed here, distance as a methodological tool could be a fruitful way of making sense of the category of the supernatural, perhaps not only in Old Norse material, and not even only in literature, but also in folklore and other fields investigating human imagination.

NOTES

1   The standard scholarly edition of *Eiríks saga* is in volume IV (2nd edition) of the *Íslenzk Fornrit* series (*Eiríks saga rauða* 1985). I will also quote from the English translation of Magnus Magnusson and Herman Pálsson (*Eirik's saga* 1965). *Eireks saga* has been published in the *Fornaldarsögur Norðurlanda* editions of C. C. Rafn (1829–1830) and, most recently, Guðni Jónsson and Bjarni Vilhjálmsson (1943–1944). The only scholarly edition is the diplomatic one by Helle Jensen (*Eiríks saga viðforla* 1983). I will also quote from the English translation by Peter Tunstall (*The Tale of Eirek the Traveller* 2005). The different editions and translations use various alternative ways to spell the saga titles (*Eireks saga víðförla* is sometimes also known as *Eiríks saga viðförla*) or the names of the heroes (Eirik, Eirek, Eirikr, Eirekr, etc.).

2   For a more thorough discussion of the notion of holiness, approaching it from a multitude of angles, see Barton 2003. A useful brief discussion of holiness in a broad Christian sense, roughly in line with how the concept is employed in this study, can be found in Thiselton 2015: 428–430 (keyword 'Holy, Holiness').

3   For a discussion of the different textual variants of the saga – some of which do not terminate with this explicit moral – see Kleivane 2009: 39–45.

4   Note especially the migratory legend type ML 4075 ("Visit to the Blessed Island"), cf. Christiansen 1958.

5   Erik Wahlgren (1969: 67) interprets this episode as Eirik's acknowledgement of the Christian sin of avarice.

6   For a discussion about the notion of Earthly Paradise and related terms in *Eirek's saga*, as well as the many learned and biblical parallels to the story, see Power 1985: 159–160 and Ashurst 2006.

7   See the many parallels with biblical and other accounts mentioned by Sayers (1993: 3–4).

8   See also Baumgartner's similar point (Baumgartner 1993: 22). This bears relevance also to the argument of Paul Schach that the transformation from heathenism (or even 'Viking-mentality' as such) to Christianity is in Sagas of Icelanders often conceptualised as a generational issue (Schach 1977: 379; Baumgartner 1993: 29).

9   Such travel-connected epithets are especially characteristic of the so-called *víðförli*-sagas ('tales of the widely-travelled'), a category which in addition to *Eirek's saga* includes three more texts, all connected to travels to the East (see Sverrir Jakobsson 2006: 936).

10 Sverrir Jakobsson (2006: 937) considers Eirek's allegiance to the King of Greeks and the patriarch of Miklagard as evidence that Icelanders were not concerned with the strife between the Catholic and Orthodox churches.

11 On different ideas of Paradise current in Medieval Iceland, see Ashurst 2006.

12 On such 'distancing markers' in sagas, see Sävborg 2009: 341.

13 Aalto 2006: 15. About these terms, see also Eriksen 2002 [1993]: 66.

14 For the theory of conceptual metaphors, see Lakoff & Johnson 1980.

Sources

Aalto, Sirpa 2005. The Digital 'Other' in Heimskringla. In *Dialogues with Tradition. Studying the Nordic Saga Heritage*. Kristel Zilmer (ed.). Tartu: Tartu University Press. Pp. 93–112.

Aalto, Sirpa 2006. Categorizing "Otherness" in Heimskringla. In *The Fantastic in Old Norse/Icelandic Literature. Sagas and the British Isles. Preprint Papers of The 13th International Saga Conference, Durham and York 6th–12th August, 2006*. John McKinnell, David Ashurst & Donata Kick (eds.). Durham: Centre for Medieval and Renaissance Studies, Durham University. Pp. 15–21.

Ashurst, David 2006. Imagining Paradise. In *The Fantastic in Old Norse/Icelandic Literature. Sagas and the British Isles. Preprint Papers of The 13th International Saga Conference, Durham and York 6th–12th August, 2006*. John McKinnell, David Ashurst & Donata Kick (eds.). Durham: Centre for Medieval and Renaissance Studies, Durham University. Pp. 71–80.

Barnes, Geraldine 2001. *Viking America. The First Millennium*. Cambridge: D. S. Brewer.

Barton, Stephen C. (ed.) 2003. *Holiness: Past and Present*. London & New York: T & T Clark.

Barraclough, Eleanor Rosamund 2009. The World West of Ireland in Medieval Icelandic Oral Tradition. In *Á austrvega: Saga and East Scandinavia. Preprint Papers of the 14th International Saga Conference, Uppsala, 9th–15th August 2009*. Agneta Ney, Henrik Williams & Fredrik Charpentier Ljungqvist (eds.). Gävle: Gävle University Press. Pp. 99–105.

Barraclough, Eleanor Rosamund 2012. Sailing the Saga Seas. Narrative, Cultural, and Geographical Perspectives in the North Atlantic Voyages of the Íslendingasögur. *Journal of the North Atlantic* 19(3): 1–12.

Baumgartner, Walter 1993. Freydis in Vinland oder Die Vertreibung aus dem Paradies. *Skandinavistik* 23: 16–35.

Christiansen, Reidar Th. 1958. *The Migratory Legends: A Proposed List of Types with a Systematic Catalogue of the Norwegian Variants.* Folklore Fellows' Communications 175. Helsinki: Academia Scientiarum Fennica.

Eiríks saga rauða 1985. In *Íslenzk fornrit IV: Eyrbyggja saga, Grœnlendinga sǫgur.* Einar Ól. Sveinsson & Matthías Þórðarson (eds.). Reykjavík: Hið íslenzka fornritafélag. Pp. 195–237.

Eirik's saga 1965. In *The Vinland Sagas. The Norse Discovery of America. Grænlendinga Saga and Eirik's saga.* Magnus Magnusson & Herman Pálsson (transl.). London: Penguin Books. Pp. 75–105.

Eiríks saga víðfǫrla 1983. *Eiríks saga víðfǫrla.* Helle Jensen (ed.). København: C. A. Reitzels Forlag.

Eriksen, Thomas Hylland 2002 [1993]. *Ethnicity and Nationalism.* London: Pluto Press.

Heide, Eldar 2011. Holy Islands and the Otherworld: Places Beyond Water. In *Isolated Islands in Medieval Nature, Culture and Mind.* Gerhard Jaritz & Torstein Jørgensen (eds.). Budapest, Bergen: Central European University/Centre for Medieval Studies, University of Bergen. Pp. 57–80.

Kleivane, Elise 2009. Sagaene om Oddr og Eiríkr. In *Fornaldarsagaerne: Myter og virkelighed.* Ármann Jakobsson, Annette Lassen & Agneta Ney (eds.). København: Museum Tusculanums Forlag. Pp. 27–47.

Lakoff, George & Mark Johnson 1980. *Metaphors We Live By.* Chicago: University of Chicago Press.

Lindow, John 1995. Supernatural Others and Ethnic Others: A Millennium of World View. *Scandinavian Studies* 67(1): 8–31.

Power, Rosemary 1985. Journeys to the Otherworld in the Icelandic Fornaldarsögur. *Folklore* 96(2): 156–175.

Sayers, William 1993. Vinland, the Irish, "Obvious Fictions and Apocrypha". *Skandinavistik* 23: 1–15.

Schach, Paul 1977. Observations on the Generation-Gap Theme in the Icelandic Sagas. In *The Epic in Medieval Society. Aesthetic and Moral Values.* Harald Scholler (ed.). Tübingen: Max Niemeyer Verlag. Pp. 361–381.

Shafer, John Douglas 2010. Saga-Accounts of Norse Far-Travellers. Doctoral thesis. Durham University. Available at Durham E-Theses Online: http://etheses.dur.ac.uk/286/ [Accessed July 10, 2015]

Sävborg, Daniel 2009. Avstånd, gräns och förundran. Möten med de övernaturliga i isländningasagan. In *Greppaminni: Rit til heiðurs Vésteini Ólasyni sjötugum.* Margrét Eggertsdóttir, Árni Sigurjónsson, Guðrún Ása Grímsdóttir, Guðrún Nordal, Guðvarður Már Gunnlaugsson (eds.). Reykjavík: Hið íslenska bókmenntafélag. Pp. 323–349.

Sverrir Jakobsson 2006. On the Road to Paradise: 'Austrvegr' in the Icelandic Imagination. In *The Fantastic in Old Norse/Icelandic Literature. Sagas and the British Isles. Preprint Papers of The 13th International Saga Conference, Durham and York 6th-12th August, 2006.* John McKinnell, David Ashurst & Donata Kick (eds.). Durham: Centre for Medieval and Renaissance Studies, Durham University. Pp. 935–943.

The Tale of Eirek the Traveller 2005. Peter Tunstall (transl.). Available at http://www.northvegr.org/sagas annd epics/legendary heroic and imaginative sagas/old heithinn tales from the north/032.html [Accessed October 16, 2016]

Thiselton, Anthony C. 2015. *The Thiselton Companion to Christian Theology.* Grand Rapids & Cambridge: Wm. B. Eerdmans Publishing Co.

Wahlgren, Erik 1969. Fact and Fancy in the Vinland Sagas. In *Old Norse Literature and Mythology. A Symposium.* Edgar C. Polomé (ed.). Austin: University of Texas Press. Pp. 19–80.

Zilmer, Kristel 2005. The Motive of Travelling in Saga Narrative. In *Dialogues with Tradition. Studying the Nordic Saga Heritage.* Kristel Zilmer (ed.). Tartu: Tartu University Press. Pp. 64–92.

Traditions and Histories Reconsidered III

Jonathan Roper

http://orcid.org/0000-0001-8807-2276

Folk Disbelief*

Aleksandr Afanas'ev (1826–1871), in addition to compiling the classical collection of Russian folktales, *Narodnye Russkie Skazki* (1855–1863), assembled a collection of obscene and erotic folktales, in a manuscript entitled *Narodnye Russkie Skazki. Ne dlja pečati* (completed by 1862). While his published collection assumed a position in Russian culture equivalent to that of the Grimms' collection in Germany, forming part of the educational syllabus and being the object of a large number of adaptations in the form of cartoons, films, retellings, etc., what became known as the 'forbidden' tales did not find their way into print in Russia until the last decade of the 20th century, and even then only with a small print-run. The long obscurity of his obscene tales partly explains the violent reaction to an English translation of some of them in a customer review by "Miss K. Shekel" of Robert Chandler's *Russian Magic Tales* on the Amazon website (with its original capitalization and punctuation retained):

> This book does not contain the russian 'Magic' folk tales it is a book of foul lies, shocking twisted ideas and swear words. this book cannot be read to children, nor does it represent russian culture or folklore. Being russian I have read many of these tales in their original form and what is printed in this book is far from the real thing. It is extremely offensive to russian culture and I sincerely hope that those who choose to read it do not believe that this is a true interpretation of russian folk tales. (Shekel 2013.)

It is not just the fact that the tales are unknown to her that prompts her rejection of them, it is the fact that they do not equate with her notion of what "russian culture or folklore" is. Needless to say, Afanas'ev's 'forbidden' tales absolutely possess a folk character, more so indeed than several members of the classical folktale canon. What explains the reviewer's shock is that her notion of what folk narratives are is somewhat more narrow than their full gamut in practice. This case is an example of the theme this essay takes up in another field, another case where ideology about what people say (and think) is not as full-spectrum as reality, where pre-existing categories (the scholarly category of *folk belief* in this case) do not always prove easy to match up with one's own experience. And again, this is a situation where our notions have been reinforced by a loop of what we as connoisseurs of folklore are usually exposed to, and what we as fieldworkers usually aim to elicit.

If called on to describe the kind of things the working class people I grew up in contact with in south-east England, and those I have known since, said and did, the scholarly category of *folk belief* would be one of the last notions I would use. These people, the kind of people our 19th century intellectual predecessors would have called 'the folk', were sceptical about much in life, including supernatural notions. They were sceptical about magic and ghosts to be sure, as well as so-called 'traditional healing', not to mention the notion of fairies. In fact, a fair few of them had an outlook on life that might better be described as cynical than sceptical. At the same time, the middle class people I was also in touch with, then as now, were not themselves, with their health scares and moral panics, entirely strangers to credulity. While it could be argued that scepticism was only to be expected at the end of the 20th century in a stable community with compulsory education, near 100% adult literacy, and good technological provision, attitudes not that dissimilar were to be found in that same part of the world over a century earlier when very different social conditions prevailed there, as regards literacy, education, and technology.

Back in October 1900, for instance, the writer George Sturt (1863–1927) was talking to his gardener, Frederick Grover (here 'Bettesworth'), and trying to lead the conversation around to discovering whether this labouring-class man knew any ghost stories. 'Bettesworth' had just been telling Sturt that the village they both lived in Surrey was, for all the rest of its faults, a very honest one, for instance, nobody would pick up tools left behind by accident:

> For a certain reason I took up this point, and hinted that Flamborough in Yorkshire must be an equally honest place. The Flamborough people, I had been told, never lock their doors at night, for fear of locking out the spirits of relatives drowned at sea.
>
> Would Bettesworth take the bait, and tell me anything he might know about ghosts? Not he. The interruption changed the course, but not the character, of his talk. He looked rather shocked at these benighted Yorkshiremen, and commented severely, "Weak-minded, *I* calls it." Then, after a momentary silence, he was off on a new track [...]. (Bourne 2010 [1907]: 40.)

This new track involves him talking about fishermen in the coastal village of Selsey, who go round all hours of the day and night. But Sturt is not really interested in listening to this, and wants another try at eliciting ghost stories:

> He had got quite away from the point in my mind. But as I had long wondered whether Bettesworth had any ghost stories, I harked back now to the Flamborough people, egging him on to be communicative. It was all in vain, however. He shook his head. The subject seemed foreign to him. "As I often says, I bin about all times o' the night, an' I never met nothin' worse than myself." (Bourne 2010 [1907]: 40.)[1]

But just as it seems that Sturt would have to admit defeat, Grover begins to tell a narrative:

"Only time as ever I was froughtened was when I was carter chap at Penstead. Our farm was down away from t'other, 'cause Mr. Barnes had two farms — 't least, he had three — and ourn was away from t'other, and I was sent late at night to git out the waggon — no, the pole-carriage. I set up on the front on the shafts, with a truss o' hay behind me; and all of a sudden she" (the mare, I suppose he meant) "snarked an' begun to turn round in the road. The chap 'long with me— no, he wa'n't 'long with me, 'cause he'd gone on to open the gate, and so there was I alone. And all 'twas, was a old donkey rollin' in the road. She'd smelt 'n, ye know; an' the nearer we got, the more froughtened she was, till she turned right round there in the road. 'Twas a nasty thing for me; they hosses with their legs over the traces, and all that, and me down atween 'em."

He was fairly off now, a tale followed of stumbling over a drunken man, who lay all across the road one dark night. (Bourne 2010 [1907]: 40.)

And so Sturt goes on to conclude "There were no ghost stories to be had" (Bourne 2010 [1907]: 39–40). But this was not a fruitless interaction – from the folklore point of view it was a highly profitable one, as Sturt *had* succeeded in eliciting a traditional narrative: a story of a seemingly frightening something (perhaps a supernatural something) that turns out to be a mundane something after all. It is to his credit that Sturt was willing to portray himself as being mistaken, in persisting in following a wrong thread, and finally in giving us the unsolicited data his interviewee provided him with anyway. This is certainly not the only such occurrence in the annals of folklore studies, but it is very rarely that are we given such full descriptions of the researcher's chasing of a hare.

It is worth noting here that George Sturt was *not* a folklorist. It is also relevant that writers we shall turn to later – John Coker Egerton, Thomas Geering and Edward Nicholson – were not folklorists either, although their depictions of village life (in Burwash, Hailsham and Golspie respectively) are full of folkloric data. It is their freedom from the contemporary folklore paradigm (that is, the Victorian and Edwardian folklore paradigm with its focus on finding the remnants of pre-scientific notions amongst the less educated) which has allowed them to record these *non-ghost* stories, stories that others would have passed over as surplus to requirements. For what would have shaped the requirements of many of their contemporaries who were folklorists? Narratives expressing folk belief. The credulity of 'the Folk' (and the concomitant lack of credulity on the part of the researcher and his folk group) was the necessary working assumption in that era. *Folk belief* had been the focus of intellectuals (themselves presumably sceptical) at least since Thomas Browne's mid 17th century work on 'vulgar errors'. Even Charlotte Burne, the author of what is perhaps the best 19th century collection of regional English folklore, could still speak of "the multitude of the superstitious fears that beset the folk" (Burne 1914: 392). But such attitudes are not necessarily confined to the 19th century – Leander Petzoldt for one has described a similar condescension to the credulous folk in research on contemporary legends, finding the attitude of the editors of such collections "much in the spirit of 19th-century collectors who noted the tales of the 'ignorant and superstitious' peasants as curiosities for more instructed people" (Kawan 1995: 107). It may very well be that the concept of folk belief

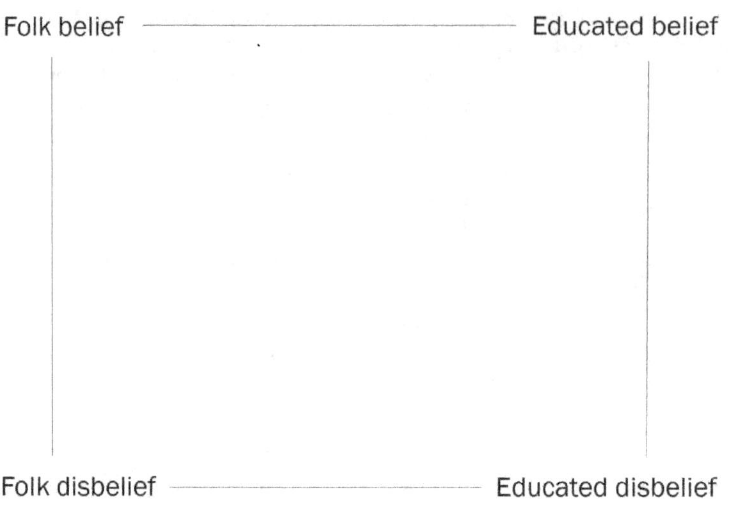

Fig. 1. The four possible combinations of the dyads folk/educated and belief/disbelief.

itself is a historical formation: a category that only came fully into being as a result of what Peter Burke (1978) calls the 'withdrawal' of the elites from popular culture, or what Max Weber terms 'disenchantment'. In this period, the newly-opened gap allowed the creation of a new subject of study – which was alternately as a site of thrills, disgust and delight.

Folk belief is always implicitly (and sometimes explicitly) contrasted with educated disbelief. But given that folk belief is a term with two members (*folk* and *belief*), we should rightly set out the permutations not as a polarity but as a logical square (as in Figure 1), the four corners of this square being: folk belief, educated belief, educated disbelief, folk disbelief.

This essay will focus on just one of the corners of this square, folk disbelief, but it will first say a word in passing about educated belief, or what one might term 'middle class folklore'. George Orwell, writing in a notebook that remained unpublished in his own lifetime, made a note of fallacies taught to him in childhood:

> That you will be struck dead if you go into church with your hat on.
> That you can be had up for putting a stamp on a letter upside down.
> That if you make a face and the wind changes, you will be stuck like that.
> That if you wash your hands in the water that eggs have been boiled in, you will get warts.
> That there is a reward of £50 for spending a night in the Chamber of Horrors at Madame Tussaud's.
> That bats get into women's hair, after which the women's heads have to be shaved.
> That if you cut yourself between the thumb and forefinger, you get lockjaw.
> That powdered glass is poisonous.
> That bulls are enraged at the sight of red.
> That swans can break your leg with a blow of a wing.

226

That if you tell a lie, you get a spot on your tongue.

That people who have a touch of the tarbrush can be detected by their finger-nails.

That orientals are not subject to sunstroke.

That dogs are good judges of character.

That all toadstools are poisonous.

That pigs cannot swim because if they do they cut their throats with their trotters. (Crick 1980: 42.)

Now, lists such as these of fallacies spread to and by middle class children (I recognise three of them from my own childhood) could serve as a useful starting point for the study that might be made of middle class folklore. Yet, 'educated belief' is unexplored territory. In fact, even the term 'educated', used here with the sense it carries in phrases like "educated person", may not be the best designation for this category of 'non-folk', as the attitudes and beliefs are already in formation before a person's formal education begins, and once that has begun, continues in parallel to it in non-educational settings such as the home, social events, etc. On the other hand, the terms 'elite' (elite itself is probably a bit too restrictive, excluding much middle class folklore) or 'official' (the beliefs are often also in some way non-standard) or 'bourgeois' (again not a term without its problems) do not seem to catch the category entirely either. Whatever doubts we might have about the term we use to denote, we have no doubts about the existence of the phenomenon itself.

The reasons for the neglect of such educated lore seem to be related to the concentration of study upon folk belief. For, while we are familiar with statements about the role that nationalism has played in folklore studies (e.g. Oinas 1978; Dundes 1985; Baycroft & Hopkin 2012), including in the studies of folk belief, a focus on nationalism alone does not provide a sufficient account of the development of folklore studies, for class as well as nation is involved. Some of the attention that the so-called 'superstitions of the folk', those vulgar errors and extraordinary popular delusions, have received is in part a function of the disenchantment of the educated, who are intrigued to find enchantment (innocence!) regarding magic, ghosts, fairies, traditional healing, etc., still present among the folk, and amuse themselves with it, horrify themselves with it, and just as often come to cherish it.

By contrast, the notion that there might be *folk disbelief* somewhat escaped many early modern and 19th century observers' attention. While popular scepticism about, for instance, politicians, or landlords, or other social actors, was well-acknowledged, scepticism (and sceptical narratives) regarding belief in magic, ghosts, traditional healing was not sought out in the same way that belief (and belief narratives) were. Without rejecting the notion of folk (popular, vernacular) belief, we should supplement it with the notion of folk disbelief.

Some Documenters of Sceptical Narratives

John Coker Egerton (1829–1888) was rector of the parish of Burwash in the east of Sussex for a substantial stretch of the late 19th century. Toward the end of his life, a series of his journal articles about the parish and his parishioners was published in book form as *Sussex Folk and Sussex Ways* (Egerton 1884). Though the book seems to have quite a folkloristic title, it gained its title from an editor or sub-editor of the journal it first appeared in; Egerton's own first intended title had been *Sussex Reminiscences*. This is one sign that Egerton was in fact not himself a folklorist, nor someone who shared the 19th century folklore paradigm. He did not belong, for example, to the Folklore Society (as some other of the clergy in his diocese did). Writing of his parishioners, he said:

> our people are of a somewhat matter-of-fact rather than superstitious temperament. Our local superstitions are few... I once asked in our school, "What is a ghost?" a question to which one of the boys made answer, "Something what somebody imagines." (Egerton 1884: 108.)

He further remarked, that despite living in Burwash for more than two decades "I do not remember having heard more than two ghost stories, and *they* are told of days long gone by" (Egerton 1884: 108).

Both of these stories, interestingly, belong to a family tradition that Egerton was told of by the granddaughter of Richard Balcombe, the man who saw these 'ghosts'. She heard these stories as personal experience narratives from her grandfather's own lips in the early 19th century about events which occurred in the 1750s. In the first instance, Mr. Balcombe, out at night, passing a reputedly-haunted stile, saw something "glowing fiercely out of the hedge":

> He put down his basket, walked quietly up to the place, and with his "bat" [i.e. stick] struck out boldly. He owned that he then felt a good deal frightened, for no sooner had he struck than flames on all sides came flying past his head. However, he held his ground, and then discovered that he had smashed into a hundred pieces an old rotten tree stump which had dried up into touchwood, and the phosphorus in which shone with such mysterious brightness in the dark. (Egerton 1884: 109–110.)

The second encounter, again at a stile (a suitably liminal location), involved him flinging newly-repaired boots at the apparition, which this time turned out to be "an old grey horse which had been standing with its tail to the stile" (Egerton 1884: 111) and which promptly ran off with the boots across its shoulders.

Thus in both these Balcombe family narratives, the supposed "ghost" turns out to have been something much more down to earth: in the first instance, phosphorescent old wood, and in the second, a horse. Egerton (1884: 111) further remarked that there were no haunted houses in the parish and that "our people are too familiar with the [churchyard, which, then as now, is crossed by a public footpath,] ... to associate it with ghosts and apparitions." Yet he is also careful to note that Burwash's lack of ghost belief is not replicated in every place and time, not even within 19th-century England (which might be taken to represent a single place and time), for in the Cheshire of his boyhood there had been ghost narratives which he, as a boy, had taken seriously.

Thomas Geering (1813–1889) who lived in the nearby small town of Hailsham published a book about his parish in 1884, the very same year as Egerton's work appeared. Geering was from a more modest background than Egerton however, he worked as a shoemaker and currier, and he was, by further contrast a local born and bred (born in fact in Alfriston, half a dozen miles away). In a manner reminiscent of Egerton, Geering (2003 [1884]: 167) stated that "Our parish is not rich in ghost lore or haunted houses." Nevertheless he also has two 'ghost stories', or rather 'ghosts who were not ghosts', stories.

The first concerns the sighting of a figure in the thickest oak clump in the parish by a young man "of an imaginative and gossipy frame of mind" called William. William's father, who clearly wasn't having any of it, made up the following rhyme in response, which he read to the rest of the family at breakfast:

> As poor Will went past a post
> There he saw a paper ghost –
> His great long teeth and rusty beard
> Made poor Will quite afeard. (Geering 2003 [1884]: 167.)

The term 'paper ghost' clearly indicates the kind of reality the father thought this sighting belonged to. And we can wonder whether the rhyme was not only recited, as Geering proposes, "as a warning and deterrent against late hours", but also as a means of ridiculing Will's delusion.

In an afternote, Geering notes that in his adulthood, Will had had another strange sighting at the same site, which turned out to be just the shadow of an owl, and so [Will told Geering] "the mystery of my youth was solved" (Geering 2003 [1884]: 169).

The second of these stories concerns a different young man, a suitor on a moonless night, who sees a mysterious figure on the road and hears a roar, only to then find that the figure is that of a donkey and the roar turns out on second hearing to be that donkey's bray.

Of course, such narratives are found elsewhere and elsewhen than late 19th-century Sussex. A recent collection of lore from the Channel Island of Jersey contains versions told in the 1980s of narratives about smugglers invoking ghost belief to be able to work under the cover of secrecy and not be disturbed by people who might otherwise be tempted to move about after dark. These stories tell of a ghostly dog who was in fact a man on all fours who would growl and even hammer on doors if necessary to keep the coast clear (Bois 2010: 175–180). Here we (apparently) get some of the sociological background to the narrative and its use: the belief is invoked to get the credulous to do what the smugglers, who lack any such illusions, want them to do, that is to sit tight. But that is only if we accept such narratives at their face value. I wonder whether we should not rather see this account itself as an origin narrative about how such now-implausible ghost-dog stories ever came into being?

At this point, having seen non-folklorists successfully documenting sceptical narratives, it is worth turning to examine in some detail how someone who certainly was a folklorist dealt with such material. Herbert Halpert (1911–2000), one of the key figures in 20th century anglophone folklore studies, touched upon sceptical narratives over the course of his career. In his 1947 Ph.D. thesis on folktales of the New Jersey pinelands (his supervisor being none other than Stith Thompson), he included a series of narratives in a sub-category of humorous stories, which he termed "humorous tales of the supernatural" (Halpert 1947: 453). In these stories, as he explains:

> people are frightened by the supernatural in several ways. One man who dresses as a ghost to scare another is himself scared by a white-robed monkey. Men think they hear the Devil dividing souls in the cemetery. One man runs from a sociable talking ghost. In most cases the frightened person takes to his heels; in one instance a man kicks a rabbit out of his path because it is too slow. Frequently a catch-phrase or retort is the climax of the story. (Halpert 1947: 453.)

Halpert went on thinking about his New Jersey material for over half-a-century, and when a heavily-revised version of his Ph.D. thesis was finally published (posthumously) in book form the comparative notes were very much more extensive, and his label for this group of narratives had changed to: "Humorous Tales about Fear of the Supernatural" (Halpert 2010: 147–151). The change in nomenclature may seem to be a minor one, but it signals what had become clearer to Halpert, namely that these stories, as he has found them, are not about the supernatural, but about the *fear of* the supernatural. And usually that fear is unfounded. For example, other versions that he located in a lifetime of applied bibliophilia have people (and not just would-be scarers) unduly frightened by a white goat, a white dog, a white (or black) cow, a white or a grey horse, a sheep or a goose; or even by a scarecrow, a phosphorescent old tree (again), or a finger post. Stories of fear of the supernatural might be told with the message that fear was an appropriate response, or, on the contrary, that fear was a foolish response. In the cases outlined above, it is apparent that the teller is saying that such fear (and the actions it provokes) falls very much into the latter category.

Those stories where the person who takes fright was himself a would-be scarer of others (i.e. those analogous to ATU 1676 "The Pretended Ghost") are, Halpert suggests, expressions of "a folk code ascribing retribution for wilful imitation of the supernatural" (Halpert 2010: 263). But, as he himself admits we also find such "scarer scared" stories "without serious consequences".[2] The stories associated with this tale-type can be told in a way which supports the belief in the existence of ghosts or, conversely, in a way which ridicules the idea of ghosts. Inasmuch as they have a common point, it is not so much a warning not to mess with the supernatural, as a warning not to mess with the minds of your friends and neighbours.

Writing back in 1947 Halpert claimed sceptical tales only exist because of the fact of belief:

> Among those who take the supernatural very seriously the depth of their belief is often concealed by a code which requires that one's fears are to be covered by treating them jokingly. [...] in communities where the belief in the supernatural is keen, there is a humorous ridicule of the absurd lengths to which some people carry their beliefs. (Halpert 1947: 465.)

But even in this, his position was to change. He later writes: "Stories of ghost that were no ghosts only existed where *there was or had been* serious belief in ghost-lore" (Halpert 1971: 54).

In other words, he now locates the belief in ghosts he sees as supporting such comical tales not just in the ethnographic present but also in the past outright (*was or had been*). It may be that Halpert is on to something here, and it would surely repay investigation if we looked into individual cases in order to gauge how frequently sceptical tales correlate with credulity and how frequently with sceptical attitudes.

Somewhen during the second half of the 20th century, Halpert read a book called *Golspie*. It is an unusual work in that the major part of it was written by seven children. Its history is as follows. In 1891, Edward Nicholson (1849–1912), the chief librarian of the Bodley in Oxford, was holidaying in the northern Scottish village of that name, and on becoming interested in the local lore of children he met there, he designed a little questionnaire-contest on it, that was administered via the local school. Children are an interesting group to collect from as they are usually not *over-fieldworked* (a parallel to being *over-socialworked*), nor indeed fully conditioned to give the higher-class outsider what he or she expects from an interaction (such as genuine ghost stories). Nicholson wrote up the results of this questionnaire together with notes and an introduction, and published it in book form in 1897. Having to classify the narratives he had received, he devised the category "ghosts that were no ghosts". Three of these stories are versions of ATU 1676, and can indeed be read, as he suggested, as cautions "against ghost-shamming" – in other words, they are narratives which function within the frame of folk belief, and warn that those who meddle with the supernatural will come to grief. But this is not the full gamut of the narratives Nicholson includes. He also mentions ghost-shammers who are simply disbelieved rather than getting any just deserts, and he prints three cases where the 'ghost' on second inspection turns out to be a horse, a goat with its horn caught in a fence, and a travelling salesman on an unshod Shetland pony. As one of the children (Willie W. Munro) remarks: "I do not belief in ghosts, and none of the stories which I am going to tell you proves contrary to my statement" (Nicholson 1897: 36). In passing, we might also note that Nicholson (1897: 53) made an observation highly apt to our theme: "Superstition exists in all parts of Great Britain and among all classes". Regretably he did not go on to observe the corollary of this: that in all parts of the country and amongst all classes disbelief in 'superstition' also exists.

It is worth saying something about the popularity of these sceptical tales – or rather to quote the words of those who have made such remarks before. Firstly Halpert (1947: 465), who, speaking of these humorous tales about the fear of the supernatural, remarks: "Oddly enough, tales of this kind are perhaps the most widely known in English-speaking America. Several similar stories are also well-known in Europe". Likewise, when speaking of the "One for You and One for Me" tale, where someone passing a churchyard at night hears people sharing out nuts (or apples) with the phrase "One for You and One for Me" misinterprets this as God and the Devil sharing out souls, the doyen of Ozark folklore, Vance Randolph (1952: 204) remarks it was "perhaps the commonest of all the Ozark tales". Thompson (1946: 214) remarks that this tale "is widely told by oral story-tellers all over Europe and, for some reason, is about the best known of all anecdotes collected in America". And finally, Linda Dégh and Andrew Vázsonyi (1976 [1971]: 114) note that many of the more elaborate of what they term 'negative legends' "are extremely popular in both rural and urban communities".

So, at the same time as these researchers note these tales' popularity, there is a hint of their bafflement that at why they should be so popular, something betrayed by the choice of such words as "oddly enough" and "for some reason". Does this stem from the expectation that the folk should be telling narratives that support 'traditional beliefs', rather than making fun of them? Is this also the reason that Halpert and Ernest Baughman had found them to be unsatisfactorily represented in the tale-type and motif indices? Halpert noted that despite its widespread distribution, the "One for Me, One for You" tale only gained recognition of its "independent existence" in the folkloristic world (and not as a peculiar version of ATU 1791) in the 1970s (Halpert 2010: 265).[3] Such a fate was not uncommon as the classificatory mechanisms devised to deal with folk narrative were not well attuned to such sceptical tales. Often such tales were merely ascribed motif numbers, rather than the fuller status of a narrative type, that is of course if they were recognized at all. Often Baughman and Halpert had to propose completely new motif numbers themselves in order to classify what are really quite popular stories (e.g. Halpert 2010: 259–267).

Many of the tales found a classificatory home under the heading J – the set of motifs that deal with the Wise and the Foolish – which is apt enough. Just as the concept of folk belief can be seen, *inter alia*, as a way for the educated to distinguish themselves from the folk, so sceptical folktales and legends can be ways for *the sceptical amongst the folk* to differentiate themselves from their credulous neighbours – to signal themselves as wise and to signal those who believe in ghosts, magic, and the like, as foolish. Indeed, it is likely that we might find *belief and scepticism* within a single community, within a single family, and even within a single individual.

A key part of the story of the development of folklore studies from the 19th to the 21st centuries is not only the widely acknowledged increase in both the number and kind of people thought to possess lore, but also an increase in the number of forms considered as being lore. This development can be observed throughout America, Europe, and beyond. If we consider the culture of a people a long way from Anglo-America, the Gagauz of Moldova, we can note that one of the main points of a sensitive study of their lore (Kapalo 2011) is that certain genres, such as toasts and non-canonical prayers, long ignored by scholars as being too Christian, literate, and ethnically widespread, and thus not pressing the magic buttons of old-school folklore studies of being pagan-derived, oral and ethno-specific, should be taken up for documentation and study. This broadening of the scope of folklore can be observed within the career of a single scholar: Herbert Halpert. Halpert famously looked to topographic works and local writings to supplement folklore collections proper. He also was prepared, like his friend Vance Randolph, to aim at something more than "selective text collecting in a few genres". As Halpert (1981: 346) wrote in his obituary for Randolph, "in his folk-narrative collections we are given every kind of story that informants tell [...] modern folklorists follow Randolph in his view that folk narrative collecting should not be limited to the tales included in the Type and Motif Indexes."

But whereas Randolph was a folklorist, although a self-trained, private scholar of unconventional bent for his time, the other writings that Halpert read, which include those of Egerton, Geering and Nicholson, were by non-folklorists, by people not on the look-out for narrative traces of folk belief, who were content to report what was of interest to them about their chosen locality. We can see that Halpert, by his promotion of these narratives from a sub-section within a miscellaneous catch-all section in his Ph.D. to a self-standing and thoroughly annotated section of their own in the book that resulted sixty years later, and by his own changing comments over this period, had during his own lifetime enlarged and sharpened his own concept of popular narrative.

The Study of Folk Disbelief

'Folk belief' is not a useless scholarly category; quite the opposite, it is a useful one, but it should be complemented by three other categories, which are also amenable to study and documentation: folk disbelief, educated belief, and educated disbelief. This examination of examples in one of these categories, folk disbelief, has focused on ghost disbelief narratives, but it could just as well have focused on traditional narratives expressing disbelief in (or by corollary, the foolishness of belief in) any other supranormal concept, such as magic or fairies, say. While our indices and articles are weighted to registering expressions of belief in supranormal concepts, disbelief in those phenomena can (and could) be found amongst what used to be called 'the Folk', as can traditional sceptical narratives.

Despite Dégh and Vázsonyi's (1976 [1971]: 113) observations that "born sceptics, searchers for truth, and knowledgeables are recognized folk characters", sceptical statements and narratives which express scepticism have not generally been the focus of folklorists' attention. And despite David Hufford's (1982a: 251) declaration that "'traditions of disbelief' make up a serious and researchable topic", little has been done to study these traditions of disbelief or their narratives. Indeed, his much-cited article entitled "Traditions of Disbelief" (Hufford 1982b) invokes them not to study them but rather to support the continued study of *belief* traditions by relativizing disbelief as a position. While Hufford briefly (a single sentence in ten pages) refers to a narrative from Newfoundland analogous to those we have presented above – in this case the 'ghost' is "the rear end of a horse seen at dusk through the ever-present Newfoundland fog" (Hufford 1982b: 50) –, this expression of scepticism is not explored at all. We are not told for example, when Hufford came across it or in what context (or perhaps rather contexts, given that he remarks that it is "a traditional example"). There is no foreshadowing of any narratology of folk disbelief in Hufford's piece.

Dégh and Vázsonyi (1976 [1971]: 112) observed that while "the folklorist has been acquainted with negative legends; he has not paid much attention to them". Just as a study of traditional expressive forms which omits obscenity is a study which does not possess the fullest breadth it might, so a study which omits folk disbelief is also selling the vernacular short. Above we have presented some such narratives in the works of local writers who were not folklorists, and have concentrated on the attempt of one great folklorist, Herbert Halpert, to find a new way to think about such narratives over the course of his career.

As it is investigated further, folk disbelief is unlikely to emerge as a monolithic entity, anymore than folk belief is, but to possess its own substantial variation. The examples presented here are from Protestant areas, and the situation may be different in Orthodox and Catholic areas.[4] But given that belief in ghosts, fairies, and so forth seems to have been quite current in Methodist Cornwall in the far south-west of England at the same time as the mid and late 19th century examples of scepticism from south-east of England, we must conclude that religion is not the only factor at work here. Incidentally, sceptical narratives about religious doctrines may well have their own traditionality and form a productive avenue for investigation as well.

In addition to geographical variation, one would expect historical variation too. Thus one would expect less (or different) folk disbelief in the 16th and 17th centuries than in the 19th and 20th. The *differential* distribution of popular scepticism might also be considered, for example with regard to different beliefs – ghosts, magic, fairies, the abilities of cunning folk, and so on. It is striking that while we can find sceptical traditional narratives about ghosts in England, the few traditional narratives that feature magic in a way that reflects the ethnographic record of actual folk magical practice take magic very seriously. That is something that might be investigated further. We might be interested in the role of sceptical narratives in folk didactics, perhaps typically related to children. Another area for investigation might be, as Halpert suggests, the co-existence of sceptical narratives in the public sphere with surreptitious belief in the private mind. And yet another avenue for investigation could be genuine scepticism versus what we might term 'entertainment scepticism', i.e. scepticism embraced for the duration of a good 'ghost who was not a ghost' yarn. Ethnographic studies might reveal

234

that what Gary Butler (1990) observed in French Newfoundland, namely that statements of belief were often made provisionally or ironically, might equally apply to statements of disbelief as well.

As a final thought, we might ask ourselves whether this heavy focus on folk belief (as opposed to folk disbelief) has been and continues to be the reason why one of the most popular vernacular senses of the word 'folklore' is of 'nonsense that sensible people reject'. All the more cause then for us to turn at least some of our attention to address sceptical narratives, both in contemporary fieldwork and in our re-envisagings of historical material.

Notes

* This research has been supported by the European Union through the European Regional Development Fund (Centre of Excellence, CECT) and by the Estonian Ministry of Education and Research (Institutional Research Project IUT2–43).

1 Martin Lovelace (1983: 578) notes that "the remark 'nothing worse than myself' is a traditional remark of a sceptic" citing in addition to Bettesworth, his own experience in Dorset in south-western England, the country writings of Thomas Miller (*Rural Sketches*, 1842) and the essay-writing of one of his students from Nova Scotia. We might add that the phrase also appears in chapter four of *Jane Eyre*, when Jane looks round the shadowy room at night.

2 To preserve his 'code' argument, Halpert chronologizes – seeing (or rather, supposing) the comic material as later, but there is little support for such a ordering from the dating of the texts as we have them.

3 This recognition (by Pirkko-Liisa Rausmaa) was limited however to the system used by the Finnish Folklore Archives; in the latest revision of the tale-type index (Uther 2004), the story is still undifferentiated from "The Sexton Carries the Clergyman".

4 The existence of popular scepticism in Catholic areas of Europe in the 19th century has been argued in Correll 2005 and Hameršak 2011. The latter for example writes that "19th century Croatian manuscripts and printed collections of folk narratives [...] suggest that scepticism was part of the traditional worldview" (Hameršak 2011: 150).

Sources

Afanas'ev 1855–1863 = Афанасьев, Александр (ed.) 1855–1863. *Народные русские сказки*. Москва: Издание К. Солдатенкова и Н. Щепкина.

Afanas'ev 1862 = Афанасьев, Александр 1862. *Народные русские сказки. Не для печати*. Рукопись.

Baycroft, Timothy & David Hopkin 2012. *Folklore and Nationalism in Europe during the Long Nineteenth Century*. Leiden: Brill.

Bois, J. G. C. 2010. *Jersey Folklore & Superstitions. A Comparative Study with the Traditions of the Gulf of St. Malo (the Channel Islands, Normandy & Brittany) with Reference to World Mythologies*. 2 vols. Milton Keynes: Authorhouse.

Bourne, George [i.e. George Sturt] 2010 [1907]. *Memoirs of a Surrey Labourer. A Record of the Last Years of Frederick Bettesworth*. Stroud: Amberley.

Burke, Peter 1978. *Popular Culture in Early Modern Europe*. London: Temple Smith.

Burne, Charlotte 1914. [Review of] Rustic Speech and Folk-Lore by Elizabeth Mary Wright. *Folklore* 25(3): 391–392.

Butler, Gary 1990. *Saying Isn't Believing. Conversation, Narrative and the Discourse of Belief in a French Newfoundland Community*. St John's: ISER.

Correll, Timothy Corrigan 2005. Believers, Sceptics, and Charlatans. Evidential Rhetoric, the Fairies, and Fairy Healers in Irish Oral Narrative and Belief. *Folklore* 116(1): 1–18.

Crick, Bernard 1980. *George Orwell. A Life*. Harmondsworth: Penguin.

Dégh, Linda & Andrew Vázsonyi 1976 [1971]. Legend and Belief. In *Folklore Genres*. Dan Ben-Amos (ed.). Austin: University of Texas Press. Pp. 93–123.

Dundes, Alan 1985. Nationalistic Inferiority Complexes and the Fabrication of Folklore: A Reconsideration of Ossian, the *Kinder- und Hausmärchen*, the *Kalevala*, and Paul Bunyan. *Journal of Folklore Research* 22(1): 5–18.

Egerton, John Coker 1884. *Sussex Folk and Sussex Ways*. London: Trübner.

Geering, Thomas 2003 [1884]. *Our Sussex Parish*. Bakewell: Countryside Books.

Halpert, Herbert 1947. *Folktales and Legends of the New Jersey Pines. A Collection and Study*. Unpublished Ph.D. thesis. Indiana University.

Halpert, Herbert 1971. Definition and Variation in Folk Legend. In *American Folk Legend. A Symposium*. Wayland Hand (ed.). Berkeley: University of California Press. Pp. 47–54.

Halpert, Herbert 1981. Obituary: Vance Randolph (1892–1980). *Journal of American Folklore* 94(373): 345–350.

Halpert, Herbert 2010. *Folk Tales, Tall Tales, Trickster Tales and Legends of the Supernatural from the Pinelands of New Jersey. Recorded and Annotated by Herbert Halpert between 1936 and 1951*. J. D. A. Widdowson (ed.). Lewiston: The Edwin Mellen Press.

Hameršak, Marijana 2011. Lowbrow Scepticism or Highbrow Rationalism? (Anti) Legends in 19th-Century Croatian Primers. *Studia Mythologica Slavica* 14: 143–157.

Hufford, David 1982a. *The Terror that Comes in the Night. An Experience-centered Study of Supernatural Assault Traditions*. Philadelphia: University of Pennsylvania Press.

Hufford, David 1982b. Traditions of Disbelief. *New York Folklore* 8(3–4): 47–56.

Kapalo, James 2011. *Text, Context and Performance. Gagauz Folk Religion in Discourse and Practice*. Leiden: Brill.

Kawan, Christine Shojaei 1995. Contemporary Legend Research in German-Speaking Countries. *Folklore* 106: 103–110.

Lovelace, Martin 1983. *The Presentation of Folklife in the Biographies and Autobiographies of English Rural Workers*. Unpublished Ph.D. thesis. Memorial University of Newfoundland.

Nicholson, Edward Williams Byron 1897. *Golspie: Contributions to its Folk-Lore*. London: Nutt.

Oinas, Felix 1978. *Folklore, Nationalism and Politics*. Columbus: Slavica.

Randolph, Vance 1952. *Who Blowed Up the Church House? And Other Ozark Folktales*. New York: Columbia University Press.

Shekel, Miss K. 2013. Shocking! [Customer Review of Robert Chandler *Russian Magic Tales from Pushkin to Platonov*] Available at http://www.amazon.co.uk/product-reviews/0141442239/ref=cm_cr_dp_hist_one?ie=UTF8&filterBy=addOneStar&showViewpoints=0 [Accessed April 14, 2014]

Thompson, Stith 1946. *The Folktale*. New York: Dryden.

Uther, Hans-Jörg 2004. *The Types of International Folktales. A Classification and Bibliography*. I–III. Folklore Fellows' Communications 284–286. Helsinki: Academia Scientiarum Fennica.

David Hopkin

Legends and the Peasant History of Emancipation in France and Beyond

Who emancipated the European peasantry? Other aspects of the process that ended the agrarian Old Regime might be debated, but the answer to the question 'who' appears straightforward. Europe's peasants were emancipated in a series of state acts stretching from Charles-Emmanuel III's edict concerning 'The freeing of property subject to feudal obligations' (*l'affranchissement des fonds sujets à devoirs féodaux*) in ducal Savoy in 1771 (suspended by his successor Victor-Amadeus III), to Prince Alexandru Ioan Cuza's decrees abolishing serfdom in the Romanian provinces in 1864 (Blum 1978: 216–218, 375–376). Credit often accrued to particular heads of state, such as the 'tsar liberator' Alexander II, responsible for the 1861 Emancipation Proclamation in Russia (Moon 2002: 56–69). Even in the case of revolutionary states, emancipation came from above. It was the French National Assembly, during its dramatic evening session of 4 August, 1789, that abolished the feudal regime, along with many other kinds of legal privilege. What the August Decrees meant in practice in the countryside took some time – and not inconsiderable violence – to work out, but the direction of travel was clear (Markoff 1996: 428–515). The French revolutionary regime was by its very essence hostile to the existence of separate legal estates within the polity, and (with some exceptions) wherever its power extended the abolition of serfdom and feudalism was enacted. Other European states such as Prussia (1807) and Bavaria (1808), in awe of the energies that the Revolution had unleashed, followed suit.

So we know the answer to the question 'who emancipated the peasants' – it was governments, autocrats, states. But why European monarchs and states chose to emancipate the peasants is less clear. In the case of France, Marxist historians such as Georges Lefebvre and Albert Soboul argued that it was the revolutionary bourgeoisie, embodied in the Third Estate (which had declared itself the National Assembly in June 1789), that sought through this action to free up the factors of production – labour, land and the capital it represented – though both were also interested in the ways that peasants themselves shaped the process (Lefebvre 1929; Soboul 1983). However, it is less easy to detect the active role of the bourgeoisie in the decisions of Frederick VI, prince-regent of Denmark, responsible for the abolition of the *Stavnsbånd* in 1788 (Horstbøll & Østergård 1990) or Tsar Alexander I's decision to end serfdom in Estland, Kurland and Livland (1816–1819) (Plakans 2011: 183–198). Other historians have posited the development of an enlightened public sphere in the late 18th century, in which educated members of the nobility and the middle classes both participated. From this world of enlightened debate emerged a new political culture of natural rights and citizenship that cannot be understood as the ideological property of any one social group, but which had its own intellectual and cultural power to mobilise supporters. Hence one finds aristocratic landowners, the very people who one might imagine had the most to lose from emancipation, at the forefront of reform: it was the declarations of the vicomte de Noailles and the duc d'Aiguillon which initiated the bonfire of privileges on the night of the 4 August 1789 (Fitzsimmons 2003: 13); Nikolai Miliutin, noble landowner and serf-holder, drafted the Emancipation Manifesto of 1861 (Lincoln 1977). A third answer might emphasise the developing significance of the state and its own concerns in this period, independent of either noble or bourgeois interests. A peasantry free of the labour demands and economic burdens imposed by the landowning nobility could become a citizenry of taxpayers and conscript soldiers. Thus there is no contradiction in enlightened despots acting as peasant liberators any more than there is in revolutionary assemblies; in this domain the French revolutionaries were the continuation of the absolute monarchy rather than its negation (or so argued Alexis de Tocqueville more than 150 years ago).

There is much else that historians do not know about peasant emancipation. We are not really sure what feudalism and serfdom meant in practice, at least in western European countries. How heavy feudalism weighed on individual peasants is very hard to calculate, not least because the forms it took were so many and varied. Compulsory labour charges might be converted into payments in money or in kind. There were also the lords' monopolies, one had to use his mill, his wine-press, his bread oven, his justice... Lords made claims over what peasants considered common land: the pastures, the woods, the water courses. Feudalism also included more-or-less symbolic privileges: the right to hunt; the right to own a dovecot; the right to carry weapons; the right to the first pew in church. But the package of burdens varied enormously not only from state to state but region to region and even village to village, as did their implementation (Sutherland 2002). Nor do we know for certain who gained and who lost from emancipation. One may have one's suspicions but in practice it can be quite hard to identify, for example, the beneficiaries of the privatisation of common land. And although we do know that agricultural production increased over the course of the 19th century, whether that was as a consequence of emancipation or of other developments associated with 'modernisation' – such as new crops, new technologies, roads, railways, market integration, capitalist farming – is not clear.

Given these doubts, one might imagine that peasant emancipation is a hotly debated topic among historians, but this is far from the case. With the exception of the 1861 Russian decree, no European example has attracted anything like the scholarly interest generated by the abolition of slavery in the new world. The latter is usually treated as an entirely separate topic, even though for contemporaries peasant and slave emancipation were linked events (Mintz 1996). The reasons for this neglect are varied but one explanation is the air of inevitability that hangs over the process – personal service was bound to give way to the cash nexus because that is what the modern world demands. Following the same teleology, peasants themselves were doomed to disappear before the forces of globalisation, industrial production and mass culture: they are a residual population, quaint but insignificant. Attention more deservedly settles on those social groups who embody the future, the middle classes or the urban workers, depending on one's point of view. Finally, at least in France which will be the focus of the rest of this chapter, many historians assume that feudalism was, by the time of the Revolution, a dead letter whose disappearance no one noticed. The current consensus among historians is that the French Revolution was an urban and intellectual undertaking fought out among competing elites. It has been characterized as "a largely irrelevant affair to the vast majority of rural inhabitants" who were either indifferent to events in Paris, or hostile to them (Woell 2008).

This view is demonstrable nonsense: peasants were active participants in the Revolution. The reason that such an interpretation has found traction among historians is best explained by the lack of sources concerning peasant attitudes and beliefs. Without these, their documented actions are difficult to interpret. Peasants seldom had much to say, or at least not in a form that is readily comprehensible. Historians need written sources but peasants were mostly illiterate, and if literate did not usually write things down. Theirs was primarily an oral culture, and it is very difficult to access past conversations, especially the conversations of the subordinate who were practiced in disguising statements that might get them into trouble. Mostly undocumented, even when their words were recorded, as in court for example, it can be difficult to extract a clear meaning from them.

For this reason the role that peasants themselves played in the processes of emancipation can easily be misunderstood, ignored or overlooked, allowing 'top-down' models of political action to go unchallenged. However, we can be fairly certain that feudalism was not irrelevant to peasants, because they remembered it and this powerful memory of exactions and the manner of their ending continued to affect their behaviour for decades to come. This rumbling antagonism was no doubt fostered by the legal hangovers of the feudal regime, which peasant communities continued to challenge both in the courts and on the ground through vandalism, arson and other "small arms fire in the class war" (Scott 1985: 1; Agulhon 1982; Blaufarb 2012). But in addition to these traditional actions, politics also came to the peasantry in the course of the 19th century. Emancipation was followed, though not always immediately, by some form of political engagement, if not the franchise then at least some token of citizenship such as participation in village councils. Some kind of village assembly had often played a part in peasant life before emancipation, but now these were drawn into the national administrative structure, under the oversight of state bureaucrats. Peasants became subject to political campaigns and governments fretted about how they might cast their vote. This happened particularly early in France where, leaving out the complicated history of voting under the Revolution and First Empire (1789–1815), male suffrage arrived with the Revolution of 1848. Thereafter peasants were scrutinised as they came up to place their ballot. And a primary motive in those choices, according to these outside observers, was hostility to feudalism and those who had benefitted from it. This is recurrent theme in the observations of justices, prefects, sub-prefects and teachers as they tried to explain what, to the modern eye, seemed peculiar manifestations of peasant politics. For instance, the assault by several hundred people on the church of Chevanceaux (Charente-Inférieure) in April 1868 was triggered by the gift by the local noble landowner of a stained-glass window containing his coat of arms, interpreted as a sign that a return to feudalism was imminent (Soboul 1968: 979). According to prefects and other observers of rural elections, nothing was more powerful in mobilising the peasant vote than a (deliberately fostered) rumour that the lords, temporal and ecclesiastical, were about to return (Corbin 1992: 4). "How many peasants threaten you still with the Convention [the revolutionary regime associated with the Terror and the guillotining of aristocrats]? How many believe in the privileged and tremble at the mention of the tithe?" wrote a rural schoolteacher in the Nièvre as late as 1861 (Price 2004: 221).

At the time some commentators argued that these memories were not 'traditional' but fostered within the feverish electoral climate of the period, as noted by the English artist Philip Hamerton resident in France during the Second Empire and first decade of the Third Republic:

> One of the strongest reasons for the increasing Republicanism of the peasantry is their recent belief that if Henri V came to the throne he would re-establish the old corvées – a very erroneous notion, of course, like all the ideas which suddenly gain currency in the uncultivated world, but it has served the Republic well. A Royalist told me that he believed this idea had been industriously spread amongst the peasants by the Republican propaganda. Very likely the Republicans may have done their best to propagate it, and yet all such efforts would be utterly useless if there were not a tide of peasant-rumour and peasant-opinion to circulate the idea, a tide which no art, craft, wisdom, or knowledge of the instructed classes can either foresee or direct, and against which even the prodigiously strong and minutely perfect organization of the Church of Rome is utterly unable to contend. (Hamerton 1877: 228.)

In other words according to Hamerton there existed a set of peasant memories of the *ancien régime* on which party propaganda could feed, but which it could not confect. We may surmise that these rumours, these memories, also explain a key feature of the 19th century – the problem of peasants' "non-disappearance", as Teodor Shanin (1990: 61) put it. Despite the hopes and expectations of both political Left and Right, both Karl Marx and state-sponsored agronomists, the peasantry did not break down into classes of rural capital and rural labour over the course of the century. In France, and for that matter other countries such as Germany, peasants appeared to be thriving right up to the First World War. They were not declining numerically, their percentage share of the national landholding was increasing, and their political clout was growing through their enrolment in cooperatives and land leagues in the 1880s and after. In order to explain this "non-disappearance" we must assume that peasants had some sense of themselves, some notion of their unity as a social group, some common commitment or some common enmity expressed in culture. It seems plausible that the memory of feudalism and subordination, continuing resentment against historical injustices and a renewable hostility to those who had lorded over their forebears, fed this peasant identity.

Historians of rural society, such as Albert Soboul, Alain Corbin, Peter Jones, Roger Price and Eugen Weber, have followed contemporaries in stressing the importance of peasant "myths" – to use Price's word (2004: 221) – or "atavisms" – to use Jones (1985: 105) – concerning feudalism to explain peasant political behaviour in the 19th century. What form did these memories (or myths, or atavisms) take? How were they transmitted from generation to generation and, in as much as they shaped a collective peasant identity, from region to region? Are we talking about a common set of narratives shared over a wide area, or a plethora of purely local narratives? Did they concentrate only on the suffering with no reflection on how that had, or might, come to an end? By-and-large historians are not able to answer these questions: they observe behaviour and offer a rationale for it, but their habitual sources have little to say about the actual form and content of such memories. Therefore we need to turn to material more familiar to folklorists, such as legends. Legends such as this one, recorded in 1903 by the folklorist Félix Arnaudin from a rural woman, Anne-Jeanne Mariolan (1822–1916, known as Marianne de Mariolan), then 81, from the Landes region south of Bordeaux. It is about a place, a supernatural place, and so falls squarely within the remit of this book.

> They say that once upon a time at Lué there was a wicked lord, really hard on poor people. This lord was owner of much territory, woods and moors, but he had forbidden the shepherds and goatherds to pasture their animals on his property, or even to pass over it.
>
> One morning he went to see a plantation of pines that he had put in, not far from Hidéou, and there he found a goatherd leading his flock. When the goatherd saw the lord, he tried to round up his goats, but the lord, mad with rage, went at him on his horse, and so both goatherd and goats started to run. The lord made his horse gallop right on the man's heels. The unfortunate man quickly begged for mercy.
>
> 'Pity, monseigneur, forgive me for the love of God.'
> But the lord paid no attention to the goatherd's words. 'You would come back here you brigand', he kept repeating, 'You would come back to ravage my saplings?'
>
> And this went on for quarter of a league. He forced the unfortunate goatherd before him, trotting on his horse. At last the goatherd was overcome with anger. He took his gun and, without a word, he fired it at the seigneur and left him for dead.
>
> Then the man, seized with fear, fled and never came back to the parish. No one mourned the wicked lord and since then the poor people of Lué have been free to lead their herds wherever they felt like on the moors.
>
> At the place where the wicked seigneur died, as no one had given him justice, the broom would not regrow, and the sand has remained red with his blood. (Arnaudin 1994: 294–295.)

This story is not without its ironies, as William Pooley has demonstrated in his discussion of this text (2014: 133–155); peasant emancipation is a tale well suited to the ironic mode. But what should we call this text – a legend, a peasant 'myth', the articulation of a 'peasant atavism'? We might simply call this peasant history, because in essence this is a true story. On 10 June 1760 Bernard de Pic de Blaise de la Mirandole was found dead on the path between the farm of Gouaillard and the church of Lué. Arnaudin had been familiar with legends of 'moussu Pic' from other storytellers around his home town of Labouheyre long before he recorded this version, and had already turned to the historical archive to learn more about the events that lay behind them. These other legends included such piquant details as the fact that the rumour was already abroad that the lord had killed a goatherd when the return of his mount, the saddle covered in blood, reversed the expectation (Arnaudin 2003 [1872]: 519–531).

Arnaudin found that the archival documents from 1760 reveal only the barest facts about the murder. They tell us nothing about how, why or by whom it was committed, because this information was not known to the authorities. This legend is, therefore, peasant history in the sense that it reveals knowledge of past events only known within the peasant community, but about which that community kept silent at the time. It is peasant history in another sense too, it is indicative of how seigneurialism, at least at this place and this time, was experienced, and how peasants responded to it. History is of course not just the recording of 'facts' but also endows those facts with significance. So again this is peasant history because it offers not only an account of events but also offers an interpretation of them: as a consequence of this event "the poor people of Lué have been free to lead their herds wherever they felt like". That mattered at the time, and it continued to matter in de Mariolan's time, for history is always present-facing even as it recounts the past.

The most striking feature of this story is that it offers a very different answer to the question posed at the start of this article, "who emancipated the peasantry?" According to de Mariolan, as far as the peasants of Labouheyre were concerned they did it themselves (the anonymity of the perpetrator serves to make him representative of the community as a whole). This was not emancipation from above but literally from below, the mounted lord struck down by the foot-soldier of the commons.

Some of my historian colleagues might object to calling this text a 'history'. It displays several faults by the standards historians claim for themselves. For example, it collapses what was, in fact, a drawn out process (the assertion of communal control over the moors) into a single event. The interpretation of the consequences is disputable, with no room for the actions of the village council, the local administration, or the national government in settling ownership of the commons. This is particularly striking because, during Marianne's lifetime, the Lande had experienced a new, and far more drastic form of enclosure. Under government pressure the communes had sold their land to private landlords, who like 'moussu Pic' had turned off the sheep and goats and planted maritime pines instead. The region was rapidly transformed into the largest man-made forest in Europe (Temple

2009). As the effective head of the Mariolan clan, Marianne was one of the agents of this process. The seeming identification with the 'poor people' of the region masks the transformation of the Mariolan family from peasant pastoralists into arboricultural capitalists. It is, in fact, not at all unusual for the richer and more successful members of rural communities to be the most articulate spokespeople for a peasant collective identity. They have the most to gain from denying the existence of 'us' and 'them', only a 'we' (Hopkin 2012: 185–209). This suggests that Marianne's narration was strategic, aimed at influencing her contemporary audience, and was not a neutral retelling of 'facts'.

However, all these criticisms might be addressed with equal validity to work of professional historians. For example, the potted history of peasant emancipation given above includes numerous examples of single events being offered as tokens of long and complex processes (emancipation almost never occurred as a result of one decree, but was drawn out over decades); facts were advanced on the literate equivalent of hearsay (I know almost nothing about emancipation in Savoy and am reliant entirely on what Jerome Blum [1978] asserts to have been the case); and interpretations proffered even though I knew these to be vexed questions. Was Napoleon really the agent of modernisation in Germany? Many historians doubt this (Blanning 1989). And all histories are written for contemporary audiences with the intention of shaping their beliefs about the past and therefore directing their actions in the present, that is not a phenomenon unique to oral culture. Even Marie's indication of a supernatural agency at work, marking the spot where murder went unavenged, is not so unfamiliar to historians: in the 19th century it was not unusual for historians to see the hand of providence at work, before replacing it with other *dei ex machina* such as national integration, class consciousness, political culture, and so on. The distinction between peasant oral legend and academic history is not so great.

19th-century folklore collections may, therefore, contain the materials for an alternative history, a more 'democratic history' of feudalism and emancipation in which the peasants were not just waiting on state action but were agents with some control over their lives. This history need not necessarily contradict those "constituted in the hegemonic centres of knowledge", but at the very least it might operate as a corrective to them (Beiner 2004: 217). Emancipation may have come from above but perhaps it was presaged by movements from below (as Tsar Alexander II warned his nobles in 1857) (Leonard 2011: 31). On the night of 4 August 1789 the deputies in the French National Assembly were undoubtedly moved by an exalted spirit of patriotic self-sacrifice, but their theatrical gestures were played out against a backdrop of widespread rural revolt (more violent and threatening in the Parisian rumour mill than it was in reality). It is easier to renounce privileges that have, for practical purposes, already gone up in flames (Markoff 1996: 427–450). And as this example demonstrates, what matters in directing one's actions is not the truth but what one believes to be true. Therefore, it is significant that Marianne de Mariolan believed that emancipation came from below, and attempted to convince others of this 'truth', even if a more sceptical historian might cast doubt on her version.

I must admit that I'm not the first to call for a legendary history of France. The Revolution itself forced French historians to reconsider the nature of their available sources and find them wanting. It is worth revisiting their efforts within the framework of Nordic, Baltic and Celtic research on legends, because it stakes a claim to a 'Celtic' character for the whole of France. Although few people outside the hexagon would consider France (with the exception of the Breton peninsula) a Celtic country, at certain periods at least numerous French people have considered themselves the descendants of Celts.

This 'Celtic' element in French national identity can easily be overlooked as it is seldom foregrounded, compared with France's revolutionary or even royal heritage. Indeed the most common contemporary reference to *nos ancêtres les Gaulois* ('our ancestors the Gauls') is as a post-colonial joke, the mythic first sentence of the primary school textbook taught to all children of whatever race throughout the French empire (Gross 2005). Nonetheless, in the 19th century, one regularly finds passing references to some sort of Celtic identity, especially among working-class and peasant autobiographers, and among folklorists. The migrant stonemason and Republican politician Martin Nadaud, for example, opened his autobiography with the claim that his family belonged to "the great and powerful Gallic race". Although reduced to slavery by the Romans and the Franks, the Gauls "always wanted the Republic" he maintained (Nadaud 2011 [1895]: 38–39). The fact that these references were so commonplace, so uncritically accepted, reveals something about the shared presumptions about history and culture at the time. It is ironic that, in a post-colonial context, "our ancestors the Gauls" has come to represent the cultural power of the metropole, because in France itself it carried the assertion of a plebeian (and insurgent) social identity. Gauls are the 'the people', the peasantry, the salt of the earth. Hence Gauloises were 'democratic' cigarettes, preferred by footsoldiers in the trenches in First World War and resistance fighters in the Second. This social identity requires another against which it is defined – the seigneur, the lord – who is both socially and ethnically excluded from the people, and therefore the nation (Viallaneix & Ehrard 1982; Dietler 1994; Weber 1991).

The rediscovery of the Celts and their take up in French popular culture arose from questions about the nature of the tripartite social and political division of France before the Revolution. As in other countries, the population was divided into three estates – the lords spiritual (the first estate, the clergy), the lords temporal (the second estate, the nobility), and the commons (the third estate). From the 16th century onwards, perhaps because the system was breaking down as a practical means of administration, scholarly attention was directed to the origins of this arrangement. Who were the Second Estate, and how did they come to have dominion over the Third? One answer, promoted by nobles themselves, was that their privileges were justified by right of conquest. They were the descendants of the Franks, the Germanic tribe that had conquered the Romano-Celtic population of Gaul and continued to hold them in subjugation. The foremost proponent of this theory was Henry de Boulainvilliers (1658–1722), an unashamed apologist for feudalism. With the Revolution, however, while this entire political and social order tottered, the logic of conquest could be reversed. As abbé Sieyès put it in his enormously influential revolutionary pamphlet "What Is the Third Estate?" the descendants of the Gauls and Romans, the Third Estate, "could again be noble by conquering in turn" (Sieyès 2002 [1788]: 11).

The French Revolution of 1789 was widely interpreted by those who lived through it as the revolt of the Third Estate against the two privileged orders. In contemporary imagery the Third Estate was always portrayed as a peasant, and even though many of its most active partisans were lawyers, administrators and so on, it was understood that peasants made up the bulk of Third Estate in the present, and peasants were the forebears of all its members (Vovelle 1991). If the Second Estate were the descendants of invading Franks "and other savages out of the forests and marshes of ancient Germany" (as Sieyès put it, 2002 [1788]: 9), then this revolt was not just against the tyranny of a privileged class, but also against an ethnic other, a foreigner. And if feudalism was not a functional (albeit hierarchical) system of exchange but rather the legacy of illegal violence, it was easier to justify its abolition.

These radical political possibilities, nourished by a current of *Ossian*-inspired romanticism, encouraged an outburst of *Celtomanie* in the Revolutionary decade. On the whole this had more to do with philology and archaeology than with racial war, although the latter was occasionally revived, for example when the French wanted to make common cause with insular Celts against their oppressors, the English. The inheritor of the Revolution's mantle, Napoleon, would give some encouragement to an imperial Celtic identity through the foundation of the Académie Celtique in 1804. The Academy's aim was twofold – first to study Celtic languages both as they existed, and as they had once existed, in France; second "to collect, compare and explain all the monuments, usages, traditions [...] and to explain ancient times through modern times" (Belmont 1995: 33; cf. Senn 1981; Ozouf 1984). It was less devoted to the reconstruction of the pre-Roman past than tracing the continuity of France's Celtic heritage into the present: in other words, they sought 'survivals in culture' in the form of peasants' legends. Although the Academy did not outlast the regime it served (its last publication appeared in 1813), it is often cited as the origins of folklore studies in France, and, thanks to its influence on one member, Jacob Grimm, not without significance in the development of folklore studies elsewhere too (Gaidoz 1904: 140–142).

I do not want to exaggerate: the narrative of Celt versus Frank was not a particularly common or powerful one during the Revolutionary period. And it was complicated by the fact that the most obviously Celtic element in the French population, the Bretons, were also among the least enthusiastic revolutionaries. Some Celtomanes, such as Jacques Cambry, would develop theories of racial degeneration to account for exactly this paradox (Bianchi 2008). Nor, is it a particularly accurate narrative. However, my point is that the emergence of 'the people' as a political entity in France, as a sovereign nation, was accompanied by a story that was not dissimilar to that which would be told in other European nations *in statu nascendi* over the course of the 19th-century – Ireland, the Czech lands, Serbia, Estonia

– that the emancipation of labour was a necessary precursor to the political emancipation of 'the people', and both could only be achieved by the defeat of a feudal oppressor who was simultaneously an ethnic other.

A problem facing the revolutionary generation was that this newly emancipated people was without its own culture or its own history. Its language was that of one invader, the Romans; its history that of another, the Franks, starting with the first king of France, Clovis 1 (466–511). France's Celtic history and culture might provide the glue that would unite the Empire, particularly as it spread to those areas outside the borders of France which shared a similar Celtic pre-Roman history (the low countries, Switzerland, northern Italy, Spain...). The attempts of the *Académie Celtique* to collect legends connected to supposed Celtic monuments might be understood in this light. Legends would provide an oral history of an oppressed people, and the history of their resistance to their oppressors. This would become the foundation charter for the new Empire. The project went to pieces on the rocks of its members' linguistic ignorance and their erroneous ideas about the pre-Roman past, not to mention the indifference of much of the educated public, for whom culture was by definition classical. Nonetheless, even in the Revolution, some people understood that oral traditions could provide an alternative history.

Their vision was taken up by romantic historians during the Restoration (1814–1848), most notably by Jules Michelet, a keen reader of Giovanni Battista Vico, Johann Gottfried Herder and the Grimms (Rearick 1974: 82–102). His aim was to use legends to write "an alternative history, that is the history of the soul of the people, and of its imagination" (Michelet 1889 [1847] II: 5). 'The people' is a useful term because it is both socially divisive – the Second Estate, the nobility, cannot belong to 'the people', at least as long as they retain their separate identity – but at the same time it is a politically unifying terminology, 'the people' are synonymous with 'the nation', obfuscating other social distinctions. The introduction to the second volume of his history of the French Revolution, published in 1847, opens with an impassioned defence of the oral tradition as a reliable source for the historian (and a rejection of the historicist school emerging in Berlin around Leopold von Ranke, which attached value only to documented facts, that is to the written archive).

> When I say 'oral tradition' I mean national tradition, that which [...] everyone says and repeats, [...] that which you can learn if you spend the evening in the village bar; that which you can collect if, on your way you meet a traveller, and you start to talk about the weather, and then the expense of foodstuffs, and then of the Emperor's time, and then of the time of the Revolution. [...] Note well his judgements: about events he can sometimes be wrong. [...] But about men he is never mistaken, and only rarely misled. (Michelet 1889 [1847] II: 6.)

Michelet was arguing that villagers not only possessed an alternative history, but also an alternative historiography, that is an alternative method to make sense of the past, and to distinguish the meaning of history from 'mere events'.

Michelet uses the word "collect", but this is something that Michelet himself did not do. Nonetheless he did inspire others, most notably the novelist George Sand, whose book, *Légendes rustiques* (published in 1858) is one of the first works in French literature to claim to be taken direct from peasant oral tradition. Sand went to her native Berry with the intention of supplying Michelet's demand for a "great legend-trove of France". In the preface she wrote "the fantastic world which enflames or stupefies the mind of the peasant is an unpublished story of times past [...] The peasant is the sole historian, so to speak, of pre-historic times." However, later in the same document she lamented that he fulfilled this role rather badly, and "no historical tradition has remained in peasants' memory". (Sand 2000 [1858]: 18, 64.)

The person who came closest to actually supplying Michelet's "legend-trove" was Paul Sébillot who, like Sand and Michelet, was also a Republican activist. Sébillot was the leading French folklorist of the late 19th century. He was responsible for dozens of collections of folktales, he founded the *Société des traditions populaires*, and he edited its journal the *Revue des traditions populaires* (Postic 2011). He was in direct contact with most regional folklorists, including Arnaudin, and helped publish their work. He was also the person who did most for 'legend studies' in France. In 1897 Sébillot used his position as editor to urge his readers to seek out what would henceforward be identified in the index of that journal as 'Little Local Legends', short narratives (sometimes no more than a sentence) that related some apparently historic (even if supernatural) fact (Sébillot 1897: 129–131). The response to this request was huge, and within a decade the journal was already publishing its 1000th *petite légende locale*.[1] Sébillot would use this material to construct his multi-volume encyclopaedia of *Le folklore de France* in 1904, and in particular to write those books (IX–XI) that took as their subject the legendary history of France. Like George Sand before him, Sébillot was disappointed that "peasants conserve a very small number of historical memories" (Sébillot 1882: I, 345). In particular, he found that legends did not supply the 'democratic history' – the history of the people by the people for the people – that Michelet had expected. Instead he noted "the people [meaning the popular classes] appear fairly often in historical legends, but only in a secondary capacity, as they orbit those who held religious and feudal power" (Sébillot 2002 [1904–1906]: 1341).

Disappointment with the peasant *qua* historian is a recurrent discourse in 19th-century folkloristics. However, as we have seen, this lament contradicts those observers of peasant political action who argued that peasants retained a vivid memory, too vivid even, of their forebears' lives under feudalism. It is not difficult to resolve this contradiction. Although Michelet used the term "alternative history" (*autre histoire*) to describe legends, the grand lines of his chronology and his concerns had been established by literary history, that is the history of the monarchy. He was not yet prepared to accept that peasant historians might have a different set of priorities, one which relegated national conflict behind social conflict. For Republicans like Sébillot, Sand and Michelet, social conflict undermined the unity of the people. What Michelet was looking for in legends was an explicitly national epic concerning great men, great events… the clash of Celt and Teuton, the reverberations of Alesia, stories in which a people united to make their own history. But what folklorists like Sand and Sébillot found when they interrogated peasants was local, short, minor, unheroic – narratives of oppression and defeat as often as inspiring tales of resistance and victory. In as much as they did find the latter these often related the counter-revolutionary resistance of peasants to the Republic – 'the people' opposed to the very regime that acted in their name (Cadic 2003 [1908–1918]; Lagrée & Roche 1993)!

The importance of the social is apparent in Sébillot's finding that historical legends revolved around those who held religious or feudal power. Another of his findings helps us to understand that legends, rather than epic, were strategic. Considering legends about war Sébillot wrote that many belonged to "what one might call the folkloric commonplaces [*lieux communs*] of battles, because one finds them at the same time in narratives from elsewhere and from antiquity" (Sébillot 2002 [1904–1906]: 1406). These commonplaces were narrative schemas which storytellers applied to events, personages and locations distant from each other in space and time. Folklorists might call these 'migratory legends'. The fact that very similar stories were told about distinct events further damaged the reputation of the peasant historian, because it undermined his claim to factual accuracy. However, more recently oral historians, observing a similar phenomenon, have proved more tolerant, and have learnt to use such narratives to explore collective concerns (Ó Ciosáin 2004: 224–225). Legends made sense of experience rather than simply recording it; in the process of endowing events with significance, storytellers drew on the existing body of collective knowledge or tradition. In other words Michelet was right, legends were an expression of a popular, collective imagination; they were both part of, and give shape to, a group ideology. Of course that is true of other genres of oral literature, but perhaps more so with legends because legend carries some kind of 'truth value', and therefore is "intimately related to cultural ideology – the norms, values and expectations of a particular cultural group" (Tangherlini 2007: 8).

This ideological dimension is another reason why historians cannot ignore legends: they help us to understand why people behaved as they did. One might argue that legends, despite their historical character, are not really about the past, they are about the present and future. They discuss the kinds of conflicts that have arisen in the past precisely because these same kinds of conflicts are likely to arise again, and at the same time they suggest strategies for surviving these conflicts. The performance of a legend like Marianne de Mariolan's was (and here again I follow Timothy Tangherlini's exposition of the significance of legends) a deeply political act: she was attempting not only to shape the audience's conception of the past, but by so doing influence their actions in the future, by highlighting particular social solidarities and social divisions. What one believes to be true directly affects the way one behaves. Therefore, those who share, or come to share through legend telling, a particular vision of the past can, as Michelet both believed and hoped, be mobilised for collective action in the present.

I cite as an example Louise Michel – anarchist, revolutionary, the 'Red Virgin' of the Paris Commune, and folklorist (during her seven years of transportation to New Caledonia she collected the material for a volume of *Légendes et chants de gestes canaques*, 'Legends and Heroic Songs of the Kanak people' [1885]). After her return to France, but during another period of imprisonment, she wrote her memoirs (Michel 1886), which are a paean to the oral tradition. Michel was the illegitimate daughter of a servant and the son of the local landowning family (the former seigneurs). Although she grew up in the manor house of Vroncourt (Haute-Marne), she went to the village spinning-bees (*écregnes* in the local patois) and participated in village oral culture. Her sense of her Celtic inheritance, and the value she attached to oral culture, undoubtedly owe much to her readings in Michelet, among others, but she also drew on the tales told to her by her peasant neighbours and mentors (Hart 2001–2002). Their stories turned her into a rebel: "From my evenings at the village spinning-bees date a sentiment of revolt that I have often rediscovered." The story she then goes on to relate concerns not a feudal lord but a grain-hoarder (though the two were often the same) who so starved the family of the storyteller that two of her children died. And the moral that narrator and listener drew from the narrative was very different: the former was not moved to revolt but rather to accept the will of God. (Michel 1886: 226–228.) However, it is in the nature of a legend that its significance will change with the context in which it is told. The same story can, with a different twist, require resignation or indignation from its audience (Gilsenan 1996: 115–139).

Historians have used the term 'atavism' to describe this peasant recitation of wrongs suffered at the hands of feudal (and other) oppressors. Atavism is usually a pejorative word: it implies that peasants were unthinking primitives in thrall to irrational urges. However, for Michel, atavism had a positive meaning; it was what gave the people, individually and collectively, their identity: "I spoke of atavism. Back there [in Vroncourt], at the very foundations of my life, are these legendary narratives." (Michel 1886: 39, 236.) Although one feature of oral culture is its ability to forget what is no longer functional ('structural amnesia'), another is redundancy. As one cannot always know what knowledge has become irrelevant, and as whatever is not repeated in an oral culture will be lost, it is not surprising that peasants continued to relate stories about feudal abuses long after feudalism itself had been abolished. However, given that the very definition of the peasant requires becoming "subject to the demands and sanctions of power-holders outside his social stratum" (Wolf 1966: 11), perhaps these stories had not yet become irrelevant. Feudalism in the Old Regime sense may have gone by the time of Louise Michel and Marianne de Mariolan, but it left profound traces in the social relations of the 19th century countryside. If seigneurs were extinct, landlords remained, if feudal tutelage was abolished, clientage and caciquismo might replace it. Legends of the past could still provide useful lessons in the present and future. All atavism means in this context is that peasant actions were conditioned by their sense of history, and that does not seem nearly so unreflective, or so unreasonable. What is the point of history if it doesn't offer some kind of reflection on the present?

This chapter is really an advertisement for a research project not yet undertaken. My hypothesis is that, in folklore archives lies the material to write an alternative history of feudalism and its destruction, a history told from the peasants' point of view. I do not claim that this alternative history would be more accurate than that preserved in the written record, but we need not assume that it would be more inaccurate either. And whatever its inaccuracies, because it would tell us what peasants believed to be true, it would help us understand their attitudes and behaviour subsequent to emancipation. As an initial foray, let us consider the series of 'Little Local Legends', which appeared in the *Revue des Traditions Populaires* between 1897 and the journal's closure in 1919, and which helped Sébillot formulate his ideas on the subject: what does this sample have to offer in the way of legends of feudalism? The recurrent themes found there might begin to give some substance to this wished-for peasant history.

The legends came from many sources. Both through the journal and his own private correspondence Sébillot had built up a substantial network of contributors in the provinces who sent him texts for this collection. The latter included Arnaudin; indeed his summary version of the legend of the murder of Lord of Lué had appeared under the 'Little Local Legends' rubric in 1899 (LLL 345). Both Sébillot and these correspondents participated in France's web of regional learned societies. Although such societies covered many subjects from agriculture to zoology, local archaeology and antiquarian pursuits formed a central part of their activity. Some organised competitions for the best folkloric texts and many visited monuments to gather first-hand information on their legendary history. Sébillot often reported their findings. Regional learned societies also drew on the 'village monographs' which the French minister of education had directed village teachers to complete in every commune across the country as part of the preparations for the International Expositions held in Paris in 1889 and 1900. The instructions specifically mentioned local legends and oral histories. Teachers responded with different degrees of enthusiasm to this request: some ignored it, some denied that there were any local legends, but some provided numerous texts. A few of these monographs were published independently and Sébillot also drew on these; however most remain unpublished in departmental archives and are an underused folkloric source. In addition, the late 19th century witnessed the beginnings of popular tourism (in its original sense of leisure touring) in France – by train, by bicycle and by car. National touring clubs were set up to advise on itineraries and local tourism offices publicised the sites to see in their vicinity. Both spawned an ever greater profusion of guidebooks which frequently made mention of local legends attached to a ruin or a church which they considered worth a visit. These too were used by Sébillot.

The collection 'Little Local Legends' is, therefore, not only a valuable source in itself, it also points to an even denser profusion of texts. However, these are often legends shorn of any contextual information and reduced to their most anecdotic and picturesque form. Yet even in this truncated state, they confirm that the crimes of feudal lords were a common topic of popular storytelling.

> They say at Coadout [Côtes d'Armor] that the seigneur of Bois-de-la-Roche retuns to his castle every night. His unquiet soul groans from the top of the narrow granite staircase and one hears the dull thud of his pickaxe as he tries to unearth his buried treasure. (LLL 47.)

Dozens of castles were believed to be the site of hoarded treasure still jealously guarded by phantom seigneurs. The source of this wealth is seldom specified, but it does not take a great intuitive leap to interpret this legend as a peasant judgement on feudal extortionists. "The manor-house of Goas-Hamon in Plouisy [Côtes d'Armor] was destroyed by lightning one Sunday during mass as punishment, so the legend goes, for the impiety of its inhabitants who preferred to play cards than go to church" (LLL 48). Seigneurial impiety was the frequent wellspring of legend. Sabbath hunters were condemned to eternally hunt through night skies, as happened to the count de Valory (from Saint-Ellier, Maine-et-Loire; LLL 295). The local origin story attached to the Wild Hunt often drew on some such legend. Hunting, as a seigneurial privilege and as the cause of material damage to crops, was particularly resented. "The baroness of Montfort [Côte-d'Or] who, when alive, imprisoned all those who did not acknowledge her as she deemed appropriate, still wanders in the form of a wolf that one cannot kill" (LLL 68). Other chatelaines bathed in the blood of maidens, ate babies (LLL 166) or threw children to their dogs (LLL 408). Seigneurs devised horrible punishments for their adulterous wives, rolling them in a barrel studded with nails (LLL 38), strangling (LLL 171), using their skin to make a chair (LLL 307).

Some legends concern charitable seigneurs, though their stories make little mention of their good works but rather concentrate on their conversion. According to Breton legends both Pierre Le Gouvello de Keriolet (1602–1660) and Marot de la Garaye (1675–1755) led dissolute lives until a ghostly warning of the hellfire that awaited them brought about a change of heart (Sébillot 1898: 159–162). Local memory needed to account for why these seigneurs, whose reputations are attested in written history too, were so different from their fellows.

As Sébillot noted, the focus in legends was on brutal and avaricious lords, not on the peasants who had to suffer them. Punishment in most cases was not human but divine. However, we do find some indications of peasant resistance. In the same year that the journal carried Arnaudin's account of the death of the seigneur de Lué, two other legends were published about the murder of seigneurs. In the first, the seigneur of Bosfranchet (Puy-de-Dôme) had ordered that no one should observe his daughter's *cortège* on the day of her marriage. Unfortunately the charcoal-burner's son, overcome by a desire to see this fabled beauty, was caught peeking and hung. To revenge himself the charcoal-burner kidnapped the seigneur's son, brought him up as a brigand, and finally urged him on to kill his father (LLL 297). In the second, the tyrannical seigneur of Moncoutant (Deux-Sévres) was shot through his window while dozing, "and this was how his people found him the next day, already cold and his heart transfixed by peasant lead" (LLL 362). I have not been able to ascertain whether either story has, as did that of Blaise de la Pic de la Mirandole, a basis in fact.

There are a lot of questions one might ask of this kind of folkloric source. Who told stories about the feudal past, to whom, when and where? Was the burden of feudalism a more frequent topic in some regions than others? How does that map onto the political choices of peasant voters? What role did external agents, such as urban politicians, play in fostering the memory of feudalism? How did peasants compare the past and the present? What shifts in social, economic, legal and cultural relations did they perceive? How did that history continue to influence peasant actions, not only in the countryside but as they migrated to the city and even overseas? Was the process of class formation among the urban migrants predicated on their historic knowledge of an earlier confrontation, that between peasant and lord?

I'm interested in peasant history, but I'm also interested in peasant historiography. What models did the peasant apply to understand events related to the past? What schema did they use to make them relevant to their own present? Certain narrative structures seem to have helped the peasant make sense of the experience of feudalism, and encode it in a usable form for another generation. Stories of haunted castles, baby-eating countesses and godless hunters were found across France, and beyond. One will find plenty of Sébillot's *lieux communs* among the legends about feudalism told across Europe, pointing to a shared social history that escapes national boundaries. It has been very interesting, in the short time I have been in Estonia, to observe the efforts being made to integrate Estonia's national history to the history of the European continent through the role of its Swedish kings or its enlightened Baltic German philosophers. Perhaps, however, it would be easier to make a common history through the epos, even in the ironic mode, of peasant emancipation.

Notes

1   This rubric appeared in almost every issue of the journal thereafter, drawing on numerous contributors. In the text I cite these as 'Little Local Legends' (LLL) and the number.

Sources

Agulhon, Maurice 1982. *The Republic in the Village: the People of the Var from the French Revolution to the Second Republic.* Cambridge: Cambridge University Press.

Arnaudin, Félix 1994. *Contes populaires de la Grande-Lande.* Jacques Boisgontier & Guy Latry (eds.). Bordeaux: Confluences.

Arnaudin, Félix 2003 [1872]. Une Branche des Pic de la Mirandole à Labouheyre. In *Journal et Choses de l'ancienne Lande.* Jean-Yves Boutet, Guy Latry & Jean-Bernard Marquette (eds.). Bordeaux: Confluences. Pp. 519–531.

Beiner, Guy 2004. Who were "The Men of the West"? Folk Historiographies and the Reconstruction of Democratic Histories. *Folklore* 115(2): 201–221.

Belmont, Nicole (ed.) 1995. *Aux sources de l'ethnologie française: L'Académie Celtique.* Paris: CTHS.

Bianchi, Serge 2008. Jacques Cambry, un Jacobin face aux populations rurales de l'Ouest? In *Jacques Cambry: Un Breton des Lumières au service de la construction nationale*. Anne de Mathan (ed.). Brest: CRBC. Pp. 179–198.

Blanning, T. C. W. 1989. The French Revolution and the Modernization of Germany. *Central European History* 22(2): 109–129.

Blaufarb, Rafe 2012. *The Politics of Fiscal Privilege in Provence, 1530s–1830s*. Washington, DC: Catholic University Press of America.

Blum, Jerome 1978. *The End of the Old Order in Rural Europe*. Princeton, NJ: Princeton University Press.

Cadic, François 2003 [1908–1918]. *Histoire populaires de la chouannerie* 1–2. Fañch Postic (ed.). Rennes: Presses universitaires de Rennes.

Corbin, Alain 1992. *The Village of Cannibals. Rage and Murder in France, 1870*. Cambridge, MA: Harvard University Press.

Dietler, Michael 1994. "Our Ancestors the Gauls." Archaeology, Ethnic Nationalism, and the Manipulation of Celtic Identity in Modern Europe. *American Anthropologist* 96(3): 585–605.

Fitzsimmons, Michael P. 2003. *The Night the Old Regime Ended: August 4, 1789, and the French Revolution*. University Park, PA: Penn State University Press.

Gaidoz, Henri 1904. De l'influence de l'Académie Celtique sur les études de folk-lore. In *Recueil de Mémoires de la Société des Antiquaires de France*. Paris, Société des antiquaires de France. Pp. 134–143.

Gilsenan, Michael 1996. *Lords of the Lebanese Marches: Violence and Narrative in an Arab Society*. London: Tauris.

Gross, Janice 2005. Revisiting "nos ancêtres ls Gaulois." Scripting and Postscripting Francophone Identity. *The French Review* 78(5): 948–959.

Hart, Kathleen 2001–2002. Oral Culture and Anti-colonialism in Louise Michel's *Mémoires* (1886) and *Légendes et chants de gestes canaques* (1885). *Nineteenth-Century French Studies* 30(1–2): 107–120.

Hamerton, Philip Gilbert 1877. *Round My House. Notes of Rural Life in France in Peace and War*. Boston: Roberts Brothers.

Hopkin, David 2012. *Voices of the People in Nineteenth-Century France*. Cambridge: Cambridge University Press.

Horstbøll, Henrik & Uffe Østergård 1990. Reform and Revolution. The French Revolution and the Case of Denmark. *Scandinavian Journal of History* 15(1–2): 155–179.

Jones, Peter 1985. *Politics and Rural Society. The Southern Massif Central, c. 1750–1880*. Cambridge: Cambridge University Press.

Lagrée, Michel & Jehanne Roche 1993. *Tombes de mémoire: la devotion populaire aux victimes de la Révolution dans l'Ouest*. Rennes: Apogée.

Lefebvre, Georges 1929. La place de la Révolution dans l'histoire agraire de la France. *Annales d'histore économique et sociale* 1: 506–523.

Leonard, Carol S. 2011. *Agrarian Reform in Russia. The Road from Serfdom*. Cambridge: Cambridge University Press.

Lincoln, Bruce 1977. *Nikolai Miliutin: An Enlightened Russian Bureaucrat*. Newtonville, MA: Oriental Research Partners.

LLL = see Sébillot 1897.

Markoff, John 1996. *The Abolition of Feudalism: Peasants, Lords and Legislators in the French Revolution*. University Park, PA: Penn State University Press.

Michel, Louise 1886. *Mémoires de Louise Michel, écrits par elle-même*. Paris: F. Roy.

Michel, Louise 1885. *Légendes et chants de gestes canaques*. Paris: Kéva et Cie.

Michelet, Jules 1889 [1847]. *Histoire de la Révolution française*. Paris: Imprimerie Nationale.

Mintz, Steven 1996. Models of Emancipation during the Age of Revolution. *Slavery and Abolition: A Journal of Slave and Post-Slave Studies* 17(2): 1–21.

Moon, David 2002. *The Abolition of Serfdom in Russia, 1762–1907*. London: Pearson.

Nadaud, Martin 2011 [1895]. *Mémoires de Léonard, ancien garçon maçon*. Maurice Agulhon (ed.). La Geneytouse: Lucien Souny.

Ó Ciosáin, Niall 2004. Approaching a Folklore Archive. The Irish Folklore Commission and the Memory of the Great Famine. *Folklore* 115(2): 222–232.

Ozouf, Mona 1984. L'Invention de l'ethnographie francaise: le questionnaire de l'Académie Celtique. In *L'Ecole de la France: essais sur la Révolution, l'utopie et l'enseignement*. Paris: Gallimard. Pp. 351–379.

Plakans, Andrejs 2011. *A Concise History of the Baltic States*. Cambridge: Cambridge University Press.

Pooley, William 2014. 'Misery in the Moorlands': Lived Bodies in the Landes de Gascogne, 1870-1914. Doctoral thesis, University of Oxford,.

Postic, Fañch (ed.) 2011. *Paul Sébillot (1843–1918): Un républicain promoteur des traditions populaires. Actes du colloque de Fougères, 9–11 octobre 2008*. Brest: CRBC.

Price, Roger 2004. *People and Politics in France, 1848–1870*. Cambridge: Cambridge University Press.

Rearick, Charles 1974. *Beyond the Enlightenment. Historians and Folklore in Nineteenth-Century France*. Bloomington, IN: Indiana University Press.

Sand, George 2000 [1858]. *Légendes rustiques*. Evelyne Bloch-Dano (ed.). Saint-Cyr-sur-Loire: Christian Pirot.

Scott, James C. 1985. *Weapons of the Weak. Everyday Forms of Peasant Resistance*. New Haven, CT: Yale University Press.

Sébillot, Paul 1882. *Traditions et superstitions de la Haute-Bretagne* 1–2. Paris: Maisonneuve.

Sébillot, Paul 1897. Les petites légendes locales. *Revue des traditions populaires* 12: 129–142.

Sébillot, Paul 1898. Les héros populaires VIII. La légende de M. de la Garaye (1675–1755). *Revue des traditions populaires* 13: 159–162.

Sébillot, Paul 2002 [1904–1906]. *Croyances, mythes et légendes des pays de France*. Paris: Omnibus. First published as *Folklore de France*.

Senn, Harry 1981. Folklore Beginnings in France, the Académie Celtique: 1804–1813. *Journal of the Folklore Institute* 18(1): 23–33.

Shanin, Teodor 1990. Defining Peasants: Conceptualizations and Deconceptualizations. In *Defining Peasants: Essays Concerning Rural Societies, Expolary Economies, and Learning from them in the Contemporary World*. Teodor Shanin (ed.). Oxford: Wiley-Blackwell. Pp. 53–73.

Sieyès, Emmanuel Joseph 2002 [1788]. *Qu'est-ce que le tiers état?* Paris: Editions du Boucher.

Soboul, Albert 1968. Survivances "féodales" dans la société rurale française au XIXe siècle. *Annales. Histoire, Sciences Sociales* 23(5): 965–986.

Soboul, Albert 1983. *Problèmes paysans de la revolution, 1789–1848*. Paris: François Maspero.

Sutherland, D. M. G. 2002. Peasants, Lords, and Leviathan. Winners and Losers from the Abolition of French Feudalism, 1780–1820. *The Journal of Economic History* 62(1): 1–24.

Tangherlini, Timothy 2007. Rhetoric, Truth and Performance: Politics and the Interpretation of Legend. *Indian Folklife* 25: 8–12.

Temple, Samuel 2009. The Natures of Nation. Negotiating Modernity in the *Landes de Gascogne*. *French Historical Studies* 32(3): 419–446.

Viallaneix, Paul & Jean Ehrard (eds.) 1982. *Nos ancêtres les Gaulois: actes du colloque international de Clermont-Ferrand*. Clermont-Ferrand: Presses Universitaires de Clermont-Ferrand.

Vovelle, Michel 1991. The Countryside and the Peasantry in Revolutionary Iconography. In *Reshaping France: Town, Country and Region during the French Revolution.* Alan Forrest & Peter Jones (eds.). Manchester: Manchester University Press. Pp. 26–36.

Weber, Eugen 1991. Nos ancêtres les Gaulois. In *My France. Politics, Culture, Myth.* Cambridge, MA: Belknap Press. Pp. 21–39.

Woell, Edward J. 2008. Review of Peter McPhee, *Living the French Revolution, 1789–1799. H-France Review* 8(46): 187–191. Available at www.h-france.net/vol8reviews/vol8no46woell.pdf [Accessed July 17, 2015]

Wolf, Eric 1966. *Peasants.* Englewood Cliffs, NJ: Prentice-Hall.

Diarmuid Ó G.lláin

People, Nation and 'Combative Literatures': Baltic, Celtic and Nordic Configurations of Folklore

Until the mid-20th century, it is probably true to say that 'folklore' was almost everywhere understood implicitly as a social phenomenon. But it also had a distinct spatial dimension since the scholarly consensus was that it was found only in rural areas among certain social strata. In the view of some scholars, it was also found in urban areas, but similarly limited to certain social groups. We say 'social strata' and 'social groups' advisedly, because, outside of the socialist countries, the social aspect was not overtly interpreted in terms of class. Sometimes this was simply because of the narrowness of focus of scholars. But more often it was – to distort the Gramscian term – because of the perceived 'national-popular' quality of folklore, which saw the national genius reflected in the poetic works of the common people and which as a result saw these works transcend that plebeian world. The spatial dimension of folklore hence was more specific than a generalized rural–urban divide since folkloristic space could be particularized by language and culture, ultimately by nation. But this was the case only in folkloristics shaped by Romantic nationalism.

The people in the early modern period often referred to a species that barely shared a common humanity with the elite (Cohen 2010: 67, 80). With the Enlightenment a conception of the people as a collective political actor emerged according to which sovereignty was vested in them, thus legitimizing government in the social contract with the ruler. But in tandem with this positive political idea of the people was a negative idea of them in terms of culture (Martín-Barbero 1993: 6–7). If the Enlightenment championed the right of the people to be politically incorporated into the state, the implication was clear that they would be assimilated to the dominant culture through a process of what would be later called 'development' or 'modernisation' (cf. Esteva 1992/1993).

The Romantics rejected this, heralding a type of populist politics inflected by questions of culture and language while, at the same time, blurring the distinction between people as nation, as *populus*, and the people as a social class, as *plebs*. Ernesto Laclau describes such a situation thus:

> [...] the *populus* as the given – as the ensemble of social relations *as* they actually are – reveals itself as a false totality, as a partiality which is a source of oppression. On the other hand, the *plebs*, whose partial demands are inscribed in the horizon

> of a fully fledged totality – a just society which exists only ideally – can aspire to constitute a truly universal *populus* which the actually existing situation negates. It is because the two visions of the *populus* are strictly incommensurable that a certain particularity, the *plebs*, can identify itself with the *populus* conceived as an ideal totality. (Laclau 2005: 94; cf. Grignon & Passeron 1989.)

This, it seems to me, points to a key characteristic of folkloristics whenever it has been understood as a 'national science': it was when a national quality was understood to be inherent to it. As is clear from William Thoms' famous letter to the *Athenaeum* in 1846, no such quality adhered to it in the English context, with the author referring to "Popular Antiquities, or Popular Literature (though by-the-bye it is more a Lore than a literature, and would be most aptly described by a good Saxon compound, Folk-Lore – *the Lore of the People*)" (Thoms 1999 [1846]: 11).

Baltic and Nordic are relatively unproblematic terms today, having a primarily geographic referent. Of course the terms have become somewhat circumscribed by history and convention. The terms Baltic provinces, Baltic republics and Baltic states refer to past or present political entities in the region south of Finland and northeast of Poland (the remaining two countries whose only coastline is Baltic), while the region in which the present or historic Baltic languages are or were spoken is even more limited. The Nordic countries include Denmark, more southerly than the Baltic states, but are commonly understood to be as much a product of historical and cultural factors – despite the linguistic difference between Finnish and Scandinavian – as of geography.

'Celtic', on the other hand, is a much more problematic term. It is used to refer to a group of languages spoken in northwestern Europe today (the Goidelic Irish, Scottish Gaelic and extinct Manx, and the Brythonic Welsh, Breton and extinct Cornish), as well as to a variety of continental European tribes and their languages in antiquity, especially as observed by the Romans. The link between the insular and the continental Celtic languages (the origin of Breton, incidentally, is more insular than continental) was established only in the 18th century and the identity of a Celtic family of languages within Indo-European only in the 19th century with the development of comparative linguistics. "The construction of the Celt, then, takes place roughly from 1650 to 1850", as Joep Leerssen outlines it.

> This means that it coincides with developments such as the invention of the Sublime, the cult of Nature and the idea of the Noble Savage. All these aspects have been written to the profile of what it means to be Celtic. The construction of the Celt in itself documents the revolt against rationalism and the Enlightenment, and the attributes stereotypically ascribed to the 'Celt' have a profile to match. (Leerssen 1996b: 5.)

It is not coincidental that the development of the notion of folklore coincides with that of the Celt, nor that "the invention of the Sublime, the cult of Nature and the idea of the Noble Savage" as well as "the revolt against rationalism and the Enlightenment" shaped folklore as much as they shaped the Celt. This was already marked out with great clarity by Giuseppe Cocchiara in

1952 in his *Storia del Folklore in Europa*, in which the very first chapter is entitled "The 'Discovery of the Savage'", and he has subsequent chapters with titles such as "Europe between Religion and Superstition", "Error in the Light of Reason", "Nature, Civilization and Progress", and "The Poetic 'Revolt'" (Cocchiara 1981 [1952]: 13–28, 44–60, 61–76, 116–134, 135–150). The development of the concept of oral tradition echoes this trajectory.

Oral tradition was initially limited to the domain of theology. According to the Catholic understanding developed in the 15th century and which later became a dogma of the Counter-Reformation, truth resided both in Scripture and in unwritten tradition. While Protestants tended to dismiss the value of oral tradition, continental jurists had nevertheless outlined the principles of an unwritten 'natural law' underlying statutory law, and the authority of the unwritten traditions of English customs and law had been invoked since the mid-17th century as the "Ancient Constitution" (Hudson 1996: 162, 164). Gradually the notion of oral tradition expanded from the theological into the ethnological domain. The book *Moeurs des sauvages amériquains, comparées aux moeurs des premiers temps* (1724), the work of the Jesuit missionary Joseph-François Lafitau drawing on his residence for several years among the Iroquois, contended that despite the absence of writing, a people could have a sophisticated culture and social system. 18th century comparisons of native American peoples to the Greeks and Romans is also evidence of a more subtle understanding of the European classical age itself. Scholars began to see the power of the language of Homer's *Odyssey* as coming from the primitive state of Homer's own society. Both Giovan Battista Vico and Jean-Jacques Rousseau had questioned Homer's literacy, but from the 1760s on, there was a dramatic increase in the number of British and especially of Scottish texts making the case for sophisticated oral societies, and one of them was made by Thomas Blackwell, James Macpherson's teacher in Marischal College in Aberdeen (McDowell 2010: 238–240).

We will return to *Ossian*, but first I would like to consider two related questions that contextualise the development of folklore studies: the development of the modern nation-state and the project of a national literature. The nation-states that replaced dynastic-religious states from the late 18th century on moved towards a capitalist economy and a civil society along two different routes, and in this I follow Miroslav Hroch and Ernest Gellner. One route is where the early modern dynastic state developed under a pre-existing ethnic high culture, as in the case of Denmark, England, France or Sweden and the modern national culture then seemed to represent a relatively uninterrupted development or flowering from the seed of earlier times. The second route involved ethnic groups that occupied a compact territory, but lacked their own aristocracy and a continuous high culture, and whose ruling class was of foreign origin. Typical examples here would be Estonians, Finns, Latvians or Slovaks. In this case a high culture did not exist and it was necessary to create one. There was also, of course, an intermediate route in which an ethnic community had its own ruling class and literary traditions, but lacked a common statehood – typically Italy and

Germany before unification, but also Poland after the 1795 partition (Hroch 1996: 79–80; Gellner 1996: 139).

To Hroch (1996: 80), a national movement involved a disadvantaged non-dominant ethnic group reaching a level of self-awareness sufficient to see itself as a real or potential nation. It had three main goals: "the development of a national culture based on the local language", "the achievement of civil rights and political self-administration", and "the creation of a complete social structure from out of the ethnic group, including educated elites [...], an entrepreneurial class, [...] free peasants and organized workers" (Hroch 1996: 81). This took place in three structural phases. The first was that of intellectuals who took an interest in the language, culture and history of the common people (the Estophiles or Fennomans providing an obvious example in this category); the second was the so-called national awakening, whereby contacts were established between the intellectuals and the people; and the third was a mass movement (Hroch 1996).

The literary scholar Pascale Casanova sees the development of national movements in the 19th century "as a symbolic assertion of equality between the various national collectivities" on the cultural, political and economic level. But, she argues, "the older powers of Europe enjoyed such an advantage that it was impossible for newcomers like Germany to compete" (Casanova 2011: 123–124) and, as Germany and Italy's belated attempts to construct colonial empires from what remained from the depredations of the older powers demonstrate, this was a lack felt as much on the political as on the cultural level. The artistic heritage of nations – their cultural capital – was accumulated over long historical periods: "[t]ime still conferred strength, and antiquity, authority" (Casanova 2011: 125). This was apparent in long established states where even political ruptures as momentous as the French Revolution did not break the continuity of an old and venerable high culture.

Historical ruptures, however, often precluded the accumulation of cultural capital, especially in the absence of a state. A historian explains the problem of Irish cultural discontinuity as follows: "[t]here is scarcely another country in Western Europe where a high culture was sustained in the Middle Ages in which less of the treasures of learning have survived", and he refers to both ecclesiastical and secular buildings, libraries, manuscripts and works of art (Ó Corráin 2004: 7). The 16th and 17th century Elizabethan and Cromwellian conquests led to the destruction and dispersal of the documents and monuments of high culture, to the dispossession and exile of the native elites, and to demographic disaster. The outcome was the blank slate of an apparently uncivilised country, saved from barbarism only by outside intervention. Hroch (1996: 84) argues that most European national movements, despite the relative poverty of their national cultural capital, long predated industrial society. There were often, he contends, antecedents for modern nation building in late medieval and early modern times: the memory of former independence or statehood and the survival of the medieval written language. The latter provided a nation-building resource for the Czechs, Icelanders, Irish and Norwegians, for example, with folklore filling in the discontinuities, as in the case of the Irish Folklore Commission, whose director, Séamus Ó Duilearga, asserted of the work of his staff: "we consider ourselves not as creators or adaptors, but as literary executors of earlier generations" (Ó Duilearga 1943: 12).

James Macpherson, the author of *Ossian*, was born in 1736 into a defiant Gaelic world that soon would be fully subdued within the British state, a Gaelic-speaker in a Scotland in which almost a quarter of the inhabitants still spoke that language. The role of the Gaels in early modern Scotland, in the words of the historian Colin Kidd (1999: 123), "defined the historical essence of nationhood, yet also represented an alien otherness". The case for the defence of Scottish sovereignty against England rested on the ancient independent origins of a Scottish polity, in the Gaelic kingdom of Dál Riada, despite the fact that the centres of gravity were all in the English-speaking Lowlands with their historical antipathy to the Gaels (Kidd 1999: 125). The linguistic and cultural affinity of the Gaels with Ireland was a given; indeed the Scots term *Erse*, 'Irish', was applied by the Lowlanders to the language of the Highlanders. Derick Thomson thinks that "the repairing and boosting of the Highland, and the Scottish, image may have been an important factor in motivating Macpherson's early work", one aspect of which "was the attempt to locate the Ossianic legend more firmly in Scotland, lessening the importance of Irish origins or denying them" (Thomson 1998: 23–24).

A dialect continuum for a long time existed between Irish and Scottish Gaelic, and the same literary language was shared until the 18th century translation of the New Testament established a new literary norm for the Scots. Macpherson grew up in a strongly oral culture: "[t]he evidence", according to Thomson, "suggests that he was not strongly literate in Gaelic" (Thomson 2006; Gaskill 1996: 264). The fact that the literary history of the shared language is mostly Irish until late is possibly one of the reasons why Macpherson stressed the orality of the sources of *Ossian*, though he was well aware of the existence of manuscripts – the most important Scottish Gaelic manuscript, the early 16th century *Book of the Dean of Lismore*, was in fact brought to light by Macpherson on his collecting tours of 1760–1761 (Thomson 1998: 20). The second half of Macpherson's life was largely British and imperial, spent in public service in the colonies (as secretary to the governor of West Florida) and in England (as a Member of Parliament). Later critics have seen him "as both cultural nationalist and cultural quisling", in Dafydd Moore's words, adding that there is a need to balance this "Anglo-British" reading of *Ossian* with the fact that its most virulent English critics were motivated to a significant extent by antipathy to Scotland and the Scots (Moore 2004: 38).

The multifarious ethnic origins of the Scots (Picts, Britons, Gaels, Anglo-Saxons, Scandinavians...) and the divide between the Gaelic-speaking Highlands and English-speaking Lowlands established from the late medieval period complicated the question of Scottish identity, which hence was above all political. To Kidd, the 19th century dominance of the idea of a Teutonic origin for the Scots short-circuited the potential use of Gaelic for cultural nationalism and "contributed to the transformation of Highland Celtic culture from a potent ideological resource into an embarrassing millstone of backwardness" (Kidd 1995: 68). The Teutonic origin thesis supported the political alliance of the Scots with the English in the construction of empire. Scotland was an integral part of the United Kingdom, the result of the union in 1707 of the two kingdoms (which had already shared a monarch since 1603). Indeed the Prime Minister of Britain in 1762–1763 was the Earl of Bute, the first Scot to exercise that office, and one of the sponsors of Macpherson's *Ossian* project; *Temora* was dedicated to him.

There was immediate Irish opposition to Macpherson's claims for the authenticity of his translations and for *Ossian*'s Scottishness. One of the most important Irish contributors to the Ossianic debate was Charles O'Conor (1710–1791), a direct descendant of the last High Kings of Ireland and an important scholar and activist for the rights of Ireland's oppressed Catholic majority. O'Conor was educated in traditional Gaelic scholarship and in his writings aimed to vindicate Ireland's ancient civilisation. This meant that he had little sympathy for Macpherson's claims, nor for his primitivist views. O'Conor could not accept the case for the oral transmission of *Ossian* since this contradicted his argument for early Ireland as a sophisticated, aristocratic and literate society (when, of course, this characterisation of the country might only hold for the period after the coming of Christianity). He saw Macpherson's argument "as part of the established British tendency to depict the Irish as barbaric" (O'Halloran 2004: 102).

One of the consequences of the debate in Ireland about Macpherson's *Ossian* was that the Anglo-Irish, recent colonists, now in possession of almost all the country's land and of the monopoly of political power, became involved in the assertion of Ireland's cultural heritage, and native Gaelic and Anglo-Irish versions of Ireland's past began to converge at least on this issue (Leerssen 1996a: 344–347). In Scotland, whose political status in the United Kingdom remained secure and, after the defeat of the Jacobite Rebellion of 1745, largely uncontested, cultural nationalism had little impact. *Ossian*, of course, appeared in English rather than Gaelic and may be contrasted with later epic poems such as *Kalevala*, published in Finnish rather than Swedish, and *Kalevipoeg*, in Estonian rather than German. In Ireland, *Ossian* helped to fuel later cultural and, indeed, political nationalism; the name of the 19th century revolutionary nationalist organisation, the Fenian Brotherhood (the American sister organisation, founded in 1858, of the Irish Republican Brotherhood), is one obvious indicator of that.

Ossian was, of course, a European literary sensation. Few intellectuals were more enthusiastic about it than Johann Gottfried Herder (1744–1803). His essay "Über Ossian und die Lieder alter Völker" (1773) was "all about literary liberation, regeneration, rejection of cultural enslavement, whether it be to France or classical antiquity" (Gaskill 1996: 260). Herder opposed the abstract universalism of the Enlightenment and its perspective on tradition as being synonymous with ignorance. He championed a German literature and art that would not be an imitation of foreign, and especially of French, models and the potential for which Ossian, Macpherson's northern Homer, had already demonstrated. Among Herder's key ideas, as outlined by Isaiah Berlin (1976: 45) were, firstly, the belief in the value of belonging to a group or to a culture; secondly, that art should express the "entire personality of the individual or the group, and are intelligible only to the degree to which they do so"; and thirdly the belief in the incommensurability of different cultures and societies. Every culture had to be admired for what it was and according to its own terms of reference.

Herder's *Volkslieder* appeared between 1778 and 1779, an anthology of poetry from many countries and many eras that included what we now call folk songs (a late 19th century English term itself modelled on the German) – including a few Estonian and Latvian examples – as well as learned poetry. The ambiguity between *plebs* and *populus*, people and nation, is inherent in the German word *Volk* (Brückner 1987: 224–226; cf. Gramsci 1991: 123), as it is in Estonian *rahvas* or Finnish *kansa*. The people in Herder's writings carried suggestions of the rural lower classes but at the same time the notion remained vague. This allowed him to include Shakespeare and Goethe, and other celebrated writers who were true to the *Volksgeist*, as authors of *Volkslieder*. He argued that these songs best reflected the character of a people and hence he lamented the decay of popular traditions.

Earlier we looked at the situation of national movements among peoples that lacked their own aristocracies and continuous high cultures. It is clear that the new and positive ideas of oral tradition, especially through a Herderian filter, provided a new resource for creating a modern national culture. According to Casanova (2004: 76–77),

> By granting each country and each people the right to an existence and a dignity equal in principle to those of others, in the name of 'popular traditions' from which sprang a country's entire cultural and historical development, and by locating the source of artistic fertility in the 'soul' of peoples, Herder shattered all the hierarchies, all the assumptions that until then had unchallengeably constituted literary 'nobility' – and this for a very long time.

Casanova draws her idea of "combative literatures" (2011) from several sources: Franz Kafka's 1911 text "The Literature of Small Peoples", in which he wrote that "literature is less a concern of literary history than of the people" (Casanova 2004: 202); Franz Fanon's reference to "literature of combat" in his 1959 address to the Congress of Black African Writers, when with regard to new national literatures, he referred to the moment when "the native writer progressively takes on the habit of addressing his own people" (Fanon 1967 [1959]: 193); and Fredric Jameson's 1986 article "Third-World Literature in the Era of Multinational Capitalism" where, in Jameson's view, "all third-world cultural productions" are national allegories (Jameson 1986: 69). Casanova's (2011: 133) notion of combative literatures then "suggests the idea of a collective movement: these literary spaces are engaged – to a greater or lesser extent, according to their degree of dependence – in struggles for recognition which are both political and literary".

In the end all of these are formulations of Herder's idea – itself articulated in the context of resistance to French cultural hegemony – that art should express the personality of the group. Since the groups in question here are, in Gramscian terms, subaltern, this art cannot but be political, and the politics populist. But the notion of combative literatures suggests a foundational phase rather than a perpetual struggle. This phase can be compared to the notion of charisma – itself personified in the great national writer – which Max Weber saw as being "sharply opposed to both rational, and particularly bureaucratic, authority, and to traditional authority", and which recedes, as do all revolutionary impulses, as new permanent institutional structures are established (Morris 1987: 72).

The question of small literatures and small peoples is, of course, more a question of position than of size: Danish has much less of a combative literature than has Ukrainian. When Herder published his *Volkslieder*, the German language itself was in the shadow of French, and the German intelligentsia, scattered and provincialised over a multitude of separate states, had a profound sense of cultural alienation (Elias 1994: 7–8). If *Volkskunde* has its origins in Enlightenment *Statistik* (Bausinger 1993: 24–25; Brückner 1987: 228) – along with *Landeskunde* and *Staatskunde* – its predominant heritage has come to us via Romanticism. The Grimm Brothers, who can be seen more than anyone else as the founders of folklore studies, were deeply preoccupied with the national question, which informed their work on law, on mythology, on linguistics and on folklore. The political dimension of this role was perhaps nowhere more obvious than in the seating arrangements of the *Nationalversammlung* in Frankfurt in 1848, where Jacob Grimm had a seat to himself in the centre between the Left and the Right, transcending these political differences in a higher national cause (Leerssen 2006: 183).

For the English or French languages, the first novel or the first play is a question of literary history. For Estonian or Finnish, it is a question of national history. A French or English speaker if asked "who was the first French or English poet?" will probably be perplexed, not least because the earliest works of poetry provide formidable linguistic obstacles to speakers of today's languages. An Estonian asked "who was the first Estonian poet" will confidently answer Kristjan Jaak Peterson, whose birthday is annually celebrated as Mother Tongue Day. Figures such as the Estonian Friedrich Reinhold Kreutzwald or the Finn Elias Lönnrot were not just writers or folklore collectors but central figures in movements that were literary, historical and political. Kreuzwald's *Kalevipoeg* and Lönnrot's *Kalevala* were read not only as literature, but as history and as foundational works of nation-building: such were 'national epics'. A little over a year after the publication of *Kalevala* in 1835, the chairman of the Finnish Literature Society (founded in 1831 to further the development of Finnish language and literature, the word for literature itself being a coinage of Lönnrot's) stated that on the basis of this work, Finland could say "I too have a history!" (Wilson 1976: 42). Folk poetry in Estonian and Finnish, *rahvaluule, kansanrunous, Volkspoesie*, was both popular and national.

In Sweden and Denmark interest in folklore was strengthened as a result of defeat. The loss of Finland by Sweden in 1809, Denmark's loss of Norway in 1814 and of Schleswig in 1864 (prefigured by the British bombardment of Copenhagen and the seizure of the fleet in 1807 along with the bankruptcy of the state in 1813), reduced these imperial powers to nation-states in which a single language and culture for the first time were overwhelmingly dominant (although Denmark held on to Iceland, the

Faeroe Islands, Greenland, and its small colonial outposts in Africa, India and the West Indies, their combined population was only a fraction of that of the metropolis). Seminal folklore works like Erik Gustaf Geijer and Arvid August Afzelius' *Svenska Folk-Wisor* of 1814 (Jonsson 1971) and Svend Grundtvig's *Danmarks gamle Folkeviser* of 1847 (Piø 1971) could not have the same foundational importance as *Kalevipoeg* and *Kalevala* in these long-established countries where writing, despite patriotic impulses, did not fit into the category of 'combative literature'.

In Spain in the late 19th and early 20th centuries, a similar criterion can be used to distinguish the folklorists in Galicia, the Basque Country, Catalonia and Valencia from their colleagues elsewhere in the peninsula. In those regions, where a distinct language and history were the focus of cultural identity, writers were the ethnographic pioneers, leading one anthropologist, Josep M. Comelles, to see anthropology as "a scientific discourse about humanity" and folklore studies "as a particularistic discourse about identity" (cited in Prat 1991: 14). The repression by the Spanish state of Basque, Catalan (in its various names) and Gallego helps to explain the 'combative' role of writing in them as well as the importance of folklore. Folklore studies were not institutionalised in the academy in Spain whereas anthropology was, and Comelles' judgement points to the importance of the state for the legitimation of scholarly disciplines.

Alan Dundes wrote about what he called the "devolutionary premise" in folklore studies, based on the idea of a past golden age and of the present being found wanting (Dundes 1975). An idealised past provided the inspiration for the future, as in the words of K. A. Grönqvist's rhapsodical account from 1884, according to which Karelia's remarkable seeing glass was such that "anyone can see hundreds of years both forward and back" (Tarkka 1989: 248). In a lecture given in 1937, the director of the Irish Folklore Commission stressed the continuity in the Gaelic tradition from a medieval aristocratic culture, explaining that after the destruction of the native elite in the 16th and 17th centuries the common people saved "in spite of all persecution some of the culture of the upper classes and admitted it into their age-old treasury of oral tradition". Thus "a large part of our medieval literature exists in oral form" (Ó Duilearga 1943: 12). Douglas Hyde's lecture in 1892, "The Necessity for De-Anglicising Ireland" (Hyde 1986), the manifesto for the language revival movement, was based on retrieving the *Volksgeist* so that an authentic Ireland that was not just a second-rate imitation of England could be reconstructed. This type of folklore studies was part of a movement in which the energies of large sections of the population were mobilized to build or to 'save' national culture. In Estonia, Jakob Hurt's appeals for the collection of folklore, continued by Matthias Johann Eisen, were launched through newspapers from 1871 and were answered by contributions from all levels of society, from country tradesmen, farmers, teachers, factory workers and school children (Masing 1984: 480; Laugaste 1986: 112–113). The Irish Folklore Commission, founded in 1935, probably reached some 40,000 informants, from a similar range of humble backgrounds, and was helped by an earlier mobilisation through the Gaelic League, which had placed folklore at the heart of a literary and linguistic project (see Ó Giolláin 2000; Briody 2007).

Metropolitan folklore studies came to be influenced by evolutionary ideas especially through Edward Burnett Tylor's *Primitive Culture* (1871), and the comparisons between peasant and 'savage' – that the possession of colonial empires made possible – were irrelevant insofar as a national high culture was concerned. Despite enjoying a brief period when they seemed to be the equal of anthropology, British folklore studies failed to be institutionalised and became, according to Renato Ortiz (1992: 56), a middle-brow science, lacking in scientific legitimacy. The journal of the Folklore Society from the beginning covered the colonies as well as the United Kingdom. Richard Dorson (1976: 109) writes of the British folklorists who "supplied the theoretical frame and the personal encouragement for vicars and country ladies and colonial administrators to collect folklore survivals from 'peasants' and 'savages'". If one type of folklore studies was framed by the nation then, the other was by the provinces and the colonies and its marginalization was reflected in its provincial-colonial, as opposed to national-metropolitan nature.

This provincial-colonial aspect was to characterise the French *Société du Folklore français*, founded in 1928 and which dedicated its initial meetings to the setting up of regional groups and committees, to the extent that the society's journal in its first issue wrote of "the point of departure of a regional movement that continued to expand" (van Gennep 1930: 5). The *Revue de Folklore français* changed its name without fanfare after its first two years, to the *Revue de Folklore français et de Folklore colonial*, the result, in fact, of a merger between the *Société du Folklore français* and the *Société française d'ethnographie*, under the new name of *Société du Folklore français et de Folklore colonial*. The *Société française d'ethnographie*, founded in 1859, was a scholarly society of mostly conservative amateur scholars, not to be confused with the ethnologists trained in the *Institut d'ethnologie* (Meyran 2002: 12–13) founded in 1925 by Marcel Mauss and Lucien Lévy-Bruhl (both of whom sat for a time on the council of the *Société du Folklore français*). A nationalism imbued with regionalism appeared in many of the classic texts of the French Third Republic (Meyran 2002: 55) during much the same period when France's colonial empire was being consolidated. While failing to be established in the universities, folklore studies in France, unlike in Britain, benefited from official support, under the Popular Front government of 1936–1938 (with the foundation of the *Musée national des Arts et Traditions populaires* in 1937) and, after the fall of France, under the Vichy government. Vichy's embrace of folklore left many folklorists, and the discipline itself, seriously compromised after the Liberation (Leibovics 1992: 135–188; Meyran 2002; Christophe et al. 2009).

The first specific chair of folklore was Kaarle Krohn's in Helsinki in 1890, following on his lectureship in Finnish and comparative folklore from 1888. Moltke Moe followed with a chair of folklore in Oslo in 1899. Other early chairs or other university positions in folklore were established in Basel, Copenhagen and Lund (Rogan 2012), but especially in the states that emerged after the First World War where independence represented the political triumph of national movements and in which folklore studies along with the study of the national language and literature could be legitimised as national sciences. While we may rightly criticise the essentialism that often went hand in hand with the notion of national sciences – by now, there is quite a substantial bibliography on the question of folklore and nationalism – we can also recognise the significant scholarly achievements that institutionalisation made possible. As I have written elsewhere (Ó Giolláin 2014), since the 1960s there has been a gradual convergence of the two orientations of folklore studies. The idea of folkloristics as a 'national science' has hardly been tenable since the Second World War. The Western narrative of progress has been challenged by decolonization and postmodernism, though renewed in a narrow economistic perspective through the concept of development, while democratization, urbanization and globalization have confounded particularistic notions of folklore and the popular (Franco 1999). But more recently, and especially since the 2007–2008 global economic crisis, we have been living through an unstable conjuncture, and it is challenging globalization, European integration and national political configurations. If we are witnessing some kind of paradigm shift, then folklore studies are unlikely to be immune to it.

Sources

Bausinger, Hermann 1993. *Volkskunde ou l'ethnologie allemande*. Dominique Lassaigne & Pascale Godenir (transl.). Paris: Éditions de la Maison des sciences de l'homme.

Berlin, Isaiah 1976. *Vico and Herder. Two Studies in the History of Ideas*. London: The Hoggarth Press.

Briody, Mícheál 2007. *The Irish Folklore Commission 1935–1970. History, Ideology, Methodology*. Studia Fennica Folkloristica 17. Helsinki: Finnish Literature Society.

Brückner, Wolfgang 1987. Histoire de la Volkskunde. Tentative d'une approche à l'usage des Français. In *Ethnologies en Miroir. La France et les pays de langue allemande*. Isac Chiva & Utz Jeggle (eds.). Paris: Éditions de la Maison des sciences de l'homme.

Casanova, Pascale 2004. *The World Republic of Letters*. M. B. DeBevoise (transl.). Cambridge, MA, London: Harvard University Press.

Casanova, Pascale 2011. Combative Literatures. *New Left Review* 72: 123–134.

Christophe, Jacqueline, Denis-Michel Boëll & Régis Meyran 2009. *Du folklore à l'ethnologie*. Paris: Éditons de la maison des sciences de l'homme.

Cocchiara, Giuseppe 1981 [1952]. *The History of Folklore in Europe*. John N. McDaniel (transl.). Philadelphia: Institute for the Study of Human Issues.

Cohen, Déborah 2010. *La nature du peuple. Les formes de l'imaginaire social (XVIIIe-XXIe siècles)*. Paris: Champ Vallon.

Dorson, Richard 1976. *Folklore and Fakelore. Essays toward a Discipline of Folk Studies*. Cambridge, MA, London: Harvard University Press.

Dundes, Alan 1975. The Devolutionary Premise in Folklore Theory. In *Analytic Essays in Folklore*. Hague, Paris, New York: Mouton. Pp. 17–27.

Elias, Norbert 1994. *The Civilizing Process*. Edmund Jephcott (transl.). Oxford, Cambridge, MA: Blackwell.

Esteva, Gustavo 1992/1993. Development. In *The Development Dictionary. A Guide to Knowledge as Power*. Wolfgang Sachs (ed.). Johannesburg: Witwatersrand University Press; London, New Jersey: Zed Books.

Fanon, Frantz 1967 [1959]. Reciprocal Bases of National Culture and the Fight for Freedom. In *The Wretched of the Earth*. Constance Farrington (transl.). London: Penguin Books.

Franco, Jean. 1999. Globalization and the Crisis of the Popular. In Jean Franco, *Critical Passions: Selected Essays*, Mary Louise Pratt and Kathleen Newman (eds). Durham and London: Duke University Press.

Gaskill, Howard 1996. Herder, Ossian and the Celtic. In *Celticism*. Terence Brown (ed.). Amsterdam: Editions Rodopi. Pp. 257–272.

Gellner, Ernest 1996. The Coming of Nationalism and its Interpretation: The Myths of Nation and Class. In *Mapping the Nation*. Gopal Balakrishnan (ed.). London, New York: Verso. Pp. 98–145.

van Gennep, Arnold 1930. Historique de la Société. Jusqu'à l'Assemblée Générale du 8 Février 1930. *Revue de Folklore français* 1(1).

Gramsci, Antonio 1991. *Letteratura e vita nazionale*. Roma: Editori Riuniti.

Grignon, Claude & Passeron, Jean-Claude 1989. *Le savant et le populaire. Misérabilisme et populisme en sociologie et en littérature*. Paris: Seuil.

Hroch, Miroslav 1996. From National Movement to Fully-formed Nation: The Nation-building Process in Europe. In *Mapping the Nation*. Gopal Balakrishnan (ed.). London, New York: Verso. Pp. 78–97.

Hudson, Nicholas 1996. 'Oral Tradition': The Evolution of an Eighteenth-Century Concept. In *Tradition in Transition. Women Writers, Marginal Texts, and the Eighteenth-Century Canon*. Alvaro Ribeiro, SJ & James G. Basker (eds.). Oxford: Clarendon Press. Pp. 161–176.

Hyde, Douglas 1986. *Language, Lore and Lyrics. Essays and Lectures*. Breandán Ó Conaire (ed.). Dublin: Irish Academic Press.

Jameson, Fredric 1986. Third-World Literature in the Era of Multinational Capitalism. *Social Text* 15: 65–88.

Jonsson, Bengt R. 1971. Arvid August Afzelius (1785–1871). In *Leading Folklorists of the North*. Dag Strömbäck (ed.). Oslo, Bergen, Tromsö: Universitetsforlaget. Pp. 81–87.

Kidd, Colin. 1995. Teutonist Ethnology and Scottish Nationalist Inhibition 1780–1880. *The Scottish Historical Review* LXXIV: 45–68.

Kidd, Colin 1999. The Gaelic Dilemma in Early Modern Scottish Political Culture. In *British Identities before Nationalism. Ethnicity and Nationhood in the Atlantic World 1600–1800*. Colin Kidd (ed.). Cambridge: Cambridge University Press. Pp. 123–145.

Laclau, Ernesto 2005. *On Populist Reason*. London: Verso.

Laugaste, Eduard 1986. *Eesti rahvaluule*. 3rd edition. Tallinn: Valgus.

Leerssen, Joep 1996a. *Mere Irish and Fíor-Ghael. Studies in the Idea of Irish Nationality, its Development and Literary Expression prior to the Nineteenth Century*. Cork: Cork University Press.

Leerssen, Joep 1996b. Celticism. In *Celticism*. Terence Brown (ed.). Amsterdam: Editions Rodopi. Pp. 1–20.

Leerssen, Joep 2006. *National Thought in Europe. A Cultural History*. Amsterdam: Amsterdam University Press.

Leibovics, Herman 1992. *True France. The Wars over Cultural Identity 1900–1945*. Ithaca, London: Cornell University Press.

Martín-Barbero, Jesús 1993. *Communication, Culture and Hegemony*. Elizabeth Fox & Robert A. White (transl.). London, Newbury Park, New Delhi: Sage.

Masing, Uku 1984. Esten. In *Enzyklopädie des Märchens* 4. Kurt Ranke (ed.). Berlin, New York: Walter de Gruyter.

McDowell, Paula 2010. Mediating Past and Present: Toward a Genealogy of "Print Culture" and "Oral Tradition". In *This is Enlightenment*. Clifford Siskin & William Warner (eds.). Chicago: University of Chicago Press. Pp. 229–246.

Meyran, Régis 2002. *Folklore, "genres de vie" et révolution nationale. Les revues d'ethnologie et l'ethnologie dans les revues sous le Régime de Vichy*. Paris: Mission du Patrimoine Ethnologique (DAPA, Ministère de la Culture).

Moore, Dafydd 2004. The Reception of *The Poems of Ossian* in England and Scotland. In *The Reception of Ossian in Europe*. Howard Gaskill (ed.). London, New York: Thoemmes Continuum. Pp. 21–39.

Morris, Brian 1987. *Anthropological Studies of Religion: An Introduction*. Cambridge: Cambridge University Press.

Ó Corráin, Donnchadh 2004. Cad d'Imigh ar Lámhscríbhinní na hÉireann? *Oidhreacht na Lámhscríbhinní. Léachtaí Cholm Cille* XXXIV: 7–21.

Ó Duilearga, Séamus 1943. Volkskundliche Arbeit in Irland von 1850 bis zur Gegenwart mit besonderer Berücksichtigung der "Irischen Volkskunde – Kommission". *Zeitschrift für Keltische Philologie und Volksvorschung* XXIII: 1–38.

Ó Giolláin, Diarmuid 2000. *Locating Irish Folklore. Tradition, Modernity, Identity*. Cork: Cork University Press.

Ó Giolláin, Diarmuid 2014. Narratives of Nation or of Progress? Geneologies of European Folklore Studies. *Narrative Culture* 1(1): 71–84.

O'Halloran, Clare 2004. *Golden Ages and Barbarous Nations. Antiquarian Debate and Cultural Politics in Ireland, c. 1750–1800*. Cork: Cork University Press.

Ortiz, Renato 1992. *Românticos e folcloristas. Cultura popular*. São Paulo: Olho d'Água.

Piø, Iørn 1971. Svend Grundtvig (1824–1883). In *Leading Folklorists of the North*. Dag Strömbäck (ed.). Oslo, Bergen, Tromsö: Universitetsforlaget. Pp. 189–224.

Prat, Joan 1991. Historia. In *Antropología de los pueblos de España*. Joan Prat, Ubaldo Martínez, Jesús Contreras & Isidro Moreno (eds.). Madrid: Taurus Universitaria. Pp. 13–32.

Rogan, Bjarne 2012. The Institutionalization of Folklore. In *A Companion to Folklore*. Regina F. Bendix & Galit Hasan-Rokem (eds.). Malden, MA, Oxford, Chichester: Wiley Blackwell. Pp. 598–630.

Tarkka, Lotte 1989. Karjalan kuvaus kansallisena retoriikkana. In *Runon ja rajan teillä*. Seppo Knuuttila & Pekka Laaksonen (eds.). Helsinki: Suomalaisen Kirjallisuuden Seura. Pp. 243–257.

Thoms, William Ambrose Merton 1999 [1846]. Folklore and the Origin of the Word. In *International Folkloristics. Classic Contributions by the Founders of Folklore*. Alan Dundes (ed.). Lanham, Boulder, New York, Oxford: Rowman and Littlefield. Pp. 9-14.

Thomson, Derick S. 1998. James Macpherson: The Gaelic Dimension. In *From Gaelic to Romantic. Ossianic Translations*. Fiona Stafford & Howard Gaskill (eds.). Amsterdam: Editions Rodopi. Pp. 17–26.

Thomson, Derick S. 2006. Macpherson, James (1736–1796). In *Oxford Dictionary of National Biography*. Oxford University Press. Available at http://www.oxforddnb. com/view/article/17728 [Accessed November 15, 2012]

Tylor, Edward Burnett 1871. *Primitive Culture. Researches into the Development of Mythology, Philosophy, Religion, Art, and Custom*. London: John Murrey.

Wilson, William A. 1976. *Folklore and Nationalism in Modern Finland*. Bloomington, London: Indiana University Press.

List of Authors

Madis Arukask, Ph.D. is Associate Professor and Senior Researcher in Folkloristics at the University of Tartu, Estonia. He has published several fieldwork-based studies on folk belief of Finnic peoples in Russia, concentrating on folk magic, human–non-human relationship, and communication with the dead. He has edited some books and collections on beliefs and different folklore genres of Estonians, Vepsians and other Finnic peoples.

Frog, Ph.D., is Adjunct Professor and Academy of Finland Research Fellow of Folklore Studies at the University of Helsinki, Finland. Frog has published extensively on mythology and verbal art. Since his doctoral dissertation, he has worked with evidence of historical contacts and exchange among pre-modern cultures of Northeast Europe, with emphasis on empirically grounded theory and methodology. His current Academy of Finland project is Mythology, Discourse and Authority in Social Impact (2016–2021).

Terry Gunnell is Professor of Folkloristics at the University of Iceland. He is author of *The Origins of Drama in Scandinavia* (1995), editor of *Masks and Mumming in the Nordic Area* (2007) and *Legends and Landscape* (2008), co-editor of *The Nordic Apocalypse: Approaches to Völuspá and Nordic Days of Judgement* (with Annette Lassen, 2013), and *Málarinn og menningarsköpun: Sigurður Guðmundsson og Kvöldfélagið 1858–1874* (with Karl Aspelund, 2017). He has also written a wide range of articles and chapters on folk legends and beliefs, disguise traditions, Old Nordic religions and belief, and performance studies in general.

David Hopkin is Professor of European Social History at the University of Oxford, where his research focuses on using oral traditions to explore the history of rural communities and marginal social groups. He is author of *Voices of the People in Nineteenth-Century France* (2012) and recently co-edited *Rhythms of Revolt: European Traditions and Memories of Social Conflict in Oral Culture* (2018). He is also interested in the history of folklore collecting and the political and cultural uses to which folklore can be put, in which connection he co-edited *Folklore and Nationalism in Europe during the Long Nineteenth Century* (2012).

Kristel Kivari, Ph.D., is Researcher at the Department of Estonian and Comparative Folklore, University of Tartu, Estonia. The article is part of her dissertation (2016) on dowsing practices and -lore in contemporary Estonia. She has published articles about the Earth radiation and energy as the bonding concept of natural and supernatural.

Bengt af Klintberg, Ph.D. h.c., Professor, is a folklorist and writer who taught folklore at the University of Stockholm in 1967–1987 before he became a full time writer. His publications amount to over forty books and numerous articles. His special field is traditional and contemporary legends.

Kaarina Koski, Ph.D., is Adjunct Professor in Folklore Studies at the University of Helsinki, Finland. Her publications embrace a monograph on death-related beings in belief tradition, as well as several articles on belief narratives, Christianity in folk culture, death and grieving, vernacular conceptualization, and internet culture. She has also co-edited three books regarding genre issues, uncanny experiences, and contemporary folklore.

Mart Kuldkepp (⬤ http://orcid.org/0000-0002-0942-717X), Ph.D. is a lecturer in Contemporary Scandinavian History at University College London (UCL). His scholarly activities have been split between modern Scandinavian and Baltic history and politics, and Old Norse-Icelandic literature and culture. In this latter field, his main areas of interest have been supernatural themes, literary geography and the translation history of Old Norse texts into Estonian.

Sandis Laime, Dr. philol. is Researcher at the Institute of Literature, Folklore and Art, University of Latvia. His research topics include Latvian folk religion and witchcraft beliefs, place related narratives and Medieval and Early Modern sandstone carvings and graffiti. Publications include the monographs (in Latvian) *The Sacred Underworld: Cave Folklore in Latvia* (2009) and *Witches in Latvian Folk Belief: Night Witches* (2013). Laime is currently preparing an online index of Latvian legends on witchcraft and sorcery.

John Lindow is Professor emeritus in the Department of Scandinavian at the University of California, Berkeley. He has published numerous works on Nordic folklore and Old Norse-Icelandic literary tradition. His most recent book is *Trolls: An Unnatural History* (2014), and he is co-editor of the forthcoming *Pre-Christian Religions of the North: History and Structures* (4 vols.).

Diarmuid Ó Gilláin is Professor and Chair of Irish Language and Literature and concurrent Professor of Anthropology in the University of Notre Dame. He has worked mainly on Irish cultural history and popular religion, and on the intellectual history of folklore studies. Among his publications are *Locating Irish Folklore: Tradition, Modernity, Identity* (2000) and, most recently, the edited volume, *Irish Ethnologies* (2017).

Jonathan Roper (ⓘ http://orcid.org/0000-0001-8807-2276), Ph.D. is Senior Research Fellow in English and Comparative Folklore at the University of Tartu. He is author of *English Verbal Charms* (2004) and editor of various books including *Charms, Charmers and Charming* (2009) and *Alliteration in Culture* (2011).

Daniel Sävborg, is Professor of Scandinavian Studies at the University of Tartu. Sävborg has a background in studies of Classical Philology and Comparative literature and wrote his Ph.D. about grief in Eddic heroic poetry. He has published several monographs and articles on medieval Scandinavian literature, religion, manuscript philology, folklore and historiography. His special research interest is the role of the supernatural in Old Norse literature in the light of later recorded folklore and folkloristic theory.

Ülo Valk is Professor of Estonian and Comparative Folklore, University of Tartu. His publications include the monograph *The Black Gentleman: Manifestations of the Devil in Estonian Folk Religion* (2001), and *Vernacular Religion in Everyday Life: Expressions of Belief* (co-edited with Marion Bowman, 2012). His current research is focused on belief narratives, folklore in social context, and the history of folkloristics.

Abstract

Storied and Supernatural Places
Studies in Spatial and Social Dimensions of Folklore and Sagas

Edited by Ülo Valk and Daniel Sävborg

This book addresses the narrative construction of places, the relationship between tradition communities and their environments, the supernatural dimensions of cultural landscapes and wilderness as they are manifested in European folklore and in early literary sources, such as the Old Norse sagas.

The first section "Explorations in Place-Lore" discusses cursed and sacred places, churches, graveyards, haunted houses, cemeteries, grave mounds, hill forts, and other tradition dominants in the micro-geography of the Nordic and Baltic countries, both retrospectively and from synchronous perspectives. The supernaturalisation of places appears as a socially embedded set of practices that involves storytelling and ritual behaviour. Articles show, how places accumulate meanings as they are layered by stories and how this shared knowledge about environments can actualise in personal experiences.

Articles in the second section "Regional Variation, Environment and Spatial Dimensions" address ecotypes, milieu-morphological adaptation in Nordic and Baltic-Finnic folklores, and the active role of tradition bearers in shaping beliefs about nature as well as attitudes towards the environment. The meaning of places and spatial distance as the marker of otherness and sacrality in Old Norse sagas is also discussed here.

The third section of the book "Traditions and Histories Reconsidered" addresses major developments within the European social histories and mentalities. It scrutinizes the history of folkloristics, its geopolitical dimensions and its connection with nation building, as well as looking at constructions of the concepts Baltic, Nordic and Celtic. It also sheds light on the social base of folklore and examines vernacular views toward legendry and the supernatural.

Index of Persons

274

General Index

Studia Fennica Historica

Modernisation in Russia since 1900
Edited by Markku Kangaspuro
& Jeremy Smith
Studia Fennica Historica 12
2006

Seija-Riitta Laakso
Across the Oceans
*Development of Overseas
Business Information
Transmission 1815–1875*
Studia Fennica Historica 13
2007

Industry and Modernism
*Companies, Architecture and
Identity in the Nordic and Baltic
Countries during the High-
Industrial Period*
Edited by Anja Kervanto
Nevanlinna
Studia Fennica Historica 14
2007

Charlotta Wolff
**Noble conceptions of politics
in eighteenth-century Sweden
(ca 1740–1790)**
Studia Fennica Historica 15
2008

**Sport, Recreation and Green
Space in the European City**
Edited by Peter Clark,
Marjaana Niemi & Jari Niemelä
Studia Fennica Historica 16
2009

**Rhetorics of Nordic
Democracy**
Edited by Jussi Kurunmäki &
Johan Strang
Studia Fennica Historica 17
2010

Fibula, Fabula, Fact
The Viking Age in Finland
Edited by Joonas Ahola & Frog
with Clive Tolley
Studia Fennica Historica 18
2014

**Novels, Histories,
Novel Nations**
*Historical Fiction and Cultural
Memory in Finland and Estonia*
Edited by Linda Kaljundi,
Eneken Laanes & Ilona
Pikkanen
Studia Fennica Historica 19
2015

Jukka Gronow & Sergey
Zhuravlev
Fashion Meets Socialism
*Fashion industry in the Soviet
Union after the Second World
War*
Studia Fennica Historica 20
2015

Sofia Kotilainen
**Literacy Skills as Local
Intangible Capital**
*The History of a Rural Lending
Library c. 1860–1920*
Studia Fennica Historica 21
2016

**Continued Violence and
Troublesome Pasts**
*Post-war Europe between the
Victors after the Second World
War*
Edited by Ville Kivimäki and
Petri Karonen
Studia Fennica Historica 22
2017

**Personal Agency at the
Swedish Age of Greatness
1560-1720**
Edited by Petri Karonen &
Marko Hakanen
Studia Fennica Historica 23
2017

Pasi Ihalainen
The Springs of Democracy
*National and Transnational
Debates on Constitutional
Reform in the British,
German, Swedish and Finnish
Parliaments, 1917–19*
Studia Fennica Historica 24
2017

Studia Fennica Anthropologica

On Foreign Ground
*Moving between Countries and
Categories*
Edited by Marie-Louise
Karttunen &
Minna Ruckenstein
Studia Fennica Anthropologica 1
2007

Beyond the Horizon
*Essays on Myth, History, Travel
and Society*
Edited by Clifford Sather &
Timo Kaartinen
Studia Fennica Anthropologica 2
2008

Timo Kallinen
**Divine Rulers in a Secular
State**
Studia Fennica Anthropologica 3
2016